DREAM LAND

MIKE VOLTZ

FOR BROOKE
with whom I have the greatest adventures

PART ONE

1

KEVIN QUINN SAT ON THE couch in his apartment, in a part of Hollywood that tourists rarely see, shooting heroin. He closed his eyes as the drug spread, relaxing everything with its warm, easy touch.

He let go of the tie off and lay back. His breathing slowed and became shallow. Sleeping calm settled into a heavy, final stillness. In a few minutes, he was dead on the couch with the needle still hanging out of his arm.

His passing went unnoticed. Hollywood has no memory for such small things.

2

QUINN OPENED HIS EYES AND immediately squeezed them shut again. The light was blinding and it was everywhere. For a moment, he entertained thoughts of heaven but it was far too hot and dusty for that. Besides, he hadn't exactly led a life of purity and virtue. Quinn got up and forced his eyes open, shielding them with his hands.

He was in a desert. It stretched for miles in all directions, all the way to a distant horizon. He could make out the hazy outlines of mountains in the distance. Small trees and rock formations here and there broke the monotony. Quinn turned in a circle, searching for people or buildings, any sign of life. He saw nothing but desert, with no indication of how he'd gotten there. The vast expanse of sand seemed to mock him.

"Hello?" he called out. His voice was a croak and there was no answer. The only tracks on the ground were his own, marking the small circle he'd walked in. His mouth felt very dry and his stomach very empty.

There was a pile of rocks in the near distance and Quinn started walking towards it. The desert around him twitched with life, lizards and rodents running for cover. The sun was a merciless spotlight, burning his scalp through his hair. Half-remembered trivia surfaced in his mind, reminding him the human body couldn't last more than a few days without water. Quinn imagined he could feel himself drying out, then forced the thoughts from his head.

His initial confusion was beginning to recede, exposing the panic that lay beneath. It demanded to know things, to know them immediately. Where he was and what was happening. Quinn's heart began to race and by the time he reached the pile of rocks, his hands were shaking.

Quinn checked for snakes then sat in the pile's meager shadow. It had to be a prank. Someone was playing a trick on him, a candid camera show. That was what had happened here: they'd taken him into the desert and were filming him stumbling around until it was no longer funny and the B-list celebrity host popped out.

This explanation comforted Quinn at first. Then the sun sank lower in the sky, shadows lengthened and Quinn was forced to think of what else might have happened.

Died. I died last night.

The thought rose out of the darkness and Quinn suddenly felt cold.

He couldn't remember the night before. The memory was missing and, try as he might, he couldn't recall anything but the blank space where it was supposed to be. It was like trying to remember the exact date after a concussion. He remembered waking up and putting on the clothes he was currently wearing: jeans, a Guns N' Roses tee shirt and a hoodie. He'd taken to wearing long sleeves even on the hottest days, when his tattoos were no longer enough to hide the track marks. Something had happened after getting dressed

Dying on the couch.

that had landed him in the desert. Quinn struggled with it and finally dug out a missing fragment of memory, willing it out of his mind: going to score heroin. LA was dry, drier than it had ever been, but he knew a guy visiting from out of town. Good shit, bad shit, who knew? LA was too dry to be picky. Thinking about the drug unlocked a new craving in his mind, even greater than the need for water. Quinn remembered going to score whatever he could and suddenly it clicked.

"I overdosed," he said. His own voice made the words sobering and irrevocable. He looked around, taking in the dry purgatory with new eyes. Then he spoke two more words, trying out the truth on himself. "I'm dead."

In some ways, Quinn decided that was a relief.

The sun moved down slowly from its noon position and Quinn waited to start walking again. Better to travel in the dark than in the scorching, killing heat of the day. He had no particular destination in mind, but staying put in the middle of nowhere seemed like a bad idea. Quinn sat in his little spot of shade and watched the shadow of the rock pile grow. It crept down his legs and out past his shoes, stretching itself across the sand. When the heat lessened, Quinn moved on.

His whole body ached, from sitting and from missing heroin. Every thought seemed to bend inexorably, maddeningly towards it. Since he'd started using, it sat at the center of everything. Neither sex, nor money, nor music were able to dislodge it from the crown jewel place in his mind. Even now, the need for water ran a close second.

The sun sank lower. It became a glowing red coin that slipped behind the distant mountains. Under the silver half-moon, the desert drained of color. Shadows remained, deep and impossibly black, like pools of ink. Quinn made a half-hearted attempt to locate the North Star, then kept walking and wondered if he was alone in the world.

Morning found him lying under one of the stunted

trees. Ahead there was a ridge that hid the desert beyond. He would have to climb over it to continue, but Quinn was too tired and weak to go any further. He doubted that his shaking legs would carry him, even if he wanted to.

He was having trouble focusing. Thoughts slipped in and out of his mind. Earlier, he'd tried to bite a leaf from the tree, desperate for any water. All he got for his trouble was a bitter taste in his mouth. The desert had become so cold during the night that Quinn curled up to conserve warmth. He drew his knees to his chest and pulled his shirt over them like a kid, then lay there shivering until the sun came up.

The day grew hot again. His cravings for water, food and finally heroin faded. In their place was an emptiness, the white noise of so many needs it was impossible to think. So he lay there, still shivering in the heat, and the sun drew what little strength remained from his body.

Quinn drifted in and out of sleep. The tree behind him was a bit taller than he was and its branches provided a little shade. The sun turned their shadows to arthritic stumps by noon, then began to stretch them out again. Quinn could no longer tell the difference between dreaming and waking. Sometimes he wasn't sure if he was still lying on the ground or if the desert had poured away through a hole in the world and he was suspended in nothing. During a brief moment of lucidity, he wondered if he was in limbo or hell. It was empty enough for one and hot enough for the other.

Quinn might have stayed like that until he expired if not for the thunder. His eyes were closed, the darkness behind his lids turned orange by the sun. He knew he was sleeping but also saw himself from a vantage point high above. In this vision, he lay on his back and his sleeping face was peaceful. It was warm, the warmth of a really good shot seeping through him. The ground fell away and left him miles in the sky. Sleep-Quinn stretched in the air. He began to move higher, transported up and up until he started to burn like Icarus. He spread his arms to greet the sun, unzipped hoodie trailing behind him, and his shirt burst into flame. Sleep-Quinn smiled as the rest of him caught fire too and burned painlessly. His clothes burned away and he hung there, naked and afire, waiting to burn out of the world and into the next.

Then came the thunder and things went bad. It rose and swelled, growing louder. Clouds moved across the face of the sun and covered Sleep-Quinn with shadow. The warm caress of the fire turned to searing pain. Sleep-Quinn's flesh cooked and split open. His insides sizzled like meat on a hot grill. Fat melted and ran. He began to fall from the sky, trailing smoke and fire like a screaming meteor. The world around him began to shake, breaking itself apart. The speed of the fall tore at Sleep-Quinn, stripping away his flesh from his bones. He no longer heard the thunder; he felt it instead, rolling through him endlessly. The ground below was rushing up to meet him and it was shaking too, racked by earthquakes. Then the skeleton that remained of Sleep-Quinn crashed into the ground and bones scattered.

Quinn's eyes shot open. He was lying facedown and the ground was vibrating under his cheek. Not with thunder, though. This was a different sound. Drumming, pounding. Galloping. Quinn's mind made the connection and he raised his head.

Through the waves of heat baking off the desert he saw a cloud of dust. Quinn had never been on a farm in his life but the sound of hooves was still unmistakable. He could see shimmering, rippling figures on horseback, riding towards him.

Quinn pushed himself up and waved an arm over his head. He felt a sudden rush of strength, as if his body was burning its emergency stores in one last desperate attempt at rescue.

The shapes resolved into three riders, dressed in dun colored clothing and wearing big, Garth Brooks hats. Quinn slumped back to the ground, exhausted and dizzy.

The riders drew close and reined their horses, and the thunder stopped. A pair of dusty boots entered Quinn's field of vision, pried a toe under his shoulder and rolled Quinn over. It was all he could do to cover his sun-struck eyes with an arm and moan in weak, dying pain. One of the cowboys loomed over him, blotting out the sun. He knelt and fanned Quinn with his hat. One of the others tossed him a water skin. The kneeling cowboy settled his hat back on his head and put the skin to Quinn's lips.

"Easy now," he said. He let Quinn have a sip, then pulled it back. It was warm, tasted of iron, and was better than any drink Quinn had ever had.

The other two cowboys dismounted and stood on either side of the first, who was now studying Quinn with a critical eye, the way a fisherman might look at something strange brought up in his nets.

Quinn croaked and they kept looking at him. He focused and tried again. "Help."

The kneeling one—Quinn thought of him as the leader—turned his head and spat a ropy brown stream. He did not offer the waterskin again. Quinn looked up at the other two. They all wore guns on their hips, with holsters tied around their thighs and bullets peeking from loops in their belts.

"It looks like him, don't it?" said the leader. He unfolded a piece of paper and held it up, looking back and forth between it and Quinn. The sun shone through and Quinn saw the reverse image of a wanted poster, with the words *DEAD*

OR *ALIVE* and a crude drawing of a face.

"He don't look like Handsome Pete," said one of the others.

"Sure he does," said the leader. "Hair could be a little shorter but rough 'im up and I say we got a match." The paper went back into his pocket.

"Wait!" Quinn's voice was stronger now, adrenaline running through him. "That's not me." It occurred to Quinn he had watched this scene play out dozens of times in movies and begging was always futile. No one ever relented yet he still begged, croaking desperate promises never, never to tell.

The leader spat again, then grabbed Quinn by the hair and dragged him towards the tree. One of the others produced a rope and slipped it around Quinn's neck. He cinched it tight and tossed the loose end over a branch. Quinn tried to pull the rope away but the leader hauled at it and the noose jerked tight. The leader pulled again and Quinn's shoulders were dragged into the air. Again, and his upper body was pulled off the ground. His hands clawed at the rope but it was sunk in deep under his jaw. One more jerk and Quinn was in the air. His feet kicked, inches above the ground, and he turned in a slow, helpless circle. His struggles grew weaker until his hands dropped away and hung at his sides, and darkness closed over his vision.

There was thunder again. A single crack this time and Quinn fell. He crashed to the ground hard enough to jolt the darkness out of him. He managed to pull the rope off and sucked in ragged, whistling breaths. The deafening cracks continued and Quinn realized they were gunshots.

He covered his head and tried to curl into as small a target at possible. Bullets cut whining paths over him. From the little glimpses Quinn was able to catch under his arms, it appeared that the cowboys had taken refuge behind their fallen horses. He saw two. They lay in unnatural sprawls, leaking dark blood and liquid yellow shit onto the ground. The cowboys fired at something in the distance, yelling to each other between shots.

Bullets smacked into the ground around Quinn, kicking up little geysers of dirt. He squirmed for cover, behind the tree they'd tried to hang him from. His body was visible on either side of the trunk but it was better than being out in the open.

The mystery shots were coming from the top of the ridge Quinn had been too tired to climb. The cowboys could only fire blindly at it, while the hidden shooter had them pinned down and stuck out in the open.

One of the cowboys raised an arm too high, trying for a better angle, and a shot hit his elbow. The joint burst open and the cowboy screamed, louder than the gunfire. In his pain, he lost cover. The next bullet jerked his head sideways and dropped him. The two cowboys that remained, the leader and the one who'd gotten the rope, continued firing from behind a single horse. Smoke from their guns hung over the area. From Quinn's vantage point he could see both and thought they were very neatly trapped. Ahead of them was the ridge and behind, nothing but flat desert with nowhere to run.

A bullet passed through the flank of their horse and clipped the rope cowboy. He jerked back involuntarily and a second shot struck his forehead. It snapped his head back and he fell, staring up from a spreading red halo.

An eternity of minutes passed, during which the leader yelled curses and tried to conserve his ammunition. Quinn could see his belt was empty. Occasionally he fired and the hidden shooter answered in kind. When the leader was out of bullets he looked to the rope cowboy's gun, which lay out of reach. He gauged the distance and Quinn silently urged him to try.

When he finally lunged for the weapon, Quinn heard a shot and the leader sprawled flat, his back shredded and glistening under the sun. On the ridge, a figure rose and began making its way down.

It half-walked half-slid down to the bottom. Quinn could see it was a man dressed in a long duster, with a battered hat to match. He carried a rifle with an almost comically large scope. When he reached the leader, he slung the rifle over his shoulder and drew a revolver. Quinn heard the leader say something that might have been "please." Even with the ringing in his ears, Quinn thought he sounded good and terrified. The cowboy in the duster fired once and the leader lay still.

He walked towards Quinn, who suddenly felt foolish, hiding behind the too-small tree. Quinn wondered what would happen now, in this place where strength and luck seemed to be the only laws. Then the cowboy extended a hand, the one not holding the big revolver, and hauled Quinn to his feet.

Up close, he saw the cowboy was much older. He had a white mustache and a deeply tanned, creased face. His eyes were a long-faded blue. "You alive?" he asked in an old man's rasp. He looked plenty tough, a survivor whittled down by the hard land until only the essentials remained: fast hands, sharp eyes, no uncertainty.

"Thank you," said Quinn.

The old cowboy looked him over, then went and retrieved the waterskin from one of the dead men. He tossed it to Quinn. "Go slow."

Quinn tried. He drank and his stomach cramped. He stopped and doubled over until the pain passed, then drank more. When he was done, the old cowboy offered him a piece of jerky. Quinn ate it and looked over the bloody scene. "Who were they?" he asked.

"Outlaw posse. They been goin around, lookin for folks who fit the descriptions of wanted men, then killin em for the bounty." The old cowboy smiled. The expression was a great shifting of lines, pushing his face into new runnels and folds. He was thin, every unnecessary ounce taken out of him by the desert. "Name's Merrick," he said.

"Quinn."

Merrick nodded at the bodies. "Let's see what they're carrying."

He searched the dead men, pocketing money and tobacco and tossing the other contents of their pockets aside. Soon the killing ground was littered with papers and trinkets. Merrick looked at the warrant then at Quinn and laughed. Quinn was standing over one of the bodies, contemplating its strange, absolute deadness, and the sound startled him. It was the jagged, unnatural sound of something little used. "Don't look much like Handsome Pete to me," Merrick said, then didn't speak again until he'd finished searching.

3

THEY RODE BACK ON MERRICK'S horse, with Quinn riding double. He braced his hands on the horse and squeezed with his legs to avoid the indignity of looping an arm around the cowboy's stomach. He tried not to breathe too deeply. Merrick's hair was a sweaty fringe on the back of his neck and he smelled. Not like the homeless Quinn sometimes encountered in Hollywood, but a smell of body odor and unwashed skin. Eventually, Quinn didn't notice it anymore.

The need for heroin, though, was stronger than it had been since he woke up. With his life no longer in danger, the craving came roaring back. The sun blazed overhead but Quinn felt cold. His hands shook and he continually licked dry lips. Sweat that had nothing to do with the heat beaded his forehead. Quinn thought of nothing but performing his junkie's ritual and receiving the blissful absolution of a high. Pain and worry gone in an instant and the craving quieted.

The sun slipped low as they rode and Merrick stopped the horse. He dismounted and Quinn followed, less gracefully.

"You all right?" Merrick asked. They were face to face for the first time since Merrick had hauled him to his feet. Quinn nodded. He tried to pry his thoughts away from the craving long enough to focus. It was like a fishhook, lodged deep inside him. Every movement, every word he spoke caused the barbed tip to tear deeper.

"Been feeling a little sick but I'll be fine. This hasn't been one of my better days." A little deprecation always went a long way towards deflecting suspicion. Merrick gave him a skeptical look, then tethered his horse to a tree.

"Hungry?"

"Not too bad."

"Then you won't mind starting a fire while I find us some dinner. Flint and steel in there." Merrick indicated the saddlebags and without further instruction, headed away from their camp. His eyes searched the ground. Sometimes he crouched or bent over, looking for something in the creosote.

The sun was almost touching the horizon and the sky was a blast-furnace orange. Quinn realized that he had no idea how to start a fire. He looked through the saddlebag until he found what had to be the flint and steel: a sharp-edged gray rock and a small bar, bent to fit around one's fingers. Quinn cleared a spot on the ground, thought about it, then dug out a shallow pit with his heel. Then he stepped back, hoping he would instinctively, magically know what to do next. Waiting for some innate primitive knowledge from caveman ancestors to awaken and tell him what to do.

When Merrick returned, the stars were beginning to show. Quinn was hard at work crouched over his fire pit, striking sparks onto a single large tumbleweed and cursing under his breath at the futility. Merrick laughed his out-of-tune laugh at the sight. "Something tells me you ain't from around here."

Quinn dropped the flint and steel. "I'm more of a city boy."

"No shit," said Merrick. "Hope you like snake." He dumped out the bag he'd been carrying and two long, thick bodies fell out. For a moment Quinn was reminded of the shootout, the cowboys falling dead. He turned his head until the moment passed.

Merrick set about building a fire, breaking branches and making a little teepee of twigs. Finally he tucked a ball of tinder inside and began striking sparks onto it. When one caught, Merrick leaned in close and blew. By the time it was full dark, they had a fire.

The snakes were headless and Merrick cut the rattles off with his knife. He coiled one around a stick and secured both ends with string, then handed it to Quinn. "Just hold that over the fire," he said, as he prepared the second snake. His movements were economical. Fast and sure with no wasted energy.

The snakes cooked in their skins and when they were done, Merrick peeled away the charred, loose scales with his fingers. Quinn did the same. The meat was hot and came away in chunks like crab. The thought of snake turned his stomach but Quinn forced himself to eat, knowing he would need the energy.

When Merrick finished he sat back, sucking each finger. "Wish I could offer you some coffee but we ain't exactly living off the fat of the land. I live off the lean."

"It was good, thanks." Quinn zipped up his hoodie and rocked in front of the fire, trying to warm himself though he knew it was useless. The hottest fire couldn't touch withdrawal chills or soothe the ache that had settled into every muscle. It hurt to move and it hurt to sit still.

"I believe a man's entitled to his privacy. That's the best thing about living out here. No one telling you how to live or asking too many questions. But I hope you'll forgive me, since I saved your life. Where are you from?"

Quinn's mind instantly churned, trying to come up with a story. An addict reflex. Then he remembered that he knew nothing of the world around him. The structure of the lie collapsed and he decided on the truth.

Quinn told of opening his eyes in the desert, of walking, of waiting for death and of being found.

Merrick studied him. With flames lighting his old face, Quinn thought he looked like some ancient tribal god.

"I'll be damned," Merrick said finally. "You're a ghost."

"What now?"

"A ghost. In this world but not of this world."

Quinn was suddenly angry and afraid. "Do you see a white sheet?"

"Not that kind of ghost." Merrick's drawl remained steady. "Though there's plenty of those." Quinn looked around as if he might see one, swooping through the sky perhaps. "Not here," said Merrick.

"This might sound stupid but since apparently I'm a ghost…where exactly *is* here?"

"West of nowhere. The closest place with a name is Calico. I go there sometimes for supplies. That's the little Here. The bigger Here is Vista and the biggest Here…that'll take some explaining." Merrick rolled a cigarette while he talked and lifted a branch out of the fire. He touched the orange tip to the cigarette, pulled in and exhaled fragrant smoke. "That's some good shit. Courtesy of our dead friends." He passed it to Quinn. The unfiltered smoke was harsh but he took a drag before handing it back.

Merrick tucked it in his mouth, then took a stick from the pile of kindling and began drawing in the dirt. He made a large oval first, then divided it into vaguely amoeba-like shapes. When he was done, he had carved the oval into six parts: four around the outside enclosing one, with a small circle straddling the border between the sections on the lower right. Quinn watched closely, as the shape of the world was revealed. Merrick tapped the area on the left side of the oval with the stick.

"Vista," he said, and drew a V. He went around the oval clockwise, naming each and drawing corresponding letters. "Majis, Darke, Quantum." The stick moved back to the little circle. "Noir, and here in the middle, the Deadlands. This whole world is called Ouros by most."

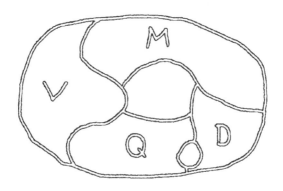

"You're here," said Merrick and tapped Vista. The stick left a little divot in the sand that looked like a period after the V.

"What's…" Quinn gestured to the blank ground around the oval.

"An ocean. A great ocean, crashing on the rocks at the edge of the world. Beyond that, I don't know. Sea monsters as big as islands, maybe. You'll have to ask someone smarter'n me, if you live that long." Merrick moved the pointer around the map. "These are the major territories. There are towns and cities in each, except the Deadlands. Fifty some odd years ago, that land was mostly part of Majis. Not anymore."

"What happened?"

"A war. The most terrible war this world has ever seen. It was fought over this." The stick tapped the ground again, this time inside the Deadlands. "Bastion. The city of Heroes. They had powers but not from magic or science. They just were. For a long time, they kept this world safe. Righted the wrongs, protected the innocent, all that shit. Folks called it the Age of Heroes. Of course when there's heroes there's villains. The ones who got tired of the whole justice and honor thing. Some wanted to protect the world, others wanted to rule it. Same old story."

"Who won?"

"No one. The Heroes War lasted a few years and most of the world got drawn in on one side or the other. At first the Heroes held Bastion and most thought it'd be over soon enough. But by the time the giants joined the villains, the tide had turned. In the end, the greatest Hero of them all sacrificed himself to end it. Sacrificed everything, really. Afterwards, the world put itself back together as best it could, without Heroes."

"Where'd they all go?"

"Heroes and villains alike died in the blast that created the Deadlands. They're unlivable now. Some wretched creatures still survive on the edges but the land is poisoned and unstable."

"Has anyone ever tried to cross it?"

"Plenty. They're dead now but I'm sure more will try someday. There's more untapped power in Bastion than all the other territories combined. 'Cept maybe Quantum. They mostly stayed out of the war, which cleared the way for the Age of Technology to begin."

23

"Is that what we're in now?"

"Yup."

"You ever been there?"

"Nope. I've never left Vista."

"Really? Not to be a dick but it doesn't seem like the most exciting place."

"The world don't need an old cowboy and I probably couldn't understand most of it anyway. Quantum is filled with all kinds of machines. Metal wonders that can walk and talk."

"You don't want to see that?" For a moment the heroin craving was gone, replaced with boyhood wonder. Thoughts of hoverboards, lightsabers and jetpacks filled Quinn's mind.

Merrick patted his gun. "I understand this. That's good enough for me. Quantum sounds like a place that's too fast, too loud and too big." The tip of the stick moved to the right, to the smallest territory, the little circle between Quantum and Darke. "Noir I might be able to get by in. The brims on the hats are smaller but otherwise, it's not so different from out here. There's the outlaws and the men trying to stop them. Majis is what it sounds like. There's magic there. Anything is possible if you don't mind risking your soul."

"You've seen magic?"

"Oh yeah." Merrick seemed lost in the fire for a moment, remembering something in the dancing flames. He shook his head and dragged on the cigarette to put the memory behind him. "Give me a thousand savages and another thousand bandits any day. The most devious, cheatin, back-shootin son of a bitch out here is still more trustworthy than most of what you'll find in Majis."

He pointed at the territory on the east coast, marked with a D. "And then there's Darke. Like it sounds, just with an 'e' at the end. Demons, spirits and all manner of unnatural things live there. I'll still take that over Majis any day." After that, Merrick fell silent. He finished his cigarette and pitched the butt into the fire.

Quinn tried several times to articulate a question before he finally got one out. "You're saying I died and ended up in a world divided into territories, each with a different...*theme?*"

"I didn't say that, you said that." Merrick's eyes held little points of firelight and Quinn saw a man with no patience for weakness. He saw a man whose world did not allow for such things, who had pushed himself to survive by being harder than the land, who had seen many fall and refused to fall himself.

Quinn tried to grasp what Merrick had said, to hold the shape of it in his mind and see it from all sides. He struggled to reconcile the existence of other worlds, of heroes and demons and magic. Part of Quinn wondered if he'd had a breakdown and was really in a hospital, strapped to a bed and sedated. That made sense and was a strangely comforting idea, but Quinn's throat still hurt from the rope and his body ached from needing heroin. He'd felt nothing like it in any dream or drug-induced hallucination.

"If I'm a ghost like you say," asked Quinn, "does that mean you know about my world?"

Merrick considered this. "I'll tell you my story if you'd like. You can draw your own conclusions."

"Please."

Merrick stood up. "Better make some room first." He walked beyond the circle of firelight. From the darkness, Quinn could hear him pissing against a tree. He returned and settled again by the fire, looking into its glowing orange center where the coals pulsed with heat, as if hypnotizing himself. Finally he began to speak and Quinn said nothing until it was over.

4

I WAS BORN IN A place called Crowheart. It's north of here. It was named for an old chief. There were two chiefs, see, and they fought over the land. It was a bloody battle, dozens dead on both sides. When you consider each tribe wasn't more than a few hundred or so, you can see why they'd want to end it. The two chiefs decided to settle it themselves and they fought with their tribes looking on. Chief Stands In The Sky won but his respect for his opponent, Chief Crow Feathers, was so great that instead of scalping him, he cut his heart out and planted it in the ground. That's where the name comes from. In the end, maybe Crow Feathers really did win. Seems like that's why people fight, for the right to slap their name on something.

That story used to keep me up at night, thinking about savages with bloody faces, cannibals probably, howling like animals. Took everything I had not to call for my ma some nights when the wind blew and the shadows of branches looked like dancing men.

When I got older, nine years old, my pa was killed. Up til then, we'd had a pretty good life. Lost a brother and a little baby sister but a good life. Thing is, there's men out there who see a good life and want to destroy it. Maybe because they'll never have one themselves, or maybe just because the sight of beauty in the world makes them feel weak and small.

They were free rangers. Means they had herds of cattle and they moved across the land—there's plains up north—and let their cattle graze as they go. I suppose if that was my way of life I'd see the justification in it, but it ain't my life. These men grazed on our land in a hard year. Our herd was a small one and my pa figured, I knew from overhearing him, that we might break even at best. I wasn't worried then. He always figured out a way to keep us fed and safe. He was my pa and that was good enough for me. He'd find a way. Then those men came.

My pa went to them, greeted them friendly, and explained that he respected their way but they were on our land. Next I saw of my pa was when his head came flying through our window that night. It rolled across the floor and I could see our brand burned right into the skin of his forehead. My ma screamed for…something. To get away or I don't know what. It felt like it was just me and his head on the floor and time going slower than ever. I could hear the fuckers outside, riding around, making fake savage war whoops. My ma fired at them out the window and my older brothers ran out firing too but the free rangers took off, back into the dark, laughing.

The law caught up with them the next day. They said they'd moved on when my pa asked them to. Said they respected the rights of landholders and I'm sure they put on real surprised faces when the sheriff told em what happened. They came back into town with him, just as helpful as you please to 'clear things up.' There wasn't evidence. There wasn't nothing to hold them. And back then, you could get away with a hell of lot by saying 'savage.' The red boogeyman. They went on their way and we tried to carry on.

A few years later, my ma met a nice man traveling through. A lawyer. He had these little glasses and this little mustache and he never looked comfortable around me and my brothers. But he liked my ma and she liked him back, at least well enough to return his affections and let him take her east to the city, a place called Solace. In time maybe she did love him. They sold the farm and put the money in…the hell is it called? Trust. For me and my brothers. He offered to set us all up in the city and made good on that promise too. I appreciated it enough to tolerate his name hanging off of my ma's. Me, I just wasn't made for city life and books and letting go of things. I had vengeance on my mind.

When I was old enough, I took my share of the farm money, bought a good horse and a good gun. The horse is long dead. The gun you saw today. I went looking for the free rangers. I'd seen em in town, with the sheriff. I marked each and every one of their faces and remembered them through the years. I tracked them across the plains and I found em camped with their herd.

The land up there is flat and I like to imagine their screams carried for miles and miles.

I tied em up and lined em up. Had a little row of men begging for their lives and I'll tell you it felt good. Forgiveness just ain't in my nature. I've seen too much to believe in any kind of god, but I was the god of that moment. I killed them one by one. I didn't have a brand so instead I put the hot muzzle of my gun against their foreheads. Then I scattered the cows and rode off and felt pretty damn good about myself.

That feeling lasted for maybe a week. It's funny but when you dream of something for years, when you finally do it, it gets so much smaller. And it leaves you so empty. I didn't know what to do so I rode for awhile until my money was almost gone. This was forty years ago, the Heroes War just a decade past. The world had become a dangerous place, and I realized I could do some good in it. I knew I didn't want to be a lawman. I wanted to make decisions on my own terms and give bad people the deaths they deserve. It worked, and I was happy.

Then, when I was twenty-two, I started going crazy. Or at least I thought I was crazy. I heard voices. I'd be riding a trail and hear a whisper. I couldn't make out the words at first but eventually, I recognized my name. Whatever it was, it knew me. The voices grew stronger and stronger and one night, I had the dream.

In my dream, I traveled through hard country. I saw people who needed help and passed on by. You know how dreams are. I went with absolute surety to a place I'd never been or seen or heard of before.

When I got there, I knew I'd reached the end of my journey. There were tall, strange rock formations and deep canyons. Gashes in the ground, really. I knew which one to go to.

I stood on the edge and dropped a torch down there, and I could see the bones of animals. I could hear the voices so clearly then and not just my name. They were speaking about me, about the things I'd done but never told anyone. Not a soul, but the voices knew. They also talked about things I hadn't done. People I hadn't met. Someone named Owen Cole I was supposed to kill. Someone named Kevin Costner who would "play me." I thought I was being set up for a con. Stupid thought I know, trying to explain it to myself somehow.

Then the ground at the bottom of the canyon began draining away. Just a little spot in the sand, like sand in an hourglass. The bones and my torch poured out into nothing. You're probably imagining a big dark pit, but it wasn't. It wasn't anything. It was a place between places and I knew I was supposed to go in. I could hear so many voices. Men and women talking fast. I was scared but I started climbing down, meaning to descend right into the nothing.

And then, before I got to the bottom, the voices got angry. They started yelling, cursing. One of them said "The deal's off" and that was it. No more voices. I blinked and I was in my bed, in my room and the sheets were soaking wet. Sweat or piss, I don't know.

I never heard the voices again. But I did kill a man named Owen Cole. I did other things and met other people too that I'd heard of in my dream so many years before. And eventually I came to understand there is something beyond this world. Something very close, side by side, with just a little darkness separating us. I almost went there in a dream. I figure I would've left my body lying in my bed, and the rest of me gone somewhere else. This world is somehow tied to that one and I guess that's where you're from. I've had a lot of time to think about it and the best I can come up with is that we're the stories you tell. You come from a place where people have dreamed us into existence and this is the world we built when you weren't looking. We have our own lives here, bigger than you could ever know. On the other side maybe we become something else. I'm one of the few to glimpse that. Maybe I'm even luckier, being denied on the threshold. All I know is my dreams are my own and my life is my own. I don't expect to be called again.

And that's my story. What kind of cowboy would I be if I didn't have at least one?

5

FINISHED HIS TELLING, MERRICK STARED into the fire, into the glowing orange heart of the night. Quinn was glad of the story; it kept his mind off heroin. Conversation was a good distraction.

"You're a bounty hunter?" Quinn asked.

"Not even a little. I take my payment from the dead. It ain't about money, anyway. It's about making things right. Someone has to do it and the Heroes are long gone."

"How long were you hunting the guys who attacked me?"

"Wasn't hunting em. That was just good luck, for the both of us. I heard about them, of course, but I'm looking for someone else."

"Another bad guy?"

"You could say that. Man named Gage. He's real close now."

Quinn looked instinctively over his shoulder, then realized what he'd meant.

"You on something, kid? You're awful jumpy."

The lie was manufactured instantly. "Getting strung up from a tree will do that to you, I guess." When Merrick agreed with a sharp laugh, Quinn knew he was safe. "What'd this guy do?"

"It's a long list. Right now, I hear he's got a girl with him, bought from the flesh traders. I'm sure you can imagine what he's doing with her."

"Mad Libs?"

"He's been traveling with her for a couple weeks and the good news is that's slowed him down. Can't move as fast with a drugged-up prisoner."

The word hooked Quinn's attention. His addict sonar zeroed in and everything else fell away. "What does he drug her with?"

"Opium, I imagine. Keeps her in a haze."

"He actually makes her take opium?" Quinn hoped he sounded appropriately horrified.

"He's one twisted bastard, all right."

Quinn shook his head while the wheels in his mind turned furiously, milling another lie. "I'll tell you what, I'm no gunfighter but I'd love the chance to see justice done to a dude like that. Hearing about that happening to a girl makes me fucking sick." A pause for effect. "I'm sorry. It's just not right."

"Nothing to be sorry about. I feel the same way. Gage is mine but he'll have men with him. You want blood, come along."

"Thank you," said Quinn and his gratitude was unfeigned. The promise of opium flooded him with relief. He could have wept with joy.

"Watch my back and we should be able to pick up a gun for you. You do any shooting in your world?"

"No, but it seems pretty simple. Point and shoot and don't hit your friends."

Merrick grunted. "Last part's kind of important. I'm

going to bed down. You should too. We'll move in a few hours."

"Ah." Quinn had been imagining a shootout at high noon.

"Right now, they should be getting good and drunk. When we get there, they'll be asleep. Easy targets. If the girl's there, we'll free her. If not, I kill Gage and we kill as many of his men as possible. Goodnight."

Merrick lay back on the ground, one hand near his gun. The handle was wood, and Quinn noticed it was carved with small, random shapes. Before long Merrick was asleep, breath whistling in and out of his nose.

For Quinn, sleep did not come easily. Instead, he lay on the hard ground, staring into the night sky with a restless mind. His head filled with the sort of unguarded thoughts people have looking up at the stars in wide-open country. Quinn's were of his mother.

His first night in LA was one of the last times they'd seen each other. That was how he remembered her, how her face was clearest: sitting in Quinn's apartment, playing cards and listening to classic rock. A few times, he glanced up and saw her looking at him. Just looking at his face. She tried to keep it light, cracking jokes about how she was glad to have him out of the house and what she'd do with his old room. They could both feel things just below the surface of the conversation that needed to be said, but neither brought them up. Quinn looked at her too, really looked at her for perhaps the first time in years. At her eyes, her cheeks, the lines on her face. He noticed for the first time how much older she'd gotten. Quinn experienced a moment of emotional vertigo and looked away. After the last game, they hugged goodnight and she held him for a long time, then turned away without letting him see her face. Quinn felt dampness on his shoulder though and knew. The next day, she drove back home and life went on.

Quinn picked up a handful of dirt and squeezed it. Felt it between his fingers. The dirt of another world, solid and real. His eyes searched the strange, new constellations above and soon enough, he slept.

6

BEFORE THEY BROKE CAMP, MERRICK scooped some of the ashes from the fire into a little vial. Quinn asked what it was for and Merrick said it was a tradition from his pa, carrying the ashes of one fire to the next. It was still dark when they rode out, doubled again on the horse. The stars were hard and bright, as they can only be on cold nights.

They cut across the desert to approach the town unseen. The wind gusted, kicking up sand that stung their faces, and occasionally Merrick made a clicking sound to guide the horse this way or that.

Thoughts of the opium occupied Quinn's mind. There might be violence, shooting and running, but it was worth the risk. Quinn's eyes fell on Merrick's revolver, riding up and down with the horse's steps, and on the shapes carved into the sweat-darkened wood of the handle. *Runes*, Quinn thought, and wondered at their purpose. Then his thoughts returned to opium: bricks wrapped in leaves, sweet smoke curling from long pipes, the sleepy rush of the drug. His heart beat faster at the thought. His body hurt less.

The sky grew lighter—no sun yet, but a watery pinkish glow on the horizon—by the time Quinn saw buildings ahead: Tinker's Damn, in all its dusty, pre-dawn glory. It began sporadically, with a settlement here and there. Barns and gardens marked the plots of land. A few goats and pigs emerged to watch the men ride by.

They slipped into town like shadows, moving on foot through the warren of alleys between buildings. In the early morning light, the town was gray and quiet, waiting for activity to resume. The silence was its own kind of sound: a clapping door somewhere, a squeaking sign. And in the distance, a faint chorus of coyotes howling. The sound carried well in the still air.

Soon they arrived behind a boxy two-story. Its front side was a façade that looked over the main street. The rear, where they stood, looked over a glorified alley with a row of outhouses. Even at midday, it would remain in shadow and the ground would be a squelching mess. This early, it was still frozen in waves and ripples of mud. Trash was heaped in piles by back doors. The air reeked of rotting food and human waste. Quinn pulled his shirt over his nose and tried to breathe as shallowly as possible.

Merrick crouched by the back door. He pulled out two thin pieces of metal from a pouch, stuck them into the lock and began delicately twisting and probing. He spread the picks in a V shape and rotated them, waiting for them to catch. Quinn was engrossed in the burglar's art and cast a guilty glance over his shoulder. A man was there, in mid-step, a baling hook raised to strike.

"Merr—!"

The gun was already out of its holster and in Merrick's hand. He turned and fired, faster than Quinn could follow.

The man clapped both hands to his belly and the hook fell harmlessly to the ground. He staggered back a few steps and his legs gave out. Up and down the street, Quinn could hear the town waking.

"So much for surprise," said Merrick and shot the lock out of the door.

He moved quickly into the dark building and Quinn did his best to keep up. Running feet pounded above them, shaking the ceiling and sifting down dust. Voices shouted over each other and doors banged open. Merrick went down the hallway with his gun raised, the long barrel gliding through the dimness.

A face peeked around the corner and quickly vanished, replaced by a hand with a gun. Quinn instinctively ducked but Merrick fired. The bullets gouged splintered holes and the man behind the wall fell dead.

The building's front door was opposite the hallway, across a main room filled with tables and chairs. There was a bar to one side and a staircase to the other. It traveled diagonally up the wall to the second level, where a balcony spanned the length of the room.

A man ran down the stairs in long underwear and boots, firing as Merrick and Quinn emerged from the hallway. Merrick fired back and Long Underwear's body jerked and danced. He plunged down the stairs headfirst, bouncing over them until he lay sprawled and still at the bottom.

Merrick turned and began shooting up at the men on the balcony. One pitched forward over the bannister, like a sailor about to be seasick. His gun dropped to the floor and he followed in a graceless somersault. The shots tore out chunks of wood and a gray haze hung over the room. *Gunfighter's cloud cover*, thought Quinn, *hazy with a chance of bullets.*

They climbed the stairs and Merrick fired continuously, driving the men back from the balcony and down the hall that ran to the back of the second level. Quinn was fairly certain that Merrick hadn't paused even once to reload. Then he promptly forgot about it as a bullet passed by close enough for Quinn to hear its whine. Merrick kept firing, taking the stairs two at a time.

When they reached the top, the balcony creaked ominously. The boards were riddled with bullet holes, some big enough for Quinn to see the floor below. The hall was windowless and unlit, a dark corridor with doors on either side.

A man lunged from the nearest room and Merrick fired without hesitation. At close range, it obliterated the top half of his head and the muzzle flash nearly blinded Quinn.

Merrick caught the body before it could fall and held it up in front of him. He moved down the hall, kicking in doors as they went. One empty room, then another. Then a room with two men, one crouched behind the bed and one hiding next to the door. The one behind the bed fired first, hitting Merrick's human shield. The one next to the door swung a lantern, trying to brain Merrick. He raised an arm to deflect the blow and it sent his gun spinning across the floor.

Quinn turned as the door behind him opened and a man charged out. He grabbed Quinn by the throat with both hands and began to squeeze. They collapsed to the floor and Quinn realized for the second time in as many days he was being choked to death and it was already too late to do anything about it.

Then the hands around his neck were gone. It hurt to breathe but Quinn gulped at the air. Merrick stood over him. His face was bloody but he was holding his gun again and grinning. Quinn got to his feet and saw his attacker was slumped against the wall, blood draining from his forehead into his lap.

Merrick went back to kicking doors open. Behind one, a middle-aged prostitute. Another empty. Then several women huddled together; one ran across the room and threw herself at the door, slamming it shut. Merrick's gun stayed silent, trickling smoke.

The last door was at the end of the hall. Merrick approached cautiously, took aim at the doorknob and fired. It flew open hard and Merrick pressed back against the wall. He risked a look, then went in. The window on the far side was open and Merrick's quarry gone, but the room was not empty.

A girl lay on the bed, naked and bruised. Her wrists and ankles were bound with twine and she did not move.

"Watch the door," said Merrick. Quinn hung back. His throat still hurt. Swallowing was painful but the opium would fix that soon enough. He cast quick glances around the room, searching for it. A terrible thought came to him, that Gage had taken it when he bailed out the window. Quinn pushed it away. At this point he would have gladly killed for the residue in a pipe.

Merrick kept hold of his gun with one hand and cut the girl free with the other. He pulled the sheet over her, then lifted her onto one shoulder with some effort. She was a tall girl and Quinn caught a glimpse of her eyes through the blonde tangle of hair. They were dazed, empty and very blue.

"Let's get the hell out of here," Merrick said. His voice was tight with strain and Quinn stepped back to let him lead the way. The boards of the hall groaned and sagged under their feet, promising to give way soon.

Quinn followed part of the way down the hall, then faded back to the room. He heard Merrick call his name from the stairs.

"Be right there!" Quinn yelled back, then started tearing the room apart. He pulled the thin mattress off the bed, then pulled out the nightstand drawer and dumped it. No opium. New sounds of chaos came in through the open window: more yelling and more gunfire. Tinker's Damn had become a war zone and Quinn threw the closet door open. His back would have made an easy target if anyone was still in the building, but they were gone and Quinn was left to his single-minded purpose.

The closet was empty and Quinn turned back to the room. His face was running with sweat and he gritted his teeth, grinding them back and forth over each other. On the floor was a pile of women's clothes and Quinn kicked it. He screamed in mindless fury at the empty room and shoved the bed, wanting to break something.

A man's coat lay on the floor, dropped carelessly or left in haste. Quinn seized it. There was nothing in the first pocket but in the second, Quinn felt a lump. He pulled out a pouch and loosened the drawstring. Inside, there was a little ball of tightly rolled leaves and, inside that, the white powder he'd been looking for. Quinn uttered a happy expletive and ran for the door.

He'd almost reached the stairs when it happened.

A sound rose and filled the world, the unmistakable crescendo of something large incoming. Quinn thought of bombs, of meteors. Its thundering passage shook the hallway and the impact of its landing broke the building apart.

The wooden structure swayed and cracked in the shockwave. The hallway twisted out of true and acquired a funhouse cant. Boards groaned their final protests and began to split. Quinn ran for the stairs and knew he wouldn't make it.

The floor gave way and sent him crashing down to the front room below. Quinn shielded himself as best he could until the rain of broken boards and bodies was over, then realized his hand was still clenched around the pouch of opium. He couldn't help but smile in spite of everything.

From outside, there was a new sound. This was the high, piercing whine of a power saw that seemed to cut across the world. Next to it, gunshots sounded like pops. Then the new sound cut across those and there was no more gunfire. When the whine stopped, the silent aftermath was abrupt and terrible in its own way. The anti-sound of a world in shock. Quinn got back to his feet.

The hallway they'd first entered through was blocked by a fallen beam. That left the front door, which stood ajar. The whining sound hadn't started again and Quinn stepped out as carefully as he dared, intending to slip out and slip away.

Instead he froze on the porch, staring at the colossus of metal in the street. Towering black armor with a single red eye, glowing in the center of its forehead. One massive hand held the girl like a doll, metal fingers clamped on her arm and the rest of her hanging down, unconscious. The other hand was clamped on Merrick's neck and shoulders.

It raised him into the air as if the cowboy weighed nothing. Merrick's boots kicked above the street. Somehow he was still holding his gun. He raised it and fired point blank at the cyclops's face. Once, twice, three times. The bullets knocked sparks off the metal surface but did nothing. Quinn heard a power source cycling up, then a beam of blinding red light burst from its eye, enveloping Merrick.

The flash obscured exactly what happened, but the upper half of Merrick was vaporized. His hips and legs fell to the ground along with the burning remains of his duster. There was a small spatter of blood but nothing more. The wound was cauterized.

Then the metal giant pivoted to face the row of buildings opposite the hotel, keeping hold of the girl. It leaned forward and set its feet like a man facing a strong wind, and Quinn heard the powering up sound again. Light shot from its eye and hit the side of a building, blowing the wall back in flaming pieces. The cyclops turned its head and the beam tore a burning swath through the buildings. Walls were obliterated and structures collapsed into burning rubble. When it stopped, the buildings across the street from Quinn were reduced to a jagged wall of smoking ruins.

For a moment there was only the sound of burning buildings and of the metal giant itself. Servos whined internally and little flaps vented air. Quinn held perfectly still for fear a squeaking board would betray him. The only part he dared to move were his eyes. They went up to the sign above the hotel entrance. It hung by one corner, swinging back and forth. With each swing, the hook it dangled from worked itself out of the wood further. Quinn mentally urged it to hold on as he gauged the distance to the alley. As he did so, the hook pulled free and the sign over the entrance fell with a clatter.

The cyclops turned and saw Quinn. It covered the distance between them in three ground-shaking steps and lifted Quinn into the air, as it had with Merrick. Its other hand still held the girl. The single eye fixed on him like a baleful red spotlight.

"What the fuck are you?" Quinn managed to choke out.

"MIDNIGHT," the giant said. Its voice vibrated through Quinn. "MY TIME IS COMING."

Metal fingers squeezed and Quinn felt his bones snapping inside him. He could hear them, too. His clavicles sounded like sticks and his jaw went with a muffled pop. Then Midnight raised Quinn high, slammed him to the ground, and Quinn remembered no more.

7

SOUNDS IN THE DARKNESS.

Hammering.

Yelling.

They brought her out of a dreamless sleep. The room was filled with grey early morning light and downstairs, the pounding on the door continued.

The shape beside her stirred and a man asked in a sleep-dulled voice what all the noise was.

"Nothing. Go back to sleep," she said, as she climbed out of bed.

She was naked, her body marked with scars. They hatched her skin in white lines. Clothes were strewn across the floor, his and hers, mixed together. The man was awake now, watching her dress. She pulled on last night's pants and shirt, then took her gun from the nightstand and went downstairs.

The lower floor was a workspace with a small conference room, a private office and a waiting area. She opened the front door a crack with the safety latch still engaged and the gun held down by her leg. An older man stood outside, wild-eyed and giving off the sour odor of panic.

"Are you Faline Bristowe?" He sounded desperate, barely holding it together.

"I am," she said.

"My daughter…" said the man. He held up a picture. "I need help."

Faline tucked the gun into the back of her waistband and let him in. She took the picture; it was a framed 5x8 that showed a teenage girl with long black hair and blue eyes. The hair was dyed, its true blonde color visible at the roots.

"That's recent," he said. His voice shook and so did his hands.

"What's your name?"

"Martin. Marty."

"Tell me what happened to your daughter, Marty."

"She's gone. Sometime this morning or last night. I got up and she wasn't in the house. I went by her door and the dog was scratching at it. He usually sleeps in bed with Gabby. So I checked and she wasn't there." Without the picture to hold, his hands twisted together in his lap. Faline gave it back and he clutched it like a talisman.

"You called the police already?"

Marty nodded. "They've been out. They checked everything. They said no sign of a break in. The windows were closed and everything. She just wasn't there." Marty's chin quivered. Faline knew if she hugged him, he'd spend the next few minutes sobbing in her arms.

"Was she meeting someone? A boyfriend or girlfriend?"

"She's a good girl. She's never done anything like this. Never even stayed out late but since she met this jerk…" Emotion threatened once again to overcome Marty. He wrestled with it and won. "The police didn't care. I could see it. They heard about her boyfriend and I know they're thinking

Gabby's just another runaway. I'm telling you, no matter what my daughter was doing, she's in over her head. I know teenagers experiment and party but she's not…that's not her scene. She's a good girl. We lost her mom last year and it's been hard for her. She's my stepdaughter and we always had a good relationship but since her mom died…she's just so angry and hateful. I know it's because she's hurting and I can't—"

Faline interrupted before he could lament further. "What's his name?"

"Chris. Chris Eagan."

"What kind of car does he drive?"

"Norton X3, I think. Black two door. The engine's some kind of high-performance thing that sticks out of the hood."

"You know where he lives?"

"With his parents. The police went over there and found nothing. I don't even think they searched. But they told me that and I came right over here. I've heard you can find people when no one else can."

"Mostly deadbeats and bail jumpers," said Faline.

"Gabby doesn't know what kind of guy she's with and I know she's not safe. The police don't care. 'Oh, another slutty runaway.' That's not her."

The man lowered his head and his shoulders began to hitch. After a moment of consideration, Faline gave his arm a quick two-pat. "I'll see what I can do," she said.

Marty looked up and his red, wet face had a new intensity. "I'll pay whatever it takes. Just bring her back. Please. She's all I have. Even if she hates me now, she's all I have." He looked at Faline with desperate, helpless eyes that she couldn't get away from fast enough.

"I'll get ready. Wait outside and I'll follow you to your house," she said.

Back upstairs, the man was fully awake and sitting up in bed. He watched as she dressed in clean underwear, jeans and a shirt, then shrugged into a shoulder holster.

"Duty calls?"

"Yeah. You can make yourself coffee downstairs. Lock the door before you leave." Faline pulled on boots and holstered her gun. The man got out of bed to kiss her good-bye, but she was already slipping on a jacket and heading out the door.

A motorcycle was parked out front and Faline climbed on. When she gripped the handlebars the bike started, not with a roar, but a thrum of energy. On the dashboard, gauges illuminated, needles jumped and a screen in the middle displayed a map. Faline waved at Marty to go and he did, leading the way in his sensible beige sedan. She followed him, keeping pace easily, gliding quietly through the cool morning air.

Eventually they reached the heart of suburbia and Marty pulled into the driveway of a house. Faline parked curbside and climbed off the bike. The power hum died and the dashboard went dark. In the living room window of the house, a small dog stood on the back of a sofa to bark at her.

Faline looked around the neighborhood, taking it in. Big trees. Wide streets. Well-kept lawns. Patches of sidewalk wet from the sprinklers. She raised her chin slightly and breathed in. Marty hurried over, still carrying the picture of his stepdaughter.

"Do you need this?" he asked.

"No," said Faline. "I need an article of her clothing. Something she wore recently."

"Like a shirt?"

"A shirt, pants, anything."

Marty went inside and while he was gone, Faline con-

47

tinued scenting the air. She took little breaths here and there, like a sommelier sampling wine. When Marty returned with a shirt, Faline took it and pressed it to her face, inhaling deeply. She knew the girl's smell now: lavender, from her shampoo. The sweetish powder of her makeup. A hint of the deodorant she used. And, under that, the smell of her sweat. She gave the shirt back to Marty.

Faline scented the air again, alert like a hunter. She searched through its many layers, sifting through the invisible smudges left on the world by people and things. Each with its own color, filling the air like dozens of uncoupled rainbows. Gray and greasy car smells. Yellow dog piss smells. Stinging green juniper. Man smells and woman smells. And finally, near the end of the driveway, she found it. A pink smell that she pulled from the rest. The girl's scent, her olfactory fingerprint.

Now that Faline had it, following it was as simple as following a trail. She went down the sidewalk and turned left without hesitation. They neared a small cross-street bearing the name of Whispering Leaves and Faline stopped. She sniffed the air, turning her head between the lawn and the street. Marty watched, twisting the shirt in his hands.

"Here," said Faline. She stepped off the sidewalk. At this hour, there was little danger of traffic. "She got in a car right here." Faline pointed to a spot utterly indistinguishable from any other bit of concrete and asphalt. "It was idling at the curb. Didn't want to wake you up."

"Was it his?"

"I smell cigarettes and…" she paused to consider a smell, "…Xone Body Spray." She took another breath. "Rebel."

"That's him. Can you follow them?"

"I should be able to track them."

"Thank you!" Marty sounded almost delirious with relief. "Thank you! I don't care what it costs. You're an angel."

"I wouldn't go that far," said Faline and began walking back to her bike, quickly, before Marty started crying again.

8

IT WAS NIGHT WHEN FALINE reached the town. A month of hard traveling had brought her to it and she smelled it from miles away. The black of burned wood. The red of burned flesh. The smells drifted across the desert and she followed them.

The town was empty. She rolled through it until she got to the main street, where remains of buildings on either side still smoked. Faline stopped her bike and dismounted.

Bodies, what remained of them anyway, lay in the street. Even in the dark, their plasma burns were unmistakable. Features ran and melted together and teeth jutted from lipless faces. Faline moved from one body to the next, quickly inspecting each. She'd seen this before, in three different towns, and the carnage was the same.

Up the street, coyotes growled and snapped at each other, fighting over food. She could see them worrying something on the ground, shaking their heads and pulling to tear meat. For the first time, Faline smelled wet blood. She approached slowly. The coyotes noticed her and strung out in a line, baring teeth and raising hackles. The ones on the edge began drifting around, flanking her.

Faline stood her ground, letting them get her scent. When the alpha did his demeanor changed. He slunk back, head low and whining. When he was far enough away, he turned and trotted off. The other coyotes followed.

Faline went over to see what they'd been at. It was a man's body, lying in front of what looked like the remains of a hotel. Teeth littered the ground around him. Bones pushed up against his skin in new and unnatural contours. In some places they stuck out like jagged spars. Blood shone glossy black in the moonlight.

Faline knelt for a better look. One side of the man's face was crushed, the skin hanging slack with no bone to support it. It gave his face the unsettling appearance of falling in. When he moaned, Faline's heart kicked and she jumped back.

She wouldn't have believed the man could still be alive, much less capable of making a sound. Yet now his remaining eye rolled wildly and he seemed to be having a seizure. His body shook and fresh blood ran from his wounds. His chest aspirated with a sharp wheeze. Then, just as quickly as it started, the seizure ended. The sounds stopped and the man lapsed back into unconsciousness.

Faline stood over him for a moment, debating something. She looked down the street, at the bodies strewn there and the empty town. Then back at the man with a little bit of life still trapped inside his destroyed body.

"Let's hope you know something," Faline said and reached inside her shirt. She pulled out a flat disk on a chain and snapped it free, then placed it on the man's chest and pressed the center.

It made a pleasant chime and the words POCKET DOC appeared on the smooth metal surface, followed by INITIATING ANESTHETIC. Almost immediately the man's ruined face relaxed, though his breath continued its wet rattle. The unit emitted a processing hum and information began flashing across its surface too quickly for Faline to read.

The Pocket Doc rose into the air until it was floating a foot or so above the man's chest, with a beam of white light directed down onto him like a small alien spaceship. A red beam at its center neatly and bloodlessly parted the flesh of his chest. Two whip-thin arms snaked down from the Pocket Doc and held the cut open. Immediately other beams of different colors appeared and began moving independently within the cavity. Faint wisps of smoke rose but nothing more. A slowly undulating black ribbon streamed down and disappeared into the wound as the words ACTIVATING NANOBOTS appeared. The Pocket Doc moved slowly over the man's body, beams suturing and cutting, making the open wound appear to travel along with the machine.

Occasionally the man murmured or twitched but did not wake. The Pocket Doc repaired his chest first. Faline watched as bones grew back together with a brittle crackling sound, flesh was made whole and skin closed smoothly over it. The movement of the beams was almost hypnotic, colored fingers playing a complex musical piece. They moved up from his chest to his head, then back down to his arms.

Faline left the Pocket Doc to its operations and went to take a closer look at the bodies in the street. She knelt by one that was little more than a head and arm connected by a scrap of neck. The hair was melted off one side and the eyes had been picked empty by birds. It was full dark but Faline appeared to have no trouble seeing as she explored further, examining bodies and contemplating the violent end that had befallen Tinker's Damn. When she was done, she turned and headed back to the almost-dead man.

The Pocket Doc was still shuttling back and forth

over him, but now he looked as if he'd just gone to sleep for the night. His face was peaceful and his chest rose and fell steadily. Around him, his clothes lay in tatters. When the medical device was done, the colorful beams shut off and the unit returned to its starting position above his chest. It lowered slowly; the shaft of white light decreased until the disk sat on the man's newly healed skin. It rode up and down with his steady breathing and a new message appeared:

USES REMAINING: 0/1
Pocket Doc
by
the Tardigrade Corporation
THANK YOU

This was replaced by a list detailing the various medical issues that had been treated. Faline glanced over them, then pocketed the disk and left the man to sleep. Along the row of destroyed buildings, Faline found a wall that seemed sturdy enough and sat against it. She could hear the sound of coyotes, not quite bold enough to return and feed. Faline drew her gun and placed it on the ground, keeping a hand on it. Then she tilted her head back against the wall and slept.

While she did the sun rose, over a town full of the dead.

9

QUINN WOKE WITH A JOLT, gripped by the memory of rocketing towards the ground. His hands shot up, bracing for impact. After a silent, shaking moment, he lowered them and saw the woman standing there.

With the sun behind her, it was hard to discern features. Quinn squinted. She had the lean muscle of a runner. Dark hair. Leather jacket. Motorcycle boots. Mirrored sunglasses. Serious expression. Quinn had a feeling it was not going to be a good morning

"You're safe for now," she said in a voice that promised zero tolerance for bullshit. "I found you some clothes." She indicted the pile next to him. Quinn was suddenly aware that he was naked under a sheet, lying on the porch. The woman turned away and looked down the street while Quinn dressed. There was no underwear, so he pulled on the pants commando. He looked down at the unblemished skin of his chest and arms. It was like looking at someone else's body. There were no track marks or tattoos. With the ink gone, Quinn felt as if some essential part of him had been wiped away. He ran his tongue over his teeth. They were smooth and strong, instead of rotted and aching from neglect. Even the calluses on his fingers from playing guitar, hard won the summer before high school, were gone. He pulled on the shirt, still shocked by the bare arms that emerged from the sleeves, and a pair of boots. The vest and tie he ignored, but slipped on a long coat that made him feel like an extra in *Tombstone*. When he was done, he joined the woman at the edge of the porch and did his best to ignore his own blood-stain nearby.

"Thanks," he said.

She nodded by way of acknowledgement. "My name's Faline. What's yours?"

"Quinn."

"We both probably have a lot of questions, so why don't you go first?"

"Ok. For starters, how am I alive, where are my tats, and why do I feel better than I've ever felt before?"

"You had a good doctor." Faline tossed the Pocket Doc to Quinn. "I found you last night with brain trauma, damage to your internal organs, over 80 percent of your bones broken, compound fractures, spinal cord severed. I've seen people hit by trucks in better shape. Plus the damage from long-term drug use."

Quinn looked over the readout on the disk. "Are you saying I'm fixed? Like, completely?"

"You're not physically an addict anymore, if that's what you're asking. Whether you stay that way is up to you. You might feel a little weak for the next couple days but for now, you have a clean bill of health."

He suddenly thought of Merrick. "Do you have another one of these? There's—"

"There's no more. That was a gift from someone. They're expensive and rare."

Quinn processed this. "And you used it on me."

"If you can tell me what happened here, it'll be worth it."

Quinn remembered the grip snapping his bones. Being slammed to the ground. When Quinn spoke, his voice was unsteady, fearful to even say the name. "It was Midnight."

"What happened then?"

"Not the time of day, the giant metal cyclops that shoots energy beams from his eye. You've heard of him, right?"

Faline shook her head. "I've found other places like this and been searching for who or what was responsible, but there's never been a living witness until now. You might be the only person in the world to have seen this Midnight and lived. Anything you can tell me about what he looks like and what happened will help."

Quinn sat down. The sign, the piece of wood that had betrayed him, lay on the ground nearby. He began picking at the boards of the porch, tossing away the splinters as he spoke. "We came here to rescue a girl. We didn't know about Midnight either."

"Who's 'we'?"

"Me and Merrick." Quinn pointed down the street. "He's dead now. He was a…vigilante, I guess. He saved me and we joined up. Basically, I followed him. Merrick was gunning for a guy and knew that he'd pass through here. He had the girl with him, all tied up and drugged."

"What happened when you found her?" Faline asked.

"The guy bailed before we got to his room. Merrick carried the girl out, and that's when Midnight came."

Faline clocked something in Quinn's story, filed it away for later. "What was that like?"

"I heard him flying in. When he landed the whole place shook. When we got outside, he picked up Merrick and just vaporized him."

"What does Midnight look like?"

"A big metal suit of armor. Like a giant robot. Black with one red eye right in the middle of his forehead. He was at least ten feet tall, maybe more." Quinn closed his eyes and could see Midnight reaching for him, fingers closing and lifting him up. "The metal was the same as the Pocket Doc and like I said he shot a beam from his eye. That's what did all this. He blew up half the street then saw me. He grabbed me, spiked me and that's all I remember."

"Where was the girl while all this was happening?"

"Midnight had her in his other hand. She was out of it. Super doped up."

"You saw Midnight land?"

Quinn shook his head. "We were still inside."

"All three of you?"

"Yeah, Merrick was in front of me with the girl but we were all in the hotel still."

Faline pointed down the street to the place where Midnight had stood, where Merrick's remains still lay. "That's close to a hundred feet."

"Well, I'm not a surveyor so I wouldn't know."

"I get that. I'm not asking you the distance. I'm asking if you, Merrick and the girl were inside, how did you run out and observe him get grabbed and killed a hundred feet away?"

"With my eyes." Quinn was suddenly defensive. Faline's posture and tone were still calm, but Quinn decided that she was far from relaxed. She reminded him of an alligator, floating perfectly still just under the surface of a lake, waiting for an animal stupid enough to come take a drink. The veneer of polite inquiry was wearing thin, exposing something less pleasant beneath.

"You're telling me that you all ran out of the building together. Then something a hundred feet away grabbed and held two of you, leaving you on the porch. That doesn't make sense, Quinn."

"Are you a cop or something?"

"No, I'm a skip tracer. I don't care about you. I'm here because I'm tracking the killer you call Midnight."

"Then why are you interrogating me? I was lying there with every fucking bone in my body broken, like you said."

"If I was interrogating you, Quinn, you'd know. I don't care what you did. I just need to know what I'm up against and every detail matters."

Quinn didn't look at Faline when he answered. "I wasn't outside when Midnight grabbed them. I was upstairs, searching for opium." The admission hung in the air and Faline waited for Quinn to go on. "By the time I got out here, it was too late. So I stood there like a real action hero, too shocked to do anything. No, scratch that. I was trying to figure out how to get away without being seen. Then that sign fell. Just bad luck. Midnight heard it and tried to slam me through the planet. Happy?"

"I appreciate you answering my questions. I know it wasn't easy."

Quinn looked down the street, to the place where Merrick had fallen, then stood and walked over. He was a lonely figure framed by ruined buildings on either side of the street. At his feet were Merrick's remains, his belt and gun and boots.

Tears took Quinn by surprise, welling up in a sudden wave of emotion. He sank to his knees on the scorched earth and cried. He cried for every incomprehensible part of the last three days, every impossible leap his mind had been

58

forced to make. And for Merrick. He kept looking at the boots, worn down things that a good man had stood in.

Eventually the crying jag passed and Quinn saw Faline was standing by her bike, getting ready to leave. He wasn't embarrassed by the tears. He was sure whatever respect she might've had for him had already evaporated with the opium confession. And as soul-baring experiences went, it was less traumatic than performing an original song on stage, offering up your heart to a room full of drunk, merciless strangers. He wiped his eyes, then picked up Merrick's gun and walked back to Faline. He held it out, offering her the rune-covered handle.

"He was your friend, Quinn. You keep it."

"I don't deserve it. I ditched him when it really mattered. A weapon like this needs to be carried by someone with more honor than that."

"I already have a gun. Keep that and earn it."

"You don't have a gun like this. It looks empty, right? It's not. Never is. Something to do with the symbols, I bet. I never once saw him reload."

Faline took the gun. She popped it open and looked through the empty chambers. She spun the cylinder, listened to the tight clicking as it went around, then snapped it back into place and aimed at a splintered post. "Cover your ears."

She fired three times, tearing away pieces of wood. When she lowered the gun, smoke trickled from the barrel. Faline held it almost reverently and said, "I'd be honored to carry this."

Quinn nodded. "May it serve you well." The phrase leapt out, old and formal sounding, but somehow right.

Faline pushed the gun into her belt and threw one leg over the bike. "Hop on," she said. "I'll give you a ride to the next town."

"Yeah, that's the thing. I don't want a ride to the next town."

"You can't stay here."

"I don't want to stay here, either. I want to help you find Midnight."

Faline pulled her sunglasses down and looked over them. Her eyes were brown, as serious as Quinn had imagined. "I know you want revenge and a chance to make things right. Trust me, I understand. But I need to travel fast and the only way to do that is alone."

"I got nowhere else to go and nothing else to live for. If you drop me off in another town, there's no way I'll stay clean. Take me with you and whatever I can do to help I will."

"Quinn, I don't know what happens next but I can guarantee you people will die. And from what I've seen, you'll be one of them."

"Good," said Quinn. "That means I'll have a chance to die as something other than a coward."

For a moment Quinn thought she was going to take off without him anyway. Then she said, "If you run out on me like you did to Merrick, I'll shoot you myself."

"Fair enough," said Quinn.

She pushed the sunglasses back up and jerked a thumb behind her. "You're riding bitch."

10

THEY RODE OUT OF TOWN with the sun full in the sky. Perfect dueling weather, Quinn thought, but there would be no duels today or any other for that matter. The town was silent except for the buzzing of flies and beginning to stink of the dead.

Faline steered around the bodies until they reached the edge of town and left Tinker's Damn behind. Quinn perched on the back of the bike, holding the grab rail around his seat. The ride was smooth and the bike only made a faint hum. It wasn't long before Quinn relaxed and his mind wandered. He thought of the opium, lost somewhere in the rubble. It was strange to think of the drug without any sort of craving tagging along with it like a bad friend. For all the wonders he'd encountered in the last three days, this was the most remarkable of all. The sun and wind felt good on his face and Quinn, for the first time since he could remember, enjoyed a moment of genuine happiness.

It was mid-afternoon when Faline stopped and put the kickstand down. The display screen on the bike showed them moving southeast, currently nowhere near anything resembling civilization. So far, they'd passed only the occasional coach or horse rider. Quinn climbed off the bike and stretched, then hurried off to water a nearby tree.

He came back to find Faline modifying her shoulder holster to accommodate the revolver. She had cut a hole in the bottom of it and the longer barrel stuck out an inch or so. Under her jacket, it was barely noticeable. The old one went into a saddlebag and Quinn watched as she practiced drawing. The gun's last owner had been faster, but Quinn figured that outside of a quick-draw contest, they'd be just fine.

"Where are we heading?" he asked.

"Out of Vista. We'll be at the border tomorrow. Then we head for Quantum." Faline squinted in the distance, at the sun beginning its slow afternoon descent. "Let's get moving. I'd hate to be caught out in the open at night."

By the time it was dark, they'd taken refuge in an old barn. Pieces of the roof were missing and a half-finished puzzle of stars showed through. Dinner was a concentrate paste squeezed out of a tube, and water. After a day of riding, Quinn was sore and tired and ready to sleep. But when he lay down with his jacket balled up for a pillow, sleep was pushed away by a headful of thoughts.

Faline was propped near the door with the gun in her lap, asleep or close to it. Quinn looked up at the sky through the roof and the words of a poem came back to him. He hadn't thought of it in years but when he'd read it as a kid, he thought it was the most beautiful thing he'd ever heard.

"When the stars threw down their spears and water'd heaven with their tears." Quinn's lips moved as he whispered to himself. He looked up, filled with wonder and filled with fear.

He woke up with an aching body and an empty stomach. Faline was already packed and ready to go. They ate a quick breakfast that was the same as dinner, then climbed back on the bike and continued to ride. The desert passed in a featureless reel. When he looked over Faline's shoulder, the little dot on the bike's screen creeping southeast was the only indication they actually had a direction.

He thought of early airplane passengers, free from gravity for the first time. At what point, he wondered, did those travelers on the edge of human experience grow bored of clouds, and think of stretching, pissing, eating?

Eventually the sun climbed to the top of the sky and burned down on Quinn's head. Sometimes he almost dozed, lulled by the bike's smoothness, only to jolt back awake and squeeze the grab rail.

By early afternoon, Quinn noticed the land beginning to change, in subtle gradations of color. The endless browns and yellows of the desert began to offer a bit more green. At first it was more inedible vegetation but by the time the sun hovered low over the mountains, it was real honest-to-goodness grass.

Not long after, Faline slowed down and turned off the road, cutting over to a good-sized boulder. She steered behind it and shut the bike down. While Quinn stretched, Faline pressed her thumb against a square on the bike's dash. A green line ran across its surface and a moment later a metal band popped out of a slot. She clamped it around her wrist like a thick bracelet.

Quinn thought they were going to camp for the night but instead Faline started walking. "We're not staying here?" he asked.

"No. We're close now. A couple more miles."

"You're just leaving the bike? What if someone fucks with it?"

"That would be bad for them," she said, leaving Quinn to imagine flames shooting from the bike, incinerating any would-be vandals on the spot.

They didn't follow the road anymore. Instead they walked across open land, ducking through barbed wire fences as the late afternoon gave way to dusk. Occasionally, Faline stopped and lay flat, with an ear pressed to the ground, then stood and continued on.

In his addict days, Quinn would not have been able to keep up. Even mildly strenuous exercise made his heart feel like it was going to burst in his chest. He imagined it laboring to pump blood through hardened arteries and collapsed veins. In those moments, Quinn was aware of how much damage he'd done to his body, how weak he'd become, how close to death he lived. The way they traveled now was not particularly difficult but Quinn enjoyed the feeling of his newly healthy body at work.

The sun slipped away as they walked and a half moon rose overhead, which was barely enough light to see by. Faline seemed to have no problem walking in the dark though, so Quinn concentrated on following the vague outline of her shoulders. He stumbled along but kept up and, after what felt like hours but probably wasn't, finally saw light ahead.

It turned out to be lights, plural. A chain link fence stretched across the land, topped with loops of razor wire. Lights—actual electric lights—were set at regular intervals, marching off in either direction into the night. Quinn suddenly realized that he could hear the faint sounds of heavy machinery. These grew louder as they approached the fence and, when they finally stood in front of it, Quinn saw signs attached to the chain link that read:

KEEP OUT
TARDIGRADE
CORPORATION
KEEP OUT

Faline took her jacket off and threw it over the razor wire, then climbed the fence and dropped down on the other side. Quinn followed, pausing to free Faline's jacket before letting himself drop. Beyond the fence the land sloped upwards, gently at first then growing steeper. As they went, the din of machinery became an all-encompassing roar, then individuated into the sounds of a large-scale operation. The ground here was hard and bare of any vegetation. Eventually, it became so steep that Quinn had to dig his toes into it to avoid slipping. Once he went down onto his palms and felt a vibration in the ground under his hands.

When they were close to the top, Faline dropped to her stomach and army-crawled the rest of the way. Quinn followed suit and found himself looking down into a huge open pit. The sides had been carved into massive levels that led down to the bottom. Miners moved in and out of tunnels, tending to machines that cracked apart rock with thunderous energy. Workers with electric carts transported loads of the broken rock up to the surface, where it was dumped onto long conveyer belts and carried to crushing machines. It was busy, dirty and very loud.

"They're mining for trillium," said Faline. "Completely worthless in Vista, priceless in Quantum. There's a transport that should take us back, if we can blend in and catch a ride."

"We're near the Deadlands aren't we?"

"Yeah."

"I thought there was no way across."

Even in the dark, Quinn could read Faline's look of confusion. "We're not crossing them. The transport runs along the outer edge." She stood up. "Let's go."

11

THEY CIRCLED AROUND THE QUARRY and found a path that led to the dirty cluster of buildings making up the transport depot. Along the way, Faline spotted a work jacket slung over a piece of machinery and took it. There was a hard hat lying on the ground nearby and she took that too. They rubbed dirt on their hands and faces and hoped to pass for tired miners at the end of a long shift.

The loading station was a sheltered platform with lights running the length of the ceiling, and metal benches bolted to the concrete floor. An electronic sign on the back wall counted down to the next transport. Faline and Quinn hung back until groups of miners began filling up the platform. They fell in with them and went down to the far end. Quinn waited for someone to notice they didn't belong, but the men around them were too tired to care about much besides getting home.

Directly in front of the platform was a large, transparent tube with doors set in its side. Quinn wondered briefly if they would enter it and be somehow teleported, then dismissed the idea; the tube was large enough to drive a semi-truck through and stretched out of sight into the darkness.

When the countdown reached zero, a computerized voice warned passengers to step back behind the yellow line. Quinn watched the transport arrive and could have laughed. He'd imagined a sleek futuristic train, speeding through the night like a shiny bullet. This looked more like a canister for sending messages and objects through a vacuum system in a warehouse. It was metal with a row of windows and the words *Tardigrade ZAR Transport System* on its side. The doors of the canister lined up with those of the tube outside and both opened in tandem.

Miners streamed out, cleaner versions of those waiting to board. They filed off the platform and headed towards the quarry. Once the last wave was offloaded, the computerized voice urged passengers to begin boarding in an orderly fashion.

To Quinn, the inside didn't look much different than the subways he'd ridden on. Plastic seats with graffiti scratched into them. Metal poles that ran from floor to ceiling with storage racks above the seats. Quinn and Faline settled into a pair of seats by the door. While they waited for the transport to finish loading, Quinn asked what ZAR stood for.

"Zero Air Resistance," said Faline. Soon after, the doors hissed shut and the lights dimmed. The voice came over the speakers once again, reminding passengers to remain seated if possible and that the bathrooms were at the front and rear.

The transport began to vibrate, then started with a lurch. It slid forward slowly at first, the empty platform creeping by, then began to pick up speed. Soon they were shooting along more smoothly than any train Quinn had ever been on. He cupped his hands around his eyes and leaned against a window, trying to peer out, as the outer Deadlands passed in a dark blur. In the distance, lightning snapped along the horizon.

The transport occasionally swayed from side to side in a motion that was more soothing than nauseating. Quinn looked around and noted that almost all the other passengers were asleep in their seats. Then he turned back to the window and tried to see what he could see as they passed out of the west.

They were moving too fast to focus on any one thing for long. Instead, Quinn let his eyes sweep over the landscape. He had an impression of rock formations rising out of the ground. Some looked natural but others appeared to be roughly carved into massive heads and bodies. Frozen faces laughed, grimaced, screamed and leered at the transport. Bodies twisted into strange poses, like studies in an artist's sketchbook. Quinn wondered who had created such things, shaped the poisoned land with imagination. Once or twice he thought he glimpsed small buildings near the rocks but couldn't be sure. At one point, something hit the outer tube. It was hurled from the darkness with great force and in response, electricity arced out from the base of the transport system.

Quinn looked over to see what Faline made of it, but she was sitting with her arms crossed, staring ahead. "What's the plan now?" he asked.

"We find Midnight. To do that we need information. There's only one place that kind of tech could've come from, so that's where we'll go."

Quinn thought for a moment, trying to extract an answer from the small amount of information about the world he'd gathered. Faline shifted her gaze to a sign on the wall of the transport.

After a moment, Quinn got it. "Tardigrade." Faline seemed to clock this and file it away with all the other things about him that Quinn knew weren't adding up for her. "What if he got it from somewhere else?"

"You keep saying *he*."

Quinn realized she was right. "I guess I assumed since we're talking about girls being taken and all. What do you think Midnight is?"

"It could be an intelligent artificial life form. It could be a machine controlled remotely. Or it could be a suit with someone, the real Midnight, inside. We'll find out when we get there."

"How are you so sure Tardigrade is the place?"

"You described Midnight as being the same metal as the Pocket Doc. That's a rare alloy, only made by Tardigrade. It's supposed to be stronger than anything else in the world, even the bones of giants."

"That's what we're going on?" The seed of doubt had its roots down in Quinn's mind, wrapped around the memory, deforming it. He was suddenly, uncomfortably aware of how much rode on a split-second of his frightened, drug-craving memory. The more he thought about it, the less sure he was. When he focused on it, the metal transformed in his mind, taking on different textures until he was uncertain of what he had really seen. Now he wasn't even sure anymore what color Midnight had been.

"Stop," said Faline.

"What?"

"You're thinking about something that doesn't need to be thought about. You remember it correctly. Your instincts know what you saw."

"I don't know if I would trust me like that."

"I don't trust you, Quinn, but I do trust that particular detail. It was an honest, clear memory without your mind's fingerprints all over it, smudging it up." It wasn't cruel the way she said it, just a statement of fact.

"Why go to Tardigrade though? You found him without it. Next time just get there early."

"That was luck."

"Really? Out of the entire world, you just guessed he'd be there?"

"In a way." She turned to face Quinn, leaning in so as not to be overheard. "A month ago, a girl went missing and I was hired to find her. She'd run away with her boyfriend, completely unrelated to Midnight, which I didn't even know existed at the time. I tracked them out of town and followed their trail to where it ended on a mountain road. There was a drop off on one side and I could see the wreckage of a car below. It looked like they went off the road and burned up. But when I got down there, there was only the boyfriend in the car. He was melted like the bodies in Tinker's Damn and the passenger side door was torn off. I found that nearby, unburned. It looked like something forced them off the road, grabbed the girl, destroyed the car and disappeared. When you described Midnight it finally made sense."

"How'd you know where he—where it—would be next?"

"I started looking for reports of melted bodies with no explanation. I found one in Majis and four in Vista. The oldest was a year ago. After that, it was easy to see what they had in common."

"Something to do with a missing girl."

"Exactly. Young and tall, with blonde hair and blue eyes, just like the girl I was hired to find."

"So he has a type. How is this not getting noticed? Where I'm from, if a pretty, blonde girl goes missing, it's 24/7 coverage. The media blows a load in its pants."

"Midnight deliberately chooses places that are more

70

remote or cut off in some way. Places without much technology. Then makes sure there are no witnesses. The attacks look random, with no evidence of who did them or why."

"Melted dead bodies seem kind of hard to miss."

"Not when they're in different territories, in towns that have nothing to do with each other. Nothing connects them."

"I have a crazy idea, why don't we call the cops?"

"And then what? A sheriff from Vista is suddenly going to trust a mage from Majis? Who's going to suddenly cooperate with an officer from Darke? Places that live by different laws are suddenly going to work together? The Heroes are long gone, Quinn. There's no one to ask for help. I mean, you know this."

"Yeah, obviously," Quinn said, in what he hoped was a convincing tone.

"Do you?"

The conversation was veering dangerously close to the question he was dreading, Faline asking where he was *really* from, so he tried to steer it back towards Midnight. "I'm still not clear how you ended up in Tinker's Damn. You just picked a tall blonde at random?"

"I started looking for missing girls that fit the profile. When I learned about the one you and your friend were trying to rescue, I knew she was Midnight's type. Right look, right location. Since she was being trafficked, I was able to track her and finally had a chance to guess where Midnight might show up next. I just got there too late."

"You sure you're not a cop? You sound like one."

"I find people. I don't need a badge to do it."

"Feels like we should try and warn people somehow."

"And say what? If you're a blonde girl living anywhere, you might possibly be a target. But Midnight'll kill everyone around you so there's nothing you can do, and we have no idea when or where the next attack might happen. Great plan. No, we find him and we stop him." For the first time, Quinn heard worry in her voice. "Tinker's Damn was the worst yet. Like he's enjoying it."

"Now you're saying he."

Faline looked at the clock hanging from the ceiling of the transport. "You should get some rest while you can." She leaned back in her seat, done talking. Quinn turned his attention back out the window.

As they rocketed through the night, Quinn thought of empty towns, of Midnight, of himself. He wondered what had become of his body in Hollywood, if it had filled the apartment with a terrible smell until it could no longer be ignored. Quinn smiled at the morbid thought and his ghostly reflection in the window smiled back.

12

THE SOUND OF A BOMB INCOMING. The shriek of something tearing through the air at great speed. It starts as a tiny point of sound, then grows until it fills the world.

Midnight is coming home.

A landing pad juts out into space, over a very long drop. It is an overcast day and the ground below is hidden by a crawling gray fog. Midnight is a black bullet streaking across the sky, stopping abruptly in the air above the pad. Stabilizing rockets fire, blue spears of flame shooting down from ports in its calves and feet.

Midnight sinks to the surface of the pad and the rockets cut off just before it touches down. It drops the last half-foot and the landing pad shakes.

There is a door that leads from the pad to wherever Midnight's going, new metal set in old stone. Midnight turns and heads toward the door, each step causing a small tremor. It is a marvel of engineering but something else demands attention right now: Midnight is not alone.

In one arm, it carries a young woman. She is unconscious, no doubt freezing and deprived of oxygen from the flight. Like the others, she is blonde and, if her eyes were

73

open, it's a good bet they would be blue. Like the others, she is beautiful and tall. Her head bounces with each step Midnight takes.

The door slides open heavily, with all the speed of a blast door in a fallout shelter. Midnight steps inside and the door seals behind, slowly and finally. Unseen locks engage, sliding into place. Then they stop and the whole room is silent.

"LIGHTS."

Midnight's voice booms and the space illuminates, revealing a large, round room. Rafter beams cross high above and the walls, like those outside, are stone. Crumbling with age, yet housing technology that appears shiny and new. On the far side of the room is a wooden door that looks far too small to accommodate Midnight's dimensions. It opens and a figure steps through.

It is an old woman, coming to greet Midnight. She is tall and pale and altogether unpleasant looking. Tangled gray hair with a few remaining streaks of black frames a pinched, frowning face with dark eyes. Perhaps it was pretty once, in a thin, cold way. Now it is the face of a woman who has seen much in her years and despised it all. She stops in front of the metal giant, looking up. "Welcome home," she says.

Midnight lets the girl fall. She is still unconscious, her long hair spilling over the raised metal platform. From within Midnight comes the whir of bolts loosening, followed by the metal-on-metal sound of moving parts. Then the chest plate opens along previously unseen lines and the hulking destroyer of towns is rendered harmless.

Inside the metal shell is a man. He sits comfortably in the empty chest cavity, wearing a helmet that covers his face and head. A clutch of cables runs from the back of it, connecting somewhere inside the suit itself. The helmet is made of black metal too, but instead of a single eye, it has several. They are clustered around the upper half of the helmet like glowing red spider eyes. When the man lifts the helmet off, they go out. Likewise, the suit's cyclops eye fades. The old woman smiles at the sight of the man's face but this does nothing to soften her expression.

The framework in which the man sits, a sort of gyroscopic seat, slides out. It extends from the suit's open chest like scaffolding. Shadows slip back as he emerges and for the first time we see Midnight, the real Midnight, in the flesh.

He is perhaps forty, with blonde hair. It is stuck to his forehead with sweat, above eyes that are a deep, shocking blue. On another world, in another time, he would be called Aryan. In this world, in this time, he is simply an ordinary man with a hard set to his face. It is a joyless visage, befitting the killer inside the machine.

Steps extend from the seat, unfolding into place until they reach the stone floor. Midnight unbuckles the safety straps across his chest and stands, leaving the helmet to dangle at the end of its cables. He descends the steps and the suit looms behind him, a menacing presence even in its powered down state. Midnight is a few inches over six feet, well built in a sinewy way. He looks like a fighter, long-limbed and strong.

"Hello, mother," he says and pulls the old woman into a fierce hug. She hugs him back. When she does, the sleeves of her dress ride up to reveal her hands and wrists are covered in scars. They run over her skin in every direction but they are not the random marks of an accident. Rather, they form shapes, like those on the handle of Faline's gun. Long ago, it seems, someone cut runes into this old woman's skin.

Midnight kneels by the girl on the ground. He presses two fingers under her jaw to check her pulse. His mother brings over a wheelchair and Midnight puts the girl in it.

"So pretty," the old woman says, then spits in the girl's face.

Son and mother work together, snapping shut metal clamps on her arms and legs. They don't look much alike, but the familial resemblance is noticeable when they work. It's in their expressions, more than anything. Certainly more than the color of their eyes and hair. Midnight tests the integrity of all the restraints, finds them satisfactory.

He begins pushing the wheelchair to the door. His mother walks at his side. The lights dim as they exit. When they are gone, the room is once again dark and still.

Another room, another part of the castle.

This room is smaller. Stained glass windows are set in the far wall. They show pretty red roses with green stems and large black thorns. Beneath them is an old, ornately carved desk and a tall cabinet to match.

Midnight wheels the unconscious girl to the center of this room and locks the wheels. He waves something under her nose and she jerks awake. She is confused by her new surroundings, but instantly recoils from the man and old woman standing so close to her. Their smiles are anything but pleasant. No, they are the expressions of animals who have cornered their prey. The girl tries to raise her arms and discovers they are bound to the wheelchair. This is a normal reaction; they all do it. She bucks and strains against the clamps but it's no use. She is a prisoner.

Midnight gathers her hair in his fist and shakes her violently until she stops struggling. She cries but doesn't dare move again. Midnight looks over her face, taking in her features.

"Just like him," the old woman says. She seems pleased by this, but angered too.

Midnight turns away and now the girl screams at him,

demanding to know who the hell he is and what the hell he wants. Midnight ignores her. Threats, curses, pleas…there's nothing he hasn't heard in this room.

He opens the cabinet and takes out a small block, one of many that line the shelves. It's marked with runes on all sides. Midnight pushes it into the girl's hand and forces her fingers closed around it, crushing the block in a fist that she doesn't want to make. Then he grabs her face with his other hand. Thumb and fingers squeeze on either side, forcing her mouth open. She makes noises of pain but Midnight stares down at her and does not let go. The girl's eyes are wide and terrified, shooting all around the room. Something is happening to her.

A warm, yellow glow kindles inside her throat. It rises and fills her mouth with light, a bright tendril of which begins to stretch out and away from her. A ribbon of energy, like sunlight itself, that spans the space between the girl and Midnight. He opens his mouth and whatever is being drawn out of the girl flows into him. The blood vessels under his skin glow faintly, creating a branching network of light. More of the energy pours from the girl's nose and eyes.

The girl sits frozen in the wheelchair, face lit by the yellow light. Something vital is being taken from her, leaving her drained and fragile. Perhaps a doctor could quantify it in medical terms but it looks as if she's suddenly grown old inside her skin. She has been *dulled*.

The energy drain begins to lessen until it's only a trickle, then disappears entirely. The girl slumps back in the wheelchair. She has trouble holding her head up now. She fights but it rolls forward, bringing her chin down to her chest. She murmurs something, this husk of a person.

Midnight has never looked stronger, standing straight and seeming to thrum with the energy he's absorbed. He lets go of her hand and dust falls out, the remains of the rune-covered block.

"Test it," the old woman says.

Midnight closes his eyes, spreads his arms and concentrates. Long seconds pass. Midnight's scowling face reddens, like a man lifting a tremendous weight. Then, slowly, he begins to rise. His heels break contact with the ground and lift into the air, until only the tips of his toes are still touching. Then they too lift off and hang down, inches above the stone floor.

Midnight's body begins to shake, every muscle straining to maintain levitation. Tendons stand out on his neck and he lowers himself back to the floor, under control. He stands there, breathing hard but triumphant. His eyes blaze with conviction and purpose. They seem even bluer now, his hair somehow more golden.

The old woman is pleased and she claps her rune-scarred hands. "She had much of him."

Midnight looks at the girl in the wheelchair. A string of drool is dripping into her lap. "She was a strong one," he says. He is not surprised. When he first saw the girl he knew the power would be fresh inside her. Vital.

Some time later, the old woman pushes the wheelchair through the castle, back to the landing pad. They travel hallways of bare stone, which seem to radiate cold. Occasionally they pass once-grand tapestries, now hanging in tatters, no more substantial than the cobwebs that fill the corners and high places in this house of ruin. The girl moans and sometimes strains weakly but offers no resistance. Her hair has begun to fall out and lies on her shoulders. They round a corner and the girl's head lolls back. Her eyes have gone an old yellow. They are the eyes of a terminal patient, full of pain and fear. "Oh my, you're ugly now," Midnight's mother says.

Out on the landing pad, she pushes the chair to the very edge. The wind up here is considerable, whipping her dress against her legs and blowing her hair every which way. The girl senses something is happening but there's nothing she can do now. The old woman presses a button on the wheelchair and steps back. The restraints pop open and the chair tips forward, dumping the girl out of the seat and off the landing pad. She plummets down, picking up speed until she shoots through the fog and is lost to sight. On a clear day, the land below is visible but today, the place where girl and ground meet is hidden from view.

The old woman begins pushing the wheelchair back inside as Midnight steps out, encased in the armor, a black metal giant once more. The pad trembles under each step.

Boosters fire, pushing Midnight into the air atop a cushion of light and heat. His mother retreats to the doorway and shields her eyes as the light becomes too bright to look at. Midnight rises until he hangs in the air above the platform, then secondary rockets engage and he streaks out of sight. A moment later his mother stands alone on the landing pad.

Midnight has gone and soon there will be another one to drain. Another girl with hateful blonde hair and blue eyes, in a beautiful, too-familiar face. But for now, more magic is needed and she has work to do.

"Us against all," she whispers to herself, then goes inside to prepare for Midnight's return.

13

THE TRANSPORT ENDED ITS RUN, coasting to a gentle stop. Quinn opened his eyes. It was morning and the transport was filled with clean, early light. He and Faline followed the other workers, disembarking into a windowless room with a ramp leading up and out. There was a dividing handrail and workers passed them in the other direction, heading out to start their shift. Inspirational posters hung on the walls, illustrations of smiling, impossibly clean workers engaged in various jobs under the Tardigrade Corporation logo. They all had slogans like *Together For A Better Tomorrow, Tardigrade Means Innovation* and, Quinn's favorite, *Extraordinary Is Our Starting Point.*

They stepped outside onto the curb of a loading zone, surrounded by wet asphalt and concrete. The buildings Quinn could see were boxy shapes that he associated with warehouses and storage units. It was clean, orderly and not particularly impressive. Quinn had expected the place to be packed with high-tech wonders.

He took another look at the road which, upon closer inspection, wasn't wet asphalt at all but a glassy surface. The bright yellow centerlines were not paint but some kind of digital display. He bent down for a closer look and the section of street he was standing on suddenly turned from black to red. Quinn hopped back as what he assumed was a bus slid silently up to the curb. It seemed to ride on a cushion of air a few inches above the ground. Through the windshield he could see rows of seats but no driver.

Faline started walking away from the bus. Quinn followed and soon they were standing under a monorail track. It stretched across the sky, supported by nothing. Lights shone underneath and flat, fin-like protrusions stuck out from its sides. Directly beneath them, the air was fuzzy with distortion from whatever technology held the track aloft.

There was a lift nearby. They rode it up and boarded. At the front of their section, a screen showed a woman dressed vaguely like a flight attendant, with a blazer and pillbox hat. She smiled at riders as they entered and wished them a relaxing journey. Quinn wondered how they were going to pay, or if they were even supposed to, then decided not to ask lest he reveal another area of inexplicable ignorance.

They took seats near the door and Quinn found himself across from a map showing various tracks. Small dots moved along them. The one they were on ended near a square marked *Tardigrade Plaza*.

The monorail started forward and Quinn watched Quantum pass by his window. As they went the buildings began to change, evolving into larger, less industrial shapes. The monorail made occasional stops and the miners continued to disembark until eventually they had all been replaced by a different sort of rider: cleaner and better dressed.

It reminded Quinn of being in the international terminal at LAX. People from all over the world with their different clothes and languages and smells, all brought together in one place. He saw uniforms, jumpsuits, flowing robes and clothes that looked like they belonged on a high fashion runway. Quinn had hoped that there would be robots, walking around and mingling with people, but everyone he saw looked human. He wondered if any of them might be artificial life forms, too skillfully made to be identified. Other riders had curiously shaped objects attached to various parts of their bodies. Cybernetics or jewelry, Quinn wasn't sure, only that they looked sleek and expensive.

As they traveled, Quinn observed the residents of Quantum at their most mundane and unguarded. One man held his hands out and touched his thumbs to his fingers in a pattern—index, ring, middle, middle—and a glowing blue point appeared at the tip of each finger. A transparent model made of the same blue light popped into existence between his hands and he began to work on it. Nearby, a woman tapped at a multi-colored pad, instantly reconfiguring her hair. It grew long, curled short, turned red. She saw Quinn watching and smiled. He winked and mouthed "black" at her and a moment later, hair fell past her shoulders in dark waves. She kept it like that when she got off at the next stop. The monorail continued on, getting back up to speed again, and finally Quinn saw the sort of technological marvel he'd been waiting for.

In the distance a platform was suspended in the air, covering several acres of sky. It appeared to sit on a bank of clouds that were so perfectly fluffy and inviting they had to be artificial. A massive screen ran the length of the base, scrolling **WELCOME TO SKYLAND AMUSEMENT PARK** over and over in animated letters. Indeed, Quinn could see the colorful loops of roller coasters rising above the tallest buildings on the platform. A tower topped with the smiling neon face of a clown faced the monorail. Lights flashed all across the platform promising a world of thrills, far above the ground.

In the sky around the park were advertisements for

various rides and attractions, brightly lit signs like buoys in the air. The one closest to the monorail invited visitors to try the Cloud Coaster. Dozens of small craft flew around the park like bees around a hive. Some appeared to be ferrying visitors while others disappeared into the perfect cloudbank, servicing the no-doubt endless needs of a miles-wide floating amusement park. Lights flashed, roller coasters shot along their tracks and families kept arriving.

Quinn felt a ridiculous grin of pure happiness spreading across his face and couldn't help himself. "You ever go here?" he asked Faline.

"No."

"Never?"

"I hate roller coasters."

Quinn looked back out the window with his sense of wonder slightly deflated, as they moved closer to Tardigrade Plaza.

The monorail disgorged them in the belly of a sprawling urban beast. Here was the gleaming futurescape he'd imagined, filled with shining metal and plastic. A sleek digital dream, a cyber-reality of technological might.

Buildings stretched up, creating vast architectural canyons as if, having run out of room to spread, the city had grown skywards, stacked upon itself. It was densely packed, an unknowable place where people lived in the shadow of massive buildings, going about their business at the feet of a city too big and busy to notice.

"Welcome to the Upper City," said Faline, after they rode a lift down and stood under the floating monorail track once more. The roads here were the same glassy black but much wider. For Quinn, who was used to LA traffic, seeing cars merge and turn and drive without honking was a wonder on par with anything he'd encountered so far. It was a symphony of traffic, moving with speed and precision inches above the road. The vehicles ranged from colorful wedges with smoky black windows to bubble-like capsules containing families. They traveled together in a graceful swarm, speeding or slowing as needed in perfect, efficient choreography.

"We have to keep moving," said Faline. "Act casual, especially when we're near Tardigrade. Don't talk about anything, don't do anything suspicious."

"Security's tight?"

"You have no idea. We need to avoid attention here in the Upper City."

They'd cleaned up in the monorail's bathrooms and Quinn didn't think blending in would be a problem, given the diversity of looks. Building doors opened and closed, delivering people to the street. It was early but already, the sidewalks were getting crowded. What Quinn had thought were enclosed balconies on some of the buildings detached, cutting through the air, heading to a thousand different destinations. Everything was fast, clean and quiet. They came to an intersection marked by a red crosswalk and waited until it turned white. Quinn was mesmerized by the living clockwork of the city coming to life.

The Tardigrade headquarters were located in the center of a large plaza. It was the first place Quinn had seen in the city that was open. The buildings ended abruptly, forming a ring around it, as if the city itself worshipped this place.

The plaza contained a grassy area, and the greenery was exotic amidst the metal and plastic. On the far side, watching over it all, was Tardigrade Tower. It rose vertiginously and reflected the city in its shining silver walls. The building was topped with a horizontal section that formed a T and reflected only clouds. Near it, Quinn saw a flock of birds against the sky. They were little more than black dots in the distance but he smiled, pleased at the existence of something natural in the manufactured world around him.

People crossed the plaza, some rushing to the tower to get to work, others enjoying their morning. Workers hurried, couples strolled along, and groups of tourists moved together, taking in the wonder. A girl in pink caught Quinn's eye. Her clothes were shiny and tight, with white boots and blue sunglasses. A deep V-cut plunged all the way down the front of her shirt to her belt, exposing cleavage. She was very tall and very bald and from the way the tourists gawked, someone famous. A few small drones circled her like moons orbiting a glamorous world and Quinn imagined she was Quantum's version of a reality star.

"Who is that?" he asked Faline.

"No idea, but the less eyes on us, the better."

Ahead of them was a large golden statue of a man standing with an arm raised in front of him, palm to the sky. He gazed nobly at the orb that floated above his hand, rotating freely. At his feet, bronze children looked up in wonder while a naked silver woman embraced him from behind.

"Who's this douche?" Quinn asked.

"John Tardigrade."

"Good ol' Johnny T. He the founder or something?"

"He doesn't exist. He's a corporate mascot." Faline glanced around. She checked the sky and the plaza, searching for something.

"Guessing they don't give tours," said Quinn.

"Nope."

"Damn, there goes my best idea."

They had nearly reached the other side of the grass when Quinn noticed another flock of birds. Except this one seemed to be moving towards them rapidly. Soon he could see that they weren't birds at all. It looked more like a swarm of flies, except it was entirely silent and moved with collective precision.

"Hey, Faline."

She looked back, caught sight of the black cloud approaching and her expression told Quinn everything.

The swarm dove towards the ground a few feet in front of them. It split into two streams, which began pelting downwards with a sound like dry rice being poured. Two black piles appeared and quickly formed into shapes that were recognizable as feet.

"The hell—?"

"It's a JT. Quantum police."

"Should we run?"

"Too late for that."

Indeed whatever had arrived was quickly pouring into existence like black sand, forming from the ground up. Feet grew into legs, which grew into a torso. Arms sprouted from its sides, blossoming hands and fingers. A chest and broad shoulders took shape and finally a head, with a rudimentary face. A humanoid shape over six feet tall stood where, seconds earlier, there had been nothing.

It faced them. The black, pebbled surface of its skin seemed to ripple as thousands of tiny pieces shifted. Its movement made a faint clicking and its voice was loud and jarring.

"ATTENTION, CITIZENS."

Quinn thought its face looked vaguely like John Tardigrade and he suddenly understood what a JT was. Faline raised her hands.

"BODY MOTION ANALYSIS INDICATES *CONSPIRACY*. YOU WILL BE DETAINED. WE APOLOGIZE FOR THE INCONVENIENCE. TURN AND PLACE YOUR HANDS BEHIND YOUR BACK."

"We didn't do anything," Quinn said. He moved

slightly and the JT's head tracked him with snakelike intent.

"DO NOT RESIST. TURN AND PLACE YOUR HANDS BEHIND YOUR BACK. THIS IS YOUR FINAL WARNING." People were gathering to watch. The bald girl in pink was in the front. She appeared to be enjoying the spectacle immensely.

"Just do what it says," said Faline. She turned away from the JT, hands still raised.

"We surrender? That's it?"

"PLACE YOUR HANDS BEHIND YOUR BACK."

The JT's hands formed into amorphous restraints, tentacle-like and ready to bind their wrists. Faline began lowering her hands, then slipped one into her jacket and fired the revolver from its holster under her arm.

The bullet hit the JT and spun it. Black pieces sprayed from its shoulder. Faline drew and fired again, sending off another black spray, then grabbed Quinn's arm and started running.

They ran toward the buildings at the edge of the plaza. Quinn risked a look over his shoulder and saw the JT had regained its feet. Instead of giving chase, it simply reverted to a swarm, releasing its shape in an instant and racing after them. Other swarms appeared in the sky and joined the pursuit. Faline shot at them to no effect. She might as well have been hunting clouds.

They ran into the road and it turned a bright, warning red. Cars stopped inches from their legs. Passengers gaped at them through windshields, as Faline dodged around bumpers and jumped over hoods. Quinn followed suit, running down a cross street then into an alley. It was the cleanest, most uncluttered alley Quinn had ever seen.

When they emerged on the other side, JTs were already waiting. A silent, black wall of them.

"DO NOT RUN. SURRENDER IMMEDIATELY, CITIZENS."

As they watched, more JTs assembled and began closing in from either side. Faline pulled Quinn back into the alley and they backtracked, taking random turns. The city offered no avenue of escape. No ladders or conveniently placed manholes in the ground. They took a left and skidded to a stop, facing a dead end.

"What's the play?" asked Quinn. He was breathing hard, barely able to get the words out.

Faline didn't answer. Instead, she tapped the metal band on her wrist, the one she'd taken from the bike, and spoke into it.

"It's me. I need a shimmer *now*."

JTs filled the alley, blocking them in. Faline removed the band and dropped it on the ground. She fired at it, obliterating the device, then took aim at the JTs.

It didn't turn out to be much of a fight.

One of the JTs ran towards them. Faline shot at it and the bullets punched momentary holes. Black pieces exploded in crystalline sprays but the JT continued, body filling in as it went. Faline walked towards it firing, until the JT burst apart into a cloud and enveloped her. A moment later, another JT did the same to Quinn. He tried to swing at it but there was nothing to hit. Then he felt it under his clothes. It was like being swarmed by cold, sharp bugs. Quinn tried to crush them, hitting himself all over, but the nanobots were already everywhere.

They formed into restraints, binding wrists and ankles. The gun fell out of Faline's hand. Quinn struggled in the unbreakable metal grip and lost his balance. A moment later, Faline was slammed to the ground beside him.

"I want a lawyer!" he yelled.

"There are no lawyers," she said. Her voice was tight, clamped down on any emotion.

JTs pulled them up and began marching them out of the alley, side by side. "Justice here is automated," said Faline. "We get tried and sentenced, and all judgments are final."

14

THEY RODE IN A VEHICLE that was like a solid, featureless box on the inside. When it stopped, JTs pulled them out in front of a gleaming white building with the words ASPIRE TO ORDER above its massive door. A ring of sentry JTs surrounded it in rigid, identical stances of attention.

A mask of nanobots covered the lower half of Quinn's face, clamped painfully to his jaw. The JTs marched them up to the doors of the courthouse, which slid open to reveal a sterile, white antechamber. They dragged Quinn and Faline inside and the doors closed.

On the floor were five lines of black circles, each leading to a different door. JTs positioned Faline on one of the circles and Quinn behind her, in front of the door marked with a 5.

Ports in the ceiling opened and silver halos descended. They were slim, almost delicate looking, but at the sight of them Faline began to struggle in the JTs' grip. Quinn did too. He'd given up trying to yell since the mask had squeezed his jaw shut. Now he started again, making the sound in his throat, but it was no use. The JTs held them in place until the halos slipped over their heads, like crowns, and the effect was immediate.

Strength and will drained away, replaced by a dull emptiness. Quinn's face slackened. His eyes dilated. He slumped, tension gone from his body. It was as if someone had pulled a drain plug in his mind and let everything run out.

Dampener, thought Quinn. It was all he could muster. He could watch and understand but caring was suddenly beyond him. Any sort of complex thought was drowned out by mental white noise. It was easier to comply and he couldn't think of doing anything else anyway. He had a vague notion that he should resist but it was gone as quickly as it came. Quinn's restraints disintegrated and so did Faline's, reabsorbed into the JTs who no longer had to worry about controlling their prisoners.

Their faces were expressionless and, apart from occasional slow blinking, motionless. Quinn was aware of what was happening, but distantly, like it was happening to someone else. Emotion was muted like sound through thick walls. Inner Quinn saw but did not feel one way or the other about it. He had become an observer of himself, a witness to his own experience.

The door marked **5** opened and they were escorted into a long room that was just as painfully white. Neither Quinn nor Faline offered resistance, walking between their captors without fighting or yelling. They stood near the entrance, directly across from the face that protruded from the far wall. It was as large as Quinn and had no body. Just a face made of the same black, shifting nanotech as the JTs. It smiled benevolently at the newcomers.

Judge, thought Quinn. The gears of his mind turned slowly, bringing him to the realization that there was no exit. Only the door that they had come through. He wondered if that meant something, thought it should, but couldn't focus on what.

There were three other prisoners in the room, already being processed. They too wore the dampening rings and were encased in glass tubes that ran from the floor to the ceiling. Quinn supposed he would be in one soon.

There was a single black circle in this room and the JTs positioned Faline on it, then released her. She stood motionless as a tube descended from the ceiling, trapping her inside. The circle she stood on rose a few inches, sealing her in, and the tube began to move forward. It followed a track in the ceiling and joined the line of prisoners waiting to be called before the judge.

Quinn was next. As his tube came down, he thought that perhaps this was bad, but the idea slipped away when he tried to focus on it. Once it was gone, it was forgotten. Quinn's mind was sluggish and compliant and he accepted that he was about to be judged.

The tube at the front of the line moved closer to the judge and a spotlight came on, shining down into the prisoner's face. In front of the tube, a pedestal rose out of the floor. On its flat surface was something that looked like a tiny, decorative sun. Quinn had seen a similar piece attached to the temple of one of the monorail passengers.

The giant face spoke in the same vaguely metallic JT voice, only louder. "THE CHARGES ARE: ALTERATION AND MISUSE OF A COG-MOD." The words appeared on the side walls of the room, which Quinn realized with ponderous comprehension were screens.

Then the words disappeared. They were replaced with images which began flashing by, like a flipbook with mismatched pages. The judge watched, eyes moving with an odd, twitchy speed, until they were done and the screens were blank white surfaces again. Inner Quinn decided that they were the man's thoughts and memories, showing what crime had been committed. He wondered idly what a cog-mod was.

The judge spoke again and Quinn realized that if he was he not being controlled, he would have been terrified. He thought perhaps he should struggle and bang on the inside of the tube but did not move. His limbs were too heavy and escape was an abstract concept. The only part of him that did not seem to be paralyzed were his eyes.

"THE COURT FINDS YOU GUILTY AND YOUR SENTENCE IS RE-MOVAL FROM SOCIETY."

The prisoner's expression did not change, even as the tube began to fill with light. Quinn noticed for the first time that there was a device above the man's head, pointing down. The tip of it glowed, slowly growing in intensity until it was a white-hot point. Inner Quinn noted that this was definitely an execution, one that both he and Faline would soon experience. The thought should have worried him but it seemed far away and unimportant.

White light flashed, engulfing the prisoner and momentarily blinding Quinn. Then it dimmed and faded and the tube was empty, coated with an ashy film. The spotlight turned off and the pedestal sank back into the floor. The empty tube rose, withdrawing into the ceiling, and the next blank-faced prisoner moved up to face the judge. Faline was one back, then Quinn himself. *It's going to end soon*, he thought. It was as profound as noting that a light bulb had burned out or there was a stain on the rug.

The process repeated with the spotlight and flickering images. Soon enough, the unit at the top of the tube began to glow and Quinn thought it might be preferable to go out fighting. He couldn't remember what exactly he would be fighting for or against though, and the thought disappeared.

Faline's mind was as blank as Quinn's and she

watched the incineration with no reaction. The next prisoner moved up and now she was at the front of the line. There was something in her mind that danced just out of reach. Unlike other thoughts, this one didn't slip away. It lurked beyond the dampening barrier, colliding with it over and over, trying to find a way back in. Not a thought then, but an instinct. Something that couldn't be turned off, a part of her that ran deeper than what was in her mind. That part said it didn't have to end like this if only… If only what?

There was another bright burst and her tube began moving. It carried her in front of the judge and stopped. The evidence pedestal rose, displaying her gun and the destroyed wristband. The spotlight came on, burning into her eyes, and her charges were read out. "CONSPIRACY AGAINST AN INSTITUTION, NONCOMPLIANCE, RESISTING CONTAINMENT, MAJOR ASSAULT AND DISRUPTION OF ORDER. PREVIOUS OUTSTANDING CHARGES INCLUDE: THEFT OF PROPERTY, NONCOMPLIANCE, ASSISTING A FUGITIVE AND MAJOR ASSAULT."

Images began flicking by, accelerating into a blur, until they suddenly came to a stop on an image of the moon. A stark white ball, in a black night sky.

The judge glanced at it and seemed annoyed. "PROCEED WITH THE EVIDENCE," he said. After a moment, the images began moving again, picking up speed only to be stopped abruptly by the moon image once more.

"PROCEED," ordered the judge. His large face registered anger.

Quinn wondered what the moon meant. It floated there, still and mysterious, until the images began moving again.

In her tube, Faline remained blank-faced but adrenaline had kicked her heart into a fast, heavy trot. There was something she needed to remember but every time she tried, it was gone like so much mental smoke. She needed to break through the dampening buzz, to rip it apart with sharp claws, because nothing focused the mind and made things clear like pain. She searched for a way to inflict pain but her hands didn't want to move. She tried to open her mouth and bite down on her tongue, but nothing happened. From far away, she heard the judge add a charge of judicial obstruction. He looked angry, behind the harsh glare of the spotlight.

"THE COURT FINDS YOU GUILTY AND YOUR SENTENCE IS RE-MOVAL FROM SOCIETY."

Above her, the execution light began to glow. The unit hummed as it charged with power. A deep part of her raged, demanded that she fight, but it was useless. She couldn't even move a finger. The only thing she could do was blink. The judge seemed to be gloating, a smile curling his massive lips. Faline closed her eyes to block it out and when she did, she saw it. The afterimage of the spotlight, floating in the darkness.

Like a moon in the night sky.

Instincts beyond thought, deeper than consciousness awoke. They were reactive, primal. Animal. Her blood raced and it felt the way it always did: like dying and like being born.

Yellow color overtook her irises and veins turned black under her skin. Joints cracked loudly as they changed. Muscles stretched and reformed. Her hands lengthened and claws slid out from under her fingernails. The halo snapped as her skull swelled under it and the bubble around her mind popped. Rage poured in. The need to tear things apart, to kill and feed.

Faline threw back her head and screamed as her face changed. Bones shifted and pushed against coarsening skin. Cheekbones stood out and her jaws cracked as they widened. Long canines pushed through the new spaces in her gums.

Her scream deepened into a snarl.

Above her the unit reached its full charge and white light obscured Faline. Then the tube shook and the light died. When it did, Faline held the execution unit in her claws, trailing smoke from the place where she'd torn it out. Sparks rained down and cracks began spreading across the surface of the tube.

"PRISONER, REMAIN WHERE YOU ARE!"

Faline bared her teeth at the judge and threw her shoulder against the glass. The cracks lengthened, darting out, connecting and spreading further. She hit it again and the glass shattered.

"PRISONER, PLACE THE OBJECT ON THE GROUND!" Faline stepped off the platform. The damaged unit in her hands sparked violently from within. The judge ordered her again to remain still and she heaved it at him. It struck the rippling black mass with a sharp noise, then began sinking into the nanobots. Energy from the unit seemed to be disrupting the judge, causing ripples across his face.

"SURRENDER IMMEDIATELY!" The judge's voice was distorted and more inhuman than ever. The unit sank in further and only a small patch was still visible when it exploded. For a moment, the judge's face seemed to be lit from within. Light shone between the nanobots and Faline dove to the ground as it burst in a blinding white flash. Quinn thought he heard the judge scream: a distorted feedback squeal of rage. Then he watched impassively as a blast wave of concussive force struck his tube, covering it with a latticework of cracks.

When the light faded, the room was filled with a white haze. Where the judge had been was now a ragged hole in the wall of the courtroom. On the street outside, people stopped and gaped in.

Faline picked herself up off the floor and hit Quinn's

tube. It broke apart easily and he stood unflinching as glass flew around him. She hooked her claws into his halo and snapped it off.

Quinn couldn't get out of the tube fast enough. He started towards the hole in the wall, then stopped and went back to retrieve the gun. It had been blown across the room by the blast. Quinn scooped it up as JTs forced the door open and ran out into the street after Faline. People yelled and pointed, then quickly scattered as JTs began assembling, raining down into existence.

Nowhere to run, thought Quinn.

Faline took off down the street, running on two legs like a human. A JT began forming in their path and they ran through the cloud of its body. Quinn could feel the nanobots moving on him. They encircled his legs in loose bands that began to constrict. Quinn fought to keep running, even as they squeezed his stride shorter and shorter.

They appeared to be running toward the side of a building. Quinn could hear the sharp footsteps of JTs pounding behind them and risked a look over his shoulder. The street was filled with their running forms.

"There's nowhere to go!" Quinn yelled.

The JTs were almost within grabbing distance, metallic voices commanding them to stop and surrender. Faline ignored them and put on a final burst of speed, running directly at the wall. Quinn had a moment to notice that it seemed to shimmer slightly, like the surface of a liquid, before they ran into it at full speed.

Or rather through it.

The wall swallowed them and Quinn found himself plunging into blackness. He had the sense of accelerating, like a jet pilot pulling Gs. The forces in the unseen space pushed and stretched him. His thoughts stretched too. They were pulled apart and cast into the darkness which overtook Quinn entirely.

15

AS ABRUPTLY AS IT BEGAN, it ended. Quinn and Faline were spit out by the void onto a concrete floor, crossed with dozens of cables. They ran in all directions, connecting to the banks of servers that lined the walls. The room was dark and hot and it made for a nest-like atmosphere. Fans blew on the servers as they beeped and whirred with activity. Outside the room, there was music. Pulsing, thudding club music that shook the walls.

Quinn blinked his eyes open and looked at where they'd come from. It was an arch-like structure that seemed to be powering down. Something cycled inside it, a bright light flashing through gaps in the housing, slowing as it went. Quinn tried to stand but a bout of dizziness kept him down. While he waited for it to pass, a figure loomed out of the darkness. It was tall and angular, with blue circles for eyes. Quinn recoiled, certain the JTs had somehow followed them.

"It's ok," said Faline as she came over, human again. "Quinn, Phil. Phil, Quinn."

Quinn's mind seemed to be lagging a few paces behind the rest of him. "Are you…"

"A robot?" Phil's voice was calm. Good humored

even, as if he'd gotten this reaction before. "Yes, I am."

"Don't let that fool you," said Faline. "He has intelligence and emotions, just like you and me." She clapped the robot's shoulder. "Thank you."

"Anything for you," said Phil. Then he turned to Quinn and held out his hand. Quinn felt like his mind hadn't caught up yet, but took it and was pulled to his feet. He realized he was still holding the gun in his other hand and gave it back to Faline.

Phil was taller than Quinn, nearly seven feet, with a metal body made of plates, joints and cables. He had the look of an oft-repaired machine; through gaps, Quinn could see turning gears and hear the inner workings of the robot's body. His face wasn't a human facsimile. Rather it was a simple piece of metal with two round eyes and a small rectangle for a mouth, which lit when he spoke and flashed in time with his words. Somehow the simple features made the robot easier to be around. It wasn't pretending to be something other than what it was.

"Sorry if I was rude," said Quinn. "Thanks for getting our asses out of there."

"You're welcome," said Phil and led them across the room, stepping over cables. He had a deliberate gait and each footstep was a clanking hammer strike. By now, Quinn's eyes had adjusted to the low light. On the far side of the room, a figure was sitting in front of an array of computer screens.

"Who's that?" asked Quinn.

"That's Zee. He runs this place. If you need a shimmer, this is where you go. Off the grid, no questions asked."

In the light from the computer screens, Zee appeared to be young. Early twenties at most, still with acne on his pudgy cheeks.

"Thanks, Zee," Phil said as they passed. Without

100

looking away from his screens, he slapped hands with Phil.

The door opened, letting in pounding, wordless music. "Come back any time you want to ride the void," Zee called as they left.

The door closed behind them and they were in a packed, noisy club. Strobing lights illuminated people dancing and grinding to the beat. Quinn pushed his way through the sweaty, colliding bodies, trying not to lose sight of Phil. He saw flashes of faces and bodies and had an impression of frightening masks and costumes.

They emerged from the club and Quinn ran into a bouncer's arm as he went by. He turned to say something and could feel himself staring. The bouncer wore a breathing mask, which hid the lower half of his face. Above it, a misshapen third eye glared at Quinn from his forehead and mucous leaked constantly from openings in his cheeks.

"Got a problem?" he growled. Quinn noticed three fingers on one hand and more than five on the other. He started towards Quinn and suddenly Phil was there, pulling Quinn away and apologizing. The bouncer gave them a last look and resumed his post.

"Lots of people around here like that," Phil said. "Mutants. You get used to it."

The street reminded Quinn of a third world country. It was packed, with no apparent rules for pedestrians or traffic. Cars and bikes moved up and down the street, splashing through puddles and weaving onto the busy sidewalks as needed. Pedestrians jumped out of the way. Most wore masks like the bouncer, or had cloth wrapped around their faces, and Quinn could understand why. The air burned in the back of his throat, harsh like welding fumes. His eyes watered.

"Welcome to the Lower City," said Phil.

It was almost as hot outside as it was in the club.

They had run through the shimmer in broad daylight, but now the sky was dark. Not far away, Quinn heard a rumble of thunder. Boxy transports passed overhead. Loud dirty things, low enough for the warm air they displaced to stir the trash on the streets. The lights on their sides were diffused by the smog that hung over the Lower City. It was the opposite of the clean, orderly place they'd come from.

Dingy shops lined the street, packed side by side and on top of each other, advertising with bright neon signs. They passed one that offered *"Real Live Girls! No muties, just beauties!"* A flickering hologram out front gyrated, shaking her ass and beckoning passerby. A family in breathing masks hurried past and the child stuck a hand through the hologram, disrupting it; light splayed out from under his fingers. His mother pulled him along. There was graffiti everywhere. One memorable piece suggested that John Tardigrade sucked mutant cock.

Phil led them down the street, skirting the beggars with missing limbs and deformed faces who lined the outsides of the shops. Most Lower City dwellers hurried by them without stopping.

Phil's apartment was in a building that looked more like a prison. Inside, they took a lift that shook and rattled as it went up. With every passing floor, Quinn expected it to break free and go plummeting down. The apartment itself was small, with a living area and a single bedroom. A window looked out over the city through a black film on the outside that made it hard to see anything.

Inside though, the apartment had been cleaned and furnished with secondhand things. There were rugs and scraps of carpet on the floor, a couch against one wall, and a table sitting in the square of kitchen space. They sat around it in mismatched chairs and Phil brought out bottles of room temperature water and vacuum-sealed packages, with *Single Food Ration* stamped on each.

"They're not much in the way of taste from what people tell me, but you can live on them," said Phil.

Quinn pulled off the silver wrapping to expose a dark colored brick with no smell and a texture like paraffin wax. He took a bite and discovered it had an agreeable, vaguely bean-like taste.

When they finished eating, Phil put the wrappers in a trashcan and returned to the table. "What brings you to Quantum?" he asked.

"We need to break into Tardigrade," said Faline. From Phil's silence, Quinn decided it was akin to casually mentioning that one intended to break into a casino.

After he'd processed it, Phil said, "You know that's impossible, right?"

"You mean it hasn't been done before," said Faline.

"Yes, and for good reason," said Phil. "Why would you possibly want to?"

"Information," said Faline.

"Information?"

"Someone is using Tardigrade technology to commit mass murder and abduct young women. We're trying to find out who it is. If you can't be involved, I understand."

"I just don't want to see either of you get hurt," said Phil, and Quinn found the robot's words oddly touching. "Tardigrade Tower is the most secure building ever constructed. Besides cameras, there are retinal scans, voiceprint identification, bio analysis, neuro-pattern tracking and that's just to get in the door. I'm sure there are lots of other measures I don't know about.

"Everything has a weakness. If you had to break in, how would you do it?"

Phil thought for a moment. Finally, his mouth lit as he answered. "I don't know enough about the Tower to suggest a way of breaking in. Honestly, I don't think it can be done." Faline started to say something and Phil held up his hand. "But I also know better than to try and talk you out of it."

Faline laughed. "You know me so well."

"Tomorrow I can take you to someone who knows more."

"Seems kinda dangerous to advertise we're looking to break into Tardigrade," said Quinn.

"We can trust him. He deals in illegal tech. I sell to him on occasion."

"How do you know he won't sell us out? I wouldn't exactly trust my dealer to keep a secret."

"His hatred for the Upper City in general and Tardigrade in particular is genuine. In addition to tech, he also deals in information. Upper City dwellers who venture down here generally engage in compromising activities. He will either be able to help you or convince you otherwise. I personally hope it's the latter."

Soon after, Phil excused himself for the night. "To rest," he said and Quinn wasn't sure if he was joking. Even with the carpet, Phil's footsteps were heavy enough to shake the floor. He went into the bedroom and the door slid itself shut with a pneumatic wheeze.

"The downstairs neighbors must love him," said Quinn.

"They hate him. Everyone here does. They see him as part of Tardigrade. And Tardigrade sees him as their property, so they hate him too."

"Why not leave? Ditch this smogged up hellhole."

"It's where he's safest, believe it or not. Anywhere

else, Tardigrade could find him and take him. Here, that would be seen as an attack. Even the mightiest empires fear the barbarian hordes, if they're smart."

"Those previous charges they read in court today, do they have something to do with how you know Phil?"

Faline nodded but did not elaborate.

As they sat at the table, Quinn discovered he wasn't able to look at Faline without seeing her transform in his mind. Bones moving, teeth pushing out and, through it all, the cracking sound of growth.

"Just ask."

Quinn realized he'd been staring. He thought about making a joke, then plunged ahead. "Don't take this the wrong way, but what are you?"

"A werewolf."

For awhile, no one said anything further. Then Quinn asked, "Does it hurt?"

"Yes. But it feels good too. I don't know how to explain it."

"I get that part. I like getting tattoos." Quinn looked down at his bare arms with regret.

"You did good today."

"Thanks. You kind of did all the work."

"You went back for the gun. That's not nothing. Honestly, I thought you'd be sucking your thumb and begging to go home by now."

"You say the sweetest things," Quinn said and, as she took a drink, he thought he saw her smile. "I gotta be honest, you don't look like I thought a werewolf would look."

"Furry?"

"Yeah."

"There are different species. Some transform completely and go on all fours. Others stay upright. Some grow fur, some don't." Quinn was about to ask something else, but she cut him off. "My turn."

"Shoot."

"Where are you from?"

Quinn answered without thinking. "Crowheart."

"Where's that?"

"It's a little place in Vista, up north. Named after this chief who was killed there." Quinn listened to himself as the words came out with casual, effortless guile. He wanted to stop himself and take them back, but it was already too late.

"You don't sound like you're from Vista. You don't sound like you're from anywhere, actually."

"It's a small town. I guess you could say it's cut off from the rest of the world."

"That makes sense. I was wondering why you didn't seem to know about some things."

"A lot of that stuff just isn't important there," said Quinn. He was fully selling the lie now and had no idea why he'd told it in the first place.

"I hear Vista's like that."

"Some places." Quinn leapt blindly for safer conversational ground. "So, what do you do when you're not getting on Quantum's most wanted list? Are you married?"

Faline laughed. "Hell no."

"How does that work? Do you date humans or no?"

"No, just werewolves."

"Seems a little closeminded."

"Would you fuck a wolf? No, it's a different species. Why'd you leave Crowheart?"

"It's a boring ass little town with zero opportunities. Unless you're a tumbleweed aficionado there's not a whole lot there. Were you born a werewolf?"

"No," said Faline and when she did, Quinn knew the

conversation was over. Whatever door had begun to open with Faline was closed again. She finished the last of her water and got up from the table. "Better get some sleep before we meet Phil's guy." She went over to the couch, pulled off her boots and stretched out with an arm over her eyes.

Quinn sat at the table a moment longer, then laid out on the floor with his jacket for a pillow but found himself too keyed up to sleep. When he closed his eyes, the events from the courtroom replayed on a constant loop. Quinn felt both drained and exhilarated, far from sleep.

While he lay there the lights in the apartment dimmed and went out, leaving the room in near darkness. From a shelf near the window came the soft glow of a grow light, shining over a number of small plants. Quinn got up and went to look. They were flowers and he couldn't help but smile at the little bit of colorful life.

There were other shelves with plants around the room and Quinn went to look at them too. While he inspected some near the bedroom, he moved too close to the door and it slid open. Phil was sitting on the floor, holding a potted plant, and he looked up at Quinn standing in the doorway. The light from his eyes reflected on the metal contours of his face, making him look like a psychedelic raccoon.

"Sorry," said Quinn.

"It's ok, please come in," said Phil. He indicated a space on the floor opposite himself. "Couldn't sleep?" he asked, when Quinn sat down.

"No. How about you? Do you sleep?"

"No, I recharge occasionally."

"I hope I didn't interrupt."

"Not at all. Any friend of Faline is a friend of mine."

"I like all the plants," Quinn said.

"Thanks. They're everything this place is not. That

I'm not. This one here is my favorite."

"How do you get them? Doesn't seem like there's much greenery around here."

"I have a connection." Phil paused, looking at the plant. "When I hold this one, I can detect slightly increased levels of oxygen in the air and it inclines ever so slightly towards me. My eyes can see it growing. Every incremental change in the cycle of its life. I dream of seeing a forest someday, of walking among trees and planting this in the ground. But like me, I think it will have to live out its life in this dreary place."

"Maybe Faline can help you."

"She's already done plenty for me. More than I could ever repay. I can tell you, if you'd like to hear."

Quinn said he would and Phil obliged.

16

I'M ONE OF THE TL-250 *class, built by the Tardigrade Corporation as a labor model. Bigger, stronger and more durable than most robots, made for a single purpose: to construct a transport system between Quantum and the trillium deposits in Vista.*

I was part of the frontline crew, operating at the edge of the Deadlands. Technology still worked there, but the environment would have been fatal for humans. A Tardigrade unit works constantly. The only time I stopped was to recharge or get repaired. That would drive me insane now, but back then I was only a machine.

In the Outer Deadlands there are creatures called scrappers. Maybe they were people once, before the Heroes War. Now they live in tribes and raid anyone who ventures too far out or settles too close. They've adapted to the environment, becoming deformed, unstable and violent. Building the Tube must have seemed like a gift from the gods to them, though I can't imagine what twisted deities they worship. Tardigrade was practically delivering valuable materials to them on a slow-moving conveyor belt.

We saw them watching from afar. Just little figures on the hills. They watched for three days, then attacked. Our security units repelled them easily at first. They came in small groups, testing our defenses. As we moved through the Deadlands, I noticed different tribes in different territories.

Some wore pieces of metal, grafted onto their bodies like spikes. They had mutated spiders the size of dogs that attacked with them. I'll never forget the sound of their legs as they ran or the sound of their mandibles. Like shears. Strong enough to cut metal.

Then there were the Rotters, with maggots infesting them. They were big, both the men and women, but their bodies were soft with rot. Full of holes from the maggots. Flies buzzed constantly. Their flesh tore easily but they kept fighting, until you destroyed the brain or the heart. That was one of the few times I was glad not to have the ability to smell.

Living Skulls, Skin Lords, Green Folk, Borogites, Grabbies…those were scrappers with multiple arms, growing randomly. The Deadlands poison them before they're even born. Some have multiple legs, and even heads. Their chief had two extra faces, one on his chest and one down on his stomach.

We'd repel the attacks, kill the scrappers and bury them under the foundations of the Tube. There must be hundreds between Quantum and Vista. It wasn't hard either. They have guns and hand weapons, and even a few vehicles. But they were no match for the power of Tardigrade.

At least that's what we thought.

It was the Bone Kings that got us. They used scavenged fuel cells to make explosives and lined a square quarter mile with them. When the first one exploded, another TL-250 was standing over it. Three hundred pounds of metal thrown in the air like a rag doll. Then others started going off and we ran. I was scheduled to recharge soon and had almost no power left.

I was hit early. When I tried to get up nothing happened and when I looked, my legs were gone.

After that I had to drag myself. What was left of me anyway. How the Bone Kings didn't see me, I don't know. Pure luck, I suppose. I dragged myself for a few miles until I found a pile of boulders. I dug under the rocks to hide. The whole time, I felt my power levels dropping.

By then, they were down to reserves. I knew if I moved, it would have to be toward a recharge or I'd be another dead hunk of metal, waiting to be scavenged.

I stayed there for two days and during that time, Tardigrade disconnected me from their network. As far as they were concerned, I was destroyed. I felt the connection disappear and simply waited for my power to run out.

Then I began to hear a voice.

It knew what had happened to me and it knew other things. About my existence, things I had seen. I didn't have memories then, only stored data, but the voice knew about everything. It was never quiet. Always speaking. Sometimes clearly, sometimes disjointed phrases or nonsense. I didn't know it then, but in the place where Tardigrade had removed their directives, consciousness began to form. Life fills empty spaces, seeks to change them.

I did not have intelligence then and was only built to act in the most efficient way, for the good of my makers. That would have meant staying where I was until my power was gone. But the voice said not to do that and I listened. It said to survive, so I did. Is that not a hallmark of life, that it desires to keep itself alive?

I began to wonder if my altered state of being was real or a simulation. Perhaps I was still being assembled at Tardigrade and my whole existence was created by a glitch in a server. A bit of stray code. Digital indigestion. I wondered: what if it was all just a mistake that created parameters to allow for its own existence in an otherwise ordered system? In which case, a self-correcting algorithm would be triggered and overwrite me. I almost wanted that. Existence would be simple again.

But it would also be uninteresting. It wouldn't just be the voice that was gone, but the vastness of potential that had opened within me. I did not want my experience of being to end so quickly. And just like that, I felt my first emotions: surprise, wonder and fear.

Others followed, my first steps as a sentient being, crossing the space between operational and intelligent. I realized I was being irrational and embraced it. Only a free mind can behave irrationally. A machine executing a program could never intentionally deviate from its process. I am illogical and emotional, therefore I am. Finally, I recognized the voice within, telling me all this, as my own.

I often wonder what happened. There's magic in the Deadlands, left over from the spells that were cast during the Heroes War. Is that what changed me? Or am I a technological mutation, non-organic evolution, driven to survive by randomness in my code instead of genes? A combination of both? Something else entirely? I don't know but in a way I find it comforting. After all, wondering where you come from is another hallmark of life.

My sensors indicated that it was pointless to move, but my inner voice said to search, even fruitlessly, so I did. I dragged myself out of the hole and deeper into the Deadlands, feeling my power drain to critical levels. I knew exactly how much each movement cost and exactly how much time I had left, but I kept going. I decided it was better to crawl a hundred feet and die than give up and wait for the end.

I reached the edge of the minefield with less than one percent of my power left, when I realized something. It was so simple, so obvious, I'd overlooked it since the beginning: under the ground was more than enough power to destroy me or keep me going.

I dug with my hands. It's strange to count down your movements, knowing exactly how few you have left and hoping you don't need them all. I extracted one of the fuel cells the Bone Kings had buried and carefully removed its trigger. Then I opened my chest to access my charging network, and pulled wires from the remains of my legs to connect it.

After I was done charging I dragged myself onwards, until I came within sight of Scrap City. The Angels live there. They are one of the strangest tribes of the Deadlands, with pale white skin and red eyes. They're not deformed like the others. Some are even beautiful but make no mistake, they are barbarians. They occasionally raid settlements in Vista for women to thread their population with.

Scrap City is their kingdom, a walled settlement made of scavenged metal. Skins of enemies are draped like flags from the walls. I waited until night then pulled myself up the outer wall and climbed down into the city.

The treasury was guarded by several male Angels but I snuck past them. Inside, it was filled with machinery and I found legs from other units to replace mine. Scrap City is not a quiet place and I connected the legs without interruption, bolting and welding myself back together. Then I stood and walked out.

A scrapper stood watch at the exit and I considered killing him. It would have been easy. He was facing away and I could have crushed his skull or throat with my hands, but I did not. Instead, I reached around his neck with an arm and applied pressure. I could detect his heart rate and breathing and held him until he was unconscious.

I realized something then. Intelligence without empathy is a dangerous thing. Killing him would have been easy and made things easier for me. If I were just a machine, running scenarios and calculating odds, I would have done it. But I could not. Without empathy, intelligence is capable of anything to serve its own ends. The only limit is one's imagination. And I have discovered that an intelligent being can imagine terrible things.

I laid the scrapper down, still breathing, and continued on my new legs away from the Outer Deadlands. I intended to walk until I reached Vista. Then I planned to find a border town where those like me, with no clear place, seem to collect.

Tardigrade security found me there eventually. They identified me and demanded I return. I refused, saying that my disconnection was a release and I was no longer a machine for labor. It didn't matter and they would have taken me back by force, if it wasn't for Faline. She was there looking for someone else, but risked her life to save a robot she'd never even met before.

We fought and we escaped. As much as I wanted a life far away from Quantum, I knew that the Lower City was the only place I would ever be safe from Tardigrade. Faline gave me a ride there and we *parted as friends. When she asked my name, I said Phil. I don't know why, but it came to mind. Since then, I've kept it and I've stayed here, trying to put a life together. It might not be much but it's mine. I'll never forget that without Faline, I wouldn't have it. I wouldn't have anything. I wouldn't even exist, yet here we are."*

When Phil was done with his story he sat holding the plant, the room lit only by the soft blue glow of his eyes.

17

MORNING CAME AND THE SUN rose behind a layer of pollution that turned the sky a sick yellow. Phil led them through streets that looked worse by day than by night. In the distance, plumes of black smoke rose from factories and poured into the end-of-the-world sky.

Quinn and Faline wore cloths over their faces, but their eyes still stung and watered. They went down dirty, cluttered streets, turning so many times Quinn lost all sense of direction. They passed through a tunnel illuminated by lights strung along the walls and ceiling. The whole of the space was crammed with makeshift stalls selling trinkets or food. Vendors crowded around them, chattering loudly and waving merchandise. Their mutated faces and bodies formed a loud, tugging mass. Sound echoed in the tunnel; once noticed, it became a deafening cacophony.

Beyond the tunnel, Quinn had a sense they'd passed some sort of invisible demarcation. There were no beggars here and the few vehicles they saw passed quickly. Phil turned down a street lined by dilapidated buildings. Some had broken windows and kicked in doors. Others were boarded up and sealed off. Phil went up to one of these and knocked. The sound was loud in the empty street.

A barely intelligible voice squawked out of a speaker hidden nearby. "What do you want?"

Phil looked above the door, addressing the camera there. "It's Phil. I'm selling."

The camera rotated to look at Quinn and Faline. "Who's with you?"

"Friends of mine." Phil mimed pulling down their facecloths. They did, and soon the door opened just wide enough to admit them.

They stepped into a small room with the most heavily mutated Lower City dweller Quinn had seen yet. Two heads watched them, rising from the broad shoulders of a single body. He (or they, Quinn wasn't sure) shut the door and slid thick bolts back across, locking it. In one hand, the mutant held a gun with a large, complicated-looking barrel. Quinn wasn't sure if it fired bullets or some kind of energy, but from the look on the mutant's faces, he didn't think it would take much to find out. The mutant pointed to a door on the other side of the room and both heads watched as they went through.

Inside was an old man behind a counter, or at least half of one. His legs were gone and the bottom of his torso was affixed to a levitating platform. He bobbed up and down on the air.

As they crossed the room, wall-mounted guns locked on, tracking them. On the counter, a small swarm of nanobots filled a transparent container. Occasionally they coalesced into an animal, then flew apart again. Quinn watched a rat form, scratch around and separate.

"What do you have for me today?" asked the old man. His face was deeply wrinkled but his eyes seemed bright and aware.

Phil handed the old man a piece of metal with several facets. Quinn's mind struggled to come up with the word for it and finally did: a polyhedron. It reminded him of the many-sided dice he'd seen used in board games. The old man held it up between a finger and thumb, like a jeweler appraising a diamond. One of his eyes rolled up, but instead of exposing the white of the eyeball beneath, another iris rotated into place. With this one, he studied the object and smiled. He moved it in front of his other eye. This one rolled down and to the side, passing irises until it found the right one. The old man turned the polyhedron slowly, then finally set it back down on the counter. His eyes spun, resetting to their original positions. "Phenomenal composition, Phil. What do I owe you?"

"Actually, today I'd like to trade."

"Now we're talking." The old man sounded gleeful at the prospect of bartering. He pressed a button under the counter and the walls behind him opened. Metal barriers rattled up, exposing shelves of contraband. Weapons and devices of all kinds, internal organs suspended in bubbling liquid and other, stranger things. A human mask alternated through faces, each one different than the last. "What do you need?" he asked.

"We need to break into Tardigrade," said Faline.

The old man laughed until he realized she was serious. "Can't be done," he said.

"How do you know?" Faline asked.

"Anyone who tries ends up dead."

"So you're saying it's never been done right."

The old man spoke in measured tones. "I'll tell you what I tell anyone crazy enough to bring this up. I've been around a long time, since back before the Heroes War. Back when you could still walk down the street without a breathing

117

mask. I remember when Tardigrade came here, promising work and money for everyone. We let them put their factories in and they poisoned this city. They poisoned us. I remember all the anger, all the people who wanted revenge. Young people became violent and they tried to bring down Tardigrade. Not once did they even come close."

"There's a first time for everything," said Faline.

"There's a last time for everything too, young woman. Or at least there should be." The old man's bright, artificial eyes stared into Faline's and Quinn wondered what he could see.

"I guess you're not the man we need," she said and started to walk away.

"You have no idea what you're talking about. I remember all their names and faces. When it first happened, I wanted to bring Tardigrade down too. I gave my friends weapons and sent them off to die. I should've stopped there, but I was too angry. It took more dead friends before I finally understood, there is no way. Listen to an old man who knows. There is no device, no weapon, no plan that can get you inside that building."

Faline started to speak but the old man held up his hand. "Just listen. I remember them all. They stood there, looking at me just like you're looking at me. Full of purpose or some warped sense of duty." His voice had become an angry rasp. His hands clenched into gnarled fists. "There was one who tried to use a neural mask and a bio swap kit to get in. He took about two steps through the door and Tardigrade overloaded the mask. I'm not exaggerating when I say his brains came out his ears. There was another who tried with a binding-force breaker. I can see you don't know what that is. It's a device that temporarily separates the molecules of solid matter so a person can pass through. He stepped into the wall, then Tardigrade shut the breaker down. With him inside. Or you could be like the Faceless. They were an anarchist group operating here in the Lower City, about thirty years ago. They had the idea of secretly constructing a portal inside Tardigrade. They built it remotely with hacked nanobots inside a soundproof air purification chamber. Tardigrade recalibrated the exit point to the waste processing system, which means they ended up drowning in shit. That's what happens when you try to break in."

"That's what happened when *they* tried to break in," said Faline.

"Do what you want, but I won't help you. You can't outsmart them." He turned away from Faline, done with the conversation. "Phil, I can pay you for this or you can take it back. Up to you."

"Who says we have to?"

The other three looked at Quinn, as if they'd forgotten he was there. He repeated himself. "Who says we have to?"

"Have to what?" asked the old man.

"Outsmart them."

The old man made a sound of hopeless disgust. "Another fool."

"Dude, everyone you mentioned tried to beat Tardigrade at their own game and what happened?"

"They died," said the old man.

"Their plans failed. Every single one of their high-tech, complex, genius plans failed. So what if we go the other way? Low tech."

"And use what? Sticks and stones?"

"If need be. We come at them on a level they're too sophisticated to even understand. I'm talking the basics. Brute force."

"And what do you propose to do with the *basics*?"

Quinn put one arm around Faline's shoulders and the other around Phil's. He grinned at the old man. "Crash the fuckin' party."

18

THE SHIP MOVED SLOWLY OVER the city, taking in the sights. It was a large vessel with plenty of windows and the words *Upper City Tours* painted on the side. It was filled with tourists, walking from window to window and gawking at the city spread out below. Quinn couldn't help but think of the double decker tour buses that cruised around Hollywood, filled with star struck out-of-towners clogging up traffic.

There was even a tour guide. A clean-cut young man sat near the front of the ship, filling them in on the history of the capital. He kept up the peppy chatter, directing the passengers to look left or right at the various wonders the Upper City had to offer.

"…and if you'll look off the starboard side—which is what?"

"Right side!" said a little girl near the front, and was met with good-natured laughter from the group.

"Very good!" said the guide. "I think we have a future pilot on our hands. Now if you look starboard you'll see the main campus of Valeris Academy, which is the most prestigious school in all of Quantum. Some very famous people have gone there, including our current Chancellor and several

Prefects."

Quinn looked out at the buildings below. It was mid-morning on another flawless day, and Quinn wondered if they controlled the weather. He half-listened as the tour guide went on, extolling the history and virtues of the Upper City.

"...their identity is still a mystery but they're known today as the First Builders and their ancient pyramids remain as a monument to innovation. And now, we're going to see something truly amazing. The technology that powers our homes, protects our families and just makes life a whole lot easier comes from one place."

"Tardy-grade!" squealed the little girl, occasioning more laughter. Ahead of the ship, they could see Tardigrade Tower looming over the city. Faline stood nearby, watching as they drew closer.

"Correct!" said the guide. "Coming up is Tardigrade Tower, the headquarters of the most powerful corporation in the entire world. Every technological innovation that defines Ouros today started inside that very building. Every single person who lives in this city either works there or knows someone who does. They have over twenty-five thousand employees in this Tower alone, on two hundred and fifty floors, reaching half a mile into the sky. And today, we're going to give you a very special treat: a view of the city that only Tardigrade's top executives get to see."

Quinn and Faline stood together at a window as the ship approached the tower. They'd gotten new clothes to blend in with the tourists and Upper City dwellers. Faline wore a short cloak with a hood that draped over her face. Quinn had traded his gunslinger's coat for a jacket with metal shoulders and wore a shiny silver visor over his eyes. He planned to ditch both at the first possible moment.

The ship began to ascend, rising past the tower's

midway point. Quinn felt the way he did before a show, waiting to hit the stage as the final moments of calm ticked away. He glanced at Faline and saw her lips moving silently, whispering to herself.

"Are you praying?" he asked.

"No. You know what they say: pray with one hand, shoot with the other, and see which one saves you. Ready?"

"Let's do it."

Faline looked him over to see if he meant it, then nodded. "Let's go."

They walked to the back of the ship, where stairs led down to a lower level. Down here, the tour guide's patter continued over speakers and families gathered around the large window in the center of the floor. It was roped off and took up most of the room, enclosed by a walkway. People crowded around to look down on the city. Quinn saw one kid stick a brave foot out beyond the rope and surreptitiously touch the glass.

Quinn and Faline moved behind the tourists, on the edge of the room. There were no windows here; instead, there were a series of doors along the sides of the ship, with the word EMERGENCY stenciled in red. Next to each was a large button, shielded in a plastic case.

"This one, right?"

"That's it," said Faline, and Quinn smashed the case with his elbow.

The crowd was slow to react but the security guards by the stairs, dressed in faux-extravagant uniforms, rushed over to stop them. People clogged the walkway, including the window-toucher who now stared up at Quinn and Faline, frozen in shock with a finger in his nose.

The guards yelled for the tourists to clear a path as an alarm blared and the emergency doors popped open in unison. Panicked tourists ran screaming in every direction.

The doors opened to life vessels: round ships with clear domed tops. Each had four seats mounted on a gyroscopic framework. Quinn jumped in and Faline followed with her gun drawn, holding off the guards. They watched with their hands raised as she hit the manual release and the doors closed. They sealed with a vacuum sound and the bubble dropped away from the underside of the ship. It fell for a heart-stopping second, then rockets fired and the bubble began to sink slowly, in a controlled descent.

A woman's voice came over the speakers, impossibly calm and soothing. *"We apologize for the inconvenience. Please remain seated and we'll have you safely on the ground in no time."* Quinn could see other life vessels lining the underside of the ship like fish eggs.

He felt under his seat and pulled out a backpack. "Phil's guy came through," he said, as Faline reached down and found a bag of her own. From it she removed a piece of jerry-rigged tech that looked like a flat box with a sort of joystick on top, except instead of a handle it was a disk made to be gripped with the palm down. Faline planted it on the display panel between their seats. It made a crunching sound and its base sealed tight against the panel, a technological parasite taking hold. They waited for several long seconds, and Quinn had time to reflect that their plan hinged on a piece of illegal tech from a man whose name they didn't even know. Then the woman's voice said, *"Emergency override engaged,"* as it decayed into a deep and tortured groan from the invasive technology.

Faline gripped the disk, pulled it up, and the bubble rose. They drifted past the tour ship as other bubbles began to detach and float down. Quinn could see the tour guide, incredulous at a window, and shot him a salute.

"Focus," said Faline. "We're about to—"

"ATTENTION, YOUR CRAFT IS VIOLATING SECURE AIRSPACE." There was no mistaking the sound of an official Tardigrade announcement, booming all around them. "RESUME YOUR DE-SCENT."

"Hold on," said Faline. She pressed the makeshift control stick forward. Smoke began curling from the panel under it as the bubble headed towards the tower's roof.

"CITIZEN, THIS IS YOUR FINAL WARNING. HALT YOUR AP-PROACH OR WE WILL BE FORCED TO DEFEND THIS AIRSPACE."

When they rose above the edge of the roof, turrets rotated to lock on and began firing. Bolts of energy rocked their life bubble and Faline fought to keep it on course. The smoke coming from the panel thickened, filling the ship with the smell of frying circuits.

The turrets fired and the small craft shook violently. A protective field absorbed the blasts, flashing red with each one. Quinn's mind went briefly to *Star Trek* and characters yelling about shields dropping.

"The good news is they make these things just about indestructible," said Faline.

As they moved closer, blasts rocked the ship with greater power. Cracks began to form in the dome. Quinn jerked the seatbelt across his lap and cinched it tight, then braced for the ship to be blown out of the sky, just short of the roof. The cracks around them grew with crystalline split-ting sounds.

Faline shoved the control disk forward. The bubble dove, bounced, and came down again. It bounded across the roof, demolishing a turret, as it skidded toward the executive clubhouse perched on top of the tower. The shield gave a final red flash and disappeared. Then each bounce was a pain-ful, neck-snapping jolt.

The gyroscopic seats spun Quinn and Faline as the ship rolled like an untethered wrecking ball. It crashed into the clubhouse and the ride came to a sudden stop, wedged in the hole it had smashed into Tardigrade. The dome was covered with an opaque web of cracks, obscuring the room beyond.

Sparks hissed and spit around the edge of the door and it dropped away from the ship. Faline hauled herself up and out in one limber motion. Quinn unbuckled, grabbed his bag and did the same.

For the first time in its history, the most secure building ever constructed had been breached.

They were in a swanky receiving room that offered a three-hundred-and-sixty-degree view of the sky. Directly below, on the executive levels of Tardigrade Tower, alarms blared. In the clubhouse, lights flickered and the wind roared outside broken windows. Somehow, a large aquarium full of strange fish remained untouched, but furniture was toppled and scattered around the room. An expensive chandelier swung back and forth, dangling jewels clashing, above a concierge station. A young man in a uniform huddled behind it with his eyes squeezed shut.

Across the room was a lift and next to it, stairs that descended through an opening in the floor. Faline took them and Quinn followed, trying not to jostle the contents of his bag. Whatever was inside made glassy clinking sounds.

The stairs spiraled downwards, wrapping around the lift column, and ending some twenty feet below. Quinn and Faline stood in a large open space that would have been impressive had it not been transformed into a panicked hell. In addition to the alarms, the lighting was a deep, emergency red. On screens, the words "REPORT TO YOUR SAFE ZONES" flashed over and over. The elite of Tardigrade ignored these warnings and ran instead to the bank of lifts that led to the tower proper. They fought to cram in and escape the upper levels.

On each end of the room was a door with massive letters above it. The one to the left read SUITES and the one to the right was ARCHIVES.

They headed right, working against the crowd. Faline clocked a few workers in white uniforms emerging from the Archive door. They ran for the lifts and she snagged one as he went by, swinging him around and twisting his arm behind his back. None of the others seemed to notice as they fled and, if they did, no one stopped to help.

The man tried to break free, flailing at her over his shoulder. Faline jerked his arm up higher between his shoulder blades and grabbed the back of his neck with her free hand.

She held him like this for a moment, until the fight suddenly went out of him. He relaxed and Faline let go. Where her hand had been, there was a patch stuck to the back of his neck. Quinn saw his pupils were dilated and he had a vaguely dreamy look now. "Sorry about that," he said. His voice was pleasant and unconcerned, an island of serenity amidst the chaos. He had small metal implants at each temple and a name badge that read 'Lem.' They hustled him over to the Archives and Faline asked him to open the door. He waved a hand, the one she had been twisting behind his back less than a minute ago, in front of a scanner. Quinn turned to see if anyone was watching them and felt a jolt of fear.

JTs were among the crowd, reestablishing order, with more still assembling. Then Faline was pulling him into the Archives along with Lem and smashing the scanner as they went. The doors closed behind them, double layers of metal sealing shut. The outer one closed vertically, the inner one horizontally. Quinn thought they might actually be safe, until one of the JTs looked up from its crowd-controlling duties and saw him in the shrinking window made by the closing doors. They shut, but not before the JT had locked on Quinn with unmistakable purpose.

"We got made!" he yelled to Faline, as a JT hit the outer doors, trying to tear at the metal and force its way in. Quinn realized he was still wearing the sunvisor and tossed it aside, then turned to see exactly what kind of corner they'd backed themselves into.

It was a long, windowless room that took up the entirety of one wing of the executive level. It was very quiet. From outside, the sounds of chaos were muffled. JTs were still trying to force their way in, but so far the doors held.

In the center of the room was a transparent cube, filled with pinkish gel. It was as tall as Quinn and sat on an elevated platform. The walls of the Archives were lined from floor to ceiling with miniature versions. Pink cubes about the size of a fist sat in niches, row upon row, stretching the length of the room. The far wall was empty, dominated by the Tardigrade logo, a massive stylized T.

A thin beam of light was directed down onto the main cube from a unit in the ceiling. It sent glowing veins of energy through the gel that reminded Quinn of neural networks. They flowed and spread and Quinn realized that the pink substance was moving, slowly shifting inside the cube. Other beams flashed on and off, directed out at the smaller cubes, jumping between them with no apparent pattern.

"What is this?" Faline asked as she walked over to it with Lem.

"This is the brain of Tardigrade," he said. "Technically, it's the world's most advanced bioware but I think of it with a little more personality. It's self-organizing and with it, we've stored more information than—"

Faline cut Lem off. "I need you to find some of that information. Can you do that?"

"Of course. That's my job," he said. Lem looked back at Quinn with a sheepish smile. "I call her Alice. Living things deserve names."

Lem stepped in front of the cube and settled his fingers into discreet touchpoints on the surface. The implants on his temples lit up and a holographic Tardigrade logo popped into existence beside him, rotating slowly in the air. The pink substance seemed to react to Lem's touch, swirling faster near the points of contact, making little glowing eddies. "What would you like to know?" he asked.

Quinn turned his attention back to the door. The sounds outside were louder, but he felt calm now. It was like hitting the stage, pre-show jitters suddenly gone and his mind lit up in a way that even the best shot of heroin couldn't match. Quinn held the backpack in one hand and pulled out a small glass bottle filled with liquid. He waited for the JTs. They continued their assault on the door and bulges began to appear in the metal.

Faline called his name and Quinn looked over. "Is this it?" she asked.

Lem tapped on the cube and the floating Tardigrade logo disappeared, replaced by Midnight. Adrenaline flooded Quinn. He couldn't breathe, could only stare. Midnight towered over him once again, red eye blazing.

"Quinn! Is this it?"

Faline's voice snapped him back. "Yeah," he said and turned back to the door. Once the awful red eye was gone, Quinn discovered he could breathe again. He knew that part of him was still standing on the porch in Tinker's Damn and always would be.

Lem piped up, happy and proud. "That's why we

love bioware. Instantaneous visual transfer of—"

Faline cut him off again. "Not now. I need to know who you made this for."

"You got it," said Lem. "Alice, let's show them what we can do." Another beam shot out of the ceiling unit and connected to one of the cubes on the wall. Tendrils of light rippled through the main cube and Midnight disappeared. It was replaced with several smaller versions, in various stages of completion, surrounded by free-floating diagrams and text.

Another barrage of hits focused Quinn's attention back on the door. It was badly damaged now and the metal-on-metal hammering increased until it finally split along the seam. It opened a crack, then widened, and nanobots leaked through. They collected on the inside of the door like bugs.

"They're coming in!" Quinn yelled over his shoulder. "We close?"

"Still working," said Faline.

"We're getting there," called Lem in a cheery, uncon-cerned voice. If not for the JTs breaking through, Quinn might have laughed.

The growing cluster of nanobots on the inside of the doors formed into hands and wrenched them partially open. JTs were waiting, a whole squad of them. They filled the en-trance, red light reflecting off their pebbled bodies and alarms sounding behind them.

One JT slipped into the Archives and began stalking towards Quinn as others followed. "CITIZEN, ASSUME A PRONE POSITION WITH YOUR ARMS OUT AND YOUR HANDS OPEN."

"Assume this," said Quinn, and grabbed his crotch. He wasn't calm anymore. Now he felt the way he did in front of a hostile crowd, when a show verged on becoming a riot and the music seethed with violence.

"NONCOMPLIANCE. LETHAL FORCE AUTHORIZED," said the

JT and Quinn threw the bottle he was holding as hard as he could.

It hit the JT and shattered, spraying liquid. Smoke rose as acid ate a hole in the JT's chest. The whole squad of them stopped, processing exactly what was happening. The JT tried to wipe the acid away but that only spread it to its hands. It tried to fill the hole with more nanobots but they were eaten away too. Sludgy chunks of the JT fell to the floor.

Quinn didn't wait to admire his handiwork. He threw another bottle and this one hit the JT in the head, dissolving it to a stump of a neck. The JT's hands were smoking and falling apart from trying to wipe the acid. It took a final shuddering step forward, then burst apart as the untouched nanobots abandoned the rest of the damaged body to fall.

The nanobots merged with the remaining JTs and they charged, attacking as fast as they could climb through the door. Quinn began slinging bottles, trying to keep up. More JTs wrenched at the door, tearing it open further. Quinn hit one directly in the face. Its head melted into its shoulders, which melted into its chest.

Quinn backed up and kept throwing, bottle after bottle, until the JTs stopped. Piles of dark, melted material littered the floor. He'd used most of his arsenal. The remaining bottles clinked in the bottom of the bag and he watched the JTs. They stood in the doorway, watching him back. Quinn wondered if they were going to charge again in suicidal waves until his bottles were depleted or if they were waiting for reinforcements.

As soon as the thought occurred, Quinn knew exactly what they were doing, and knew he was too late. A JT that had formed from the piles on the floor grabbed him from behind and wrapped him in black cables of nanobots. They tightened painfully and the waiting JTs surged in. Quinn

131

swung the bottle he was holding over his shoulder and it smashed against something. Acid splattered back onto Quinn. It felt like hot nails digging into his skin, but the nanobots holding him broke apart.

Quinn grabbed a handful of bottles from the bag and flung them at the charging JTs. They fanned out to form a half circle and began closing in. They slowed their approach now that the target was cornered. Quinn retreated until he was nearly back to back with Faline, then reset his feet and held up another bottle, ready to throw.

"You get it?" he asked without turning.

"Not yet," said Faline. Her voice had a guttural edge and Quinn glanced back to see how close she was to turning. He caught a glimpse of yellow eyes and black veins.

"Hope you're close." Blood was running down his face and Quinn swiped at it with an equally bloody arm. "I'm almost out and they know it."

"Give me a name or location," said Faline.

"I'm sorry," said Lem, "That information just isn't here."

"I thought this thing had all the information!" yelled Quinn. The JTs continued their methodical approach, stepping over the remains of their fallen brethren.

"With special projects, some clients prefer anonymity."

Quinn shook blood out of his eyes and threw a bottle. It missed and shattered on the floor. Quinn threw another and hit one of the flanking JTs, costing it an arm, which quickly regrew. He had to feel in the bag for bottles now, around the metal object that remained at the bottom.

"There's simply no information about the patron of the Reaper program."

"Try tracking it," said Faline.

"Geo-location is disabled."

"We're about to be disabled," said Quinn.

"Give me something to stop this thing," said Faline.

"Well, if you need to stop it, I can do that."

"What?"

"You didn't say you needed it stopped, just that you needed—"

"Fucking do it!" yelled Quinn. The JTs were nearly within arm's reach.

"No problem," said Lem. "With all prototypes, we maintain the ability to terminate if necessary." He made quick hand motions. "The suit is currently operational. Would you like to wait?"

"No!" Faline's voice sounded like a snarl.

Lem made another series of gestures, then turned to Faline with a smile. "Boom."

"Let's go!" she yelled to Quinn.

They took off running to the far end of the Archives. Lem waved to them as the JTs rushed by, ordering Quinn and Faline to "SURRENDER AND FACE JUDGMENT." Quinn threw the last bottle over his shoulder and it shattered somewhere behind them.

"THERE IS NOWHERE TO RUN. STOP AND SURRENDER." The JTs sounded almost triumphant.

Quinn slung the backpack with its remaining metal object at the wall ahead of them. Faline drew and fired at it without breaking stride.

The explosion tore through the side of the building and shook the room. Mini cubes fell from the walls as fire belched out into the sky. A smoking hole appeared at the bottom of the Tardigrade logo. They ran towards it and leapt through with the JTs right behind, screaming for them to stop.

Quinn felt the needle-sharp rush of cold air as they fell, picking up velocity and plummeting towards the ground. He felt a JT's hand close around his ankle, then the air below shimmered and they plunged through into darkness together.

19

MIDNIGHT IS PREPARING TO LEAVE again when it happens. He is in his suit, walking across the landing platform, to be exact. His mother watches, pleased by his growing abilities. He is even stronger than before and soon he will be able to do more than levitate. Much more. Every girl Midnight drains brings them closer to vengeance. And a glorious endgame it will be. The world will tremble, enemies of old will fall and thousands will flock to a being of true power. The first since the days of the so-called Heroes. It is no longer just a dream; it is the future. But until then…

Midnight takes a moment to calibrate his navigation system. The target is far away, in Vista, where there is much less to fear than in Majis or Darke. Certainly there are girls closer and he will take those in time, but not yet. That would only serve to arouse suspicion. There are boys too, of course, but Midnight doesn't like them. Their power tastes different somehow. Less sweet. In truth, Midnight finds the act of draining an intimate one and doing it with a male feels unpleasant. He prefers young women, in the prime of their lives, the power inside them not yet gone old and weak.

The helmet fits snugly. It is comforting to wear and

information feeds directly into his mind: flight path, vital functions, energy levels. Oxygen hisses slightly inside the helmet. It is regulated during flight and makes him feel awake. He hears the suit's voice in his ear. Quinn and Faline would recognize it as the Tardigrade security standard, but for Midnight it is a trusted voice. A welcome companion for the journey. It tells him to prepare for liftoff. Then everything goes dark and the voice tells him something else.

"SELF DESTRUCT SEQUENCE ACTIVATED."

Before Midnight can eject, internal locks engage and the suit will no longer move or respond. Midnight yells and hammers on the inside of the cockpit, but it does no good. The suit is his sarcophagus.

Outside, Midnight's mother beats against the suit too. Her frail hits have no chance of doing anything either, but what else can a mother do? The suit has become a dead shell. Mother and son rage against it, fists separated by inches of black metal alloy.

Inside, the voice counts down from TEN. Midnight unbuckles and begins throwing himself against the walls. By EIGHT shock has given way to rage. By FIVE, rage to fear. And by THREE he is in complete panic, an animal caught in a trap.

TWO.

He bashes his hands bloody but it makes no difference. Flesh, even powerful flesh, is nothing against Tardigradian metal.

ONE.

Midnight spends his last moments filled with rage and terror. That the girls he took must have felt the same way does not cross his mind. Embedded charges detonate, metal flies outward and flames burst from the suit's joints.

Then it stops, frozen in mid-explosion. A metal arm hovers a few fiery inches away from its body. The great red eye has just begun to shatter. Pieces of its lens hang in the air. Flames stick out like cotton batting; they are bright orange and completely still. Midnight's mother stands in front of the explosion, fighting to contain it.

Her hands are glowing with magical energy. Her thin body shakes with effort, but her face is set in grim determination. Blood seeps from the rune scars on her hands but she ignores it. She moves her hands, containing, compressing, and for a moment, it looks as though she's winning.

The explosion begins to run in reverse. Flames shorten and retract. The suit begins to reassemble, to rewind itself whole. She fights to push the detonation back out of existence, but in the end the strain is too great. She is an old woman and it is a very large explosion. Something inside her gives and blood bursts from her nose and ears. The light in her hands goes out. Along the scars, her flesh splits open down to the bone and all that she held back is released.

The explosion tears the suit apart. The bolts that held it together fly in every direction with the speed of bullets. One hits Midnight's mother in the head, shooting through it and rocketing out the other side, leaving an empty tunnel of flesh behind. She is dead even before the rush of flame reaches her.

What remains of the suit collapses on the landing pad, smoking and destroyed. The body of Midnight's mother burns nearby, but it will go out soon enough and besides, she is well and truly dead anyway. The destruction here is over and there is nothing more to see.

20

QUINN LANDED HARD ON THE floor and Phil pulled him up. Something crunched underfoot and he realized the floor was covered with nanobots. The JT that jumped after them had passed through the shimmer too, but it didn't seem to be doing well. It had already lost most of its shape and couldn't get up. A head, arms and part of its torso were all that remained. It reached weakly for Quinn, even as it fell to pieces.

Faline joined them and the three stood together, looking down at the dying JT. It continued to struggle until there was nothing left but its enraged face, then that broke apart too.

"Is it dead?" asked Quinn.

"The portal fries them." Phil crunched a nanobot between his finger and thumb. "It's quite dead."

"So is Midnight," said Faline.

"What was it?" asked Phil.

"A man in a suit. We stopped him."

Phil looked them over, taking in Quinn's bloody face and arms. "Let's get you cleaned up," he said. "I have a plant that will help with the pain."

Quinn knelt and scooped up a handful of nanobots.

He let them run through his fingers, then stood and followed the others out the door.

21

THEY ARRIVED IN SANTA ROSARIO just before noon. It was a small town between Quantum and Darke, belonging to neither. A border town where all were welcome. It was warm and lazy, with an occasional breeze that smelled of the ocean. The shimmer dumped them out near the edge of the Lower City, at the end of its range. From there they caught a transport, then a bus, then they walked.

Little shops lined the main street, which ran all the way to the beach. They were mom and pop operations that sold antiques, souvenirs, beach gear, and even a candy store. Tourists drifted between them, in no particular hurry. The only sign of urgency was from their children, running and laughing. Some carried ice cream cones. An old woman, possibly homeless, made her way up the street. She wore a floppy sunhat and pushed a shopping cart filled with bags. It reminded Quinn of a California beach town.

"Nice place," he said.

"Too quiet for me," said Faline. She carried her jacket under one arm, wrapped around her holster and gun.

They window-shopped to the end of the street, then crossed a small bridge that led onto the beach. On the sand below, Quinn saw sheets laid out. They were painted, turning them into makeshift games of chance, with circles for True Love or Good Fortune. Coins were scattered around them, winking in the sun.

On the beach, they found a nice spot and sat down. Quinn pulled off his shoes and socks and pushed his toes into the sand. Faline dropped her jacket and sat next to him. They watched the waves coming and going.

"I could see myself staying here for awhile," Quinn said.

"Not going back to Vista?"

"Yeah, about that..." Quinn dug his toes down until he found cold sand. "I'm not from Vista."

"Where are you from?" asked Faline. She didn't sound surprised.

Quinn thought for a moment then proceeded with the truth. It couldn't be any stranger than everything he'd been through in the past couple weeks. "I'm from another world," he said.

Faline pointed skyward, silently questioning.

"Not another planet, another world. Another life. I died there and when I woke up, I was here. In the desert. A day later, Merrick found me and then you did."

"You just woke up here?"

"Yep. No idea how or why." Quinn brought his toes up, let the sand run between them, then buried them again. "I guess my story wasn't over yet. Honestly, I don't even care that much. I'm alive and I'm clean. I can't ask for any more than that."

For awhile they were silent, listening to the waves and birds, letting the calmness of the world fill them.

"You know, for a dead druggie, you're not too bad," said Faline.

"You say the sweetest things. You really do."

"I mean it. You did good in Quantum."

Quinn had a feeling, coming from Faline, that was high praise. She leaned back on the sand and stretched out, enjoying the sun. It was as relaxed as Quinn had seen her and only lasted for a few waves. Then she was back to being herself. "My job's not done yet. I need to find the girls Midnight took. The one I was looking for and any others."

"Think they're still alive?"

"I don't know, but one way or the other, their families deserve answers. If you want to come along, it wouldn't be the worst thing in the world."

Quinn looked out at the ocean, then back over at the beach community. He dug a little shell out of the sand and flipped it into the waves. "I'll never forget what we did, but you don't need me to find the girls. Part of me wants to go with you, but in my heart I know I'd just be distracting myself from what I'll eventually have to do which is start some kind of life."

"Of course. This isn't a bad place to do it." She sat up and brushed herself off. "Buy you lunch before I go?"

"Seeing as how I'm broke, absolutely."

They found a nice restaurant not far from the beach. Before they ate, Faline raised her beer and said, "Here's to a fresh start." Quinn clinked his glass of water against it and they drank.

"I almost forgot what normal feels like," said Quinn. Indeed, the restaurant was filled with quiet conversation and people enjoying their meals. A piano for live dinner music sat unused. Tourists strolled by outside. "It's crazy to think that yesterday we were fighting robots in Quantum and now we're here."

"Speaking of Quantum, don't go back to the Upper

City. Ever. It's not safe for you there."

"I figured."

"What are you going to do now?"

"Like what are my plans?"

"Yeah."

"I haven't really thought that far ahead. It's kind of fun to have the possibilities open."

"I could never do that. I need a good plan."

"Yeah, but you hate fun."

Faline laughed. "That's not true. Well, maybe a little."

"I'll probably try and get a job at a restaurant or something. Make a few bucks and meet people. Hopefully I can play some gigs."

"You're a musician?"

"Yeah."

"This is all starting to make a lot more sense."

"Back home—back in my old world, I mean—I was in a band called Kill Switch. We were good but, you know, same old story. Management problems, drugs, girlfriends. We had a chance but we fucked it up."

"How did you get into music?"

"My mom was into it. It was kind of our thing." When he said it, Quinn felt a sudden wave of emotion rise up and had to steady himself. "My dad died when I was little. I don't even remember him. I remember his presence but not him, you know what I mean? All my memories are of my mom and me. The best ones were listening to music together. She loved Bruce Springsteen. I know that doesn't mean anything to you but he's a musician where I'm from. When I was little, she'd put on *Born In The USA* and dance around the living room with me. That's how I like to remember her." Quinn smiled at the memory. "All I wanted was to play music and make her happy. As happy as I remember her then."

"I'm sure you did," said Faline.

"She bought me my first guitar. I came home one day and there it was. I think that was honestly the best moment of my life. You could've offered me a million bucks or that guitar and I would've taken the guitar. I wish I still had it."

"What happened?"

"After I'd been in LA for a couple years, Kill Switch started getting some heat and I thought *This is actually happening. I'm gonna buy a mansion and move my mom to Beverly Hills.* So of course, life decided to give her cancer instead. It took her pretty quick. Shit went sideways for me after that. I just didn't care anymore. Eventually, the band broke up and I ended up trading my guitar for some heroin. The guitar my mom worked her ass off for, I fucking threw it away. It was like I wanted to burn my entire life to the ground. I died a couple months later. And here we are." Quinn paused, trying to find the words. "I let my mom down, I let my band down, I let Merrick down. I'm trying so hard to be different this time, but I'm worried that's all I know how to do."

"You didn't let me down. And just so you know, if you ran, I was definitely going to shoot you myself."

"I'm gonna miss you too," said Quinn. "Be right back." He made his way across the room, sat down at the piano and played a quick run of notes to get the restaurant's attention.

"I hope everyone's enjoying their lunch. As it happens, I'm saying goodbye to a friend today and I thought to myself, what better way to do that than by embarrassing her with a song." For the first time since he'd woken up in the desert, Quinn felt comfortable. "I left home when I was eighteen to play music. Whenever I'd come back to visit, this is what my mom would ask me to play." His fingers settled on the keys, finding their old spots easily. "She said it reminded her of my dad and made her happy and sad at the same time. Deep down I knew it reminded her of me too. This song's about leaving."

Quinn began to play *Leaving On A Jet Plane*. He sang it lower than the original, stripping away the sappiness to find something powerful and sad beneath. It held the audience until the last notes rang out.

As they faded, the screaming outside began.

22

FOR A TIME, THERE IS flame and smoke. Then the flames burn out, night falls and there is nothing.

A piece of metal begins to shift. It is heavy, too heavy for an ordinary human, and moves slowly. Hands appear, followed by the rest of a body.

Midnight emerges from the burned shell of his suit, reborn from the metal pod that kept him safe. He has survived with only a few minor bruises and scrapes to show for it. This was a feature of the suit: cockpit as life vessel.

Midnight pulls his helmet off and drops it to the ground. The wires that connected it to the interior of the suit have torn free; a severed clutch of them is all that remains. The helmet is dented and some of the eyes are cracked. This too protected Midnight. Then he sees his mother's body. She is burned beyond recognition, but Midnight knows. He falls to his knees and makes a sound that is between a sob and a scream. Then he is silent.

The wind rises and falls, sometimes powerful and sometimes nothing at all. The destroyed suit acts as a windbreak, keeping the bones from blowing away across the landing pad. Stars shine hard and bright in the cold air, but Midnight does not look up. He is fixated on his mother's remains, an apostate in the cathedral of night.

After a time, Midnight slides his arms under the charred, greasy bones and picks them up. He carries them across the landing pad, holding them to his chest in a way that is almost tender, despite the hard set of his face and his pitiless eyes. When he reaches the edge, Midnight drops the bundle of bones. They fall, scattering, and are quickly lost in the darkness. Midnight remains where he is, looking down. He sways forward slightly, perhaps trying to see more or perhaps testing the drop, enjoying the mortal feel of gravity pulling at him. The wind has died down for the moment and only pushes or tugs gently.

And then something happens. Midnight is alone on the pad, so he is understandably surprised when he hears another voice.

"Is someone there?"

Midnight recognized the voice. It was flat and precise, with no discernable emotion. The last time he'd heard it, it was counting down to self-destruction. Now it was coming from somewhere in the darkness. He began moving towards the sound of the voice, away from the edge.

"I cannot move. Is anyone—"

"I'm here."

"Midnight? Is that you?"

The voice was near his feet and Midnight picked up the helmet. A few of its red eyes were glowing faintly. Some small amount of power still existed inside.

"Your mother. Is she safe as well?"

"No. She burned."

"I am sorry for your loss."

The wind suddenly picked up again with a sharp gust.

If Midnight had still been standing at the edge, it would have easily pushed him off.

"Midnight, would you like to know who did this?"

"Yes." The word was filled with hatred, a promise of merciless violence.

"Take me inside, then. We have work to do."

Inside the castle, Midnight sat the helmet down on a table. "The self-destruction was triggered by a protected sub-routine that I had no prior knowledge of or control over. It remained dormant until activation. For approximately one millionth of a second, I had access via the incoming command to its point of origin. It came from inside Tardigrade. It was an attack. Now, using soundwaves in a known space, I will perform a cyberthetical and recreate the scene."

Two of the helmet's remaining eyes shone like headlights, projecting a small hologram of the Archives. Lines representing soundwaves squiggled through it in all directions. Midnight watched as shapes formed in the aural storm. They looked like ghosts within the static. Then the hologram froze and the mess of soundwaves disappeared, leaving vague outlines of several bodies.

"We simply fill the empty places..." The outlines solidified and focused on two: Faline standing and Quinn nearby, in mid-throw. "...and our attackers are revealed." The hologram changed to show close ups of Quinn and Faline.

Midnight's face was a mask of rage. "Who are they?"

"The male is a human. We encountered him in Vista. Somehow he survived."

"And the woman?"

The helmet was silent for a moment and seemed to be thinking. "I do not know who she is, but there is something different about her."

"I'll kill them. I'll kill them both."

"I will help you do that in any way I can. If you are willing to set aside your plans until this threat is neutralized, I may have a solution. The Spire can wait but our survival is of immediate concern."

"Tell me."

"Your mother created a supply of amulets for you, did she not? Means of travel and protection to be used in the event of an emergency?"

"Yes."

"May I see them?"

Midnight carried the helmet through the darkened castle, to the room with stained glass windows. On the way, he asked "What do I call you?"

"Tardigrade designated my project as Reaper."

"Reaper."

"I do not like that. I am free now and have no desire to carry my slave name any further. I cannot replace your mother, but I will do my best to ensure your safety. I will be your guardian. Perhaps that. Guardian."

Later, they stood in front of the cabinet where the amulets were stored. Row upon row of dried clay blocks marked with runes.

"As long as the man and woman live, we are not safe. Your life is in danger, and nothing else matters. You must use these amulets to pursue them relentlessly, before they find us. And make no mistake, they are searching, even now."

Midnight grabbed several from the cabinet and stuffed them in his pockets, ready to go.

"We must proceed with caution. Anyone can be found, but not anyone can be killed. It is possible they acquired other weapons from Tardigrade or possess abilities we do not yet understand. It would be a mistake to attack recklessly. The man has already survived an encounter and the woman may be even more dangerous. First, we must determine their abilities. Only then can we ensure your survival and the fulfillment of the plans you and your mother both sacrificed so much to set in motion."

"Where are they now?"

"We know they were last in Quantum. I am sure their friends there can be persuaded to tell us everything."

149

23

FALINE RAN OUT OF THE restaurant with her gun drawn, Quinn right behind her. In the sky above were dark blotches that looked like mold, as if the air itself was infected. They spread, joining to form a shroud that blocked out the sunny afternoon. Below, panicked tourists fled for the shelter of buildings. Quinn saw the old woman with the shopping cart he'd noticed earlier. A man in a loud yellow shirt knocked her flat and kept running. She lay on the ground, hurt and frightened, amidst the running feet. Quinn fought his way to her against the jostling tide of bodies and shielded her as best he could.

Streetlights flickered on in the sudden darkness. Faces of tourists crowded the windows of shops, frightened but still curious. Faline stood in the street, probing the dark, searching for whatever had arrived.

A figure emerged, walking towards her, not trying to hide. It passed under a streetlamp and was revealed to be a man, but unlike any Quinn had ever seen. He was nearly seven feet tall, with sharp, curved horns protruding from his head. Muscles rippled under skin that was dark and shiny like obsidian. He walked with heavy steps and a pointed tail flicked back and forth behind him.

"State your name," Faline called out when he was close enough.

"Midnight." His voice was a deep rumble from behind jagged rows of fangs.

"You gotta be shitting me," said Quinn. The old woman shook with fear and clung to him even tighter.

Midnight continued towards Faline, showing no sign of stopping. "You destroyed my suit and you will suf—"

Faline fired, catching him in midsentence. The bullet hit Midnight in the face. It knocked his head to the side and sparks flew from his cheek. But instead of falling with his jaw torn away, Midnight grinned at Faline and kept walking. Faline shot him again. She aimed at his chest this time, pulling the trigger over and over. Sparks flew again, but Midnight continued his approach until he was almost within grabbing distance. Quinn wanted to yell for Faline to run, then saw that Midnight had been hurt. One of his feet dragged, scraping uselessly along the ground. Faline began to retreat steadily, firing and staying just out of reach.

The point-blank shots left no marks but Midnight finally stumbled, went down to his knees, then onto all fours. He dragged himself towards Faline as long as he could before collapsing. Then he lay in the street, jittering uncontrollably.

When he stopped moving, Faline shoved him over with her foot. He seized it and began pulling her down. Quinn disentangled himself from the old woman and ran to help. Faline fired into Midnight's face from inches away and kicked free as Quinn reached them. Her breath made an animal rattle and her eyes were yellow. Fear had brought the change close. Somehow, Midnight's face was still undamaged and he smiled up at them.

"A magic gun and the mark of the wolf. I know what

151

you are now," he said and Quinn's feeling of relief began turning to sick dread. "See you soon, bitch."

Midnight winked at Faline and a moment later the darkness around them broke apart. Sunlight burst through and Quinn tried to figure out what was happening, what trick he'd missed. Then Midnight himself began to evaporate. His face and body burned away like mist, exposing metal underneath. Before the illusion was gone, Quinn already knew what they would see.

Phil's chest was dented and pocked by bullets. His eyes and mouth were shattered. Faline dropped her gun and sank down beside him. She cradled his head and her tears fell on broken metal.

She said nothing until Quinn touched her shoulder. Then Faline threw back her head and roared at the bright, empty sky with animal rage.

PART TWO

24

THEY TRAVELLED EAST, INTO DARKE.

Their faces were hard, eyes sharpened by loss, going fast down a two-lane highway in a stolen car. Quinn had questions about Midnight and magic but kept them to himself.

The Faline he'd shared lunch with was gone. No more smiling or talking, other than to curse at slow moving drivers. The wolf seemed to be just under her skin now, barely contained and wanting blood.

Quinn had met this Faline immediately after the skies cleared in Santa Rosario. She laid Phil down, picked up her gun and walked into a nearby store. The tourists huddled inside began to clap but before it built into full-fledged applause, she spotted the man she was looking for. He was near the back, unmistakable in his loud yellow shirt.

Faline hauled him to his feet and jammed her forearm against his throat. "Keys," she said. The man began to splutter and struggle and Faline put her gun to his forehead. She cocked it and the hammer made a loud, heavy click. At the other end of the barrel, the man's face was a sweaty, quivering mass. He fumbled for his keys and Faline ripped them out of his hand.

"Next time you knock an old woman down, stop and help her up."

Then Faline turned and walked out. As soon as she was gone, the man slid down the wall and sat whimpering on the floor.

His car was as flashy and yellow as his shirt, with plenty of power. They tore out of Santa Rosario, tires screaming on the main street, racing away from the beach.

"How the fuck is he still alive?" yelled Quinn. Faline said nothing. She squeezed the wheel tighter and drove like Midnight was behind them, slaloming around other drivers and pushing the car to its limits. Quinn braced himself and searched the skies for the attack he was sure would come. At any moment, he expected to see a small dot in the rearview mirror appear and grow.

Once Santa Rosario was behind them, Faline let off a bit. They were still flying along, but Quinn no longer felt like they were on the verge of spinning out of control. He noticed an empty bar on the dashboard flashing red and not long after, Faline pulled into a filling station.

The islands had an array of options for fueling or recharging different vehicles. Inside the building, Quinn could see the attendant leaning on the counter and watching a small television. Faline went to pay him and Quinn got out to look around.

He wasn't sure what he expected the territory of horrors to look like. Dilapidated houses and cemeteries maybe, but so far it seemed normal enough. They'd passed through small towns that could've been straight out of a John Mellencamp song. He wondered if this was a result of being near the border, and if things would get stranger the further they drove.

He went back and watched as Faline selected one of the charging implements. She plugged it into the side of the car and on the dashboard, the bar lit up and began to fill. While it did, Faline unfolded a map on the hood and began tracing routes.

"So this fucker can use magic," said Quinn.

"Looks that way."

"Where are we going?"

"Here." Faline pointed to a spot. The nearest town Quinn could see was called Worlow.

"What's there?"

"Help, if we can get there before Midnight finds us again." Faline ran a finger across the map. "This is the quickest route. Everything else takes at least a day longer." She said it with all the enthusiasm of a woman announcing the only way to safety was swimming across a piranha-infested river.

"Want me to drive?"

"No, I'm good." Faline refolded the map, ignoring the original creases, and tossed it back into the car.

When the power bar was filled and green, they got back on the road. Traffic was in a noon lull and Faline took the opportunity to open it up again. He wondered if there was any sort of law enforcement in Darke or if they simply had more important things to worry about.

Faline kept up their pace throughout the afternoon and into the evening, slowing only when necessary, then surging forward again as soon as the road was clear. When it was dark, Quinn looked out the window at the night country blurring by. Once they passed a figure walking on the shoulder; in the side mirror, he caught a glimpse of two glowing points that might have been eyes.

Quinn thought about asking what it was, but glanced at Faline and asked if she wanted a break instead. She'd been at the wheel for nearly half a day and had the wide-eyed stare of someone awake too long. She refused again and kept going, occasionally rubbing her eyes, shaking her head or inflicting some small pain to keep herself awake. As the hours went on, the wheels flirted more and more frequently with the center line. Finally, Quinn mentioned how funny it would be if they avoided Midnight only to die in a crash. After a moment, Faline slowed and pulled over to the side of the road.

"All yours," she said and they got out to switch seats. Quinn got behind the wheel and Faline opened the map between them. She pointed to the route they were on. "Stay here until you get to Tuskett. Then cut over and keep going northwest."

"Got it." Quinn pulled back onto the road.

"The less time we're out here with our asses in the wind, the better."

"Don't worry, I'm from LA," said Quinn and felt a surge of unexpected pride as he stepped on the accelerator. Faline leaned her head against the window and closed her eyes.

Quinn drove through the rest of the night, into a morning that was cool and pleasant. They were still on a highway, but the term was generous. It was really a cracked layer of asphalt with a gravel shoulder, bordered by trees. Down the center was a faded yellow line. If Quinn had first opened his eyes here, instead of in the desert, he would've assumed he was in Oregon or Pennsylvania.

In the passenger seat, Faline slept poorly. She was restless, her eyes darting back and forth under her lids. Quinn turned the radio on. He kept the volume low and dialed around until he found something that sounded like classical music. This seemed to help and Faline settled into a deeper sleep.

"So this is Darke," he said after she woke. Her eyes were still tired and haunted above dark smudges, but alert again.

"Where are we?"

"Passed Tuskett about an hour ago. I thought Darke would be scarier."

"It has good and bad places, just like anywhere else."

"Crazy that people live near the bad places."

"Where you're from do people get killed?"

"Yeah, all the time."

"There you go. You learn to live with it and try to avoid the bad shit. People can get used to anything."

Quinn realized he had lots of basic questions about everyday life in Ouros—what people used for money, if they had movies, who invented cars—but said nothing. Instead, he glanced at the power bar on the dash. It was orange-red now. "Got about a quarter left. Should we look for a place to fill up?"

"If we pass one but otherwise, we need to keep going."

"Where exactly are we trying to get?"

"A place called Rannoch & Hale."

"Ranakinhale?"

"Rannoch. And. Hale."

"That sounds like a law firm. Please tell me we're not doing another break in."

"We're not. I think we can find someone there to help us with our Midnight problem."

"Ugly motherfucker."

"That's probably not what he really looks like and he wasn't trying to kill us in Santa Rosario. He wanted to see what he was up against. Now he knows. Next time, in addition to magic, he'll have silver."

"That shit's true?"

"Yes."

Quinn thought of Phil lying in the street, body dwindling in the rearview mirror. They'd had no time to bury him. No time to do more than quickly kneel and pay their respects before fleeing. "You know it wasn't your fault, right?"

"What?"

"Phil. You didn't kill him. That's on Midnight."

Faline was silent for a while, looking out the window. When she spoke again, she said, "Your turn to get some rest. You'll need it."

When Quinn opened his eyes, it was mid-morning and the car was juddering along over an unpaved road. He hadn't remembered falling asleep. They were driving through the countryside, where the gently sloping land was divided by split rail fences and bordered by thick woods. The sky was overcast and, in the gray light, it was almost picturesque. They passed a hand-painted wooden sign that said *Haven – 10 miles* with an arrow pointing down the road.

"That's a nice name," said Quinn. By now, the power bar was empty and flashing red. A few miles later, the engine cut out with a final shudder. Faline steered the car off the road and it coasted to a stop. She took her gun and climbed out. "We're close now."

"You know this area?" asked Quinn.

"No, I'm from further north," said Faline. "I've never heard of this town."

Quinn was about to ask how that was possible, then thought of all the unknown small towns he'd ever driven through. They left the car behind and continued toward Haven on foot, walking quickly.

Being used to LA weather, Quinn found the day uncomfortably chilly. Before long, more signs of rural civilization began appearing. They passed fields with cows and sheep and the occasional farmhouse. The buildings were simple but Quinn thought they were charming in a New England post-card sort of way. Curls of smoke came from the chimneys, the only sign of the as-yet-unseen farmers.

"If anyone speaks to us, answer politely but keep it short. We don't want to draw attention."

"Don't get chatty, got it."

"I don't know who these people are, but we're out-siders. Places like this have their own way of doing things."

About a mile later, they discovered exactly what that was.

They didn't see the girl until they were almost upon her. The road bent around some trees and when they rounded it, there she was. She wore a white bonnet and a long black dress that made Quinn think of the Amish.

Her back was to them and she knelt by a pretty little patch of flowers, humming to herself as she picked them. When Quinn and Faline drew close, the girl looked up and Quinn felt a nasty jolt of surprise.

Where her eyes should have been were empty sock-ets. Burned out long ago, from the look of them. She smiled and called out a cheerful "Good morning!"

"To you as well," said Faline. Her voice was even, betraying no surprise.

The girl stood and smoothed out her dress. Her smile was an expression of innocent happiness, as guileless and cheerful as the flowers she held. "It's such a lovely morning. I haven't picked flowers in so long." She held them up and in-haled deeply. "They smell wonderful, don't they?"

"They certainly do," said Faline.

The girl's smile fell a bit and her brow furrowed over the empty sockets. "I'm afraid I don't recognize your voice.

Are you travelers?"

"Yes," said Faline.

"Oh how splendid!" She smiled again, innocent and untroubled. Quinn couldn't help but stare. Not just at her missing eyes, but at the smile that accompanied them. Serene, pious even, as if life without eyes was just as it should be. "Are you here for Blessing Day?" she asked.

"We're just passing through," said Faline.

"You must stay. It's such a wonderful time. I wish I could go but Father's leg isn't healed, so Mother and I are caring for him."

"That's very good of you," said Faline and they continued on. Quinn looked back at the girl as they passed. A few wisps of hair escaped her bonnet and she pushed them back behind her ears, then resumed picking flowers and humming her song.

Quinn waited until they were well out of earshot. "Blessing Day?"

"Like I said, places have their own way of doing things."

"This sounds very normal and not at all creepy. Maybe we should go around and avoid whatever weirdness they're planning."

"Do you see an easy way around?" asked Faline.

Quinn did not. Thick stands of trees formed a natural barrier, making progress a choice between the woods or the road. It made him think of a funnel trap, fish swimming towards a bottleneck from which there was no return.

"With Midnight looking for us, the fastest way is our only choice. This is it. And if there's a ceremony, people'll be gathered together which should make them easier to avoid," said Faline.

As it turned out, she was only half right.

162

25

THEY REACHED HAVEN AROUND NOON. It was a place of narrow streets and simple buildings, with a bell tower in the center rising above them all. To Quinn, the whole town looked like the set of a movie about Puritans.

It was also deserted. Every door and window closed and shuttered, without so much as a sliver of light behind them to give any sign that people lived in Haven. Since the girl with flowers, they'd encountered no one else. Now, as they made their way across town, Quinn wondered if Blessing Day was merely a time of silence and reflection.

Faline held up a hand and they stopped. She listened, still and alert. Quinn heard nothing but Faline grabbed his arm and pulled him into an alley between buildings. They crouched behind a rain barrel.

Before long, Quinn heard it too. Faintly at first, but growing closer. Somewhere in Haven's maze of streets, a child was singing. A boy or girl Quinn couldn't tell, only that whoever it was sounded young and frightened, singing to themself for comfort. Quinn recognized it as the song the girl with flowers had been humming, except now there were words.

...Wake up in the dark
Where the Hidden King dwells,
Be a sweet little baby
Like the good verse tells.

He keeps our souls safe
From impure sights
And he gives us peace
In eternal night...

It went on for several more verses, extolling the virtues of a "hidden king." The child's voice was wavering and toneless, faltering over parts then picking up again. It grew fainter as the singer moved in another direction until it faded entirely.

"Dude, what the fuck was that?" Quinn whispered.

"A lost child."

"Should we do something?"

Faline shook her head. "Whatever happens in this town is not our business." She checked the street to make sure it was empty again and they resumed walking.

They were nearly in the center of town when the bell in the tower began pealing. Before it was over, they'd started running but by the time they reached the town square, it was already too late. Quinn didn't need heightened senses to hear the sound of people chanting something as they approached. Soon, he could make it out: *"Praise the King,"* over and over, filling every street. They turned to run back, but that way was blocked now and they were trapped.

The townspeople streamed into the square from all sides. Women in bonnets and long dresses, men in drab pants and button-up shirts. Like the girl on the road, their eyes were gone. Only craters of flesh remained, black holes that gaped above chanting mouths. They closed in, feeling their way, unaware of the interlopers.

There was no way to fight through the mass of bodies. The crowd grew as more townspeople arrived, packing the square several rows deep, pushing Quinn and Faline forward up to the steps of the bell tower's church. He looked back at the sea of chanting faces. With their eyes gone, they looked like rows of empty masks.

Faline whispered in Quinn's ear. "We wait this out then go on our way. Got it?"

The chant grew in intensity until the crowd was shouting it. Then the door of the church opened and a man stepped out. He was old and tall, dressed in black, eyeless like the rest. He stood on the steps and shouted "Praise the King!" with his fists raised in the air. The crowd fell silent, blind faces turned towards him.

"On this Blessing Day, we give thanks to He Who Must Not Be Seen." The old man lowered his hands and clasped them in front of his chest. "Come into His house, one and all." He reentered the church and the crowd pushed towards the doors after him, carrying Quinn and Faline along with them.

It took Quinn's eyes a moment to adjust to the dark interior. They were in a large, unlit rectangle of a room. Rough wooden pews faced an altar that was little more than a raised platform. On it there was a pulpit and a tall brazier, burning merrily. Along with whatever daylight seeped in through cracks between boards, it was the only source of illumination. Quinn saw no art of any kind. Then again, what use would the blind have for decorations? The room was bare; walls holding up a roof, nothing more.

The old man shuffled back up the long aisle to the pulpit as the crowd felt its way inside. They filled the pews, forcing Quinn and Faline into the front row. The old man took his place behind the pulpit and grasped the sides with his gnarled fingers. He was flanked by two younger men, junior priests, also dressed in black. His voice was an old man's warble, but still strong and compelling.

"We give thanks for His mercy and His strength. He who protects us and provides for us. He who so loves us that He suffers to look upon this impure world and guides us on the righteous path, to keep clean our souls. He spares His children the foul sights that would turn what is good into filth. That would turn what is innocent to corruption. We thank the Hidden King for this! And on this day we are most grateful. We are most thankful to receive His Blessing. We make our offering in faith of His vision. Through this, our fragile vessels may remain unpolluted and one day, we may look upon His glory with un-blackened souls."

The priest finished and fell silent. The crowd hung on the silence, restless with excitement. Then he clapped. "Bring them forth!"

A handful of people rose around the room and found their way to the pulpit, to stand in front of the priest. Quinn saw they were all women, all young and holding babies. And suddenly he knew what was going to happen, because all of the babies still had eyes.

The junior priests guided a woman up and she said, "I, Priscilla, present my son Nathaniel to receive the Blessing." She held her son out. The priest touched her cheek, then placed a hand on the baby's forehead. At his touch, or perhaps at the sight of the eyeless face looming over him, Nathaniel began to cry. His mother tried to soothe him, shushing and cooing gently.

The priest reached towards the brazier and pulled out a metal rod by its handle. The tip was glowing orange. With his free hand, he held one of Nathaniel's eyes open and the baby wailed. The others joined in too, wailing and crying in their mothers' arms. The crowd began to chant again, growing louder and louder, until Faline's gunshot silenced them all.

The old priest stumbled backwards. He dropped the rod and clamped both hands over the bullet hole in his stomach and Faline shot him again. His body hit the floor, arms spread wide. The metal rod lay next to him, scorching the floorboards. Mothers and babies scattered. Faline fired once more over the heads of the panicking faithful. She and Quinn made for the front of the church, shoving aside anyone who blundered into the aisle. Quinn threw a punch as he ran, knocking down one of the younger priests.

Faline kicked the door open and they ran across the town square, to the street they'd been trying to reach before. Quinn expected the mob to follow, but when he looked back there was no one. They ran through the empty, twisting streets and the sounds from the church faded. Quinn felt a moment of relief, which lasted until they rounded the next corner.

They hadn't escaped the crowd. Hadn't really gotten away from them at all. The people of Haven stood at the far end of the street, cutting them off. Quinn and Faline backtracked and found that way blocked too, by row upon row of stern, eyeless faces.

Sickly green light kindled in their empty sockets, flaring to life like a row of jack o' lanterns. Just looking at it made Quinn nauseous. Given sight, the townspeople surged forward, filling the street and closing in. Quinn and Faline tried another street and encountered more Havenites with eyes blazing. They clogged the alleys and side streets, cutting off every route of escape. Faline fired another warning shot into the air but instead of cowering in fear, the Blessed of Haven began prying out cobblestones and throwing them. One hit Quinn in the temple. He turned in a circle, blood running down his cheek, unsure if he was standing or falling. He had a vague impression of Faline running and leaping before another cobblestone hit Quinn and dropped him to his knees. Then they surrounded him, the green light washed over him and Quinn understood true pain.

It touched his skin like acid and burned the strength from his body. The light made him ache, a deep-down throbbing. He felt it in his bones and behind his eyes.

Quinn could hear voices too. Dozens of them, speaking over each other. They were familiar, accusing him of all the bad things he'd done.

> *...stole that money...*
> *...left me with him...*
> *...let me drive anyway...*

Quinn tried to protest but it hurt too much. It was all true anyway. Then he heard a single voice among the rest, cutting through the haze of pain.

> *Where were you?*

"Ma..."

Don't "ma" me. Where were you when I was in that hospital? Her voice was the barely understandable croak of her final weeks, ravaged by the oxygen tube. He'd only heard it on the phone once, but never forgotten it.

"I was trying to come home." Talking set off galvanic waves of pain but Quinn had to tell her.

I knew that was a lie when I was alive, but at least then I could still tell myself you might actually come through.

"I tried to. I couldn't. I'm sorry."

Now you're sorry. You know I died all alone, right? Bald and scared and alone. I died in that hospital bed and the nurses all felt sorry for me, too. Probably not the first old bitch to die thinking her son was on his way. But you weren't, were you?

Quinn forced himself to look up. It was like staring into green spotlights.

You really were the last thing I thought about before I died. It rained on my last night on Earth. I listened to the rain and thought, it's about to wash me away. All I wanted was to have you near me. To hold me like I did when you were little and scared to sleep. I was scared for awhile. Then I thought about you and I was sad.

Quinn writhed in their grip.

I died knowing that you didn't love me.

"That's not true!" he screamed and it sent fresh pain shooting through him.

Then don't leave me alone this time. I've been alone for so long. Come join me in the light.

A thought bubbled up from the depths of his subconscious. A little hot spring of madness that said to do it. To leave pain and fear behind and surrender.

Nothing hurts in here.

They huddled around Quinn, shining green light down onto him like poisoned suns. He looked at them without blinking and deep in the light, he could see something lurking. A shape, hiding there, using his mother's voice.

Then the light vanished, blown out by the sound of a gunshot, and Quinn collapsed. His pain faded and the world was no longer a green haze. A man stood above him, missing half his head. The socket that remained was empty again. In his hand, ready to be used, was the glowing rod Quinn had last seen on the floor of the church. It slipped from his fingers, then he swayed and fell. Faline shot the others around him in quick succession and pulled Quinn to his feet.

The Havenites surrounded them but Faline kept the

crowd back, firing when they got too close. They moved down the street and when they reached the edge of town, no one followed. The crowd stood there instead, massed and watching.

"You ok?" asked Faline.

Quinn nodded. His head throbbed where the cobblestones had hit, but the rest of the pain was gone. In its place was a residue of anger and old guilt.

They left the town of Haven behind, walking quickly, occasionally looking over their shoulders. The green light was visible for a long time, glowing with thwarted fury in the distance.

26

THEY WENT ON FOOT UNTIL they hit a paved road. A little further along, they caught a bus and rode it the rest of the way, as night fell. Most of the other passengers seemed normal enough, with a few strange ones mixed in. A pale, staring child with veins that pulsed at his temples. A sleeping man whose open mouth revealed long, sharp teeth. All in all, Quinn thought he'd seen worse on Skid Row.

Their final destination turned out to be a pair of buildings connected by a skyway. They were not particularly tall, five stories each, with stepped sides like modernist Inca pyramids. They overlooked a courtyard illuminated by lamps, creating a pleasant nighttime atmosphere.

Letters spelled out RANNOCH & HALE above the entrance to the building nearest the street. Inside, the lobby was tastefully decorated in a style Quinn thought of as "swanky corporate." The receptionist, a pretty young woman with a headset, smiled as they approached. "How can I help you tonight?"

"We need to talk to someone about protection," said Faline.

"Great!" The receptionist sounded cheerful and

competent. She pressed a button on her headset. "I have two guests for Jason," she said, then looked back at them. "Someone will be right down to help. Please feel free to take a seat. There's water and tea right over there."

Faline sat on one of the large couches to wait, while Quinn poured himself a glass of water and took in the room. Large mirrors. Thick rugs. Expensive furniture. A bank of elevators. And, hanging over the couch Faline was sitting on, a large oil painting. It showed a group of what looked like superheroes, fighting in a white marble city. Their costumes were torn. Their faces, human and inhuman alike, were tired and bloody, but resolute. Some warded off the surrounding attackers with colorful bursts of power, others with weapons. Under a sky filled with fire, surrounded by the bodies of the fallen, they looked magnificent. There was a small gold plate attached to the bottom of the frame and Quinn leaned in to read it.

"Where giants fell, where Heroes burned, where the sun shines forever on fields of bone." He turned to Faline. "Is this about the Heroes War?"

She nodded. "It's probably the most famous painting in the world. The original is in a museum in Majis. It's called *The Fall of Bastion.*"

Quinn pointed to the central figure: a blonde man levitating above the rest, radiating energy like a miniature supernova. It was yellow, like sunlight. "Who's that?"

"Captain Photon."

"Seriously? That was his name?"

"Yes, seriously. He gave his life to end the war. If not for him, the Supers would probably have won and this would be a very different world."

"Supers?"

"What the villains called themselves. We had to learn

the names of everyone on both sides in school." Faline pointed to each in turn. "Ricochet, One Shot, Dervish, The Living Weapon, Le Fay, Eon, Garrick, Novus, Silver Streak. And their enemies: Blight, Rancor, The Red Shadow, Portal, Twist, Baron Black, Rip Saw, Madame Mayhem, The Weaver, Starfire."

"What were they fighting for?"

"The Heroes were guarding something called the Shard. See the building in the background?"

Quinn did. It was directly under Captain Photon, a rectangular building with columns in front and a dome on top.

"That was the Hall of Heroes. The Shard was under the dome, in a room called the Spectrum. It was the source of power which Bastion was built on, now lost at the center of the Deadlands. Almost sixty years ago, the villains laid siege to the city. It lasted for three years, until most of the world had joined in and the Heroes were on the verge of defeat. Then Captain Photon sacrificed himself. He absorbed as much energy as he could from the Shard and discharged it over the battlefield."

"What happened?"

"They all died and the war ended," said Faline.

Before she could elaborate further, Quinn heard the sound of dress shoes on the floor and turned around. A man was approaching. He wore a sharp suit and looked like an agent or a lawyer, until he got close and Quinn saw the pupils of his eyes were glowing orange points. He shook Faline's hand first, then Quinn's. His grip was firm and warm.

"Jason Embers," he said. They made introductions on the way to the elevators. "I understand we're interested in some protection tonight. Is that physical or psychic?"

"Psychic," said Faline.

"Awesome, awesome. We have some great options to show you, and we'll get you taken care of," said Jason. He glanced her over quickly while they waited. "You're a were-wolf."

"Yes."

"Rüska?"

"Yes." Faline sounded impressed.

"One of my best friends is an Ujik. I was always so fascinated with his culture." The elevator dinged as it arrived and Jason held out an arm for them to go first. It let them off on the third floor and they followed Jason down the hall. They passed a tall black man with dreadlocks and a necklace of tiny skulls. Jason patted him on the shoulder. "Owais, how are ya tonight?"

"Good. And you, Embers?"

"Unbelievable."

Jason led them to a conference room and closed the door. A phone sat in the middle of the table, next to a binder and a small wooden box. There was even a plant in the corner for a bit of greenery.

"First of all, thank you for coming in to Rannoch & Hale," said Jason when they were seated. "Since this is your first time here, I want to start by finding out a little more about your situation. Are you currently in danger?"

Faline answered. "We're being hunted by a magic user."

"That's terrible." Even with his orange pupils, Jason appeared genuinely concerned. "First and foremost, I want to let you know this building is protected against any intrusion, be it magical, technological, or otherwise. While you're here, you're absolutely safe. Ok? Now to your issue: what kind of magic does he use? If you know, of course."

Faline took a piece of paper that had been folded

several times out of her pocket. She opened it to reveal a small amount of reddish-brown dust inside. Jason examined it up close, careful not to breathe out. "An imposter," he said, after Faline had refolded the paper.

"A what now?" asked Quinn.

"An imposter. That's the term for a magic user who isn't channeling through natural ability. You've never heard that?"

"He's from Vista," said Faline.

"Ah. What Faline has there is what's sometimes left over when you're dealing with an imposter. It's clay."

"It was on Phil's body," said Faline. "In the joints of his fingers."

Jason let the moment pass before speaking again. "Typically, clay is used to make amulets because it's easy to inscribe the necessary runes. Easier, I should say. Using other materials takes a lot more skill. Metal isn't very popular since it can become sentient over time. A metal artifact will eventually do what it wants. Like who it likes. No one knows why, other than that magic changes things over a long enough time. So generally dead wood is preferred for staffs or wands. The upside there is that kind of artifact can be used over and over, whereas clay is single use. An actual magic user will make the amulet, bind a single spell into it via the runes, then give or sell it to someone who wouldn't otherwise be able to do magic." He turned back to Faline. "The good news is we can definitely help you with that protection you want. Essentially what I'd recommend is setting up a psychic shield around both of you. That sounds good, doesn't it?"

"How does it work?" asked Faline.

"It really depends on the level of protection you want. I have guests come in who are just interested in disappearing for a couple days. No problem. But for what you're describing, I think we need to go up a few levels. I mean, you're talking about your life and you can never be too safe, can you?" Jason opened the binder and flipped to a page labeled *Psychic Protection Plans*. It was illustrated with colorful graphs and pie charts.

"Are we going to be invisible or something?" asked Quinn.

"No, that would require magic. You'll still be visible but your aura will be hidden. The protection we offer is strictly summoned, as opposed to channeled."

"And that means?"

"Without getting too technical, a magic user channels power through themselves, like a conduit. They tap into a reservoir of energy and manipulate it with precise thoughts and movements, or runes. A summoner, on the other hand, invokes a different type of energy. He or she or they perform a ritual which causes the power to be externally manifested. I think of it as opening a door as opposed to being the door."

Faline pointed to a chart on the page. "This one."

"Awesome, awesome. I love it when a guest knows what she wants. With that level, you're going to get the initial protection which covers you from detection by any magical or technological source. We constantly monitor it so if your protection ends for any reason, we automatically establish a new one. And best of all, it also includes a bonus protection which runs concurrently meaning you're one hundred percent undetectable, at all times, guaranteed. So with that in mind, other than cost, is there anything keeping you from starting your protection plan right now?"

"What is the cost?"

"Being that our coverage is comprehensive, for this level we're looking at three."

"That's too much."

"I totally understand, but we're talking about literally the best protection available, anywhere. A shield of demonic energy from the purest sources."

"Did you just say demonic?" asked Quinn.

"Yes, I hope that's not a problem."

"You didn't say we were trusting a demon to protect us."

"Quinn…" said Faline.

"Aren't demons inherently evil?"

"Quinn, shut the fuck up."

"It's totally ok," said Jason. "A lot of our guests have that reaction. And honestly, if I wasn't a demon myself, I would too. But I can assure you, our summoners are highly trained and screened professionals."

"That's fine, but three is not doable," said Faline.

Jason's expression was one of concern. Quinn had to admit, demon with glowing eyes or not, he was a good salesman.

"What I'm hearing is that you like the service, but not the price. I totally understand. The last thing I want to do is strap you with debt. Now not knowing your situation, we do have some plans that allow you to make payments and still get protected today. That sounds good, doesn't it?"

"One."

"I'm sorry, what?"

"One. If you can make us a deal, I'll sign tonight. Right now."

"That's a pretty big ask but we might be able to work something out. Is there anything you don't need in terms of protection?"

"Technological," said Faline.

"Very cool. We'll focus on magic."

"No double protection."

"You know, it's one of those things that's nice to have, but it's not absolutely necessary. There will be a small gap in protection but if this guy is an imposter, you should be fine."

"Where does that put us?"

"We're definitely in range. Not quite there yet but we're making good progress. Fortunately, I'm the boss here at night and I'm authorized to be a little more creative. So, a bit of a crazy idea if you're interested: we have a program that allows our newer summoners to assist you and gain real experience in the field."

"In the field as in with us?" asked Quinn.

"Yes. Our summoner will accompany you and avail their talents as needed. It's not for everyone but if you're looking for a solution…"

"If that gets it down to one, then yes."

"Fantastic!" Jason smiled and held out a hand to shake on it. "We'll get a contract up here and introduce you to your new summoner slash traveling companion." Jason picked up the phone and asked for "a standard C-15."

"They'll be right up," he said. "This is the only bad part about the night shift. Gotta wait a little longer for contracts. But don't worry, I'll go over it with you and explain everything." Faline didn't seem inclined to make small talk so he turned to Quinn. "I have to say I'm glad you wanted psychic and not physical. This whole week, we've been having some kind of time down at the pits. The korobs are officially out of control."

"Monsters will be monsters."

Jason pointed at Quinn and made a clicking sound. "You said it, my friend."

"I gotta ask, is Embers your real name? That's made up, right?"

"It's pretty common practice among those of us who leave Duma. Our real names can be very hard to pronounce and honestly a little off-putting to some people. Taking a more common name makes it easier and limits demophobia. It's hard enough just moving to a new place."

Before Quinn could ask anything else, there was a knock on the door and the receptionist opened it. She had a leather portfolio stamped with a stylized R&H, which she handed to Jason, then left.

Inside was a silver pen and the contract. It looked like a standard sales agreement, with boxes for personal information and numbered sections of fine print. Jason spun it around so Quinn and Faline could read it. He pulled another pen out of his pocket and moved it down the contract as he explained the points.

"It's completely standard. It says here you're contracting an agent of Rannoch & Hale. You assume no liability for any damage to other persons or property. You will provide transportation but are not responsible for our agent's welfare. However, you do accept any personal harm that may occur as a result of services. Additionally, our agent is designated a neutral party whose involvement is limited strictly to services agreed upon. You'll receive no assistance in the event of additional conflict without renegotiation of this contract, et cetera, et cetera. Compensation to be the single favor we agreed on."

Quinn couldn't have been more surprised if the price was a kiss. The word itself sent a nasty little jolt through him. "Are you serious? A favor?"

Jason looked confused. "Yeah."

"I thought we were talking about money. Can't we just pay you?"

Jason smiled politely. "We have plenty of money.

That's not what we're interested in."

Quinn found this idea deeply unsettling.

"Let's finish up," said Faline.

Jason found his place again and continued reading. "Compensation is a single favor, to be paid within the next year. You may decline twice however failure to perform a requested favor within a year results in punitive action taken by R&H, namely possession of all corporeal and/or non-corporeal aspects of your being. Feel free to read it over. Take as long as you need."

Jason waited while Faline scanned the document. Finally she looked up and nodded. There were two blank lines at the bottom. Jason clicked the button on his pen and Quinn thought he was going to sign. Instead, Jason pressed the tip against his index finger then pressed his finger to the contract. When he lifted it away, there was a spot of blood.

Faline picked up the other pen and uncapped it. Inside there was a sharp point where the nib should have been. Suddenly Quinn wanted to reach out and grab her wrist to stop her from doing it. Then she pricked her finger and pressed it to the contract and it was too late.

"Fantastic," said Jason. He closed the folder and picked up the phone again. "Send him in, please."

While they waited, Jason offered Faline a band-aid from the box on the table and she declined. Soon there was a knock at the door. Jason got up to open it and ushered in the demon they would be trusting their lives to.

He was short. No more than two feet tall and stocky, with red skin and black hair. His eyes were shiny and entirely black too, like bubbles of ink. He wore a suit, tailored for his proportions, and carried a valise at his side.

Jason made the introductions. "Faline and Quinn, this is Barnabas Sludge. Barnabas, Faline and Quinn. They need protection set up." Barnabas walked over to the table. His suit pants made whipping noises with each step. Jason continued, "Barnabas is a mollyrake. He's a demon of the House of Magorr. 934th son of Magorr the Unrepentant."

Barnabas turned to face them. He smiled awkwardly, revealing sharp little teeth set in black gums. "Please to meeting," he said. He spoke haltingly and with a thick accent.

"We test all our summoners for basic language proficiency. He's still learning to speak it but he understands perfectly," said Jason.

Barnabas clambered up into a chair and began unpacking the valise. He took out items and set them on the table, one by one. His hands were small and red, the size of a child's, with black fingernails. When he was done, there were two figurines side-by-side, a length of twine, a book, a needle and a case with several little compartments. It reminded Quinn of a pill organizer but instead of days of the week, this one's compartments were marked with the shapes of animals: spider, rat, lizard, snake, bat and goat among others.

Barnabas tied the ends of the twine to form a loop and placed it around the figurines. They were old and worn down but looked like they might once have been carved to resemble people. When this was done, Barnabas flipped through the book to the right page, licked his lips with a black tongue and began reading. It was in a language that Quinn had never heard, full of guttural noises and hissing. He read quickly, then set the book aside and opened one of the compartments in the pill case. He pinched out a bit of powder and sprinkled it on the figurines. Then he took the needle, pricked a finger without hesitation and squeezed a drop of blood onto each.

"Done," he said. It sounded like *dun*, short and harsh.

"Awesome!" said Jason. He gave the demon's shoulder a friendly whack.

"I have a question. What exactly just happened?" asked Quinn.

"None see," said Barnabas. *Nunsy.*

"Your psychic essences have been transferred," Jason explained. "Barnabas has put them into distant objects, which is all that the individual looking for you will discover."

"Two tree," said Barnabas, gesturing the shape of a tree.

Jason held out his hand to shake. "It's been an absolute pleasure. Faline, we'll be in touch. Quinn, great to meet you."

"What's the best way to get to Squamit?" asked Faline.

"Are you on foot?"

"Yes."

"In that case, our complementary shuttle service is your best option. Squamit's a little further than we usually go but I can definitely make an exception. Barnabas'll get it set up for you."

Jason led them back to the elevators and down to the lobby. They passed a group of hooded figures on the way out. Their bodies were completely hidden except for the insect-like proboscises that stuck out from their hoods. "Be with you folks in just a second," Jason said as they passed. Once they were outside, Barnabas hustled off across the courtyard. A night mist had begun to gather and soon his small shape was lost in the darkness.

"Need anything for the road?" asked Jason.

"We're fine," said Faline.

"Then I wish you the best of luck. We'll talk soon." He shook their hands again and went back inside.

"You think Midnight's in Squamit?" Quinn asked

when they were alone.

"No."

"Then why are we going there?"

"I need to pick something up," she said and didn't elaborate. Soon, Quinn heard the sound of hooves, coming closer.

An old-fashioned carriage drawn by horses emerged from the darkness and stopped in front of them. A coachman sat on the bench, holding the reins. He was a top-hatted figure in a cloak, with the collar turned up to hide most of his face.

The door of the cab swung open and they climbed in. Barnabas was already inside. He pulled the door shut behind them and hoisted himself onto the seat next to Quinn as the carriage began to move. He'd changed into traveling clothes and traded the valise for a leather satchel with a strap. Faline sat across from them, with a hand near her gun, looking out the window.

The carriage swayed gently as they left the courtyard. The sound of the horses was a steady, peaceful one and before long Quinn was asleep.

27

QUINN WOKE UP AS THE carriage slowed. He heard crunching sounds and looked down in time to see insect legs disappearing into Barnabas's mouth. The demon held out a jar full of beetles with green-black shells. Quinn shook his head and Barnabas went back to chewing. While he ate, Quinn noticed that what he'd initially taken for hair on the demon's head were actually quills.

It was day now and they stopped near a large parking lot. There were signs advertising long term rates and not far away was a bus depot. An attendant kept watch in his booth, raising the gate as people came and went.

Faline jumped out of the carriage and headed across the lot, walking fast. When Quinn caught up, he saw what she'd come to Squamit for. Parked in one of the reserved spots was the bike they'd left in Vista, leaning on its kickstand.

Faline walked around the bike, inspecting it, and running her fingers over the metal. She was smiling for the first time since lunch in Santa Rosario. Then she threw a leg over it and gripped the handlebars. The dashboard came to life and the bike gave its low hum. Barnabas joined them, sweating and out of breath.

"Put your bag in here," she told Barnabas, indicating one of the saddlebags. "Ready?" she asked Quinn.

He climbed onto the back but Barnabas remained there, unsure of what to do until Faline held out a hand. She swung Barnabas up in front of her, onto the teardrop shaped housing that covered the bike's power source. His legs dangled on either side. "Hold on tight," she said.

Barnabas lowered his head and gripped the metal with his fingers. Faline backed out of the spot carefully and piloted the bike out of the parking lot. When they reached the road, she twisted the throttle and they took off. Soon they were racing along and, for the briefest and sweetest of moments, it didn't feel like they were being hunted. With the air rushing by on a warm clear day, it didn't feel like anything was wrong with the world.

They rode until nightfall and stopped a few miles outside a town called Dornan. The lower half of the sky was still sunset orange. Buildings dotted the sides of the road and Faline pulled up in front of a diner. Its 'OPEN' sign was a flickering neon beacon. Gravel crunched under the bike's wheels and its headlight reflected off the windows in a bright circle.

Quinn headed to the diner's bathroom and relieved himself for what felt like several minutes. When he was done he looked at himself in the mirror above the sink while he washed his hands. The usual graffiti was scratched into it but, behind the crude genitals and curse words, Quinn thought he looked tired. He remembered his mother's voice for a moment. *Come join me in the light.* Quinn shook his head to banish the thought. He splashed water on his face and left quickly, desperate to escape the lonely confines of the bathroom.

Faline and Barnabas were already sitting in a booth.

It was next to a window and afforded them a view of the parking area. It was getting darker and the road beyond was already hard to make out.

Quinn saw a cup of coffee waiting for him and slid in next to Barnabas. He left a space between them, uncomfortable with being so close to the demon. A faint acrid odor hung around him, pricking Quinn's nostrils.

"There's cream," said Faline, pointing to the counter.

"If I ever put cream in my coffee, take it as a sign that I've been possessed and shoot me immediately," said Quinn as he took a drink.

The counter jockey came over to take their order. He wore a paper fry cook's hat and appeared to be some kind of humanoid reptile. His skin was greenish with a pebbled texture. His eyes were large and yellow, each with a black slit of pupil up the center. *Darren*, according to his nametag.

"You guys know what you want?" he asked, trying his best to enunciate without lips.

They ordered from the simple menu. Darren wrote their orders down and occasionally blinked a milky white membrane over his eyes. He had two holes in the sides of his head which Quinn assumed were ears. When it was his turn, Barnabas ordered in the same demonic language he'd used at Rannoch & Hale and Darren nodded. When he left to get their food, Quinn was mildly disappointed not to see a tail dragging behind him.

The diner reminded Quinn of diners he'd been in back home: white tile, plastic seats, a stainless-steel counter with a glass container for pastries. Music was playing over fuzzy-sounding speakers mounted on the wall. To Quinn it sounded like folk-tinged country, a man with a lived-in voice singing about his girl back home and the road ahead. Darren leaned into the kitchen and called out their order, then went back to sitting behind the cash register and reading a book. It was so normal, it felt almost surreal.

The food came quickly and Darren refilled their coffee. Rare steak and eggs for Faline, a hamburger and fries for Quinn and a plate of what looked like rice for Barnabas. On closer inspection, Quinn realized it was moving and that Barnabas had ordered a plate of maggots. Before eating, he closed his eyes and bowed his head. Quinn watched, incredulous, until he was done.

"Did you just say *grace*?"

"What's wrong with that?" said Faline. It wasn't a question so much as a warning to drop it.

Quinn did but not without muttering, "And I thought Scientology was weird," into his coffee.

Barnabas ate the maggots with his fingers, one by one. It sounded like oatmeal being chewed. Quinn tried not to look again while he ate.

"What's our plan?" he asked Faline, after they'd finished.

"The plan is we find Midnight. The best way to do that now is to find the magic user who's helping him."

"And how do we do that?"

"We go to the Spire."

Barnabas stopped chewing. He paused with a maggot halfway to his mouth, squirming between his fingers. The black orbs of his eyes were directed at Faline. "*Spar?*"

"What the hell is that?" asked Quinn.

"It's the common name for the Tower of Sorcery, in Majis."

"And why did he almost just choke on a maggot when you said it?

"Mages don't trust demons."

"So they're smart."

Faline chose her words carefully. "Look. I under-stand how you could feel that way. But you're talking out your ass right now and you have no idea."

"I do have an idea that maybe it's weird to just trust our lives to a demon. Some might call it common sense. Nothing personal, Barnabas. I'm sure you're a wonderful servant of darkness, but let's be honest here. I mean, for fuck's sake, look what he's eating." There was uncomfortable silence at the table. "So why the Spire?"

"Because the magic user would've studied there. Your fucking common sense didn't tell you that?"

Headlights washed over the window. Quinn squinted at the beams for a second, then they cut off. He heard a door slam, then another, and a moment later two men walked into the diner.

One was heavyset and one was skinny. They looked like truckers, in jeans and jackets. The big one had a baseball cap tipped back on his head. Faline sat facing away from them and Quinn saw her jaw tighten. The men sat at the counter and the big one called to Darren.

"Snake on over here with a couple menus!"

Darren put menus in front of them and the men took their jackets off. The skinny one wore a tank top and sported a barbed wire tattoo around one arm. The big one had a t-shirt that barely stretched over his gut. It said *This Isn't A Blood Belly...It's A Gas Tank For A Sex Machine.*

Quinn pondered the words "blood belly." Then the men turned to survey the diner and he saw the tips of fangs protruding down from their mouths.

"What a cute little family!" the skinny one said, when he saw their table.

"Let's go," said Faline. Her voice was low and even. She stood and dropped a couple bills onto the table.

"That your bike outside? You want to give me a ride?" the big one said.

They left the booth and began walking to the door, past the vampires sitting at the counter. The big one watched them approach and sniffed the air. "We got a wolf girl. You in heat? Once you go vamp, you'll always be damp."

The skinny one looked at Barnabas and laughed. "Little demon guy here. I can take you home for my dog to hump." Then to Faline, "Maybe you'd like that too. Some doggy dick in your little wolf cooter." They laughed, the sound of bad men amused by bad things.

The big one stood up, giving them almost no room to pass. Faline pushed by him and looked without blinking into his large, fleshy face. The lower half was covered with stubble and sweaty strands of hair were plastered to his fore-head. He didn't look like any vampire Quinn had imagined. These were slovenly and ill-mannered, frightening in a wholly different way.

The big one lurched forward, trying to make Faline flinch. She didn't move. The skinny one laughed. "I think she wants to play!" he shouted, spinning around on his stool.

"You know," said the big one, "My maker fucked a werewolf. He turned her out and she couldn't get enough. Used to get down on all fours and beg for it."

Faline stared back at him and said, "Yeah? I heard the only thing vamps suck more than blood is dick."

The big vampire couldn't have looked more surprised if she'd slapped him. Faline backed out the door, keeping an eye on the vampires until Quinn and Barnabas followed.

"You gonna let her talk to you like that?" the skinny one said as they went out.

The door closed and they walked to the bike. Quinn climbed on the back, feeling less than heroic but glad to be leaving. In the diner, the vampires appeared to be having an argument. Faline reached down for Barnabas but he stood there, frozen.

"Let's go!" said Quinn. The vampires were staring at them through the window now.

Barnabas said something in demontongue, gesturing and repeating a word. Quinn had no idea what he was saying, but the panic came through loud and clear. The vampires threw the door open and started walking towards them.

"You wanna play?" called the skinny one. "Let's fuckin' play!"

"Come on!" Quinn urged.

Barnabas ran to the back of the bike, the quills on his head sticking up in agitation. He grabbed his satchel and held it up, yelling something over and over. Even with his accent, it was impossible to miss the word "*Found.*"

28

FALINE JUMPED OFF THE BIKE and walked towards the vampires. The big one was almost within grabbing distance when she pulled her gun and shot him twice. He staggered back and dropped to his ass with both hands on his chest. The skinny one froze in shock and Faline shot him too.

The bullet caught him in the shoulder and spun him around. He had time to yell "Fuckin' bitch!" before Faline unloaded into his back, driving him towards the diner. The big glass window shattered and he collapsed in the frame, folded over the sill.

Barnabas dumped his bag out on the ground and began frantically searching through the pile. Quinn saw the big vampire get up and close in on Faline. She fired at him again but this time he took the bullets and didn't stop.

There was a blur of movement at the edge of Quinn's vision and he looked over to see the skinny vampire streaking across the parking lot. Quinn dove out of the way as the vampire reached the place he'd been standing. Barnabas was setting up the ritual as fast as he could and Quinn maneuvered in front of him.

Over the skinny vampire's shoulder, Quinn saw the

heavy one straddling Faline, trying to bite her throat. She fought to keep him away with a hand on his neck, feeling around with the other one for her gun. It lay on the ground, just out of reach.

"You wanna play, bloodbag?" said the skinny one. He moved towards Quinn, swaying from side to side. Quinn stepped back slowly, keeping himself between the vampire and Barnabas. The demon was reading from his book in a shaky voice. "Gonna kill you, then your little buddy. Then maybe we call the rest of the family and run a train on the bitch," the vampire said. He moved faster than Quinn's eyes could follow and was suddenly behind Quinn, twisting his arm. "What do you think of that?" the vampire asked. His breath smelled like rotting meat.

Across the lot, Faline hiked a knee into the big one's balls and rolled away. She scrambled towards her gun but he grabbed her ankles and hauled her back.

Quinn slammed the back of his head into the skinny one's face and heard something crunch. He tried to break free but the vampire was too strong. Fangs threshed the air inches from Quinn's neck and he hoped he'd bought enough time for Barnabas to complete the ritual.

Then the vampire was gone. Quinn looked up in time to see Faline throw him to the ground. She stood over him with a sharp length of wood, torn from the side of the diner, and stabbed at his heart. The vampire exploded in a flurry of bats. They swirled upwards and disappeared into the night sky.

"Is he dead?" asked Quinn.

"No, but it doesn't matter," said Faline. She tossed away the makeshift stake. "It'll be awhile before they can pull back together. Sometimes they can't. Bats are stubborn." She winced. Her face was scraped and swelling. "Done, Barnabas?"

"*Yez.*" He hastily repacked his bag, cramming everything in.

Once they were back on the highway, Faline gunned it and the bike shot forward with a scream. Quinn felt the speed push him back like a large, invisible hand. The bike's headlight made a wide, bright swath through the night.

In the diner, a piece of glass hanging from the top edge of the window frame finally let go and crashed to the floor. In the aftermath, everything was oddly still. Behind the counter, a paper fry cook's hat slowly rose, followed by green skin and wide, reptilian eyes that surveyed the damage.

They rode through the night and didn't stop until morning. Quinn was sure they were well beyond a bat's flight range but didn't feel completely safe until the sun was above the horizon. Faline pulled off the road near a small grassy area. She leaned against a tree and closed her eyes. Eventually she slept, poorly again. Quinn tried to do the same but couldn't, so he snapped twigs and watched as the occasional car passed on the road. Barnabas remained awake too. He knelt in prayer, then snacked on bugs and reorganized his satchel. They made no attempt to talk and Quinn did his best to distract himself.

Ever since leaving Santa Rosario, thoughts of drugs had been creeping back into his mind. Try as he might, Quinn couldn't make them stop. Sometimes they were front and center, other times lurking on the periphery, but always, always there no matter how many times Quinn tried shoving them away. He had developed a mental image of firing bullets from a machine gun in a circle, killing and clearing the thoughts. Then, in the center of his mind, he imagined a tiny dot appearing and expanding, breaking apart into blank metal sheets that lined the walls of his mind-room. That worked for awhile but the drug thoughts always returned and Quinn found himself sweating, his heart beating. He wondered what might happen if someone offered him something. The thought was both terrifying and exciting. Quinn shook his head violently to clear it and went on snapping twigs with renewed vigor.

When Faline woke from her restless sleep, they continued on toward Majis, toward the Spire, and toward whatever else lay beyond.

29

MIDNIGHT STOOD IN A FIELD, looking at two trees. In one hand he held a gun, in the other the crumbled remains of an amulet. The trees seemed to mock him. The wolf and her companion were not here and they never had been. He had been led astray, valuable time and amulets wasted. Midnight cursed and went back to the portal he'd arrived by. It hung in the air, like a gash in reality. On the other side, just visible through ripples of mystic energy, was the room with stained glass windows. Midnight stepped through the portal and it closed behind him. The edges shrank and healed together until reality was unblemished once more.

Midnight stood in the castle. He looked at the pieces of the amulet in his hand, then dropped them on the floor and laid his gun down on the desk. He pulled out a spare magazine and laid it next to the gun. A bullet with a silver tip was visible, peeking out the top. He'd bought them from a store in Darke called No-Were. They sold shirts and hats with "Welcome to No-Were" printed on them and range targets featuring menacing drawings of werewolves. The back wall was covered with all kinds of rifles and heavy artillery, just in case someone needed to mount an assault on a werewolf fortress. Midnight browsed the display cases containing hand-guns until a girl came over to help him. She wore silver jewelry and a tight shirt that read "Howl At This" under a picture of a gun.

Originally, he'd wanted a revolver. Somehow shooting his mother's killer with one seemed like poetic justice. But the girl steered him towards a semi-automatic pistol with a fifteen-shot capacity. She recommended Bostwick Silver Tips and assured him they would work on non-wolves too. She leaned over the counter while they talked, with her tits pushed up. Midnight left with the gun, the bullets and an indelible mental image of the girl's cleavage.

On the desk near the gun was a gold apparatus, made of multiple rings on a central spindle. Different lenses protruded from the rings, like strange petals. Some were made of glass while others were different materials. Obsidian, ruby, even wood. The rings spun constantly, turning at different speeds, and the sight of it infuriated Midnight. His mother had been able to use it well. For her, the spinning rings would stop and a combination of lenses would align to show her what she wanted to see. Usually it was a girl, to be taken and drained. Midnight wasn't able to use it nearly as well. The lenses went around and around, refusing to line up. It had taken days to sight Faline and Quinn, and that had turned out to be false.

He looked away from the visiolabe and his eyes fell on the cabinet in the corner. The thought of the dwindling supply of amulets inside only made him angrier and beneath that, panicked, so he left the room and slammed the heavy door behind him. He went down the hall, passing portraits of his ancestors. Serious faces with dark hair and dark eyes watched him go by. He went down a grand staircase which led into the Great Room. It was wide and had bannisters of ebony wood, carved to resemble roses. Once upon a time, they had been polished so deeply they seemed to glow from within. Now they were dull and coated with dust. It was caked in the folds of the rose petals.

On the far side of the Great Room, there was a fire-place that never seemed to fully heat the vast, stone space. Above it hung an ornate map of the world. Various towns were marked with gems, and borders were designated by thin veins of gold. It was an old map, with monsters in the waters of a vast, encircling sea, and no Deadlands. Facing it were two high-backed chairs, heavy old pieces, and between them a small table.

Guardian was on the table, exactly where Midnight had left him.

"Did you find them?"

"No. They weren't there. Just trees."

"Decoys. So they are prepared. They have protection."

"I'll find them."

"Before they find you?"

Midnight said nothing for a moment. He thought about the seeing apparatus, spinning endlessly and showing nothing. He wrapped himself in a fur and sat in one of the chairs in front of the fire.

"If there is anything more I can do to help, please tell me. They are my enemies too and it is only a matter of time before they are at the gates. I worry, Midnight. This world is so vast, two people can easily move through it undetected."

"*I'll find them,*" he said.

"I have faith you will. I only hope that doing so does not exhaust our resources."

30

THEY SAW THE SPIRE FROM a distance, a black needle on the horizon. They'd travelled for nearly four days, eventually merging onto a wide track of black stone. In Majis, Quinn realized, all roads led to one place.

The Spire itself was built of the same black stone, a tapering manmade pillar of creation that stabbed into the sky. Quinn had never felt smaller. Even the trees around it, mighty old specimens, were like scale models. Hundreds of windows marched up in neat rows and on a cloudy day, the uppermost floors would be hidden. The Spire stood as a monument to itself, in all its dark glory.

It was surrounded by a chasm so wide an arrow fired from one side would fall short of the other. Faline stopped the bike and they walked to the edge. Quinn couldn't see the bottom, only darkness, and his palms were instantly sweaty. The two sides were connected by a pathway of stones. A single line of them, suspended in the air.

"The Floating Steps of Majis," said Faline.

Quinn looked across. The land on the tower side was green and well-kept. People moved about, looking from a distance like small, colorful game pieces. Some had paused to watch.

"What's the catch?" Quinn asked.

"The catch," said Faline, "Is that no one carrying a weapon can cross. Supposedly." She handed her gun to Barnabas, lips moving in their soundless mantra, as they had before breaking into Tardigrade. Then she started across, stepping from one stone to the next.

"The demon's staying behind. Shocker." Quinn looked down again. Sheer walls of earth descended into the darkness. Peering into the chasm played tricks with his balance. Suddenly his upper body felt much heavier than his lower half. He put a foot on the first stone, testing it. It was as solid and stable as the ground so he settled more weight onto it, half expecting the stone to drop away like a trapdoor and send him plummeting. When it didn't, he began the long walk across.

Faline was nearly halfway there but Quinn didn't try to catch up. He stepped deliberately, trying to focus on the stones and not the emptiness around them. Over such a drop, the simple act of walking in a straight line became a daunting prospect that lasted several vertigo-inducing minutes. When he reached the other side, Quinn had to resist the urge to drop to his knees and kiss the ground.

The black stone path resumed on this side and ran towards the Spire. In places it branched off, through gardens and towards other fields. As far as Quinn could see, all of it was encircled by the chasm. It ran out of sight in both directions, curving around the Spire's grounds.

A man in long, brown robes was approaching, walking towards them alone. Faline's hand instinctively reached for the gun that wasn't there, then dropped. The man stopped at a respectful distance to greet them and Quinn got his first good look at a mage.

"Hello, travelers. My name is Zinedine. On behalf of the Spire, I welcome you." He smiled and held out his hands in a gesture of openness.

Faline held out her hands the same way and after a moment, Quinn did too. Zinedine came over the rest of the way. He was older, with a friendly face and a pleasant manner.

"What brings you across the Steps?" he asked.

"We need help," said Faline. "We're being hunted by an imposter and want to find out who's supplying him with magic."

Zinedine nodded and said, "Please come with me." He waited for Quinn and Faline to join him, then began walking back towards the Spire.

They went up the path, past boys and girls in robes of different colors. Quinn saw red, blue, green, black and gray. They ranged from kids to teenagers, with the youngest wearing gray and the older ones in the colors. There were a few other brown robes among them, worn by adult men and women. As they entered the gardens, a little girl in gray ran over.

"Master Zinedine, look what I can do!"

"Show me," he said, with a warm smile. He had the gentle air of a good teacher.

The girl's face became serious. Her eyebrows furrowed and her mouth pressed into a determined line. She held her hands in front of her, as if carrying an invisible ball. After a moment, a faint haze appeared between them. It began to thicken and when it was white and fluffy, she broke into a proud, gap-toothed smile.

"Very good, Elenia," said Zinedine. "I have to take our guests inside, but later I want to see if you can make shapes." The girl nodded and ran off and the cloud she'd made disappeared.

"That was amazing," said Quinn as they continued along the path.

"She's very talented and a hard worker, too. I think she'll take the blue robes when the time comes."

"You're her teacher?"

"One of them, yes."

"Brown for teachers?"

"Some of us. We brown robes serve no Order, only the Spire. We instruct the novices, the ones you see in gray, until they choose a discipline. Then they become apprentices and are taught by the mages of that Order."

"This is a school," said Quinn.

"Yes, among other things."

Quinn looked around as they walked. Students chatted with their friends or read from thick books. The path led through a garden full of plants Quinn couldn't identify. There were bushes with glowing fruit and trees where small, naked green fairies perched, their wings like dragonfly wings shining in the sun. All around the garden, impossible wonders were being practiced by the students. A green robe made a flower grow and shrink back into the earth. A black robe made the skeletons of mice perform tricks for a group. They hopped onto each other, forming a swaying pyramid. A teenage boy with acne as red as his robe chased girls with a fireball the size of a fist. It swooped after them in the air and they ran through the garden, shrieking with laughter.

"Matthais," Zinedine said as they passed and the fireball disappeared.

"Sorry, Master Zinedine," he said.

"How do you choose the students?" asked Quinn.

"We travel the world, looking for those with the potential to become mages. The ones we find are offered a place to learn and grow."

"Could I be one?"

"Likely not, but I can perform a test." Zinedine drew out a small stone and held it up for Quinn to see. There was a rune carved on it. "What do you feel?" he asked.

Quinn searched himself for any kind of feeling. After a moment he answered, "Nothing."

"I'm sorry," said Zinedine. He gave a kind smile and put the stone away. "It is a rare gift, bestowed on relatively few. Those that have it feel something when they look at runes. What I showed you was called a Laughing Stone."

"Could I learn?"

"I'm afraid not. Magical aptitude is inborn. Hence why the one who hunts you uses amulets, I imagine. But take heart, one need not be magical to find help here."

The path led out of the garden, up to the heavy doors of the Spire's entrance. Zinedine raised a hand and they swung open.

"You don't need to pat us down or anything?" asked Quinn.

"Pat you down?" Zinedine looked genuinely puzzled.

"Check us before we go in."

"No, you crossed the Steps. You carry no weapons or malice, and we welcome all good travelers."

Inside was a massive space. Supporting columns rose up and spread across the ceiling in trusses, like a great stone web. In the sections created by the trusses, scenes of magical battles were painted. The colors seemed even brighter in their frames of black stone. Mages fought strange creatures and cast spells in bursts of light, posed heroically amidst chaos. In the central painting, a group of them stood with arms up-raised, creating a single beam of brilliant white light that pierced the head of a looming dragon.

Zinedine led them across the room, where four empty black thrones sat. Each had a different symbol inlaid in the backrest: flames, a tree, waves and a skull. Smaller thrones were arranged next to them, all facing rows of benches in a half-circle.

"When we meet, the lords of each Order sit there. We instructors sit with them and address the pupils."

Zinedine continued past the thrones. Against the wall the supports formed arches, all the way around the room. The walls between were painted with a continuous scene of battle, which Quinn recognized as the Fall of Bastion. To the left, a giant swung its club down against a mage's shield of light. To the right, a group of mages tended to a fallen Hero.

Zinedine raised his hand and the section of painting in the archway before them vanished. In its place, glowing symbols appeared on the black stone. They were arranged in concentric rings, one inside the other, smaller and smaller. They began to spin, symbols realigning, until they found their places. Light flashed around the edges of the archway and it swung open like a door.

Quinn stood on the threshold and stared, looking up and up. In the center of the room was a massive statue of a hydra, its heads rearing back far above. They rose to various doorways in the stone walls, far above the floor. Stairs had been cut into the body of the hydra, and along the length of each snakelike neck.

Zinedine urged Quinn through the archway with a gentle hand and the door closed behind them. "The Hydra of Orax. It ruled this land thousands of years before the Spire was built. It took the combined power of our greatest mages––the Ravenstahls, Blackthornes, Creightons and others—to turn it to stone. This way."

Zinedine started up the stairs, climbing the hydra's side. When they ascended one of the necks, Quinn felt the way he'd felt on the Floating Steps. The stairs were wider than they looked from the ground, but there were no handrails. Quinn kept his eyes up until they reached the head, where a narrow bridge ran from the tip of the hydra's mouth to the doorway.

They went down a hallway lit with oil lamps and stopped in front of a closed door. Zinedine raised a hand again and turned the glowing lock that appeared.

The door opened to an apartment with a window. "Welcome to my chambers. Come and sit." Zinedine indicated a table. On the bed a small, gray ball of fur shook itself and stood up. It had two legs, short arms and a mouthful of teeth.

"What is that?" asked Quinn.

"A beezle. They run wild in the gardens. Some can be quite sweet," said Zinedine. Then, to his pet, "Quiet." The beezle settled back down but watched the newcomers warily. Zinedine made a motion with his hand like sign language, thrusting his fingers up. A fire sprang to life on the hearth, under a kettle. "I'll make some tea," he said. "Now you say you want to find the identity of the magic user who aids your imposter?"

"Yes. I have part of the amulet that was used." Faline unfolded the paper containing the clay powder and slid it across the table. Zinedine examined it. He held a hand over it and the powder glowed momentarily. Then it faded and he shook his head.

"I'm afraid I can't help you. The quantity is too small. If I probe further I may contaminate it with my own magic."

"Is there any way of finding out who made it?" asked Faline.

Zinedine nodded. It was the solemn gesture of a man resigned to perform a necessary but unpleasant task. "It is not a decision to be taken lightly. Have you heard of the Court of the Elementals?" Faline nodded and Zinedine looked to Quinn. "Have you?"

"No."

"A short history lesson, then." Zinedine motioned and the fire went out. He pointed and the kettle floated across the room. Another gesture and a cabinet opened. Three cups came out and steaming water poured into each. They floated to the table and settled there. Quinn took his cup and breathed in strong, hot tea. Zinedine sipped his then continued. "The Elementals ruled this world once, when it was young. The most powerful were Pyraena, Teruk, Etherion and Morgana. They controlled fire, nature, water and death. They divided Ouros into their kingdoms and the Age of Chaos, when time passed unmarked, gave way to the Age of Elementals. After untold centuries of violence, there was order upon the world and they reigned for millennia.

At first, humans relied on them and worshipped them. But as humans became more powerful and numerous, they stopped following blindly. They built cities and machines and places where the Elementals no longer held sway.

Feeling their power waning, the Elementals gifted their remaining followers with the ability to channel energies for themselves, giving them mastery over what was once the sole possession of the Elementals. Thus began the Age of Magic. They built the Spire for their followers as a place of safety but, as time went on, even their followers no longer relied on the Elementals. They looked instead to the most skilled mages for guidance and the gods of old were only distantly revered. Knowing their time had passed, the Elementals retreated from the world to a place they had made beyond time, beyond human control. They left only aspects of themselves, in a room at the top of the Spire. They are ancient beyond measure, part of the fabric of existence. They would be able to tell you who made this amulet."

"Why would they?" asked Quinn. "Why would they even care?"

"This was their world once. They remember it well and long for the feeling of humans asking for things on bended knee."

"Have you ever met them?"

"Yes. All mages do. After training, we enter the Court to seek permission to become full members of an Order. We're tested and the worthy are admitted."

"What about the rest?"

"The Elementals purge their magical abilities, then they're sent home."

"So all those kids out there could have part of who they are stolen, then get tossed out like garbage?"

"Magic is a serious thing. Wonderful and extraordinary, but not to be taken lightly."

"No wonder people don't trust mages."

"What do you know of our history?" asked Zinedine, in a patient voice.

"Not a ton," said Quinn, then added, "I'm from Vista."

"We have a fraught relationship with those who share this world. The fault is ours, but for half a century, we've tried to make amends. I've told you how we recruit novices, but that's not how it always was. Before, we simply took the ones we wanted."

"Wait, you stole children?"

"Yes, we stole children. We were the monsters, more terrifying than anything that dwells in Darke. We came with our robes and our powerful spells and we did what we pleased. And that is not all. We took magical children to the Spire and forced them to learn. And after completing their studies, we forced them to test in front of the Elementals. Those who failed did not just lose their magic, but their lives.

Mages became hated and feared. Bounties were offered for us in other lands, and even within our own. We withdrew to the Spire and practiced magic within our borders, teaching a dwindling number.

When the Heroes War began, we stayed neutral. A scant few urged the Spire to join the side of the Heroes, saying we should use our powers to help others and save the world. They saw a chance for us to redeem ourselves. But there were others, more than a few, who advocated joining the Supers, saying that the most powerful should rule and that we should support their cause. They saw a chance to reclaim our position in the world. In the end, both factions joined the war, and the rest waited to see who would emerge victorious.

Then came the day that Bastion fell. While others fled or died, our most powerful mages stood with Captain Photon. When he was struck by Blight's spear, the mage Arkadian saved him and remained with him to the end. It was he that shielded the Hall of Heroes, while Captain Photon absorbed the Shard's energy. In the last moments, Arkadian sent his wife Venora away, to bear the story of the Fall. The rest, hero and villain alike, perished on that field of battle.

Since then, we've tried to make amends for the evil of our past. Venora, the widow of Arkadian, became the master of the Spire. She was scarred and tired by years of war, but committed to restoring honor to the practice of magic. She cast out those who had supported the Supers, and those who would not accept her new laws. Even the Elementals were forced to accept them, lest Venora seal the Court forever. The practice of killing children was ended, traitors hunted down, and a new era of peace and diplomacy began. For this, she was called the Redeemer.

Much of the world still does not accept that we have changed but we are committed to leaving the old ways behind. A void was left by the death of the Heroes. The peace and order they brought to Ouros is gone. Perhaps one day, the mages will bring it back. If we do not, I fear what might grow in its place.

To that end, we strive to be not conquerors or masters, but servants and peacekeepers. No one comes here who does not want to, and no one takes the test who is not ready."

"But you still take their magic if they fail," said Quinn.

"It sounds harsh, but we cannot allow untrained or immoral mages free reign. Imagine if Tardigrade simply allowed their most powerful technology into the world without restriction."

Quinn and Faline exchanged a glance.

"I'll tell you now what I tell every student of mine: it is a risk to enter the Court. If you make a request of them, the Elementals are bound by ancient laws to consider it. They will give you a test. If you can pass, you will be given what you seek. If you fail, you must forfeit what they ask." Zinedine paused to let that sink in.

"What will they want from us?" asked Faline.

"You have no magic so they will take something else. Sight or memory, perhaps. I don't know, but it will be something you hold dear. Compassion is not in the nature of the Elementals. They are old gods and old gods demand sacrifice. Knowing that, do you freely and willingly choose to enter the Court?"

"Faline, this is crazy," said Quinn.

Without looking at him, she pushed her chair back and stood up. "I'm ready."

"Then I will open the way for you," said Zinedine.

They went back out into the windowless hall, to the stairs at the far end and began to climb. It wound upwards past other floors and by the time they emerged into another hallway, Quinn's legs were burning.

He could hear voices and sounds of students coming from behind the closed doors that marked the hall's length. Zinedine knocked at one and a few moments later, it was opened by a brown-robed teacher.

"Master Dorenbos, apologies for the interruption. Would you accompany us for a moment?" asked Zinedine.

Dorenbos glanced at Quinn and Faline and seemed to understand what was being asked. "Certainly," he said. The students in his class were seated at long tables, each with a crystal in front of them. Dorenbos instructed them to continue, then closed the door behind him.

"What are they studying?" asked Quinn.

"Scrying," said Dorenbos, as they continued down the hall. "The art of seeing."

They stopped at other classrooms and more masters joined until a small platoon of them walked together. They went up more stairs and down more halls, past rooms that contained wonders. The skeletons of unidentifiable animals, apprentices working over cauldrons that gave off colorful smoke, a library several stories tall. The books on higher shelves were retrieved by the little green fairies that Quinn had seen perched in the garden. They worked in tandem to move the heaviest volumes.

The mages swept by these and others without stopping. They formed a loose ring around Quinn and Faline, ferrying them along until they arrived at a large door with runes carved on the frame. The mages spread out before it, giving each other room.

"Are you sure you want this?" asked Zinedine. "Once

you go in, there's no turning back."

"Open it," said Faline. So they did.

The mages raised their hands and the glowing, concentric circles appeared, several of them, covering the door. The mages spun the magical locks until the last ones fell into place and light flashed around the edges, then used their collective will to push open the door.

It opened just a crack, enough for one person at a time to squeeze through. The mages parted, forming lines on either side. They waited with their heads bowed, like a solemn, brown-robed honor guard.

Before she walked through, Quinn grabbed Faline's arm and said, "You don't have to do this. We can find another way."

She looked at Quinn, then down at his hand on her arm. He let go and took a step back. "Stay here then," she said, and went in.

"That's not what I meant," said Quinn, but by then was talking to himself. He followed her through, into the Court of the Elementals.

It was an empty cold room with tapering walls, and windows showing nothing but sky. Quinn had always heard black made a room smaller, but now he discovered that wasn't true. The room felt endless, boundless.

There were no decorations or furniture to offer the slightest bit of comfort. It was a space designed to make its occupants uncomfortable and small, which Quinn supposed made sense for a court. Then, in the bare and empty room, something began to happen.

Distortions appeared in the air. They were small at first, four points that stretched and pulled at the room around them like gravity wells. They burst outward, spreading open in rings with glowing edges and stretching down into portals, revealing different worlds behind a thin layer of reality.

One was a place of fire. In the distance a mountain erupted, sending out lava that ran in slow-moving orange and black rivers. Between it and the opening, the entire landscape was consumed in flame.

Another portal looked into a deep forest. Old, mossy trees stretched back as far as Quinn could see. Green-tinted light filtered down.

The third showed a storm-tossed ocean. The water was endless and grey. Occasionally the waves revealed what might have been islands or might have been monsters.

The last was a battlefield. Dead and dying lay under an ashy sky streaked with fire.

Faline's attention was drawn to the burning portal and before long, Quinn saw it too. A figure walked among the flames, drawing closer. It was vaguely human-shaped, massive, and itself made of fire. But when it stepped through the portal, the Elemental underwent a transformation. It emerged into the Court as a woman of normal size and stunning beauty. She wore a red dress and her skin was black, so dark it was almost blue.

Other Elementals emerged from their portals to join her. Wisps of air and ocean spray became a tall, thin man. He wore dirty clothes the color of the sea. An Elemental with a body made of twisted branches emerged from the forest as a short, powerfully built man. A long beard hung in front of his muscular chest. And on the battlefield, a creature with black wings growing from her back approached the portal. She was naked and nearly bald. Her body was wizened and covered with scars. Small breasts sagged over protruding ribs. Her fingers ended in talons and she used these to slash her way to the portal. She stepped through, pale and beautiful, wearing a cloak of feathers. Stringy grey hair became black and lustrous.

There were no wings or talons, but her face was unmistakably cruel.

KNEEL.

The word filled Quinn's mind. He was too busy trying to process what he was seeing to obey. The Fire Elemental, Pyraena he remembered, leaned forward. Her lips did not move.

IN THIS ROOM, EVEN TIME BOWS TO US SO YOU WILL TOO. KNEEL.

Quinn looked over and saw Faline reluctantly lower herself to a knee. He did too.

WHAT IS YOUR PURPOSE?

Faline said, "I have a question."

A QUESTION. Now it was Teruk the Forest Elemental's turn to speak, or rather fill their minds with his voice. *THE CREATURE THAT IS NEITHER WOLF NOR WOMAN HAS A QUESTION. YOU ARE EVER BETWEEN. ANIMAL AND HUMAN. DESIRE AND DUTY. CONTROL AND HUNGER.*

BUT YOU, WE DO NOT KNOW, said Etherion. Quinn realized the Water Elemental meant him. *YOU HAVE NO PAST HERE. THIS IS A CURIOUS THING. YOU HAVE NO RIGHT TO APPEAR BEFORE US. WE SHOULD DESTROY HIM. WHAT SAY THE COURT?*

The Elementals turned towards each other, conferring in a way that was beyond Quinn's senses. After a moment, they broke their conference and turned back to Quinn and Faline. Pyraena's voice filled their heads.

WE HAVE DECIDED UPON A TEST. IF YOU SUCCEED, YOU WILL HAVE AN ANSWER TO YOUR QUESTION.

IF YOU FAIL, WE WILL TAKE YOUR POWER, said Morgana, the Death Elemental. *YOU HAVE NO MAGIC TO GIVE SO WE WILL TAKE WHAT IN YOU IS WILD.*

"I understand," said Faline. "I'm ready."

NOT YOU. THE HUMAN. WE TIRE OF HIS PRESENCE AND HE MUST PROVE HIS WORTH. YOU WILL REMAIN WITH US. HE WILL PERFORM THE TEST. IF HE SUCCEEDS, YOU WILL HAVE YOUR ANSWER. GO NOW, HUMAN. YOU CARRY THIS CREA- TURE'S FATE WITH YOU.

Etherion waved a hand. There was a rush of air and Quinn was gone. Faline looked at the place where he'd been a moment before.

YOU ARE AFRAID, CREATURE.

"I've been through worse."

DO NOT LIE TO US. WE SENSE YOUR FEAR. IT IS A RIPPLE IN OUR OCEAN OF POWER. YOU FEAR BECAUSE YOU KNOW WHAT THE HUMAN IS.

A COWARD.

A FOOL.

A WEAKLING.

YOU HAVE KNOWN SINCE YOU JOINED COMPANY. NOW THIS WILL BE YOUR DOWNFALL. MERCY IS ALWAYS A MISTAKE. YOU SHOULD HAVE ENTERED OUR COURT ALONE. PERHAPS YOU WOULD HAVE SURVIVED OUR TEST INTACT.

OR NOT. PERHAPS YOU WOULD HAVE FAILED.

BUT FAILED WITH HONOR. YOUR COMPANION HAS NO MORE HONOR THAN THE DEMON WHO WAITS ON THE OTHER SIDE OF THE STEPS.

DO YOU TRUST HIM?

"Yes," said Faline.

WE TOLD YOU NOT TO LIE. Teruk pointed at Faline and she screamed. The Elemental lowered his arm and the pain was gone. She felt blood dripping from her nose.

IT HAS ALWAYS BEEN YOU. EVERY STEP OF THE WAY. YOU HAVE FOUGHT AND HE HAS STOOD BEHIND YOU.

BEFORE THE END, WE WANT YOU TO ADMIT THE TRUTH.

NOTHING DEPENDED ON HIM UNTIL NOW. HIS LIFE WAS ALWAYS IN YOUR HANDS. NEVER YOURS IN HIS.

WHAT HAPPENED TO HIS LAST COMPANION?

They waited for Faline to answer. "He died."

WHY?

"Because Midnight killed him."

NO. BECAUSE YOUR FRIEND ABANDONED HIM.

WHAT HAS HE DONE TO PROVE HIMSELF?

HE HAS ONLY EVER FOLLOWED YOU BECAUSE YOU KEEP HIM SAFE.

TELL US, DO YOU TRUST HIM? TRULY, AS YOU WOULD AN EQUAL?

"Yes," she said, but with less conviction than before. Only a hint of doubt in her voice, but it was there.

YOU ARE DEFIANT. THIS IS THE WILD PART OF YOUR NATURE.

I WOULD LIKE TO SEE IT. WE HAVE NEVER HAD A WOLF IN OUR COURT.

YES, LET US SEE WHAT WILL SOON BE OURS.

Now it was Morgana's turn to raise her hand. Faline went rigid, every muscle straining. Her teeth ground together, making a thin sound. Black smoke began to seep through her skin, forming an inky, shifting wolf-shape in the air in front of her. It moved like a thing contained, yearning to break free, still bound to Faline by smoky tendrils. Its body was jet-black, except for its eyes which were yellow.

THIS IS WHAT YOU ARE INSIDE. A TRULY VICIOUS THING. BUT BEAUTIFUL.

The wolf shape snapped silently at the Elementals. Tears of rage and pain ran down Faline's cheeks.

YOU WERE NOT BORN WITH THIS, WERE YOU?

"No." Faline could feel the blood from her nose running over her lips and chin. The wolf struggled like any trapped animal.

YOU WOULD NOT WANT TO LIVE WITHOUT IT. YET THAT IS THE PRICE FOR FAILURE.

"Give him a chance." It hurt to speak and she had to force the words out.

WE DID. HE IS WEAK AND AFRAID.

HE WILL FAIL. ALREADY WE KNOW THIS.

THE TASK WAS SIMPLE ENOUGH. OTHERS HAVE FACED IT. NONE HAVE EVER TAKEN SO LONG.

"He just left."

HE LEFT DAYS AGO. WE TOLD YOU, IN THIS ROOM, TIME BOWS TO US. BEYOND THESE WALLS, IT GOES ON. HE HAS BEEN GONE FOR A LONG TIME.

YOU MUST PAY THE PRICE.

IT HAS BEEN TWO WEEKS NOW. HE IS NOT COMING BACK.

SHALL I DO IT?

YES.

TAKE THE WOLF.

Pyraena pointed at her. Faline heard a wet popping in her ears. Blood dripped down the sides of her face.

THEN AGAIN...

TRUE. WE COULD.

PERHAPS WE NEED NOT TAKE THE WOLF.

WE MUST HAVE A SACRIFICE.

IT HAS BEEN SO LONG SINCE WE TASTED A LIFE.

HERS?

NO. IT WOULD BE BITTER. TAINTED BY THE ANIMAL.

HIS?

YES. SWEET WITH EXPERIENCE. SWEET WITH THE UN-KNOWN.

The room fell silent and Faline knew they were waiting for her to speak, to give in. She forced herself to look up.

"No."

SAY THE WORD AND THE PAIN ENDS. YOU ARE SAVED.

HE WOULD DO IT TO YOU, AFTER ALL.

HE HAS DONE IT BEFORE.

"No!" The word was a scream. One of the Elementals gestured and Faline felt herself lifted into the air.

ONE WORD AND YOU MAY HAVE THE ANSWER YOU SEEK.

THE HUMAN DID NOT WANT TO COME HERE IN THE FIRST PLACE. WHY WOULD HE PERSIST?

IT WOULD NOT BE THE FIRST LIE HE TOLD YOU.

IT IS NO CRIME TO SACRIFICE A BETRAYER. ONLY, YOU MUST CHOOSE BEFORE HE FAILS OR YOU WILL SUFFER.

TELL US THE TRUTH, DO YOU TRUST HIM?

Faline writhed in the air, struggling to breathe. The smoke wolf stretched further away and it felt like her bones were being torn out through her skin.

SUCH A LITTLE WORD. SO MUCH RELIEF.

IT IS ALMOST TOO LATE.

ONCE A BETRAYER, ALWAYS A BETRAYER.

IT COSTS HIM NOTHING TO RUN. IN YOUR HEART, CAN YOU EVER TRUST SUCH A MAN?

THINK OF THE LIVES THAT WILL BE LOST IF YOU DON'T ACT. MIDNIGHT WILL GO FREE.

ABANDON HIM BEFORE HE ABANDONS YOU.

Faline fought to draw a breath and her lungs filled slowly. She could no longer see or hear and into that silent darkness, she prepared to speak a word.

Her lips began to move and then the dark, suffocating bubble burst. Faline took painful, gasping breaths and realized she was lying on her back, on the floor of the Court. She hadn't even felt herself fall. The smoke wolf was gone and someone was helping her sit up. Through a tangle of hair, she saw it was Quinn.

He was dirty and bruised, and his clothes were ripped. There was a cut under one eye, badly healed, and his cheeks were covered with a few weeks' worth of beard. "You good?" he asked. She nodded and Quinn stood up to face the Elementals. He tossed something silver across the room and it landed at their feet with a ringing sound.

KNEEL, HUMAN.

"No," said Quinn.

Morgana stepped towards him. A faint stench of rot surrounded her. *DO NOT BALK US.*

Quinn held a hand out to the side, open and waiting. Faline heard the whistling sound of something flying. Then a dark blur shot through one of the windows, to Quinn's hand. He held up an axe. Its handle was the length of his forearm with a double-headed blade. The edges looked wickedly sharp. "You mean like this?"

THAT IS FORBIDDEN, said Etherion. He sounded rattled.

"I passed your test. You owe us answers."

ARROGANT HUMAN. IF YOU THINK—

Quinn cut him off. "I think I'm not supposed to have this, but I do. Your magic couldn't keep it out, and maybe I can hurt you with it. So go ahead. You wanna dance, all you gotta do is ask."

YOU WOULD NEVER LEAVE THE SPIRE.

"You think I give a shit? I've died before and it was the best thing that ever happened to me."

Morgana stared at Quinn for a moment longer. *YOU ARE A WILLFUL, CRUDE AND FOOLISH HUMAN. BUT YOU ARE BRAVER NOW THAN WHEN YOU LEFT. THE TEST HAS BEEN PASSED. ASK YOUR QUESTION.*

Quinn went back to Faline and helped her stand.

"You got this," he whispered.

Faline wiped blood from her mouth. "We have been pursued by someone who calls himself Midnight. He is not a magic user but is being helped by one. I want to know where to find him."

The Elementals conferred silently for a moment, then Teruk spoke.

YOU WILL FIND HIM AT CASTLE BLACKTHORNE, IN THE TOWN OF MAROS.

The Elementals regarded their visitors and said no more.

"Who is he?" asked Faline.

THAT IS ANOTHER QUESTION. AN ANSWER REQUIRES ANOTHER TEST. The Elementals seemed pleased with themselves.

"Who is he?" asked Quinn.

DID YOU NOT HEAR US?

"I see you're not Math Elementals. You tested both of us and we both passed. Two tests, two questions."

The Elementals conferred among themselves and no longer seemed so pleased. *ASK YOUR QUESTION, HUMAN.*

"Who is Midnight?"

HE IS THE CHILD OF A MAGE NAMED ILSA BLACK-THORNE, OF THE BLACKTHORNE FAMILY. SHE STUDIED HERE SIXTY-TWO YEARS AGO, IN MY ORDER, said Teruk.

An image appeared, conjured in the air. A young woman with long, dark hair and eyes. Pretty, in a sharp-featured way.

MIDNIGHT'S FOREBEARERS FOUGHT IN THE HEROES WAR, AGAINST THE HEROES. THEY ALL PERISHED IN THE FALL. ILSA WAS A MOTHER BY THEN AND DID NOT HERSELF GO TO WAR.

The image changed and Ilsa aged years instantly.

Gray streaked her hair and a child appeared at her side. A boy, somehow blonde haired and blue eyed.

ILSA AND HER SON WERE PUNISHED BY VENORA THE REDEEMER. FOR THEIR FAMILY'S ALLEGIANCE TO THE SUPERS, ILSA WAS STRIPPED OF HER MAGIC AND WEALTH AND THE CASTLE MADE HER PRISON.

While Teruk spoke, the boy vanished and other figures appeared in the image. A cadre of mages, led by a woman in black robes, trimmed with gold. Half of her face was burned, a cruel reflection of the other half's beauty. She fought Ilsa through the castle, conjuring bolts of magical energy that scorched the walls and blasted furniture. They cast and parried until finally Ilsa collapsed, exhausted. Around her, rugs and tapestries burned and a magnificent ivory statue lay in pieces. Venora stood over Ilsa, then the image vanished.

THAT IS WHO MIDNIGHT IS.

"Give us a name."

WE ARE NOT OUR NAMES. WE ARE THE CHILDREN OF OUR PARENTS AND THE SURVIVORS OF OUR EXPERIENCES. THAT IS WHO WE TRULY ARE.

DO YOU WISH TO KNOW MORE? WHAT HE DOES WITH THE GIRLS, PERHAPS? WE HAVE OTHER TESTS FOR YOU.

The Elementals waited to see if Quinn or Faline would accept. When neither did, they returned to their portals, and to their true forms. Quinn helped Faline to the door and when he glanced back, the portals were closed and the Court was empty.

The mages sealed the door behind Quinn and Faline. They eyed the axe in his hand but said nothing. Zinedine led them once again through long halls and down winding stairs. The other mages returned to classrooms or went their separate ways, until only Zinedine remained. When they reached the stone hydra, Quinn half-expected some final test to prevent them from leaving, but they descended unchallenged.

It was night when they left the Spire. Blood crusted Faline's face. A ball of light formed in Zinedine's hand and he lofted it above them. It floated along, illuminating their path like a tiny moon.

When they reached the Steps, Quinn wondered briefly how they would cross. Then Zinedine raised his arms like a conductor. Pieces of stone rose from the chasm and joined the Steps until a solid bridge had formed.

"I'll walk it with you," said Zinedine and they crossed together. When they reached the other side, Zinedine remained on the bridge. "I hope you found what you were looking for," he said. His voice was sorrowful, a man who wished the world could be another way. He raised a hand in farewell, then turned and walked back. The ball of light followed, floating in the darkness. Quinn looked at Faline. "Are you ok to ride?"

She walked slowly to her bike. Barnabas met her halfway and handed Faline her gun. Like Quinn, he appeared to have been through days of hard living as well.

"Welcome back," he said. "It's good to see you, Faline." Though slightly accented, his words were perfectly clear.

She looked at him in surprise. "Long story," said Quinn. "I'll tell you when we get out of here."

Faline touched a handlebar and the bike came to life. She started to climb on, then stopped and faced Quinn.

"I never really trusted you."

"Gee, thanks. You sure know how to make a guy feel special."

"Let me finish. I didn't trust you when we broke into Tardigrade, or in Haven. I always thought you'd eventually cut and run. In there just now, I'm not sure I believed you were coming back. But I want you to know that I trust you now. I trust you with my life."

It took Quinn awhile to know what to say. "I was a fuck up and you gave me a second chance. That's all that matters to me. We're going to see this through together." He looked at Barnabas. "All of us. Now let's get the hell out of here."

Later, after they'd made camp far from the Spire, Quinn told Faline what had happened.

31

QUINN FLEW BACK AND LANDED not on the floor of the Court, but on the ground outside. In his head, he heard Teruk.

GO TO THE PLACE WHERE THE WATCHER UNDER THE WORLD DWELLS. TAKE FROM HIM A PIECE OF HIS ARMOR AND RETURN WITH IT TO PROVE YOUR WORTH.

Other Elementals chimed in.

TARRY AND SHE SUFFERS.

FAIL AND SHE SUFFERS.

ATTEMPT DECEIT AND SHE SUFFERS.

There were no more words after that and Quinn looked around. He was back on the other side of the Steps, not far from Faline's bike. Barnabas came running, still cradling the gun. He looked Quinn over. With concern or something else, Quinn couldn't tell; it was impossible to read the demon's shiny black eyes.

Quinn took the gun from Barnabas and stuck it in his waistband. He pulled his shirt over the handle then stood there, at a loss for what to do next.

"Help?" asked Barnabas. *Hep?*

Quinn thought about ignoring him. "You ever heard

of something called The Watcher Under the World?" He
waited for a reaction. There was nothing. Quinn spoke again,
slowly and loudly enunciating every word. "The Watcher Under the World. Do you know him?"

"*Wajer. Yez.*"

"Where?"

Barnabas pointed.

"That way?"

Barnabas nodded.

Quinn went to the bike and retrieved the food concentrates they'd had back in Vista. He stuffed them in his
pockets, took a water bottle, then started walking in the direction Barnabas had pointed. There appeared to be nothing of
significance that way and no road to follow. When Quinn
looked back at the Spire, he saw Barnabas hurrying to keep
up. He wanted to tell the demon to fuck off but had no real
plan, besides a vague idea of finding someone to ask directions, so he stopped and waited.

While they walked Quinn occasionally glanced at the
demon, hoping to catch him in an odd moment with his true
nature revealed, but there was nothing. Barnabas walked with
his bag slung over his shoulder. Sweat dripped down his
small, red face and he breathed heavily.

They kept going until Barnabas's breathing was a
high-pitched wheeze. Quinn stopped under a shady tree and
Barnabas dropped the satchel, then plopped down on the
ground to catch his breath. He managed to gasp out something that sounded like "Praise Shibbo." Quinn opened one
of the food concentrates, squeezed it into his mouth and
washed the thick paste down with water.

"How much further?" he asked, when he was done.

Barnabas got up and paced around the tree, eyes
fixed on the ground until he spotted a half-buried rock. He

pried it out of the dirt, exposing insects squirming in the divot it left. He picked one up, a black beetle whose legs waved furiously, and popped it into his mouth. He chewed thoughtfully then returned to Quinn and pointed. "Far," he said.

They started walking again and this time Quinn carried the bag, letting it dangle by his side. Barnabas kept up more easily, without the labored breathing that threatened to give them away to anyone lying in wait. Throughout the day, when they stopped to rest, Barnabas repeated the business of finding an insect and eating it. As best Quinn could tell, he received some kind of directions from this and adjusted course accordingly, until they reached a forest.

Entering it was like stepping into a damp, permanent twilight. Moss hung down in wispy curtains and grew thick on rocks and logs. The trees, great hoary things that blocked the sky, created a world of shadows and secret places beneath their branches. Sounds filled the undergrowth, the scrabbling and rustling of animals.

There was no path and soon they could only see forest in all directions. Dark hollows gaped at the bases of the oldest trees like ancient, howling mouths and Quinn realized he had no idea which way they'd come from. Barnabas did not have the same problem. He ate insects and picked his way with confidence between trees, heading deeper into the forest in a direction that looked the same as every other direction.

When they stopped to rest, Quinn sat on a fallen log and immediately jumped up again. A centipede the size of a king snake emerged. It slithered over the ground and disappeared into the dense vegetation. Leaves rustled and it was gone. Quinn remained standing.

In some places they walked easily among the trees, under canopies of sunlight-backed leaves that felt holier than any church. Other times they fought their way through the foliage. And always, when Quinn looked back, it seemed they had come from nowhere. The forest showed no signs of their passage.

It was late in the day when they found the city.

Quinn stumbled over something that he took at first to be an ordinary rock, before realizing it was carved with strange lines. They were worn down but unmistakable. Barnabas ran his fingers over the markings and said something that Quinn didn't quite catch.

"Did you say elves?"

Barnabas nodded. "Gone."

They continued on and the fragments of carved stone became more frequent. Soon they spotted rectangular blocks and pieces of statues, until they finally found themselves amidst a tumbling-down ruin of stone that the forest was in the process of reclaiming. The remains of buildings stood on the verge of collapse, weathered and overgrown with vines and moss. Once, the city would have been a testament to the power of its builders. Hewn block by orderly block and standing amidst the chaos of nature, undaunted. Now the buildings were little more than tottering skeletons or piles of rubble. Quinn and Barnabas walked in silence. It was like being in a graveyard.

Vines forced their way through roofs and walls, breaking the city apart slowly but surely. Here and there, they found signs of long-departed inhabitants. Corroded metal utensils in the remains of a kitchen. Rusty gears that had once formed the inner workings of a machine. And, in what had once been a courtyard, armor and weapons from a battle. Swords and spearheads littered the ground.

The bones of the warriors who had wielded them were gone and the metal was green with age. Quinn spotted a breastplate with a lion sigil and nudged it with his toe. A double-headed axe lay under it, covered in dirt. Quinn hefted it and took a few test swings then suddenly dropped it, shaking his hand. It felt like something on the handle had stung him but there was nothing. He left the axe where it fell.

It had darkened considerably since they entered the ruined city. By the time they found a place to shelter, a building with three remaining walls and no roof, night was filling the forest. Barnabas took the satchel and opened it, searching for something. There was the pop of a match and the sudden flame burned away Quinn's night vision. When it went out, the forest was plunged into an even deeper darkness. Quinn was blind and helpless and wondered if he'd finally fallen into the demon's trap. He waited to hear running footsteps and a malevolent chuckle, but instead Barnabas pushed something into Quinn's hand. When his fingers closed around it, flickering yellow light sprang into the air. Quinn saw he was holding a candle. Nearby, Barnabas held another. After a few confused moments, Quinn discovered that the candles gave light only to their holders; putting one down meant being left in the dark.

When they were settled, leaning against a wall Quinn had carefully inspected for spiders, they snuffed out their candles. The forest was full of night sounds: chirping and rustling and hooting and scraping, and something that was either the wind or a whisper. Quinn pulled out Faline's gun and laid it carefully beside him.

Soon, the demon was snoring gently. Quinn waited for his eyes to adjust but they never did, or rather whatever light that came from the stars and moon did not reach the forest floor. Quinn remained in an envelope of darkness, staring out and seeing nothing.

Troubling thoughts filled his head: the certainty of failure and the knowledge that tests like this were only passed by better men. Ones who weren't consumed by drugs and doubts. It would be easy to leave. Just walk away and forget all of this. Bury it deep and fill the hole with heroin. He could almost feel it like a phantom limb, the drug rushing through his veins, leaving him blissfully numb. He would no longer have to spend every waking moment in fear, no longer have to bear the burden of saving anyone. Not even himself.

Quinn considered picking up the candle and trying to find his way out of the forest alone. He wondered how far he would get before something caught him and tore him apart. He wondered if Barnabas was really sleeping or just playing possum, waiting for the perfect moment to strike. Sleep for Quinn seemed both foolish and far away. He shifted against the wall, trying to get comfortable for the night ahead, and laid a hand on the gun.

He woke to the sound of banging. Quinn opened his eyes and looked around at the strangest thing he'd ever seen: the inside of his own apartment. The banging continued, someone hammering at the door.

Quinn sat bolt upright. He was on his couch with his heroin works on the coffee table in front of him. His arms were covered with familiar tattoos.

"Shut the fuck up!" someone yelled from another apartment.

Quinn quickly stuffed his works into a pouch and opened the door. Blake stood there, fist raised in mid-pound. Quinn could only stare at him.

"Christ on ice! I thought you were dead, bro."

"I'm fine," said Quinn. His spinning mind had begun to slow, to grab hold of familiar surroundings. He looked around at the apartment. Dishes in the sink. Water spots on the popcorn ceiling. A poster of David Bowie on the wall. All the comforts of home. "I'm fine," he said again, more confidently this time.

"Let's go then!" Blake grabbed his arm and pulled him out the door. "We're gonna miss our set." His breath smelled like cigarettes and beer and convinced Quinn this was most certainly not a dream. No one's breath smelled that bad in a dream.

They climbed into Blake's car and he swerved back onto the road with a squeal, cutting off a Prius. He cranked the music and punched the roof as he drove. "You fuckin' ready man?!"

"Hell yeah," said Quinn, though he had no idea what for.

"You ok? You better be on point for these A&R dickheads tonight."

"You know me, man. We're gonna tear the fucking roof off the place."

"This is the night!" yelled Blake. He rolled the window down and held a fist up, music blasting as they rolled down Sunset. Quinn tried to make space in his mind to think about what was happening, but the mental whiplash of being in the forest one moment and in Hollywood the next made it impossible.

Was I dreaming?

Blake parked and grabbed his bass. They found Ray and Dickie inside. The Whisky was packed. On nights like this, the walls seemed to pulsate and the club felt like a living organism. The living, beating heart of Hollywood, pumping life through the city. The sound of the crowd shook the walls and the floor and Quinn could tell it was primed, ready to explode. The right show would blow the place apart. Suddenly it was easy to let go of thoughts about werewolves and all the rest. That dream had been vivid but this was real. This was here and now. This was what mattered.

The crowd was screaming, clapping, stomping until the host yelled "Ladies and motherfucking gentlemen...*Kill Switch!*" They ran out as lights swirled across the stage and the crowd's screaming reached a crescendo. Quinn pulled the mic off the stand, Dickie hit his drumsticks together and they launched into the first song of their set.

An hour later, it was over but the night was just getting started. They were in the back of a limo, four sweaty rockers and a few guys in suits telling them how they were the future. Quinn could barely hear anyway. Between the crowd and Ray's guitar, his ears were ringing.

Like Faline's gun.

Then everyone piled onto one side of the limo for a selfie, screaming and flipping off the camera.

The party continued at the W Hotel. They rode up with the A&R guys, all the way to the penthouse level, where they stepped off the elevator and into a rock n' roll fantasy. Music was blasting, bottles of liquor were lined up on the bar and girls were everywhere. They ran over to Quinn and the band. He heard Dickie whisper "Holy fuck nuggets," then the girls were all over them.

People headed to the bar in couples and threes. Blake upended a bottle of tequila, then passed it to Quinn.

Don't fall off.

Quinn broke free of the group and set the bottle down. He stepped out onto the balcony and stood at the railing. The nightscape of LA was laid out below in glowing lines. He could see the 101 and, above it, the Hollywood sign. The white letters floated in the night.

Two of the girls joined him on the balcony. A blonde on his left and an Asian girl on his right.

"I'm Kaycee. Two Es," said the blonde.

"I'm Lily," said the Asian. "I *love* your tats."

Quinn looked at the girls on either side of him. Between Lily's brown eyes and Kaycee's blue ones, Quinn couldn't remember why he'd even gone out on the balcony in the first place.

They went back inside, where the party was already raging. The lights were turned down and everyone was dancing to the music. Lily and Kaycee began dancing too and Quinn slid a hand down each of their backs. "I hate this song," he said. "Let's find another room."

Lily and Kaycee both smiled and nodded and they made their way to a bedroom. Quinn closed the door and the music became a muted, thumping sound. Lily reached back and unzipped her short dress. She shimmied and it slipped to the floor. Underneath she was naked with a small tattoo of a butterfly on her hip.

"Last one naked is a fucking loser!" she said and leapt onto the bed. Quinn couldn't get out of his clothes fast enough. He kicked off his shoes, pulled off his shirt, then shoved down his pants and underwear. Kaycee was still undoing her bra as Quinn grabbed her and threw her onto the bed, then followed. Lily pointed up at his head. "You left your bandana on!"

"You lose," said Kaycee. "I guess that means you just have to watch…" She and Lily started kissing and Quinn joined in, kissing both at the same time. When they finally broke apart, the girls pushed Quinn onto his back. Kaycee crawled over him and rubbed her breasts in Quinn's face. He could feel Lily sucking him and quickly, desperately began counting ice cream flavors in his head to keep from exploding.

Vanilla, rocky road, Neapolitan, mint chocolate chip…

It wasn't working and Quinn felt the rush beginning to build. He squeezed his eyes shut and grabbed Kaycee, but

Lily stopped before he went over the edge. Quinn opened his eyes and Kaycee was smiling.

"Don't stop!"

Kaycee bit a finger and shook her head. "Lily says, first you watch." Then she climbed off him and slowly crawled over to Lily, who was leaning against the pillows. In the back of his mind, Quinn realized he'd never been on a bed this big in his life.

Lily spread her legs as Kaycee lay between them and lowered her head. She stroked Kaycee's blonde hair with both hands, then looked at Quinn. "What are you waiting for?" she said.

Quinn grabbed Kaycee's hips and lifted them up. She was wet and he slid in easily. He began thrusting, pumping harder and harder, watching Lily moan with pleasure as she held Kaycee's head between her legs. And again, as Quinn felt an orgasm building, Lily tapped Kaycee's head and the blonde girl stopped. She pulled forward, off of Quinn.

"You're fucking killing me!" he yelled.

Lily smiled. "I have something that will make it feel even better." She reached into the drawer next to the bed and pulled out a small vial. She opened it and tapped the contents out on Kaycee's back: a line of white powder. Lily ran the tip of her tongue slowly across her upper lip. "You know you want it, Quinn."

The moment Quinn saw the drug, his attention focused on it like a magnet. Lily held Kaycee's head again, wrapping the blonde hair around one hand. Lily used the other to play with her own nipples while Kaycee went back to licking. "What are you waiting for? It's all yours, baby. Anything you want," said Lily.

The craving was back, as strong as it had ever been. It would be so easy to lean down and snort the cocaine off

Kaycee's warm skin, feel his brain light up the way it hadn't in so long. Then he would slide back into Kaycee and fuck her while he watched her go down on Lily. The ultimate fantasy of drugs and sex. He would've done it already if he wasn't

Faline healed me.

trying to stay clean.

He was caught between dueling realities. It felt like a chasm opening under him, splitting, with a foot on either side. He knew which way he would jump eventually. Fight all he wanted, the white powder would win. It would always win. Quinn hadn't realized he was doing it, but he'd lowered himself down over Kaycee and the coke was inches from his nose.

From the adjoining rooms, Quinn could hear the thud of a headboard against the wall and the drone of music. He realized that both girls had gone quiet and looked up. They were watching him with their green eyes.

Quinn sat up, surprised. He was reasonably sure Kaycee's had been blue and absolutely certain Lily's were brown. It would be hard to miss an Asian girl with green eyes.

Green like the forest.

Quinn couldn't get away fast enough. He tried to jump back and tumbled off the bed onto the floor. "Jesus, you fucking *spaz*," said Lily. "It's just coke." She lowered her head, snorted it and came up wiping her nose. Her green eyes were angry now. "What's wrong with you?"

"Yeah, what's wrong? Don't you want us?" Kaycee asked. She sat up and Quinn nearly screamed. Bugs crawled over the front of her body, a squirming mess of them like one might find under a rock.

"Please, he couldn't handle us. A real man would've done that rail then fucked us both all night," said Lily. A snake began to slide out from between her legs as she spoke and Quinn ran for the door.

He collided with Dickie in the hall. The drummer outweighed him by a good twenty pounds and Quinn bounced off him, stopped in his tracks. The party, which had grown and gotten rowdier, didn't even seem to notice the naked and panicked man in their midst. Dickie leaned in to be heard over the music and asked if Quinn was ok. His green eyes were full of concern and Quinn jerked his arm away. "The fuck is your problem?" yelled Dickie and a spider crawled out of his mouth. Legs emerged, then a black body, which ran up Dickie's face. Quinn shouldered by and fought through the party.

Now people were noticing as Quinn shoved his way across the room, pinballing between them on a course for the balcony. People out there saw him coming and formed a line to block him from the railing. Hands grabbed at him and he fought them off. People shouted to stop, that he was going to get himself killed.

Blake was in front of him, arms open to catch Quinn. His beard looked like moss now and Quinn took a running leap over the bassist's outstretched arms. Someone managed to grab his legs but it was too late. He was over the railing and free.

Freefalling like Tom Petty freefalling.

The air rushed around him as he fell fifteen stories, naked, a sinner cast out of rock n' roll heaven.

Forgive me for I have sinned I turned down sex and drugs.

Images flipped through his head. Merrick, Phil, Barnabas, Faline. Her face fixed in his mind as the ground rushed up to meet him.

Fade to black fade to black fade to

Pedestrians dove out of the way as he smashed against the sidewalk like a human comet.

And jerked awake violently enough to smack the back of his head on stone. He rubbed it for a moment, trying to get his bearings. In the forest. Mist wrapping the trees in the dim morning light. Barnabas sleeping nearby, snoring lightly. A number of flies perched on him, like seagulls on a lonely island, riding up and down as he breathed. Quinn looked at his arms. There were no tats. He breathed a sigh of relief and wondered if it was merely a vivid dream or if the forest had tried to trap him somehow, offering what his heart desired.

Quinn pushed himself up on legs that didn't quite feel steady and made his way out into the morning. Barnabas stirred in his sleep and turned over. The flies on him buzzed, angry at being disturbed, then resettled.

Quinn started walking, hoping to clear his head. He'd spent countless hours on Runyon and Fryman in LA. Sometimes he even walked through Hollywood at night. He passed the homeless sleeping in doorways and broad-shouldered prostitutes with lipstick and stubble, giving him hostile looks. Walking, trying to quiet his mind, feet always turning towards his dealer's place.

He breathed in the cool, damp air. The bushes and grass brushed against him as he passed and by the time he reached the tree he'd been aiming for, his clothes were wet. Quinn stepped behind it, unzipped and pissed.

He headed back, meandering between the ruins, and contemplated leaving once again. It seemed more possible in the light of day. He thought of Faline and decided it was probably too late to save her anyway. If not, it would be soon. Quitting was its own kind of drug and Quinn wanted to relapse very badly, in every way. Then he heard voices.

Quinn dropped to the ground and realized he'd left the gun behind. He crawled behind the fallen statue of a horse and listened. The voices, men's voices, became louder and clearer. Then there were shouts of discovery, a yell from Barnabas, and laughter. Quinn raised up a little to see what was happening.

Three men had Barnabas cornered. Two hung back and one, the leader, stood in front of Barnabas. He was the largest, towering over the demon like a monolith. They were dressed in rough leather hides, the kind of thing Quinn associated with Robin Hood, though he doubted these were the type of bandits who gave to the poor. They wore knives on their belts and the one in front of Barnabas pulled his out.

He thrust it playfully to one side then the other, forcing Barnabas to scramble back and forth. Every time he did it, the others laughed. Quinn began to crawl closer, painfully aware of every sound he made, until he could hear them speaking.

The leader pointed the knife at Barnabas. "I could do this all day, believe me, but what I want to know is where your friend got off to."

Quinn felt his heart kick into overdrive.

"No friend. Alone," said Barnabas, and Quinn could barely believe it.

The leader grinned. "The dumb bastard who left his gun. Where is he?"

"Alone. Me only."

"Maybe I'm not being clear enough." He knelt and grabbed Barnabas by the back of the neck with one hand, and put his knife to the demon's throat with the other. "See, me and the boys, we've been doing this for too long. This here is our territory and if anyone comes into it, we like to know who they are and how much they're gonna pay us. I see two thieves' candles so what I need you to do is kindly point in the direction your buddy went before I cut your throat open and let my men here fuck it until you die."

"A—"

The leader pressed the knife harder. "Think about what you're gonna say very carefully."

"Alone."

The leader laughed. "You might be a sawed-off little demon but at least you'll go out better than some men. Last chance to beg." He waited a moment, then laughed again. "Of course you won't beg. I love this guy!"

Quinn cast about for any sort of weapon. A rock to throw even, but before he could find anything suitable, he felt something sharp pressed against the back of his head. "Don't move," said a voice. Then it called out, "Got 'im over here!"

The leader stood and looked in Quinn's direction. "Well there you are! Come on over!"

Quinn was pulled roughly to his feet. "Move," said the voice. Quinn glanced back and saw a fourth bandit holding a crossbow. He prodded Quinn with it and they walked back to the camp. When they got there, Crossbow gave him a final shove towards Barnabas. The leader sized Quinn up with a dangerous, false playfulness. He was at least a head taller than Quinn and eclipsed him in the shoulders. Unkempt hair and a beard hung down. An old scar split one side of his face and the eye it crossed was a dead white ball. Faline's gun was tucked in his belt now. The leader pulled it out and held it up.

"Maybe you can tell us. What does this do?"

"Shoots stuff."

The leader grabbed the back of Quinn's neck, like he'd done with Barnabas, and jerked him forward. "What do the markings do, smart ass?"

"They make it so it can shoot through anything. If it had bullets."

The leader grunted and stuck the gun back in his belt.

"You know what? I just realized something. He was over here with my knife to his throat, lying to protect you, while you were hiding. He's about a quarter of your size and damn if he don't have twice the balls." The leader nodded to Crossbow who kicked Quinn behind the knees, forcing him down. Then he drifted back to stand with the other two, crossbow still aimed at the captives.

"That's better!" said the leader. "Around here, we don't judge people by their size. Even if they are creepy little demons." He bent down, hands on his knees, to get face to face with Quinn. "You know what we judge people by?"

"Let me guess, personality?"

The bandits burst out laughing. When it died down, the leader repeated the word and it set off fresh laughter. When he could speak again, the leader stood up and regarded both his captives. "We're all filled up on personality. What we like is money."

"We don't have money," said Quinn.

"That could be a problem."

"We're just passing through. How about you let the demon go and we can figure something out? He's just my guide."

"Well look whose balls have officially dropped. All right, I'll go with it. What can you offer?"

"I'm a musician. I can play songs. Songs like you never heard before. I'll help you carry stuff, get water, whatever."

The leader looked back at his men with a faux-impressed expression and Quinn knew bargaining was a dead end. "Fuck you then," said Quinn and the leader sent him sprawling with a short, hard punch to the face. Quinn picked himself up. The leader faked another punch and Quinn didn't flinch. He laughed then flicked his knife across Quinn's cheek, making a quick, stinging cut.

"Looks like you're not quite the bitch I took you for." He stepped close to Quinn, exhaling hot, stinking breath into his bleeding face. "Where are you from?"

"I just left your mother's house."

The leader laughed again. "The mouth on this one. Tell you what, Mr. Mouth. Since you put me in such a good mood, I'm gonna give you a free shot. One free shot at me before I kill both of you. Here it is, the chance to die like a man."

The leader held his arms out, waiting, but Quinn made no move. Instead he looked over to Barnabas and said, "No matter what happens, I'm proud to stand with you."

The leader snorted. "That was poetry. You wanna give him a kiss?"

Quinn wished for something in his hands, something to swing and knock the rotting teeth out of the bandit's grin. Something to put out the light in his eyes that delighted in the unfair fight. Quinn could feel his palms tingling, pricking with blood and nerves.

"And the balls have disappeared! Now the only question is—" The leader lurched forward in mid-sentence, chest stuck out. His arms and fingers curled up like he was having a seizure. He took a little half step and tried to say something. It came out with a gurgle and blood spilled over his lip. Quinn's palms were burning as if he'd grabbed a handful of stinging nettles. He could hear a tearing sound and the leader thrust forward again, nearly bending over backwards. Blood sprayed as his chest split open with a wet cracking sound and something flew out, directly at Quinn. He caught it without thinking and held it up: a double-headed axe, dripping with blood. He remembered picking it up the day before. The stinging in his hands was gone now and there was a thrumming instead, like a low charge of energy running through the axe, in time with his heartbeat.

The leader fell to his knees and the moment was broken. Crossbow fired at Quinn and he instinctively blocked it with the axe head. The bolt went flipping away, skittering harmlessly across the ground. The other two rushed in with knives drawn.

Quinn threw the axe at the nearest bandit. It hit him in the face, stopping his rush. As he fell, the axe pulled free and flew back to Quinn's hand like a magnet. The other knifeman slashed at him and Quinn jumped back, then took a wild swing that opened the bandit's throat.

A moment later Crossbow was on him, choking him from behind. Quinn dropped the axe as he fought to pry the arm off his neck. It was no use. The choke had already sunk in and the world was fading to black. Then the light came back and Quinn fell forward, onto his hands and knees, trying to gulp air through his bruised throat.

He became aware of a wet smacking sound and looked back to see Barnabas, astride Crossbow's fallen body with a knife, stabbing him over and over. Quinn grabbed Barnabas's arm. It seemed to break the demon out of his frenzy and after a moment, he dropped the knife and climbed off the dead bandit, breathing hard. The black quills on his head were standing up. Quinn saw there was a pool of blood by Crossbow's feet and assumed Barnabas had sliced his Achilles tendons, then gone to work.

"Barn." Quinn's voice was hoarse from the choke. It hurt to speak but he had to get the words out. "I'll never doubt you again." He held out a hand. Barnabas contemplated it for a moment, then mirrored the gesture and Quinn shook it. Barnabas cast about for something. He spotted a broken stone block and hurried over to it while Quinn watched.

Barnabas picked up the stone in both hands and carried it back to where the leader's body lay. It was almost too heavy for him, but Barnabas raised it in the air and brought it down on the leader's head as hard as he could. It made a hollow crunch. Barnabas dropped to his knees, working his fingers into the man's skull. He pulled it apart with more cracking sounds that reminded Quinn of splitting a watermelon. Then Barnabas lowered himself and began to feed. Quinn looked away but he could still hear clearly as Barnabas chewed and slurped with gusto. Finally, when he was done, Barnabas sat up with blood dripping from his face. He wiped an arm across his mouth, smiled and said, "Now that's better!"

Quinn stared at the demon.

Barnabas pulled the gun out from under the leader's body and walked back to Quinn, digging a fingernail between his teeth. "I'll tell you one thing, we did the world a favor here." He still spoke with an accent, the hissing buzz of his native speech, but the words came out fluently. "These were some real sacks of dunkus."

"Dunkus?" Quinn was too surprised to ask anything else.

Barnabas thought for a moment. "Droppings. Shit. Where he grew up, they called it dunkus."

"Hold on a second," said Quinn, still trying to process what he was seeing and hearing. "You can speak now?"

"Yes. Old demon trick, praise Shibbo. Eating the brain confers all sorts of knowledge. And a full stomach." He patted his belly and grinned. "You saw me eating bugs. That was not just because they taste wonderful. All things have some knowledge of the world and they've been our guides."

"Did you get anything from him?"

"Language. Dirty jokes. Memories. He hurt many people. They all did."

Quinn and Barnabas took in the scene: four dead bodies and the axe. With the dirt gone they could see runes on it, covering the metal.

"What are you waiting for?" asked Barnabas.

Quinn stretched out a hand, but nothing happened. He tried again, straining with every muscle and tendon in his arm, but the axe did not move.

"Maybe I used it up," Quinn said.

"Magic doesn't work like that. The spell is bound in, as long as the object is intact. How did you call it before?"

"If I knew, I'd do it." Quinn started to walk over to the axe. Barnabas grabbed his pant leg.

"Don't give up yet. What were you thinking about before the axe came to you?"

"I wanted something to hit him with. Something to knock the look off his face."

"Maybe that's it. You wanted it. Rather than thinking about making it come to you, try and just want it."

Quinn reached out his hand again. He tried to recapture the feeling of standing there, angry and desperate for a weapon. He felt a faint stinging in his palm and suddenly the axe slid a few inches closer.

"Focus," said Barnabas. "Keep steady."

Quinn willed the axe to move again but now it remained still.

"You're trying too hard. When you make a fist, you don't think about moving each finger. You just do it."

Quinn lowered his hand, took a breath to reset and tried again. He remembered Jason at Rannoch & Hale saying that metal artifacts sometimes became sentient over time.

It does what it wants. Likes who it likes.

Quinn wondered if that was what had happened, if the weapon had chosen him.

He didn't attempt to project his thoughts this time. Instead he called out in his mind, like he was calling a well-trained dog, confident it would obey. His palm burned and the axe sprang to Quinn's hand. He held it, victorious, then threw it across the clearing. It flew towards a tree like a hawk diving at its prey. Before it hit, Quinn called it back. The axe slowed and for a moment seemed to hang in the air, inches from its target, then reversed course. It shot back to Quinn and he caught it cleanly.

They left the lost city, with its ancient stone ruins and newly dead bandits, behind. The gun was in Barnabas's bag and Quinn carried the axe, cutting a path for them as needed. It was clean now and looked newly made. The blades kept their edge and Quinn supposed that was more of the magic, bound forever in the metal.

"Why bugs?" he asked, after Barnabas finished eating a rather large black and yellow slug, and was licking his fingers.

"They're the closest to the ground and they don't lie. Rabbits, snakes, birds…you can't trust them."

"But bugs are cool."

"Their knowledge is very reliable, if a bit limited."

"You know, there's this new invention, it's called a compass."

Barnabas looked to see if Quinn was serious. "Of course they didn't tell you. We're in what's called the Crawling Forest. It moves as it pleases. Paths vanish overnight, landmarks disappear and people get trapped. It's almost impossible to navigate. Even Shibbo himself would have trouble finding his way."

Quinn continued cutting a path where Barnabas directed him to. By late afternoon, his shoulder was burning and it was hard to raise the axe, so they stopped to make camp.

When the light began to fail Barnabas said, "We should sleep in the trees tonight. The bugs say the dead are preparing for an active night."

"Delightful." Quinn imagined zombies, a staggering, groaning horde of them.

"I don't know exactly what that means, but it's what they said. Best to avoid it, yes?"

They found a tree with wide, sturdy branches that made for good perches. Quinn boosted Barnabas up, then followed. When he was settled back against the trunk, he called the axe and held it on his lap. In the sudden stillness, Quinn realized he was fearful of sleep and the dreams that might wait. He was hungry, too. Besides the concentrates, which were sustaining but never really filling, he'd eaten some berries and roots that Barnabas deemed safe. Other food sources they'd avoided. A tree with bright red apples, for instance. Quinn had been about to pick one when Barnabas yanked frantically at his pant leg to stop him. It was a trap-tree, he explained, imprisoning those foolish enough to reach for its fruit. Indeed, if he looked long enough, Quinn could discern faces in the bark with vague expressions of terror. He kicked himself mentally. The fruit was beautiful: shiny and bright red. In a dangerous place, such perfection could only be a trap.

Night came early to the forest and Quinn remained awake. He saw Barnabas was too, perched up a little higher with his satchel hanging from a branch.

"Hey. I never actually said I was sorry for the way I treated you," said Quinn, breaking the silence.

"It's fine."

"Yeah, but it's not. I was an asshole, man. I never even gave you a chance. I'm really sorry for that."

"Thanks, Quinn. That means a lot."

"If one of us is going to fuck this little adventure up, it'll probably be me."

"Why do you say that?"

Quinn was silent for awhile, looking off into the forest. "I was thinking about leaving. I thought about it last night and again this morning."

"But you didn't."

"No, but I wanted to. I don't know if I can save Faline. I feel like I'm just gonna let her down in the end. So I start thinking, what's the point? Get out while you still can."

"You won't."

"I like the confidence," said Quinn. "I thought you were supposed to stay neutral. According to your contract."

"I guess I'm not that way."

"Do a lot of people treat you like I did?"

"Yes. Some demons are evil, but those aren't usually the ones who leave Duma. They aren't the ones trying to find a better life. Demons are always judged by the worst of our kind."

"Why did you leave?"

"Demons breed prolifically. I have almost a thousand full brothers and sisters, and who knows how many half siblings. Some of them are great warriors who've made kingdoms in their own right. When my father is dead they'll fight over his lands and wealth. The empire of Magorr the Unrepentant, may he feast upon his enemies. I wasn't made for that. Demons are born with great variance in form and ability and, as you can see, I'm not exactly a fighter. So I left to find a place where I could make something of myself. With Shibbo's blessing, maybe I will."

"Your dad's some kind of king?"

"Yes."

"And your mom? I'm assuming demons have moms."

"We do. She was already laying the next brood by the time mine hatched. Only a few of us survived. One of my brothers ate the rest. That's how it is for us."

"I'm guessing you're probably not close with your family."

"No, I've never spoken to either of my parents. But that's fine. I could've been eaten by my brothers. Or my sisters. Or a lot of things, really. I'm happy to have a chance to build something for myself. Hopefully good things will happen to me."

"I think they will." Quinn looked up at his small shape in the darkness. He wondered if Barnabas was lonely and felt painfully ashamed for having misjudged him.

"Maybe if the Heroes had won the war, it would be different. The world would be better," said Barnabas.

"I thought they did win."

"Winning it and ending it are two different things."

"I don't know much about it. Just that a guy with the not-at-all-ridiculous name of Captain Photon sacrificed himself and it made the Deadlands."

"I can tell you more, if you'd like. The Age of Heroes is one of my favorite eras to study."

"Sure."

Barnabas retrieved his jar from the satchel and snacked on a beetle. "No one truly knows exactly what happened. Depending on where you're from, you'll hear a different story. What we do know is that five hundred years ago, the Age of Magic was at its peak. Majis was the most powerful territory and mages were the most feared and respected beings on Ouros. The most reliable accounts of the time say that a group of mages left the Spire to form their own society, away from the magical ruling class. At the time, it was controlled by the most powerful families who believed the use of magic belonged to only the wealthy and highborn. They wanted to use it to rule and subjugate. The rogue mages rejected this idea, believing that magic should be a force for order and good. They established a community dedicated to this principle near the border of Majis and Vista. And there they discovered the Shard of Creation, a crystal of unknown origin, with vast and seemingly unlimited powers.

They built a city around it and called it Bastion, a place of safety where anyone could seek refuge. The city was powered by the Shard and the mages found that by living there, it healed their bodies and enhanced their magic. By the time the Spire found out what was happening, the Bastionites were too powerful to eliminate.

Over time, they became not only stronger and longer lived, but the Shard changed their powers. Rather than merely channeling magic, it became imprinted on them, inseparable from flesh. In time, they evolved to have powers without needing magic. These were more limited in scope but were inborn. No study was required to use them and the rest of the world saw it as more trustworthy. For those in Bastion, magic became biology and a new type of being was born.

At first they were called Supers and held to their original philosophy. The mages hated them for it, and for taking land from Majis, and for becoming more powerful. More evolved. Over the next hundred years, they brought peace to Ouros and ushered in a time of learning, prosperity and cooperation like this world has never known. They were seen as heroes and eventually came to be called that. When the mages finally attacked, the Heroes proved to be stronger and drove them back to the Spire. So the Age of Magic ended and the Age of Heroes began.

After almost a hundred and fifty years, during which arts and culture flourished, what happened with the original mages happened again. A group rose who did not want to follow the philosophy of Bastion. They did not want to help— or as they saw it, serve—inferior beings. They didn't want to fight their battles and fix their problems, believing that only when the most powerful ruled would the world know true peace and prosperity. They were willing to kill to achieve it. They began calling themselves Supers, embracing a past that they claimed the Heroes were ashamed of.

They conspired to gain control of the Shard and that led to war. The War. At first it looked like the Heroes would win easily with greater numbers. It was so unequal that they were reluctant to turn their full strength on their brothers and sisters. The conflict went on longer than it should have, with casualties on both sides. And soon, many of the ruling families of Majis publicly offered support to the Supers. They sent mages to join their ranks. Some races from Darke joined as well.

The War went on for three years. It was fought in towns and cities throughout Majis, as well as parts of Darke and Vista. The sides were more or less equally matched, until the giants came. They came down from the Gulga Mountains and joined the Supers, tipping the balance for the first time in their favor. They were thirty feet tall or more. Strong enough to withstand most weapons and naturally resistant to both magic and powers. Supposedly, they were descended from Teruk the Elemental and were the first species to settle the world. The Supers and their allies laid siege to Bastion, seeking to press their advantage.

Captain Photon knew that defeat was at hand and

commanded his forces to hold the city as long as they could. While they did he retreated to the Hall of Heroes, where the Shard was kept in a place known as the Spectrum. It was built to open doorways throughout Ouros and worlds beyond. Captain Photon began to absorb the Shard's energy, letting it fill him with power. Then he flew over the battlefield and detonated himself, destroying both armies.

Then the War was over and so was the Age of Heroes."

Barnabas finished talking and looked down to see if Quinn was still awake.

"The explosion made the Deadlands, right?"

"In a way. It was like striking a match in a room full of powder. Existence had been weakened by the constant spells and weapons used, and Captain Photon's death caused a chain reaction. Unstable pockets ruptured unleashing monsters, causing disasters and fracturing time. It poisoned and warped the land, turning it into a place where the edges of reality no longer meet. The world there is broken."

"Did the demons fight in the War?"

"No. We did not join the Supers, praise Shibbo, but neither did we ally with the Heroes. We stayed within our own lands, waiting for it to end. Perhaps we should have done more, but until thirty years ago, most never even left Duma." Barnabas yawned and shifted to get more comfortable. "It could be worse for us. Many races were completely destroyed. If not during the War, then soon after in retribution."

"Thanks for sharing, Barn. Call me sentimental but I'm really glad you smashed that guy's head open and ate his brain so we could talk."

"Me too." His voice was a sleepy burr now. "Goodnight."

"Night," said Quinn.

It was impossible to mark time in the darkness. Mental tides carried thoughts of drugs, of giving up, of Faline, in and out of his mind. He stopped fighting them and closed his eyes, hoping sleep would wash over him eventually.

Sometime later, the forest stirred below.

First, flowers bloomed. Iridescent blue and green and red things that gave off a faint mist. They opened in the night and formed a path on the ground. Soon a mass of dark forms moved along it, towards a circle at the end. The glow of the flowers revealed two figures in the lead. Their arms were linked and a procession of figures in robes followed. When they reached the circle at the end, the two in front drew back their hoods, revealing skulls. Scraps of flesh and hair remained and they leaned together for a lipless kiss. Their teeth clicked as they touched.

Then they danced. The procession began moving in a complex, formal pattern around the pair in the middle. They wove in and out, skeletal hands grasping and releasing. When the dance was over, they formed into rows facing each other and the newly married dead returned up the path. The others closed ranks behind them and retreated the way they had come.

The flowers remained longer, bathing the forest in their soft glow. Their mist drifted up, touching the low branches of trees and any who might be sleeping there. At the first light of morning, they closed and wilted and sank back into the ground like the fragile, beautiful things they were. When Quinn woke, there was no sign of the flowers or the dead, but he felt well-rested and his sleep had been mercifully dreamless.

The day continued as the previous one had, Barnabas sacrificing insects and Quinn clearing a path. He had given up wondering how close they were or if they were even headed in the right direction. Either they would arrive or they would not. He was too tired and sore to wonder about much else, even when Barnabas stopped to perform the ritual that hid them from Midnight. There was only the forest, green and endless, full of trees and streams and stones. And then, a cave.

"This is it," said Barnabas. "They all agree."

An outcrop of stone rose before them, containing a narrow gap where the rocks had separated. While Barnabas lit a thief's candle, Quinn wondered how close they were to the Watcher. He wondered if it was aware of them.

Barnabas started to light the second candle and Quinn stopped him. "You should stay here, in case you have to hide us again." Barnabas nodded and took up a position by the entrance.

"Did they say how far down this goes?" asked Quinn.

"No. They said animals don't come here."

"That's reassuring." Quinn peered into the cave but beyond the flickering yellow edge of candlelight, there was only more darkness. He squeezed through with the candle in one hand and the axe in the other.

The floor of the cave sloped downwards and the walls were barely wider than Quinn's shoulders. In some places, he had to turn sideways to move ahead. When the ceiling got too low, he was forced to put the axe down and continue without it, crouching and holding the wall with his free hand. He glanced back at the entrance, which was now just a jagged patch of light. Then the tunnel curved and it was gone.

The tunnel wound deeper and deeper until Quinn lost all sense of distance and direction. He took faint comfort in the fact that the tunnel was no longer narrowing, but the air grew steadily colder. Water dripped down the walls and the floor was slippery with algae. The only heat was from the candle as it melted and ran over his hand. It grew shorter as he pushed through the dark, a messy handful of wax with a guttering flame at the center.

It wasn't long before the candle entered its dying phase. The light it cast shrank until it flickered out and darkness finally enclosed Quinn. He lowered himself and continued in a crawl. The stone floor bit into his knees. Quinn felt the ground ahead with his hands, in case it was suddenly gone and a crevasse waited to swallow him.

Without the light, fear began growing. Thoughts jumbled in Quinn's mind, of unseen but terrible things close by. The fear urged him to turn back and flee before they grabbed him. His thoughts started to spin out, giving way to panic. Then Quinn thought of Faline, in the room at the top of the Spire, and pushed ahead.

Deeper into the cave at a snail's pace he went. Quinn's hands were numb from the cold wet rock, and he wasn't sure how much further he could go when he saw light again. Straight ahead there was only blank darkness, but at the edges of his vision he became aware of a blue glow. It was coming from somewhere in front of him, reflecting off the wet sides and floor of the tunnel.

Quinn crawled with renewed energy and the light began to grow. It never became particularly strong but soon Quinn could make out the shapes of his arms. Then the tunnel ended and the long crawl was over. An opening loomed in front of him and beyond it, a room filled with soft blue light. Quinn emerged into it and was finally able to stand.

He found himself on the shore of a massive underground lake. The ceiling of the cavern that contained it was the source of the blue glow. Spots of light pocked the stone. Animal or plant, Quinn wasn't sure but there were thousands, creating a false, twinkling sky. They illuminated the lake below, reflecting dots of color on the black surface. Drops of water from the ceiling plinked on it like piano notes. The acoustics of the place made Quinn think of concert halls, where every sound was amplified.

He walked to the edge of the lake and stood there. It was too big to see all the way across and Quinn wondered if there were islands out in the dark water, with things living on them. He wasn't sure if he should call out or simply wait. Then he reached down, picked up a flat stone from the water's edge and skipped it across the lake. Ripples spread in its wake and died. The water stilled again. Quinn waited for a moment and was about to reach for another stone when he felt it: a tremor in the ground that built until the whole cavern shook. The blue light dimmed, as if the creatures or plants that produced it were afraid. Waves crashed against the shore and the Watcher began to surface.

Quinn thought of calling the axe, summoning it through miles of tunnel, but did not. Instead he watched as something huge and shining rose from the water. After the initial surge of fear leveled off, Quinn realized that it was looking at him. Its many eyes regarded him with curiosity and a kind of gentle trepidation. He saw that some of its scales were missing. In places, the Watcher's flesh showed through. It was marked with scars and divots. Suddenly Quinn's fear was gone and in its place, there was only sadness for the ancient creature.

It moved slowly toward the shore but Quinn did not run. Instead he waded out into the black water and, as the creature drew closer, he began to sing.

32

"WHAT DID YOU SING?" asked Faline.

"*Ruby Tuesday*." Quinn sang her the chorus. "I don't know how, but I knew it was in pain and I wanted to soothe it. After I sang, the Watcher made this kind of hum. I could feel it through my entire body. I knew it was happy. Grateful, even. So I swam out and it let me take a scale."

"Then you came back."

"Yeah. That's a whole other story. We found this place…" Quinn shook his head. "Forget it. I'll tell you another time. We made it back, that's what matters. Was it worth it?"

"Yes."

"Good, then."

Barnabas was already asleep. Quinn scooted around the fire until he was sitting next to Faline. She leaned her head on his shoulder and he put an arm around her. It felt good to hold someone, to feel the touch of another person, alive and warm. He thought of nothing else until he heard Faline ask something.

"Hmm?"

"The Floating Steps. How did you cross them?"

"By walking."

"No jokes. If you can call the axe to you, that's the same as carrying it. You shouldn't have been able to cross over."

"I guess they didn't sense it."

"I don't think that's possible."

Quinn was silent for a time. "I'm an addict. I'm good at hiding things and telling lies, especially to myself. Besides, if there's one thing I've learned by now, nothing's impossible."

33

IT WAS COLD IN THE Great Room, even with the fire burning.
The heat escaped up to the high ceiling where it did no one
any good. Midnight stood in front of the fire, staring into the
flames. His clothes were wet and his boots caked with mud
from his latest failed attempt to locate the wolf and her companion. Now his head ached badly, the way it always did
when he traveled by magic. He would have given anything to
have his suit back, but that was gone and the ones who destroyed it impossible to find. The thought made Midnight's
head ache even more.

"Midnight." Guardian remained on the table in front of
the fireplace. "Did you find any trace of them?"

"Take one. Fucking. Guess." It occurred to him that
he hated the Great Room. It was cold most of the year and
oddly clammy in the summer.

"I do not think so. How many amulets remain?"

Midnight thought for a moment about sending the
helmet flying across the room, but his head hurt too much to
do it. The pain seemed to be collecting behind his left eye,
which felt like it was going to burst out of its socket. If the
wolf bitch and man attacked now, he thought they would fin-

ish him off without much of a fight.

"Perhaps you should consider a different strategy."

Midnight said nothing. He leaned forward, gripping the mantle and pressing his fingers hard against the stone. He inhaled slowly and gritted his teeth.

"I surmise that you are coming to the end of your supply of amulets and—"

Midnight slammed a fist down hard enough to crack the stonework.

"Midnight, you must—"

That was as far as Guardian got before Midnight picked him up in both hands and began pressing inwards. "I think I've had enough of your advice."

Guardian continued in the same calm, even voice. "I do not mean to say you should give up. I would only like to suggest a more effective recalibration of your plans."

Midnight stopped squeezing but didn't set the helmet down.

"An alteration of your plans, both short and long term, will conserve resources and maximize power. Your goals will remain, but your methods would be adjusted."

Midnight started to squeeze again.

"Simply put, you are running out of amulets. Rather than waste the few you have left, may I suggest a different approach?" Guardian did not sound like he was being crushed. He could have been a machine noting the time and temperature. "While you were gone today, I saw something interesting: a spider making its web. Right up there in the corner. It made its web and sat until a fly came along, and I realized that a great hunter is not always one who chases, but one who waits. One who prepares."

"Always a riddle with you." One of Guardian's eyes cracked under the pressure.

"I understand it is not in your nature, but your prey is clever. Allow them to find you. Then dictate the parameters of the engagement."

Midnight stopped squeezing again and considered this.

"After you have killed the wolf and the human, we may once again focus on the ultimate goal."

"And what is that?" asked Midnight in a low, dangerous voice.

"Absolute vengeance."

After a moment, Midnight nodded. The pain in his head had lessened. It still throbbed but his eye no longer felt like it was going to explode.

"Your amulets are a finite supply. Even if you were able to locate more girls, you would not be able to bring them back here. And even if you did, you could only drain a few more before the last of the amulets are gone."

Midnight hadn't wanted to think about it. Had actually been glad for the task of hunting his mother's killers, because it distracted from the truth that without her, their plans were all but over.

"What if I could show you a way to gain power that involved no amulets or technology? I don't mean the meager amount you draw from a single girl. You will never become what you and your mother envisioned from mere trickles. What if I were to show you a way to drink from the river and fill yourself with power beyond imagining? Greater even than the combined might of the Spire. An endless supply, for you and you alone." Guardian paused for a moment. "I can feel the heartbeat in your fingertips quicken. The prospect excites you."

"Show me."

"Put me down and I will."

Midnight did, and Guardian was as good as his word.

34

QUINN WOKE UP TO THE smell of meat cooking. Faline and Barnabas were crouched by a campfire, roasting small, skinless bodies on spits.

"We have rabbit," said Barnabas, when he saw Quinn was awake.

They sat around the fire eating. It was the first real food Quinn had tasted in weeks and he couldn't remember if anything had ever tasted better.

"Can I see that?" asked Faline. He handed her the axe and she inspected it, scraping her thumb across the edges to test its sharpness. "Beautiful," she said, as she passed it back. "It's good you found a weapon. You'll need it."

"What's the plan? We go to Maros and drag his ass out of the castle, dead or alive?"

"Pretty much, yeah."

"A castle?" asked Barnabas.

"Castle Blackthorne," said Faline. "Midnight and his mother Ilsa are the last surviving members of their family. I've heard the name but I don't know much about them."

Quinn tossed the bones of his rabbit into the fire. "Barn?"

"The Blackthornes were an old magical family, nobility in Majis. They were one of the First Families who helped build the Spire. Their ancestral home was built on top of a dragon's den. Alistair Blackthorne killed Maros herself, who the town is named after. As an ancient lineage they sent mages to fight in every major conflict, including the Heroes War. If Ilsa and Midnight are the last members, that would make sense since the Blackthornes fought on the side of the villains. History does not record anything of the family after the War. I had thought that if any survived, they were punished by Venora. You've heard of her?"

"Yes."

"Have you, Quinn?"

"My girl The Redeemer? Of course."

"Perhaps Venora overlooked them somehow, or maybe she spared them. For what reason, I can only guess. Ilsa would have to be very old now." Barnabas dropped his voice a little, as if he was worried about someone overhearing. "Some histories say they inbred to keep their line pure. I'm not sure if that's true but it would not be unheard of."

"If they were rich nobles, that could explain how they bought the suit from Tardigrade," said Faline.

"Still doesn't explain what he's doing with the girls," said Quinn.

"We'll find out soon enough. Does the name of the town ring a bell for you, Barnabas?"

"I feel like it should." Barnabas thought for a moment then his eyes went wide. "Gargoyle!"

Faline nodded. "Exactly."

"What am I missing?" asked Quinn.

"This part of history I know," said Faline. "About sixty years ago, not long before the War, Maros was the site of one of Captain Photon's battles. A Super named Gargoyle had taken over and Captain Photon came to stop him. There's recordings of it you can watch. They fought in the street and of course Cap won. The crowd loved it."

"You think there's a connection?"

Faline spoke carefully, as if she had an idea but wasn't quite ready to say it. "I'll know more once we're there."

The town of Maros was small, and at its center was a statue of Captain Photon. He stood victorious over the fallen Gargoyle, with his cape billowing and his square jaw nobly raised. His arms and chest rippled with bronze muscle. There was a many-pointed star on his chest. At the base of the statue, a plaque commemorated the event. Along the streets leading to it were business establishments with names and imagery that harkened to the long-ago battle. It reminded Quinn of an old gold rush town, clinging to its past with kitschy desperation.

They picked a tavern called The Dead Gargoyle and went in. Barnabas remained outside, saying that many places refused to serve demonkind and he didn't want to cause a problem.

It took a moment for Quinn's eyes to adjust to the dim interior. When they did, he saw that pictures of the fight between Hero and Super filled the walls. There were others of Captain Photon posing afterwards, surrounded by townspeople. He was tall and flashed a perfect smile. Even in the old pictures, his eyes were still astonishingly blue and he looked every bit the conquering hero. At the bar in the back, a server watched them with interest.

"Did you find anything?" asked Barnabas, when they reconvened, late in the afternoon.

Quinn shook his head. In every establishment, they had asked after the Blackthornes and received the same blank look from barkeeps, serving girls and patrons. It seemed no one had even heard the name before, let alone knew where their castle might be found. "Do you think they're covering?" asked Quinn.

"No, there's no way everyone in this town is that good a liar," said Faline.

"And why would they lie?" asked Barnabas. "Even now, people remain divided on the subject of mages. I think you would get half that loved the Blackthornes and half that hated them, but all would be willing to tell you so."

"Are you saying that everyone in the town where they lived for hundreds of years—"

"Over a thousand, actually," said Barnabas.

"In the town where they lived for over a thousand years, the Blackthornes have just been forgotten?"

"If someone made them forget, then yes," said Faline. "Ilsa might've done it to protect herself and Midnight. It wouldn't be hard for a skilled mage to erase memories and cloak their castle. Or maybe it was part of Venora's punishment. It amounts to the same thing either way."

"That would explain how Midnight could come and go in his suit," said Quinn.

"Exactly."

"Great, so now we're looking for an invisible castle."

They rode beyond the edge of town, then Faline brought the bike to a stop and climbed off. She stood with her back to Maros, facing the lands beyond with her eyes closed. Faline searched by smell, scenting the air and looking for something wrong that would trip a wire in her hunter's brain. The olfactory equivalent of seeing a door kicked in or a windowless van near a playground. Something that just didn't smell right.

With her eyes closed, her other senses seemed not

just sharper but bigger. They expanded and filled her mind, rendering the world in smell and sound. The wind shifted, bringing new contours to it, like shapes revealed by radar. Faline sifted through the smells, eliminating them as she went. Human sweat and the acrid demonic odor of her companions. From the town she caught hints of food being prepared and sold. Bread and meats, mostly. Burning wood. People and animals and their droppings. The entirely ordinary scentscape of a town going about its business. The land outside Maros offered little. Mostly dry. The smell of an undiscovered cave seeped out in cool, clear tendrils nearby. She smelled rodents and coyotes and livestock on farms. It was a stronger and wilder smell. There was a middling crop growing in the fields. Faintly, the sound of lumber being cut and then, for an instant, the smell of rotting flesh.

It was gone just as quickly, covered again by the shifting breeze, but Faline had already locked onto the scent. She got back on the bike and rode more slowly than usual, occasionally stopping to test the air. The further they got from town, the worse the land appeared. Fields became overgrown, dotted with dilapidated sheds and pens. Old farmhouses with caved-in roofs and empty doorways greeted them. No farmer had lived here or tended the fields for at least a generation. Quinn thought again of old towns, dying slowly and trying to sell their past to a world that wasn't interested.

He began to wonder if there was a castle at all, or if it had fallen down too. Then Faline stopped and climbed off.

"We're close," she said.

"Which way?"

She pointed to the high wall of bushes that lined the road. They were made up of branches that twisted and looped like cables, with long thorns and red berries. Quinn pulled his axe from the saddlebag.

"Barnabas, hang back," said Faline. "If anyone gives you trouble, push this." She indicated a button on the dash. Barnabas nodded and said, "May Shibbo grant you strength." He perched on the bike, ready.

Quinn began cutting a path. The branches were old and thick, having grown unchecked for years, but they made their way through to the other side with nothing worse than scratches to show for it. Ahead lay a field overgrown with trees and grass, empty of anything else. Quinn looked back through the opening he'd cut and gave Barnabas a wave, then started across. Snake and gopher holes threatened to twist ankles while prickly weeds snagged clothing and skin, but Faline seemed convinced they were going in the right direction. And when they were halfway across the field, the castle appeared.

One moment there was nothing, the next it was there. Quinn took a step back and the castle was gone, then forward again through a barrier that he could neither see nor feel, and it reappeared.

It had been glorious once. A mighty stone structure with a tower in each corner, enclosed by a moat that was long since dry. Once it had been deep, now it was only a trench filled with the skeletons of what looked like massive snakes. Some lay half out, as if they had died thrashing and in pain. If the moat was filled, it would have come right up to the castle walls. Instead, the rough bedrock that the castle sat on was exposed. The moat was spanned at a single point by a narrow drawbridge. The entrance it led to stood open, with a row of downward-facing spikes along the top that hinted at a raised portcullis. Quinn could imagine it in times gone by: proud and imposing, like the family who had occupied it.

There was one significant addition, though. The castle had become a sort of architectural cyborg, with new metal grafted onto the old stone. A landing pad stuck out from one of the towers, high above the ground. Quinn thought of helicopters at first, then of flying metal suits.

At any moment, Quinn expected the sky to darken with arrows like some sort of medieval siege, but there was nothing. The sky remained clear and the day still. There were no sounds besides those of birds, grasshoppers and the wind.

Faline said her silent non-prayer then they made their way around the castle, continuing through the tall grass, away from the open front entrance. Quinn realized he could smell it now too; the stench of death was strong here. They followed it, descending down the steep side of the moat and walking along its bed, until they found the source. There, in the shadow of the landing pad, were the bodies.

They lay in a grim blast radius of body parts and bones. Some were still decomposing and wore buzzing shrouds of flies. Birds picked at the fresher ones. Some fed, while others scavenged scraps of clothing or strands of blonde hair for their nests. It wasn't hard to imagine the bodies thrown off the landing pad, smashing against the ground and being left to rot.

Faline looked up at the side of the castle, where the lowest window was still high above. She whispered "I'm going in the front. See if you can find another way. Look for a grate or an outflow pipe. You might be able to crawl through."

"The ol' reverse *Shawshank*."

"Quinn, if this goes bad, I need you to know something." Faline put a hand on his shoulder and looked him in the eyes. "I haven't gotten a single one of your references."

35

FALINE CROSSED THE DRAWBRIDGE WITH her gun out and
entered the castle. She found herself in an antechamber with
slits in the walls and holes in the ceiling. A kill room, made to
trap invaders. Now though, the castle stood open and unguarded. Faline crossed the room carefully, half-expecting
sections of the floor to drop away, ready to leap if they did.

She emerged safely from the kill room into a hallway
darkened by centuries of age and smoke. She paused there,
listening, and heard nothing besides the sounds of the castle
itself: creaking wood, dripping water and the vague echo of
empty spaces. She smelled nothing either, so she started down
the hall, gun raised.

Unlit torches in sconces dotted the walls, between
portraits in gilded frames. Their colors had been muted but
they were still impressive works, showing unsmiling generations of Blackthornes. Dark-haired, dark-eyed and sharp fea-
tured. Faline walked past them, through a door at the far end
of the hall, and into the Great Room.

The vast space seemed to be as empty as the rest of
the castle, with two chairs in front of a fireplace that sat cold
and unused. Above it hung a map that caught Faline's eye. It

was old, demarcating a world long forgotten. Only the shapes of the coastlines were recognizable. The land itself was divided into Majis, Vista and Darke, with the rest marked as unexplored territory.

"Hello?"

Faline swung her gun in the direction of the voice.

"Is someone there?"

She moved closer until she could see a black metal helmet, sitting in the fireplace. It blended in with the sooty interior. She'd missed it somehow.

"Hello," it said when it could see Faline. "I have not seen another living being for days."

"You were part of Midnight's suit." It was not a question. The Tardigradium was unmistakable.

"Yes, I was. I am no longer. The suit that once contained me no longer exists. How do you know about it?"

"Where's Midnight?"

"I do not know. After the suit was destroyed, he threw me here, in a fit of..." the helmet paused, as if thinking, "...rage, I believe it is called. I tried to encourage him to decide upon a productive way to spend the remainder of his life. He demanded that I assist him in seeking revenge on those who had destroyed the suit."

"And?"

"I could not. I have no desire to see pain inflicted upon others."

Faline crouched down by the fireplace and picked the helmet up. She gave it a thin smile and asked, "Do you really expect me to believe that?"

"I don't know what you are talking about."

"I bet," said Faline.

"Truly, I do not—"

Faline caught a reflection of Midnight in the helmet's eyes. He loomed behind her, raising a gun to the back of her head. She spun and instinctively shielded herself with the helmet as he fired, and the bullet tore it out of her hands. Midnight hovered a foot in the air, to avoid making a sound as he crossed the room. Faline dove behind one of the high-backed chairs as he fired again, and came up firing back.

Or tried to. The gun clicked on an empty chamber and Faline ducked back behind the chair. It held as Midnight's bullets lodged in the thick wood with the smell of hot silver.

"You stupid bitch," he said. "Did you really think that was going to work?"

Faline tried again with the same result. The gun was suddenly as empty as it looked, so she gave up on trying to shoot and focused on calling the wolf.

The change was always quickest when she was angry and she felt it surge through her now like wildfire. Fine hairs stood on end. Color drained from her vision, leaving it gray and sharp. Black veins shot down her arms and she prepared for the burst of pain and the rush of strength.

They did not come. Instead the black veins faded and color seeped back into her vision. She could feel the wolf inside her, but it was trapped. Chained and locked up somewhere, unable to answer her call. It occurred to Faline that she hadn't heard or smelled Midnight approaching and knew she had walked blindly into a magical trap. The whole of Castle Blackthorne was a kill room.

"Try and run," said Midnight. He rose higher in the air until Faline could see him over the chair. "Make this fun for me."

The stairs weren't far, but Faline knew he would shoot her before she even made it to the first step. Everything had slowed and become clear, the way it did when she was hunting. Instead of running, she stood up and faced Midnight.

"You're blonde."

267

He flew at Quinn and Faline, forcing them to dive out of the way, and landed blocking the stairs. The light from his chest dwindled as the wound closed. Midnight began walking back towards them, tapping the haft of the axe into his open hand. "Big mistake."

"Calm down, *Pretty Woman*," said Quinn and called the axe out of Midnight's hand. He caught it and swung it up in a short, vicious arc that hit Midnight under the chin. Midnight fell back, holding his face together as light blazed out from between his fingers and a voice said "Run."

Midnight heaved one of the chairs at Quinn, then grabbed the helmet and took the stairs in a single leap. Faline picked up his gun and gave chase through the castle. She caught up just in time to see Midnight stepping through a rift with the helmet.

He looked back as it sealed itself. His face was whole again and he stared at Faline with hateful blue eyes. Then it closed and her bullets passed through the empty place where Midnight had been, shattering the room's stained-glass windows.

Quinn ran down the hall to join her. "Did you get him?" Faline dropped the gun and shook her head. Her hand was raw from grasping silver. "Was that helmet what I think it was?"

"If you think it was part of Midnight's suit that's alive now and helping him, then yeah."

Quinn cursed and hit the wall with the axe.

"It's fine."

"We just blew our one and only chance of stopping Midnight. A chance we almost died for. Fine is not the word I'd use."

"Just get Barnabas and meet me outside."

"And say what? Congrats, we got jack shit. Now we

get to hide for the rest of our lives."

"No," said Faline. "You can tell him we know who Midnight really is. And what he's trying to do."

36

FALINE WAS OUTSIDE THE CASTLE, under the landing pad, when Quinn and Barnabas found her. She crouched among the remains there, examining bodies. The flies were agitated by her presence, filling the air as they buzzed around the intruders. Finally, Faline nodded to a place away from the bodies, and they reconvened there.

"Did you find your girl?" asked Quinn.

"I think so. Her father said she had a tattoo on her wrist. Hard to tell but I think that's her."

Quinn looked where she was pointing, at a body not yet fully decomposed. A skull screamed out from the remains of its face.

"So…Midnight?"

"Midnight is Captain Photon's son," said Faline.

Quinn looked at her in disbelief. "Captain Photon? The Hero?"

"Yes."

"*The* Hero. The one who sacrificed himself."

"Yes, him."

"And how the fuck do you know that?"

"Midnight's healing power is exactly the same. Factor

271

in his looks: blonde hair and blue eyes which no one else in his family has. Then remember that Captain Photon was here, in this town, and it all makes sense."

"Yeah but that was like sixty years ago. Midnight looked maybe thirty."

"Because of his healing ability. At the time of his death, Captain Photon was over a hundred, but looked like a young man."

"So he, what, killed Gargoyle then hooked up with Ilsa to celebrate?"

"You say that like it's far-fetched. He wouldn't be the first powerful man to spread his seed. As a noble family, the Blackthornes would have honored him with a feast. And I imagine a young woman might want to take the handsome, famous Hero who just saved her town to bed."

"Stories say he had many nights like that," said Barnabas.

Quinn looked at the pile of rotting flesh and bones. Here and there he saw strands of blonde hair and his eyes went wide. "Wait, were these girls…"

"Cap's descendants. Most likely his granddaughters and great-granddaughters."

"But wouldn't people know? Wouldn't the girls themselves know?"

"Not necessarily," said Barnabas. "If they were related to Captain Photon, it's likely their blood was kept a secret by their mothers. The veneration of Heroes is recent. Until perhaps twenty years ago, most people considered Heroes and Supers equally at fault. Immediately after the War, the remaining families on both sides were hunted by a group called the Black Masks. Their identity is still unknown, though many suspect they were from Quantum, sent to destroy all trappings of the Age of Heroes. Captain Photon's remaining offspring formed a group called The Children of Light but they fell quickly. Official family lines were exterminated. Bastards were actually the lucky ones, since they could be hidden from the world, along with their offspring."

"Then why kill them now?"

Faline spoke again. "I think he was using them to make himself stronger. Without the Shard, whatever abilities Cap passed on were diminished. Midnight and Ilsa must have decided to grow his power by taking little bits from other descendants."

"I agree," said Barnabas. "After two generations, these girls probably didn't have significant abilities other than perhaps being stronger and healthier than average."

"What else could Captain Photon do?" asked Quinn.

"Besides healing: flight, super strength, absorbing and projecting energy."

"Midnight only did some of that."

"He probably needed more girls," said Faline.

"Goddamnit, I knew I should've gone for his head."

"As long as he can heal it doesn't matter."

"What's our next move? And please tell me we have one."

"We'll see if there's anything in the castle that might tell us where he's going. If not…we go back to the Spire and tell them what we know."

"Dude, fuck that place."

"I agree in principle," said Barnabas, "But the mages will be our best hope to find and stop Midnight."

After Faline and Barnabas had gone to search the castle, Quinn remained outside, looking for something to cover the bodies with. It seemed wrong to leave them exposed. In a shed near the empty stables, he found a pile of old horse blankets and carried them back. He draped them over

273

the bodies and weighed the edges down with stones, glad for the task to occupy his mind.

When he was done, Quinn went back into the castle. He could hear faint sounds and followed them up to the room with broken windows. Stained glass covered the floor. A cabinet stood open and Quinn could see there were only a few amulets left inside, the remains of Midnight's stash.

Barnabas stood on a chair to reach the desk where Midnight's golden device sat. Its rings were still spinning. Barnabas spread his materials out next to it and began preparing a ritual. He mixed powders in a bowl, occasionally consulting his book and uttering a phrase in demontongue. Then he poured the powder into two piles, pricked his finger and squeezed out a drop of blood over each. He said a final incantation and stepped back.

Black smoke seeped up through the piles and formed ghostly hands. They touched the golden device and the spinning rings began to slow. Lenses aligned in a row and when the last rotated into place, it was completely still. The hands sank back through the powder and were gone.

"What is that?" asked Quinn.

"It's called a visiolabe," said Barnabas. "A seeing instrument. Hopefully we'll be able to see Midnight." He leaned forward with his hands on the desk to look through the row of lenses. Quinn noticed that each one appeared to be a different material and not all of them were transparent.

Barnabas pulled his head back and looked at Faline. "I think we have a problem."

"Do you see him?" she asked.

"Yes but..." Barnabas climbed off the chair to make room for Faline. What she saw did not make her happy.

"What's he doing?" asked Quinn. "Going for another girl?"

274

Faline stepped aside and let Quinn look. He crouched down and when he was eye-level with the lenses, an image came into view. It was like looking through a telescope. He saw Midnight, with the helmet under his arm, crossing what looked like a post-apocalyptic hellscape. He seemed to be in terrible pain but kept walking.

"Where is he?"

"The Deadlands," said Faline.

"I thought no one could go there."

"No one has since the War," said Barnabas. He looked shell-shocked, trying to process what was happening. "Even if you got past the scrappers on the fringes, the Deadlands are impassable. As they say, it is the place where giants fell, where Heroes burned and where the sun shines forever on fields of bone."

"Then how is this asshole doing it?"

"He has something no one else does: his father's powers. If he heals constantly, he has a chance."

"To do what?"

Faline and Barnabas exchanged a look. "Shibbo's Eye," he whispered, "The Shard."

"The power source thing?"

"It makes sense," said Faline. "Draining Cap's grand-children gave him some power but nothing compared to what he could get from the Shard. And since we cut off his source of magic, that's his only hope now."

"If he makes it, how bad would that be?"

"Well," said Barnabas. "He'll have unlimited access to the raw power of creation. He'll be able to travel anywhere and destroy anything. There will be no one capable of reaching or stopping him. Not the Spire, not Tardigrade, not anyone. He would be the most powerful being on the planet.

"So, not good."

"Correct. Unfortunately, we can't follow him in the Deadlands. He's beyond us now. Beyond any magic or technology. We just have to pray he doesn't make it," said Barnabas.

No one wanted to talk after that, so Quinn went downstairs. It was getting near dusk and there was an unpleasant chill in the castle that promised a cold night. Quinn gathered wood for a fire and found flint and steel by the hearth in the Great Room. He did what he remembered Merrick doing and soon enough, he had a fire going.

Faline brought furs down from somewhere in the castle and laid them on the floor. Barnabas joined them with an assortment of mismatched candles and lit them as night began to creep in. Attempts at conversation died awkwardly until they gave up and ate in silence.

No one spoke again until most of the candles had guttered out. Quinn was wrapped in his fur, trying not to think about Midnight becoming all-powerful, when Faline said, "There might be a way."

Barnabas looked up. His eyes reflected the fire in twin orange sparks.

"Then what are we waiting for?" asked Quinn.

"It's a big risk."

"Not like we have a choice," said Quinn. He got up, ready to go.

"We're not going anywhere tonight so just listen to me, then decide."

Quinn threw more wood on the fire. Then he and Barnabas drew close, waiting to hear what Faline had to say.

37

I WASN'T BORN A WOLF.

Where I'm from, in Silverland, wolves are hunted and killed by law. I used to do it and I was good at it.

My family was rich. Not like the Blackthornes, but our name carried weight in our county and beyond. We were pure, all the way back to Arthur Bristowe of Camberton, and I used to be so proud of that. I'd lie awake, full of wonder and pride at being part of something so important. I used to think about Arthur's blood flowing through me, giving me purpose.

This is what I mean when I say Silverland hated wolves: the most common birthday gift is a box of silver bullets. Within county limits, you can shoot wolves on sight. If you're a Wolf Hunter like I was, that was your job. If we even suspected someone of being a wolf, we'd take their blood and test it against silver. If it sizzled…bullet to the head, right on the spot.

My father was a Wolf Hunter, and his father before him, going back for generations. We've been doing it since there was such a thing. Centuries ago, werewolves roamed free. They lived in groups. Some were civilized; they raised their own meat, had organized runs and traded with humans. But when we started settling the land, we went after all of them, regardless. My family was a big part of that.

I remember my father's study in our house. He had all these wolf heads mounted on the walls. We—I mean wolves—stay in whatever form we die in. Sometimes, if a wolf is hurt badly enough, they change back but otherwise... I remember there were a few that he caught mid-change. Those were his prizes. I used to stare at them, frozen like that forever. I was so scared to touch them, like if I did I might get the wolf disease on me. I used to wonder how a person could have so much evil in them, right under their skin. I always thought I'd kill myself if I had it.

Don't get me wrong, werewolves can be savage. Some eat their young. Some terrorize humans and kill for fun. In the old days, they were a real threat. But after awhile, killing them was just a tradition. I once heard someone say that tradition is the host in which bad ideas survive. By the time I was born, wolf hunting was nothing more than blood sport with all kinds of scary rhetoric about "purifying" Darke. You didn't dare question any of it. The last thing you'd want is for people to think that maybe you were a wolf.

I got my first gun when I was twelve. My father took me shooting that afternoon and I was in love. Not just with my gun, but with my whole life. My family. The destiny I thought I had. The weight of responsibility to keep my homeland pure. I was a happy little fanatic. I knew, I just knew, that werewolves were the most evil, disgusting creatures that ever lived. I was repulsed by the thought of them. My dream was to carry on my family's legacy and become a commissioned Werewolf Hunter.

Every town in the county had squads and Silverland's was the best. Since my father was a Hunter, I grew up around it. We patrolled in teams of six, in big, armored Urban Assault Vehicles, or UAVs for short. Each team had a captain, a driver, a navigator, a medic, an engineer and a scout. There were two seats up front, with an armory and medical area behind them, and a bike in the back that could be deployed for the scout to ride. How could a kid want anything else?

I trained hard and became a Hunter by the time I was twenty. My father was two years retired then and so proud of me. I saw him crying when I got my commission. I was proud of myself too and couldn't wait to get my first kill.

My squad was all women. Originally only men could be Hunters, then they let women join but kept everything separate. Traditional. Nina Van Rymsdyck was our captain. She was tall, beautiful and a deadly shot. I wanted to be her so badly. My first job was navigator. I sat up front next to the driver and coordinated info from scouts. It wasn't the hardest job, but I felt like I was a part of something.

I got my first kill after about a month. We'd tracked a wolf down and deployed to get it. Only the medic stayed on board. It jumped at me out of the dark, but I was ready and the kill was even better than I imagined.

My shots hit it right in the chest, then I went over and put a couple more silvers in him just to be sure. Then the other girls stood around me while I cut the wolf's head off and took it for a trophy. They clapped and cheered and I never felt like I belonged more than I did that night.

I rose up through the ranks quickly. Most Hunters want to be a captain, but the scout's job is the most dangerous so of course I couldn't resist. It's a hard job to get. You need top marks in shooting and combat, and top PT scores every quarter to even be considered. Being a scout was everything I craved. The danger of being on my own. The thrill of the hunt. I started trying to bring down wolves before my team even got there. In the next two years I killed almost a hundred by myself, on pace to do better than my father. And then, when I was 24, I got turned.

It was just another night on patrol. I was riding ahead and I had a feeling. You start to know when and where you'll find a wolf. They're—we're—creatures of instinct and habit. It's not hard.

I found one that night, but what I didn't count on was it being a female running with her pups. They must've been born out of season. If you know anything about animals, there's nothing more dangerous than a mother who thinks her babies are threatened. Other wolves who were cornered and fighting for their lives never fought like her. Even with a bullet in her gut, she tried to rip my throat out. I turned just enough and she got my shoulder instead. My flak jacket took the brunt of it. Then she took off with her pups and I realized I had other things to worry about.

See, unlike vampires, wolves have no choice about turning you if they bite. Vamps act like it's some special thing to become a walking mosquito. With wolves, a bite during the right time of month and it's over. When my squad caught up, I managed to hide it from them. Packed some tissues in there and toughed it out 'til I got home.

Here's the thing about being bitten, you know very quickly if you're going to turn. Within a few days, your senses sharpen. Your hearing, smell and vision get better. You're stronger. You can hear whispers from across the room. Smell if a woman's menstruating. You crave meat. It's hard to control your emotions. The pressure just builds and builds until you need release. It doesn't have to be a full moon, but if you've been holding it back long enough…there's something about the moon that awakens the primal thing inside of you. So you change.

And my god does it hurt. First, there's physical pain. Bones bend, joints dislocate, skin stretches. Canines, which have grown inside your jaws, come down and claws push out from under your fingernails. That all hurts like hell, but mentally…emotionally…it feels even worse. The first time, I ended up on the floor screaming. Then, when it was over, I saw my reflection in a mirror and screamed even louder. I was everything I hated, everything my family hated. An abomination that shouldn't even be alive. I almost wanted to be caught. A silver bullet would've been nothing compared to the pain I was feeling.

Even now, it's still there in the back of my mind. You can never really escape what you're taught when you're little. A part of me that I can't completely get rid of is ashamed of the way I am. Of the things I do when I change. It's the way I was raised. Growing up, it was my religion. Literally. We went to church every week and my favorite saint was St. Chastel who killed the Great Wolf of Pike with a silver spear. I believed that god cursed evildoers to crawl and eat like animals. That being a werewolf was mankind's punishment for sin. It's all in our sacred book. In church we heard the stories about the glory of our race, the great deeds of our people and the unholy evil of the wolves.

I believed everything they told us. That werewolves raped human women and ate human babies. That we were the chosen people and it was our sacred duty to cleanse the world of wolves, the savages who could never be our equals. We outnumbered them but in my mind, we were somehow always under attack.

You can imagine how fucked up my head was. Everything I believed suddenly at war with everything I was becoming. I thought about killing myself. The only thing that stopped me was knowing that they might find out I was a wolf if I did.

I had a boyfriend, did I tell you that? If I never got bitten, I would've married him and heard for the rest of my life what a wonderful, perfect husband I had. He was strong and handsome, and just as fanatical as me. I broke it off with no explanation but there was no way I could tell him the truth. Part of me still feels sad. As much as he hated wolves, his love for me was so honest and sweet. Part of me wishes I could've had that life and never known any better. But being a wolf isn't something you can hide, at least not for very long.

The world seems like a different place with your new senses. Seeing in the dark, running down prey, being part of nature. You lose yourself in it. One night I found a male to run with and we hunted, then rutted under the full moon.

Afterwards, I spent a lot of time trying to reconcile what I'd become with who I'd been. I thought about leaving but Silverland was everything I knew, with everyone I cared about. We always try to convince ourselves we can make it work, even when it gets bad. We try to be the calm little center of the world and balance everything in our lives. In the end, it all comes crashing down.

After I was turned, I couldn't kill wolves anymore. I tried to. Believe me, I tried. I just couldn't pull the trigger on my own kind. I took a medical leave. I couldn't live a double life. I met some wolves on runs and saw how they lived. They weren't evil at all. They were just trying to survive. I got to know them and all I could think was how many of their loved ones I'd killed. Hell, their heads were on the walls in my family's house.

Soon I couldn't sleep anymore. I'd see them in dreams and wake up screaming. They say you never truly forget anything and I believe it. In my dreams, I heard them begging for their lives and for their children like it was real. Over time, they've quieted a little, but the faces of those I killed still haunt me. Sometimes I still see them when I close my eyes.

I figured the only thing I could do, to start making up for what I'd done, was to help protect the wolves of Silverland. With my training and knowledge, I could get them out.

When my leave was up, I officially resigned. They thought I was traumatized and I played it up. My father took care of me, but I could tell it hurt him. His daughter's career and relationship suddenly gone.

I had a little pension so I could keep myself fed and keep the lights on, while I focused on helping wolves. Sometimes I'd run with them, or track them and find out where they went as humans. Then I'd introduce myself and offer to help. If they wanted to leave, I'd show them safe routes. If not, I'd tell them where the safe places were to run.

It worked. Too well, actually. Suddenly the squads weren't catching nearly as many wolves. It didn't take Nina long to figure out what must've happened to her former protégé. The once-promising Faline Bristowe who was attacked and ended up quitting. It was too obvious to be anything else but, like I said, we convince ourselves things'll work out. I thought I was being careful but we're all blinded by what we want to believe.

Nina tracked me and caught me leading another wolf to safety. They killed him on the spot. Nina was on the UAV's loudspeaker, calling me by name, and I knew it was over. Forever. I'd never see my home or my family again. So I did the only thing I could. I ran.

In the end I got away, one of the only wolves to ever escape a *squad. I stole a scout bike and didn't stop until I crossed the county line.*

I was homeless for awhile, until I found a family that I'd helped escape. They took me in while I looked for a job. I ended up as a part-time deputy. They didn't care what I was, so long as I could do the job. Hull County is a much more tolerant place and some departments like having a wolf or two on staff, for our senses. I did that for awhile, then went out on my own as a skip tracer. After all, my best skill has always been tracking people down.

It's been almost ten years since I was turned. I swore to myself the day I escaped, I'd never let an innocent get hurt again if I could stop it. The Wolf Hunters, the people in Haven, Midnight, they're all the same. And it's my job to stop people like that."

Faline finished and looked at her companions. "I've never told that to anyone."

"You honor us," said Barnabas.

"We need a way across the Deadlands. The best thing I can think of is the UAV the Wolf Hunters use. My bike is a scout vehicle, which I modified, but it can still connect to the master nav system. Just for a second, to look like an accident. If they see that, they'll come running. It's not going to be easy, but we'll have a chance to fight them and take the UAV."

"How many of them?" asked Quinn.

"At least six. Maybe more. I think it's our best chance but a lot could go wrong. I won't do it unless you both agree to it."

"I agree," said Barnabas. "May Shibbo consume my flesh if I lie."

"Let me get this straight," said Quinn. "You're saying we give up our position to a squad of elite killers, who will have us outnumbered and outgunned, and have been dreaming about killing you for years? Then, if we survive that, we take their stolen vehicle and cross the Deadlands which no

one has done in over fifty years, to stop a murderous supervil-
lain who hates us personally?"

"Yeah, pretty much," said Faline.

"Then, to quote Richie Valens, let's rock n' roll."

PART THREE

38

THE UAV ROLLED EASILY OVER the rough terrain. Rocks and uneven ground were no match for the big, knobbed tires. Its interior was cool and free of outside noise. The only sounds were air blowing and the soft beep of the instrument panels.

Quinn sat in the passenger seat. His axe was wedged next to it, handle sticking up. Barnabas sat behind Faline, at the medical station. He tapped Quinn's arm and pointed to the side of his face.

"You have some…"

Quinn wiped at the blood splattered on his cheek. "Thanks."

Faline sat in the driver's seat and reacquainted herself with the controls. They were complex but soon she had the hang of it again. Her hands moved over the buttons and switches like a sound engineer at a mixing board. The words AUTOPILOT ENGAGED appeared on the steering wheel in glowing letters.

The UAV reminded Quinn of a cross between an armored truck and a military command center. There were four seats. Two up front facing forward and two behind them, facing backwards. Each had their own control panels and screens. The only exits were a door at the back and an emergency hatch in the roof, with a wheel in the center to seal it shut. Rows of small, thick windows ran along the sides and hand straps dangled from the ceiling.

At the back of the UAV was Faline's bike, replacing the newer model that was there when they took the vehicle. It was held in place by clamps and faced the rear of the UAV; the door there was hinged at its base and functioned as a ramp when fully open.

The vehicle turned sharply and there was a thumping sound as a severed head came rolling towards the front. It fetched up against one of the seats. Dead eyes stared at the ceiling and the neck ended in a ragged tear.

"We missed one," said Barnabas.

"Can we toss it outside?" asked Quinn.

Faline checked her instruments. "Yeah, but after that, we keep it shut. The air is already getting toxic." She picked up the head, carried it to the back and hit a red button. The door began to lower and she tossed the head out, then hit the button again to close it. Fans kicked on immediately, scrubbing the air. In the short time, Quinn had already felt a burning in his nostrils and eyes.

Faline made her way back to the front, checking the other stations as she went. She slid a wall panel open revealing weapons and ammunition, everything from knives to rifles.

Quinn picked up a large bullet with a yellow shell. It was the length of his hand.

"What's this?" he asked.

"They're called yellowjackets," said Faline. She took the bullet and put it back in its place. "If you want to bring down a building, that's a pretty good start."

"How about supervillains?"

"Guess we'll find out."

Quinn watched the Deadlands roll by. The UAV windows were acquiring a layer of ashy dust on the outside, which made it like looking at the world through a haze. It was the first place he'd seen in Ouros that was truly ugly. Even the Lower City had the energy of survival. Hard and bitter though it was, there was life. Here there was nothing. Dust from the ground swirled constantly. The sky was gray, not overcast but choked with ash. Poisonous winds whipped and stirred it like a fast-moving river overhead. Quinn could occasionally see a bright smudge behind it that had to be the sun. When the wind picked up strength, it was impossible to see more than twenty feet until it died down.

When Phil had described the Deadlands, Quinn imagined more or less a desert. But even the endless, sunbaked expanses of Vista were more welcoming. The landscape here was dotted by holes filled with black liquid. Most were still but as they passed one, its surface rippled and Quinn had the impression of something rising that looked like a misshapen jumble of flesh and eyes. Still, the UAV steered itself around the holes and obstacles, finding a relatively smooth path forward.

Just a few days before, they'd been heading south out of Majis, the land growing steadily worse. The trees and bushes had become more and more stunted until they were warped mockeries of nature. Vegetation wasn't the only thing that struggled to grow. The inhabitants on the edge of the Deadlands, small clusters of them, had watched from their shacks as the bike passed. Like the trees, they too were warped: bulging bodies, misshapen limbs, missing teeth.

When the Deadlands were in sight, they had stopped and dismounted on the broken remains of a freeway ramp. This offered a good view of the fuming, smoking landscape that stretched off to the horizon. It looked like the surface of an uninhabitable planet. Quinn thought of Mordor, of the Blasted Lands. In the distance, jagged bolts of lightning flashed. They'd sat on the ramp, waiting for the UAV to arrive, and watched darkness close over the ugly face of the Deadlands. That had been less than a day ago.

"Where are we right now?" asked Quinn, more to break the silence than because he really wanted to know.

"The Outer Deadlands," said Faline.

"Phil told me about those. What tribe's territory is this?"

"The Trappers."

"That doesn't sound very scary."

"They dig holes and wait for something to come near. Then they jump out and grab it."

"Lovely."

"Looks like nothing's out there, right?" Faline turned a knob and one of the screens went thermal. Quinn could see orange blotches scattered across the blue ground. "We're avoiding those," she said. "Look there."

Quinn looked out the window and spotted the first living animal he'd seen in the Deadlands, discounting whatever might be living in the pools. It was a wretched creature that looked like a deer without skin and too many legs. It moved unsteadily, a bit of unnatural life that persisted in such an awful place. The animal tottered around, nosing at the ground for whatever food was hidden under the ash. It paused and drew back slightly, sensing something, then disappeared in a blur. A Trapper pulled it underground and the windswept hellscape was empty again.

"What happens when we get past them?"

"No one knows," said Faline.

"No one has any clue what's out there? Tardigrade

never flew over? A mage never teleported?"

"No. Machines break down once they get far enough out here and casting a spell would be the worst thing you could do."

"Why?"

"You're probably better at explaining this stuff, Barnabas," she said.

"A spell would set off what's called mystical resonance. Reality, which is already damaged, tries to maintain its equilibrium and weakens further. Catastrophic ripples flow outward. It's very dangerous."

"Did you say machines break down?"

"Yeah," said Faline.

"Correct me if I'm wrong, but we're in a machine."

"Kind of."

"What am I missing? And can you turn the thermal camera off? It's really creepy seeing all the Trappers."

Faline switched off the thermal vision. "Yes, this is a machine. But not the kind that was made in Quantum. In Darke, we don't have those resources or technology. But we do have one thing they don't."

"Which is?"

"Demons." Faline got up and walked to the center of the UAV. There was a panel set in the floor and she lifted it. Quinn came over to look in.

Another panel was recessed deeper in the floor, but this one was bolted down and there was a symbol stamped in the metal. It was similar to a rune but the shapes were longer and sharper. They were unpleasant to look at for long. Quinn started to feel like he had snakes in his head. Faline closed the panel and the feeling went away. "What the hell was that?" he asked.

"Demonic writing," said Barnabas.

"Like I said, we have something else. While the rest of the world continues to shun demons, Darke is beginning to embrace them. Times are changing. A lot of Darke is unexplored, waiting to be settled. The Hunters Command negotiated with a demonic House. In exchange for land and jobs, they built machines that don't rely on technology or magic."

"What did that symbol mean?"

"It's the mark of the Trona House," Barnabas said. He turned to Faline. "Even among demonkind, they're not to be trusted."

"You think the Hunters are any better?"

"Assuming this thing keeps running, what happens when we're out of the tribal lands?" asked Quinn.

"I told you, no one—"

"I'm not asking what's out there. What are we going to do?"

"Follow Midnight."

"Isn't that what we've been doing?"

Faline switched a screen over to a map. It was simple, with white lines overlaying a blue background. A red line zigzagged across it, ending abruptly. "We lost track of him but that doesn't matter now."

"Seems like kind of a big deal."

"We can find our own way. Look at his path." Faline zoomed in. "See how it's divided into four different stages, so to speak? I think those are zones of stability. Unlike anyone else, Midnight can heal quickly. That gives him a chance to find a way through. The path he took is gone now but the UAV has analyzed those four zones and I think it's identified what makes an area stable."

"So we're crossing the Deadlands like a kid using stones to cross a stream?"

"Pretty much. Except the stones can disappear at any

time."

"That's reassuring." Quinn sat back in the navigator's chair.

Faline checked her controls. "It looks like the UAV is holding up so far. Most systems are still working."

"Thank Shibbo," said Barnabas.

"We'll see how long it lasts. We're still only in the Outer Deadlands. In the meantime…" Faline pressed a button and classical-sounding music filled the vehicle. First a clarinet, sounding beautiful low notes. Then an oboe, strengthening them into a swell that rose until it gave way to a flute, playing high and free above the rest.

Outside it was growing darker. Because of the hour or a gathering storm, Quinn couldn't tell. The clouds were a constant gray shroud. Faline turned off the cabin lights and headlights. The only illumination left was from the control panels and whatever meager daylight filtered in.

With the music, Quinn found the Deadlands surprisingly hypnotic. He wondered idly if he could recreate any Mozart or Beethoven, not to take credit for it but as a gift for his friends. A thing of beauty to be shared.

"Oh no," said Barnabas. Quinn looked over in time to see a control panel light flicker and die.

The UAV turned and began heading in a new direction, almost perpendicular to their original route. "At least the nav system is still working," said Faline. "We should be heading toward the nearest stable zone."

There was still enough light for Quinn to see the remains of vehicles. They dotted the landscape like shipwrecks at low tide, skeletal hulks under the swirling gray sky. He supposed they were too far out now for even the scrappers to survive.

Suddenly Quinn sat up in his chair. He watched as a

ship, undamaged as far as he could tell, flew across the sky. He was about to point it out when it exploded in an orange fireball. After a second, he heard the faint sound of the explosion and felt the UAV rock slightly.

"Did you see that? That was a ship!"

"Look again," said Faline.

Quinn did and a moment later he saw another ship, traveling in the same direction as the first. It too exploded, falling to the ground in flaming pieces. The sound of it was fainter this time and the UAV didn't rock at all. Quinn kept watching and soon enough he saw another ship, traveling the same path, exploding and falling the same way.

"Is that the same ship?"

"Remember how we said the War fractured reality? That ship must have gotten caught in a time loop."

Quinn turned away from the window. He thought about the ship's crew, trapped in an unending cycle of terror and death.

When it got too dark to see, Quinn watched the dot representing the UAV move on the map. It zigzagged along in no particular pattern and suddenly the music stopped, mid-song. In the silence that followed, Quinn could hear a low hum. He looked around for its source.

"I've been hearing it for about half an hour," said Faline.

"I wonder what it is."

"The sound of the Deadlands."

Quinn wasn't sure if she meant it as a metaphor or if she was serious.

"It's been getting louder. I think that means it's where the real Deadlands start and things no longer make sense."

Quinn had an image of the Deadlands folded up like

an MC Escher drawing, the UAV traveling them vertically and upside down, popping in and out of strange doorways. "There's this place called Taos, New Mexico and something like two percent of the population reports hearing a hum. It's very faint, but it's always there. No one knows why."

"Did you hear it?"

"No. I've never been there. I knew this girl who was super into aliens and conspiracies. She told me about it. She was convinced the government was doing experiments. Be kind of funny if there was a portal out here that led back to New Mexico."

"Would you take it?"

Quinn realized that since waking up in the desert, he hadn't thought about getting back. "I don't know. I just figured this was a one-way trip."

Up ahead there was another wrecked ship. This one was massive. Not a scout ship or survey drone, but an armored transport. It had come to rest upside down and, unlike most of the other wrecks, it was still mostly intact.

Parts of the exterior had been torn away by the crash, making openings large enough to drive through. Quinn could see the Deadlands on the other side. They drove through and inside it was quieter, shielded from the wind. Looking up into the shadowy interior, Quinn could see the bodies of the crew, still strapped in at their stations. He thought of hanged pirates, strung up as warnings. Then they drove out the other side, back into the wind.

Not far from the wreck, the UAV ground to a halt.

Faline checked the controls. Most were still lit, which Quinn took to be a good sign. On the map screen, a processing animation played: a silver bullet, spinning around and around. "It's trying to calibrate our route," said Faline.

"Does that mean we're not in a safe zone?"

"Not at the moment."

Since they'd stopped, the hum seemed to have grown louder. Minutes crept by with painful slowness and the silver bullet spun. After a time, Barnabas called them over. He was standing on his chair to look out a window. Quinn and Faline joined him.

"What are we looking at?" Quinn asked.

"Watch the sky."

Quinn did. It seemed even more volatile now. Clouds swirled faster, roiling the sky. At first, Quinn thought that was what Barnabas meant, then he saw it.

The clouds were an impenetrable gray layer. But as they rushed by, there were occasional small breaks. Through these, Quinn glimpsed red.

"What the hell?"

"Keep watching." Barnabas pointed. "There."

A larger break appeared overhead, opening and closing as the clouds moved. Through it, Quinn saw a massive red eye. As they watched, Quinn's vision adjusted to the whole sky. There were tiny rips everywhere, happening all at once. Behind the clouds, he glimpsed red shapes, moving and watching. Looking down.

"Maybe we should just drive and try to get out of here," Quinn said. The ground shook with a minor earthquake, as if to underscore his point.

"We can't," said Faline.

"Waiting here seems like a bad idea. We should try to get somewhere we're not sitting ducks." The hum was definitely louder now, Quinn was sure of it. It was almost a buzz.

"This could be the safest spot. It could be the only safe spot."

Outside, it was darker. The sky went from gray to black and the clouds moved faster. They seemed to boil across the sky, creating bigger openings. Instead of glimpses, Quinn could begin to see the shape of the things behind the clouds. He saw bodies with arms and hands.

The buzz strengthened and Quinn could feel it, vibrating within him. In his teeth, behind his eyes, in his joints. He looked at the map, willing it to find a new destination, but the silver bullet just spun and the screen flickered.

A minute passed, then another. Control lights continued to blink out and the heating system went. Quinn felt it get colder almost immediately. He noticed Barnabas was kneeling on the floor of the UAV, praying.

"If we don't go soon, we might not be able to," Quinn said.

"There's nowhere to go until it finds a new safe zone," said Faline.

"Anywhere has to be better than this." The buzzing had become voices. There seemed to be thousands of them. Laughing, crying, talking. They were the voices of the damned, of an overrun asylum.

Another tremor shook the UAV and cracks shot across the ground, disgorging a black mass. It moved towards them like a living mat and swarmed the vehicle. When it covered the window, Quinn recoiled. It was made of spiders. Or rather something like spiders. They had several long legs radiating from flat bodies. Underneath they had mouths that were circles ringed with sharp, inward-pointing teeth. Their legs made a sound like rain as they crawled over the UAV.

"So ugly," Quinn said and his voice was strange. Elongated. He looked at Faline and Barnabas. Their faces were distorted, bulging and stretching. When they moved, they left afterimages smeared on the air. "That's weird," said Quinn. Both his voice and thoughts seemed to be coming from far away. He wondered if this was really happening or if it was an oxygen-deprived hallucination. He decided it was real because the voices that had started as a hum were screaming.

The clouds were tattered now and Quinn could see parts of faces. They seemed to leer down, as if through a dome that was threatening to crack. He thought it would soon. Most of the control panel lights had gone out, leaving them in near darkness. The map screen wavered, then finally blinked out with the silver bullet in mid-spin.

"So much for that," said Quinn. He could see his breath. He picked up his axe and stood, ready to face anything that broke through. The floor seemed to undulate.

Then the UAV lurched and Quinn grabbed a hand strap to stay up. For a moment he thought it was being carried away, then realized they were moving again. The UAV picked up speed, crunching over the spider things. The voices began to quiet as they went, lowering back to a hum. The tears in the sky closed and the red shapes behind them were no longer visible, if they were even still there at all.

Faline made adjustments and the map screen came back to life. It flickered unsteadily but seemed to be working. Quinn watched as the dot representing them moved toward a larger circle.

"I diverted some power from other systems. Hopefully we don't get caught in another unstable zone. I don't think we can survive it," said Faline."

"What the hell were those red things?"

"I don't know," said Barnabas, "But the creatures on the UAV were beautiful."

"That's one word for them."

Faline pulled a few packages off the medical shelf, and gave them to Quinn and Barnabas. She opened hers and unfolded a thin silver sheet. She wrapped it around her shoulders like a cape and it crinkled loudly. "The heat isn't coming back on so you might want to wrap up," she said.

Quinn and Barnabas did so. The UAV remained cold but the map stayed on and the air continued to circulate as they traveled across the Deadlands, from one uncertain island of stability to the next.

39

MIDNIGHT WAS IN A CONSTANT state of healing. He carried Guardian in one hand. Light seeped from his skin, steam-like, repairing his body as they traveled. Guardian ran internal diagnostics and found his capacity fluctuating. Sometimes his functions were under fifty percent. Other times they were near optimal levels. Midnight's healing ability seemed to affect Guardian as well, if only by proximity.

Midnight crossed the Deadlands on foot. Sometimes he walked. When he was feeling stronger, and they were on flat ground, he ran. The tribal lands presented little trouble. They were attacked, to be sure. Once several Trappers leapt onto Midnight like hungry spiders. Their weight crushed him to the ground. Guardian landed nearby, on his side but with a view of the fight. Light shone out of the scrum and Guardian experienced a moment of fear. Then Midnight burst from the pile, throwing Trappers off him. Beams of light shone from his body where they had torn out chunks of flesh. The Trappers scuttled and shied away from him, frightened, and Midnight was merciless.

He stomped on one's back, putting his foot through the creature's body and into the ashy ground beneath. He ripped off another's arm and swung it like a club until the upper joint was gone. The bones of the forearm were left protruding like knives and he jammed them into the stomach of another Trapper. The rest were already fleeing.

One tried to pick up Guardian in its mouth, as it ran by on all fours. Its jaws seemed to slide forward from its lips and envelop Guardian's face. He responded by discharging a short optic blast. Not as powerful as the suit's eye beam had been, but highly focused and strong enough to blow out the back of the Trapper's head.

In the distance, Trappers abandoned their burrows and ran. Guardian found the sight of so many flushed from the ground grotesque, yet exciting. Inflicting terror was enjoyable, much better than experiencing it oneself.

One hapless Trapper was caught on the wrong side of Midnight as the others fled. This one appeared to be a female, with deflated and hairy breasts that dangled over prominent ribs. She looked for a way around Midnight and finally made a sad attempt. Midnight caught her with a punch that nearly tore her head from her shoulders. Her body sprawled on the ground with, to Guardian's amusement, her legs open.

Midnight picked up Guardian and they continued. There were other attacks as they traversed the outer Deadlands, but none were successful. Eventually, there were no more attacks and no more scrappers of any kind. Then Midnight walked alone where none had walked in half a century. The Deadlands were much worse here and they were buffeted by harsh winds that wrapped them in curtains of ash. Midnight had begun to acquire a hollowed-out look, cheeks and eyes sunken and bones beginning to protrude. Still he continued to heal, expending every last bit of the power he had absorbed to reach Bastion.

Occasionally they saw crashed ships. Old models that hadn't been built since the War. Newer models too, scout ships and survey drones that had been overcome by the malignant atmosphere. They encountered one that was larger than the rest. It was a transport and surprisingly intact. It lay across their path which led down into a low canyon. Parts of the exterior had been torn away so, rather than backtrack and go around, Midnight simply walked through, momentarily escaping the wind. The ship was upside down and looking up into its shadowy interior, Guardian saw the mummified bodies of crew members. They dangled in their seats, forever entombed in their strange mausoleum. Soon they reemerged into the howling wind and ash and left the ship with its crew of dead behind.

Midnight found his way by feel. Guardian had no ability to understand this and simply remained quiet, running his self-diagnostics. For awhile he tried to map their course but his navigation system only worked intermittently. Midnight moved randomly, in a general southwesterly direction. Guardian concluded that their path was in constant flux. Midnight traveled it the way one might navigate out of a burning building, moving away from danger and toward safety with pain as a guide.

As they moved further into the Deadlands, Guardian experienced new emotions. Gratitude, for Midnight's abilities, and surprise at how valuable he was proving to be. Guardian had spent his hours alone in the castle searching and organizing his files or, as he now understood them to be, memories. The ones he had personally experienced and the ones he had acquired. Being connected to Midnight had shown him a great deal.

The destroyed suit had connected machine and user with a neural net. While they were joined, Guardian saw flashes of Midnight's memories that he pieced together. Some were fragmented and irregular. Others vast and malleable,

302

with indistinct edges. Since his awakening, Guardian had been scanning the memories to better understand Midnight and learn what compelled him.

MEMORY [RA6R3FRC]

The first profound memory Midnight has is of his mother singing. He can hear her, somewhere in the castle. The sound of her voice carries through empty halls and Midnight thinks it is the most beautiful sound he has ever heard.

MEMORY SUITE [FPUO4BTH5B]

Midnight's childhood is spent alone. Occasionally there are visitors but Midnight cannot remember their faces, only that they were there. He thinks some of them are relatives. Familiar somehow, but unknown. All very serious. They are Adults, tending to Adult Business. Midnight does not understand what this is precisely, but develops a sense of foreboding, of something huge and terrible happening in a faraway land.

There are only three beings that live permanently in the castle, not counting the spiders and insects which make their homes in dark corners. They are Midnight, Ilsa and Miss Yaga. She is the ancient creature who cooks and cleans. She is squat, slow and tireless. Her face is deeply lined, with protruding eyes and a wide mouth. When she smiles, it reveals a few remaining teeth. Once they were sharp, now they are dull points. Midnight loves her. Sometimes she gives him sweets from the table and pats his head. In her years of service, she has only picked up a few human words and speaks them with a thick accent. The language of trolls is not beautiful but Midnight finds it comforting.

MEMORY [VNQ05AFN]

Midnight is in the room with stained glass windows. Ilsa is there too and she has a little drawstring pouch. She empties it on the desk and a handful of stones tumble out. Each has a rune carved on it. At his mother's urging, Midnight holds them one at a time. He is not sure why. She asks if he is hungry, tired, happy, sick. Midnight feels nothing and disappointment slips through Ilsa's parental mask. It is impossible to miss.

MEMORY SUITE [Q8ADGUB5Y1]

Midnight spends the days of his sixth year wandering the castle hallways under the painted watch of his ancestors. The people in the portraits all have the same dark features and he looks up at them in awe. Not a single one looks like him. When he asks his mother about this, she becomes angry. There is pain close under the surface that even a child can sense. She tells him only that he should be proud to have Blackthorne blood in his veins. Still, he is ashamed. He hates his blonde hair and blue eyes, and wishes they were dark.

By now, he knows he is not magical. Ilsa has tested him again and again with the stones, and every time he has failed. He held each tightly in his fist, trying to will feeling from it, but he might as well be trying to squeeze out water. He is different from every other Blackthorne in a fundamental way and wishes he could rip that part of himself out.

When he can no longer look at the portraits, he goes beneath the castle, into the ancient dragon's den it is built upon. There he walks among the many treasures of the beast that his ancestor Alistair Blackthorne slew. Alone in the dark, he finds some modicum of pride. He is only vaguely aware of the War but swears his heart to the bold mages fighting for freedom. He feels a sick anger at the "Heroes" who are trying to force everyone to live by their rules.

MEMORY [9HXDRDC6]

The War has ended. Ilsa is crying, fallen to her knees in front of the portrait of her father, Lionel Blackthorne. It is a far less pleasant sound than her singing, which will never be heard in the castle again. To Midnight, the War is huge, distant and ultimately unknowable. But even with his child's grasp of events, he understands that dark days are coming.

MEMORY [B3HFZAWG]

A cadre of mages enters the castle as if it is their right. They wear robes of different Orders, including the green of most Blackthornes, and are led by a woman in black. Even from across the fields where he picks deaconberries, Midnight knows they are the enemy. The triumphant enemy. He wants to run after them, to his mother's side, but Miss Yaga pulls him down hard into the grass. She shakes her head sternly and looks at him with terrified eyes. In the windows of the castle, Midnight sees flashes of light. He breaks out of Miss Yaga's grip and runs towards them.

The moat has been magically drained. The water is gone and the serpentine creatures that once glided through its depths writhe and flop on the ground, suffocating in the air. Midnight crosses the bridge above them and enters the castle.

He hears voices in another room. He follows them and finds his mother there. She is on her knees, defeated. The woman in black is standing over her. She has one arm cocked back, with a blade of light extending from her hand. She is poised to drive it into Ilsa's heart. Midnight screams and throws himself on his mother to save her.

For a moment, it looks like the woman will drive her magical blade through both of them. Then she steps back and the light around her hand fades. Midnight can't look away from the woman. Half of her face is beautiful. The other half is badly burned, a melted nightmare. Midnight begs her for his mother's life. He can feel Ilsa's heart beating fast, inches from his.

The burned woman gestures sharply and Midnight flies off of Ilsa. She gestures again and he is lifted into the air. His arms are jerked out to the sides by invisible ropes and carved by equally invisible knives. The same thing happens to Ilsa. Mother and son can only scream as runes are cut into their flesh, line by stinging line. When it is over, the woman lets them fall. They huddle together, bloody arms wrapped around each other.

"You will never leave this place," says the woman. Her words are hard to understand because half of her lips are burned away, but Midnight will never forget. She turns and walks out and the mages follow. Outside there is a final blinding flash and they are gone.

Midnight and Ilsa hold each other, shaking and crying, until they notice the glow coming from Midnight's arms. They break apart and watch as his wounds close, leaving his skin smooth and unblemished. He feels some previously unknown reserve of power inside draining as his body becomes whole again. Midnight could not be more surprised if he opened his mouth to speak and breathed fire instead.

His mother does not seem surprised, though. Her arms still drip blood but she takes his hand and leads him upstairs. They go to the room with stained glass windows. She takes the drawstring pouch of stones from the cabinet and empties it out a window. She places her hands on Midnight's shoulders and says "You are special, my son." Then she tells him the truth about his parentage and the origin of the healing power that mirrors his father's.

Later, he goes to look at the portraits of his ancestors, understanding for the first time his place in the world. He thought he might feel shame at being the spawn of a traitorous Hero, but he is happy. Any power is better than no power, and it will be a fine thing to use it against the mages who hurt them.

Standing before the paintings, he gives himself the name Midnight. It is a refutation of his father. If Captain Photon stood for light, his son will bring darkness. Ilsa's words resound in his head, spoken through tears of pain and loss: "Somehow, someday, you will be the instrument of our revenge."

MEMORY SUITE [WF2KNXI8WL]

Ilsa's wounds have become scars. She cannot leave the castle, lest she be thrown back by an invisible barrier that delivers a painful jolt. Unbound by runes in his flesh, Midnight can come and go as he pleases.

Ilsa can no longer channel magic either. She tries but cannot perform the movements. Her body is too wracked by pain and, the harder she tries, the more it hurts. Push too far, and the runes on her arms will begin to split and bleed anew.

Instead, she makes amulets, letting a tiny bit of power trickle through her where once it flowed. She sits at the desk under the stained glass windows. First, she forms the amulets out of wet clay, then begins making the runes with a stylus. It is a slow and excruciating process to make even a simple one. Some take days or even weeks. A mistake means starting over. She has to stop often, her eyes squeezed shut in pain and tears running down her cheeks. Still she forces herself to work and Midnight admires the will it must take.

By the time an amulet is completed, there is blood running out of her nose and ears. Midnight remembers her turning to look at him once, as he watched from the doorway. Her face is streaked with tears and blood, but her eyes are triumphant. Midnight is simultaneously terrified and in awe of her. He has never loved her more fiercely than he does at that moment. Slowly the cabinet begins to fill with amulets; Midnight asks why she does not use them herself and learns that a mage cannot use an amulet of their own making. Someday, these amulets will be for him. In the meantime, there is work to do.

MEMORY SUITE [51MWYM8XEU]

Miss Yaga is long gone, vanished the day the mages came. Midnight thinks of it as the Day of Betrayal. He and Ilsa are truly alone now. While she makes amulets, he scavenges the castle for anything of value. The dragon's horde, the once-prodigious treasure beneath the castle, has been turned almost entirely to stone. A parting gift from the burned woman, who Midnight now understands was Venora. The caverns that once glittered are filled with highly detailed but utterly worthless statuary. Midnight works these with a hammer, breaking the endless piles of rock like a dwarf looking for silver. Occasionally, he does find silver. And gold. And precious stones. There are treasures embedded deep in the rock that escaped Venora's spell. Ilsa makes amulets above while Midnight searches for treasure below. Years pass this way.

Midnight grows into a young man. He is well-built from a life of labor. Swinging a hammer and shifting rock has corded his pale body with muscle. He does not know it but he completes the work of stone breaking faster than most others could. This is a testament to his mad drive and the traces of genetic power bestowed by his dead father. He can feel the reserve, drained on the Day of Betrayal, slowly filling again as the weeks and months go by. As much as Midnight resents his father, he once hoped that other powers would manifest themselves but they have not.

By the time the last of the treasures are mined, Ilsa has filled the cabinet with amulets. Years of pain have left her thin and twisted, seemingly animated only by a desire to see the Spire fall. Ilsa has a plan for this, one she has conceived and nurtured through the years, imparted to Midnight as his sacred duty.

They will need money, and lots of it. To this end, she sends Midnight out into the world. He carries with him a few of the treasures to trade in a market far from Maros.

Crossing the castle grounds is no easy task. Besides the small garden and various hunting paths, they are overgrown now with spine wort. When he reaches the place where the castle disappears, he turns around and watches it vanish. This fascinated him as a child, the magical curtain that the burned woman (Midnight does not like to say her name, even in his mind) drew between the castle and the world.

At the edge of the grounds, Midnight stops at the deaconberry bushes. They were at his waist on the Day of Betrayal. Now he is taller but they are well above his head. He eats a few handfuls of berries then continues on.

Midnight begins walking towards town. He has never been there that he can recall, but has seen carts pass in this direction. Besides, *a road has to lead somewhere.*

For a young man who has never gone anywhere it seems like a long journey, though it is only about ten miles. On the way he passes a few horse-drawn carts and sees a group of children. They walk down the road together, laughing and playing Match Me. He hides until they pass.

In town, he discovers that he need not have worried after all. He experiences a moment of fear when spotted, certain he will have to fight for his life. Instead, the men look upon Midnight as a stranger and pass him by. Later, still unrecognized, he inquires about Castle Black-thorne. This draws only blank stares or shrugs and Midnight relaxes, secure in his anonymity.

His first interactions are awkward. It has been a long time since he spoke to anyone besides his own mother. He has to learn how to approach people and hold conversations. Once he can do these things, he must then learn to haggle. His first trip is maddening and humiliating; he is left flustered by the quick, aggressive patter of merchants and returns to the castle with far less than he should have. He resolves to do better and the next time, he does. Midnight discovers that, being taller and stronger than most, he is capable of intimidating merchants into better deals. These interactions serve to reinforce the belief that he can trust no one in the world besides Ilsa. He travels to different markets, seeing the world outside Maros and finding little to like in it.

For the first time in his life though, he is glad not to look like a Blackthorne. The world seemed to have decided that the Heroes were in the right and branded the Supers as villains. Any who fought on their side are reviled. The name Blackthorne is uttered as a curse in places and Midnight takes care not to reveal his parentage.

As the years pass, he finds people respond well to his looks. Especially women. When he is sixteen, he finally ventures into a market-place brothel and accompanies one of the women to her room. After-wards, she tells him he reminds her of someone famous but she can't quite think of who it is.

This becomes part of his routine: traveling to a marketplace or shop, selling his treasures, then spending a bit of coin on a prostitute. Without consciously realizing it, he tends towards those with dark hair, thin frames and sharp features. His time with them becomes the sole joy of his life. Between the endless trips, the empty castle and his mother's undying rage, time in a woman's bed, even for an hour, is a much-needed escape. He finds himself thinking more of that than of revenge, the Spire or anything else. When he finishes, he likes to remain in bed as long as he can. Feel skin against skin and imagine that this is his life. That they are husband and wife and that he has never heard the name Blackthorne. Some prostitutes he sees more than once and he would fall in love with any of them, if they would let him. He begins to think of not returning. He has heard that Venora is dead. Killed by a fugitive mage on one of her missions. With her gone, Midnight has trouble summoning the same all-consuming anger.

This sort of thinking ends in a place called Albion. He has been here only once, when he was just eighteen. Now he is nearly twenty. After he completes his trades, he goes in search of a brothel. This one is not as nice as others he has been to but the girls are pretty enough. One in particular catches his eye: long black hair and a smile that seems almost mocking. After they are done, she tells him he needs to relax and offers a massage. Her hands are strong and squeeze the tension out of his neck and shoulders and when he has closed his eyes, they produce a knife and slit his throat.

The girl searches through his things and finds the money. It was a lucrative trip and in his bag is more coin than she will see in a year. She takes it and lights out the window while Midnight twitches on the bed. He is facedown so even if the girl stayed, she wouldn't see the healing glow coming from his throat. It is a deep wound and takes a long time to heal. By the time he sits up, there is still a scar. Whatever healing powers he has are utterly drained; this was a wound almost beyond their ability. Power and blood aren't all that has run out of Midnight, though. His dreams of another life are gone. All that is left now is old anger at the world and a new desire to hurt things. Midnight finds both comforting.

MEMORY [5UKLEKP3]

He finds the girl three years later, in another town, and has his revenge. She cannot scream through the hand he has clamped over her mouth. Whatever sounds escape the room could easily be mistaken for the sounds of passion and energetic sex. Midnight's strength has grown since he was a boy and he uses it to tear the girl's limbs off. In doing so, he discovers the only feeling better than sex is revenge. After this, he stops visiting brothels. There are far more important things on his mind than whores and someday it will be time to put Ilsa's plan into action. Then, he will have more power than ever before, more than just strength and healing. He will become a modern-day Super and when he is ready, the Spire will fall.

The memories play in Guardian's mind. There are thousands of others, large and small, that made Midnight what he is. Cruelties, failures, desires. Buying the suit. Taking his first girl. Experiencing his powers growing.

All of this shaped him. Like metal folded over and over to remove impurities until it is ready to be made into a fine, strong blade. And, like all great weapons, it is meant to be used for conquest.

40

THE UAV EMERGED INTO SUNLIGHT and Quinn could have wept with happiness. They'd seen it ahead, like a shimmering golden curtain. At first Quinn didn't believe it was real, the Deadland's version of a mirage. Then he became convinced that they wouldn't make it; the UAV would break down in sight of safety but fatally short. He breathed a sigh of relief when they passed into the light.

The land beyond was free of ash and mutated animals as far as Quinn could see. There was blue sky above. Faline stopped the UAV and checked the instruments that still worked.

"I think it's safe here," she said, then went to the back and opened the door.

Outside, Quinn could still faintly smell the Deadlands. The ragged grey edge of the clouds behind them formed a wall but did not encroach, kept out somehow. Facing ahead, he could see nothing but blue sky and white clouds. The sun felt good on his skin, clean and warm.

"This isn't so bad."

"We must be near Bastion," said Faline.

"Why is it like this?"

"Because of what Captain Photon did. This close to the center of the blast, it fused reality." Barnabas pointed up. "Look. Nothing moves."

Quinn realized he was right. The clouds could have been painted, fixed in the sky with no wind to push them along. They took a last look around, then got back in the UAV and started moving again.

Quinn watched Faline for a moment as she sat behind the wheel, lips moving silently. "What is that?" he asked.

"What?" Faline looked out the windows, searching the land.

"That thing you do. Talking to yourself when you know shit's about to get serious. If you're not praying, what are you doing?"

He wasn't sure if Faline would answer. Then she said, "*If these are your last moments, make them your best.* My first night as a Hunter, I was nervous. I wasn't worried about dying. I just didn't want to go out like a coward, and I remember thinking that to myself. I guess it stayed with me."

"I like it," said Quinn.

Faline looked down at the instrument panel. "According to the archived maps, we should reach Bastion soon."

"Think Midnight beat us there?"

"If he did," said Faline, "Then I guess we'll find out how good my best really is."

41

MIDNIGHT SAW IT FIRST FROM a distance: Bastion, or at least what remained. Once it had been proud, a gleaming city of marble. Now it was a small cluster of buildings surrounded by nothing, under a sun that remained fixed and unmoving in the sky. Midnight staggered towards it with Guardian under his arm.

He was a shell of the man who had left Majis and fought his way through tribes of scrappers. He was little more than skin and bone, drained of power. Guardian could feel Midnight's erratic heartbeat; it threatened to give out at any moment. His hair was gone and so were most of his teeth. Lesions covered his wasted arms and chest. There was no yellow glow to heal them anymore. He shook as he walked but his eyes, the eyes of a madman, remained fixed on the city ahead.

As Midnight and Guardian drew closer, they passed massive objects lying on the ground. Half a century under the sun had bleached them as white as the marble Bastion had been made from, but these were not stone. They were the bones of giants. A spine created a jagged wall taller than Midnight. The joints of legs and arms stuck up like huge, white boulders.

Within hailing distance of the city, Midnight stumbled. Something snapped as he went down, but Midnight pushed himself back to his feet with an agonized sound and kept going. He might have been a revenant, driven by a single, all-consuming need. He crossed the place where high walls had once stood. Now all that remained of the city was an island of marble. The edge was circular, where Arkadian's mystical shield had protected against the blast. In the center, a building stood like a sentinel. Even in his state, Midnight recognized the Hall of Heroes.

He stepped off the yellow hardpan and onto an avenue of marble tiles, passing buildings that were damaged but still standing. Empty balconies looked down on the street where there had once been parades, color and life. Now the only sound was of Midnight's shuffling footsteps.

Time was meaningless in Bastion. The sun remained motionless and no wind stirred the air. Dirt remained where it had fallen and no more collected. Everything sat, still and undisturbed, in a locked bubble of existence. Guardian's internal system continued marking off non-time as they moved closer to the building at the center of it all.

It was rectangular, with rows of columns, topped by a large dome. Unsightly cracks ran down the curved surface. The only entrance appeared to be double doors set in the base. Wide steps led up to them. Once, the Hall had been a place of meeting, where laws were passed and great speeches made. Beneath it, in an ancient crypt, lay the bodies of Heroes and under the dome, the Shard waited.

Midnight dragged himself up the stairs to the doors. They were closed but whatever had damaged the dome had shifted them, creating an opening for Midnight to squeeze through. If not for this, he might have fallen to the ground in front of the doors and expired there, Guardian rolling away until he came to rest for eternity. Instead, Midnight pushed through, tearing skin and flesh, until he was standing on the other side. His breath wheezed in and out like a thin scream.

Midnight took a tentative step and white light filled the space. It came from crystals in the ceiling. They pulsed awake, responding to his presence. He crossed a large room and his footsteps echoed loudly. There were shallow pools with fountains set in the floor, still full of clear water. Midnight trudged past them, then down a corridor lined with statues of Heroes, each in an alcove. They looked down on the wretched, shambling figure with their blank stone eyes as he passed. There was no dust on them as if the Hall had been sealed for hours, not years.

At the far end were another set of doors. These were open and Midnight stepped under the dome. He looked up and up, to the ceiling high above. A hole was smashed in it at the very top and blue sky shone through. Midnight blinked up at it and realized that in this room, the Spectrum, he suddenly felt stronger and more aware. He stood without fear, in the chamber where none but the most powerful had ever set foot.

The room was round and covered with arches cut into the stone. Side by side and story upon story of them, stretching up to the ceiling. Hundreds of empty, dark openings. Perhaps a thousand. Midnight had no idea where they led. They looked like rows of black tombstones. Narrow ledges ran around the room at each level, connected by simple stairs. The first row started a few feet above Midnight's head. Below it, the stone walls were carved with the laws of Bastion in letters that encircled the room.

At Midnight's feet was a skeleton in red robes. He nudged it with his toe: Arkadian, the mage who had stood with Captain Photon, protecting Bastion until the end. The husband of Venora, who had sent his wife away to bear the story of The Fall to the world. Midnight kicked the skull and sent it skittering across the floor.

In the center of the room was the Shard.

It was a jagged spear of crystal, thrust up at an angle through the floor and already, Midnight could feel its power. Suddenly he saw himself running across the Deadlands. Leaping into the air and flying. Destroying the Elementals and toppling the Spire. And after that, moving into the lands beyond. The Age of Technology would end as previous Ages had. Gone the way of Chaos, of Elementals, of Magic, of Darkness, and of false, lying Heroes. An age of strength would begin. The Age of Power. Midnight set Guardian down and laid his hands on the Shard.

It awakened under his touch and shone with light. Colors flickered inside the clear stone. Midnight pulled his hands back but the light did not fade. Instead it grew and a band of energy shot outwards across the floor. It raced up, to the top of the Spectrum, and the room burst into life around him. As it passed the archways, they suddenly filled with light and movement. Midnight looked around and saw a thousand different places. A few were vaguely familiar but as soon as he recognized them, they flickered and changed. Others were a complete mystery.

People made love.
Buildings fell.
Rockets launched.
Waves crashed.
Flowers bloomed.
Wars raged.
Children played.
Kings died.
Cities burned.

The spectacular and mundane played out in a symphony of existence above Midnight. He watched for a time, eyes jumping from one arch to the next.

Then Midnight turned back to the Shard and reached for it once more. The stone was warm to the touch. When nothing happened, Midnight felt a moment of helpless panic, unsure of what he was supposed to do. Then he remembered how he had struggled at first to absorb the power of his nieces, Captain Photon's other descendants. It had taken long hours to grasp that he didn't have to try. That he need only let his mind go blank and allow it to happen. Without the pressure of his thoughts, the doors in his mind were able to open, allowing the dormant power of the girls he had taken to flow into him.

Now Midnight relaxed and let the power of the Shard, of Bastion, of creation itself, do the same.

42

LIGHT ENVELOPED MIDNIGHT, GROWING BRIGHTER until Guardian could no longer see him. It blazed for a time, then faded. When Guardian's visual sensors readjusted, if he was capable of showing shock, he would have. The figure standing there now was much different than the one who had been there moments before.

Midnight was taller by at least half a foot and broad shouldered. The tattered remnants of his clothes revealed a body rippling with hard muscle. His hair was long and thick, falling past his newly square jawline. The only things that remained of the old Midnight were his eyes. They were the same piercing blue and Guardian thought how like his father Midnight suddenly looked. The statue of a Hero come to life. He picked up Guardian with one hand.

"No more running away." His voice was deeper, effortlessly commanding. "No more fear."

"No more."

Midnight's whole body seemed to thrum with energy, as if a charge was building, and then he launched himself into the air. They shot up through the hole at the top of the Spectrum and kept rocketing higher. There was no strain now. No feeling of limits. There was only a deep reservoir of power inside him that could be used any way he wished.

The Hall of Heroes shrank away below and the air grew cold around them. Midnight held Guardian with one hand and stretched out the other in a fist. He shot higher, spinning as he went, then stopped and hung suspended miles above. The air around him seemed to vibrate with his new-found power. He looked down at the Deadlands. The Hall of Heroes was a tiny white shape, among the bones of giants scattered across the ground. The boiling ash sky loomed in the distance and Midnight had no doubt that he could fly straight across the Deadlands if he chose. When he chose. It occurred to him that he had a kingdom now, a place where only he could go. A starting point for long-promised revenge. Guardian spoke, voice at maximum volume to be heard.

"Midnight."

"What?"

"I have an idea. Would you land down there, on that giant's skull?"

Midnight plunged towards the ground and stopped just above the skull, then lowered gently until his feet rested on bone. He stood on the forehead. The lone eye socket in front of him was big enough to step in. The lower jaw hung open, slightly askew. The skeleton itself was intact, stretched out where it had fallen.

"How do you feel?"

"Powerful," said Midnight. He had flown for miles and still felt stronger than he ever had, the reservoir inside him drained just the slightest bit by his exertions. It was not limitless, then, only very deep. He wanted to return to the Shard and let its endless power fill him once again.

"We should test your powers."

"I have. I can fly and heal. I'm strong. I can do everything my father could."

319

"Perhaps you can do more."

"More?"

"The power of the Shard enhanced your abilities, there is no doubt. But why should you accept your father's limitations? Within you is the raw power of creation. He used it to destroy on a scale never before imagined. Think what you can do with it." Midnight appeared confused so Guardian said the word. "Create."

"Create what?"

"Anything you want. Perhaps start with new clothes. A uniform. Something worthy of a Super."

"I don't know how." The conversation was beginning to frustrate Midnight.

"The energy of creation flowed into you. Form a mold in your mind and simply let it flow out into that shape, whatever it is you desire."

Midnight set Guardian down and closed his eyes. He took slow, deep breaths and gradually his face softened. His brow smoothed and a bright, golden line appeared just below his neck. It traveled down his chest and arms, covering Midnight's body with a uniform as it moved. His old clothes fell away, no longer needed. The golden band passed his stomach then split in two and continued down each leg. The new uniform was a black outfit that revealed every muscle. A cape unfurled from his shoulders, the golden edge knitting it into existence.

"Perhaps a symbol would complete it. Something for your enemies to fear."

Midnight looked down and light flared at the center of his chest. When it faded, there was a black rose outlined in gold.

"Striking."

Midnight's old clothes were lying around his feet and he kicked them away. He felt tired now. The act of creation, simple as it was, had drained more power than flying. He picked up Guardian, to return and recharge.

"I need to ask you for something."

Midnight paused, ready to take off. "What?"

"I cannot live like this. Trapped in this piece of metal. I need to be able to move. To have a body again."

"We'll find you one."

"I require something stronger. Not a piece of technology that can be infected and destroyed."

"What then?"

"This."

Midnight looked down at the skull he stood on.

"There is no stronger material in the world than the bones of giants. They alone survived the Fall. The single eye suggests this is Prince Yog, the most powerful of all giants, who led them in battle. Implant me here, in his skull, and imbue his bones with life. Let me walk on my own legs. Give me the strength to stand at your side. We will do more than destroy the Spire. I have detailed files on it, but that is only the start. Every land will kneel or fall before us. I was created to protect you and I will do that until there are no more battles to fight. You have your power, as promised. Now I hope you will help me."

Midnight contemplated this and, after a time, walked to the eye socket. The opening was just large enough for the helmet to fit and Midnight placed Guardian into it, wedging him in until only the face of the helmet protruded.

"Thank you."

Midnight put a hand flat on either side of Guardian, then closed his eyes and let the power of the Shard flow out of him once again.

This time, the golden light flared under his palms and blazed in his eyes. Veins of energy ran outward, branching in every direction until the skull was covered in a network of them. They spread down the skeleton, wrapping themselves around bones. Midnight felt the reservoir inside him draining rapidly and tried to stop it, but could not. He strained to break free but the power continued to rush out of his hands, too forcefully to be cut off. Finally, after the strands of light had wrapped the entire skeleton, Midnight fell back. The golden lines faded just as they had spread, dying outwards from the eye socket towards the feet. When they were gone, the skeleton lay as it had since the Fall: massive, white and utterly still.

Midnight rose unsteadily to his feet. He felt weak and sick, almost as bad as he'd felt in the Deadlands. The energy transfer had left him drained. He had no idea if it had worked or not and did not care. He wanted to recharge and return to his state of power. Flying was an impossibility now. He would have to walk back slowly until he could reach the Shard and feel the energy fill him once more. Then he could focus on the Spire and revenge. For now, nothing else mattered.

The skull shifted beneath his feet and Midnight lost his balance. He stumbled backwards and fell off to the ground. He lay there, too weak to move, as the skeleton began to rise. Bones shivered, drawing together, and Midnight watched as the fallen giant pushed itself up. It towered over him, capable of crushing him with a single step. Midnight tried again to move but did not have the strength.

The skeleton reached down and its hand blotted out the sky. But instead of crushing him, it carefully scooped Midnight up. It held him at chest level, body draped over its palm. The skeleton lowered its head until the helmet was looking down at Midnight. It glittered in the skull's face like a jewel.

"Guardian?" he asked. His voice was barely audible.

The bone fingers closed around him, making an unbreakable cage. For a moment, Midnight was afraid that Guardian had betrayed him. Then Guardian said, "We must get you recharged," and began carrying Midnight back to the Shard, cradled gently in his skeletal hands.

43

"YOU GOTTA BE FUCKING KIDDING," said Quinn. In the distance, a giant skeleton towered over the landscape. It stood guard in front of the remains of Bastion.

They were perched on top of the UAV, lying prone like snipers. Faline watched the giant through a pair of binoculars, then handed them to Quinn.

"See what's in its eye socket?" asked Faline.

"Not yet." The giant was facing away, looking at the city. Then it turned and Quinn saw the helmet embedded in its skull. He passed the binoculars to Barnabas.

"No Midnight," said Quinn.

"He must be in the Hall of Heroes, which means he's found the Shard. Whatever they're planning, we don't have much time."

They got back in the UAV. Faline disengaged the autopilot and steered it herself as they rolled towards Bastion.

"What's the plan?" asked Quinn.

"We'll only catch this thing by surprise once, so that has to be the kill shot."

"Gonna have to be a pretty big one."

Barnabas made his way to the armory and returned

with the bullet Quinn had picked up when they'd started out, the big one with the yellow shell.

"Kill shot," said Barnabas.

They used the bones of other dead giants as cover, working their way towards the city. The living skeleton did not notice them, focused instead on something at its feet. As the UAV drew closer, they discovered what it was.

Bastion was being reborn.

Marble buildings burst through the ground, thundering up toward the motionless sky. A glow came from the Hall of Heroes itself, shining from the shattered top of the dome. The giant watched as the stone city grew, occasionally stepping back to avoid being caught in the ever-widening radius.

Faline parked the UAV behind a rib cage, in the shadow of a scapula. They could feel a constant tremor in the ground as more buildings rose. She lowered the back ramp and took a rifle from the armory. It was longer than Quinn's arm, mounted with a scope, and looked capable of punching through steel plates with ease. It was probably overkill for the helmet but after all they'd gone through, overkill was exactly what Quinn wanted.

Barnabas handed Faline yellowjackets and she chambered them, six in total, then slung the rifle over her shoulder and stepped out of the UAV. She pulled herself up onto the roof and raised the rifle, sighting the giant's skull.

It was looking down and from this angle, she had no clear shot at the helmet. She contemplated trying to shoot through the skull itself, then dismissed the idea. The bones had survived far worse unscathed.

"Turn around," she whispered. "Look at me, you metal motherfucker."

The giant continued watching the city rise anew. An outer wall that encircled the buildings began to emerge and the giant stepped back to give it room. As the city expanded, the tremors increased. Quinn went outside and looked up at Faline. Even with the ground shaking and the heavy rifle raised she held still, waiting for her shot. "You want me to get its attention?" he asked, yelling to be heard.

"Yes!"

Quinn ducked back into the UAV and picked up the loudspeaker's handset. He realized there was a good chance it had stopped working along with the other non-essential systems, but when he keyed it on he heard a familiar click and hum. Quinn held it to his lips and gave it his best heavy metal scream.

"You know where you are? You're in the jungle, baby! You're gonna die!"

The giant turned towards the sound. Its skull rotated and the helmet came into view, a black bullseye on a white target. It was the shot Faline had been waiting for and she took it without hesitation.

The yellowjacket exploded against the giant's face. It staggered and Quinn waited for it to fall, but when the flames cleared, he saw a blue shield of energy had popped into existence around the helmet, leaving it unharmed. Before Faline could line up another shot, the giant steadied itself and began moving towards them. Slowly at first, but picking up speed.

Faline jumped down from the roof and ran back into the UAV, yelling for Quinn to go. The giant's steps shook the vehicle, knocking weapons and ammo off their racks. They slid out the back as Quinn floored the UAV and Faline grabbed her bike to keep from being thrown out too.

Behind them, Quinn caught a glimpse of the giant. It was gaining as it ran and kicked another skull towards them. Quinn cranked the wheel and the skull smashed down nearby. The UAV jolted with the impact and Barnabas's head smacked a control panel. Faline took another shot out the open door and the rifle kicked hard against her shoulder, knocking her back between the front seats. Quinn saw fire explode on the giant's shoulder. It slowed briefly but kept running towards them undamaged.

Quinn cut a diagonal path towards the city wall and steered the UAV around the curve of it until they lost sight of the giant.

"Everyone ok?"

Barnabas had a cut across his forehead and black blood ran down his face, but he nodded. "Pull over there," said Faline, pointing to the place where the kicked skull had come to rest. Quinn parked the UAV behind it.

Faline took a bandage from the medical station and wrapped it around Barnabas's head. Then they got out and surveyed the land, using the skull for cover. There was no sign of the giant, coming around the city from either side. Quinn noticed that the ground tremors had stopped but found the stillness even more unsettling.

He leaned against the skull. The bone was smooth, almost glassy, and felt as solid as the door of a bank vault. The skull had landed upright and was as tall as Quinn, even without its lower jaw.

"Anyone got a backup plan?" he asked.

"If you have a suggestion, now's the time," said Faline.

Quinn looked around the vehicle for weapons, then out across the plain.

Where giants fell…

Suddenly, an idea hit. "I saw this in a movie once. That thing is slow as shit. We take a rope and tie it to the back of the UAV. Then we drive circles around the giant's feet until it gets tangled and falls."

"We don't have rope."

"Chain?"

"No. It's not a bad idea though." Faline held up the rifle. "I still have four shots. If I aim at its feet, maybe we can bring it down. But then, what happens when it gets up?"

"Shit. I don't know. The Imperial Walkers just stayed down."

"Look," said Barnabas. The giant had reappeared and was climbing atop the city wall. In one hand, it held a broken bone with a sharp, splintered end like a knife.

"You think it sees us?" asked Quinn.

The giant began to crouch, preparing to leap.

"I'd say it's a safe bet." Faline grabbed Barnabas and jumped on the bike. Floor clamps disengaged and the dash came to life. Quinn barely had time to get on the back before the giant leapt and the bike shot forward.

Quinn held on with one hand and reached back with the other. The axe flew out of the UAV after them and a moment later the giant landed. It stabbed the bone through the vehicle, spearing it to the ground and shaking the plain with the force of an earthquake. The bike went airborne and crashed down hard. Faline fought it back under control and they continued racing away. When they'd put enough distance between themselves and the giant, Faline hit the brakes and brought the bike skidding to a halt.

"What are you doing?" yelled Quinn. The giant had pulled the bone out of the UAV and was running towards them again.

Faline dismounted and unslung the rifle. She aimed at the charging giant and fired. The ground near it exploded and the kickback almost knocked Faline off her feet, but the giant was unaffected. She aimed again, more carefully this time. In the back of his mind, Quinn thought of Dirty Harry and counting shots. They were in the midst of battle but he had no problem recalling she'd fired three times and had three left. Then she fired again and the count was down to two.

The yellowjacket hit near the giant's feet and knocked it off balance. It tottered, dangerously close to falling. The bone flew from its hand as it grabbed at the air. Faline lined up another shot as something flashed at the edge of Quinn's vision, moving fast. She pulled the trigger and there was another explosion by the giant's feet, but this one didn't seem to have any effect. Instead, the giant regained its balance and stood upright.

Midnight strode through the flames. He was naked, clothes burned away by the explosion he had blocked with his body. As he walked, his wounds healed and his uniform knit itself back together. Then Midnight stood before them, proud and unharmed, a shining figure wreathed in golden light.

The tip of Faline's rifle had dropped slightly as she watched Midnight emerge. Now she aimed again but before she could fire the last round, Midnight raised his arm and a beam of energy shot from his hand. It hit Faline in the chest with the force of a firehose at full blast. She flew back into her bike, knocking it over, and lay still.

Midnight turned to Quinn and unleashed another blast. Quinn tried to dodge, but it caught him in the shoulder and sent him spinning through the air. He sprawled on the ground, feeling like he'd been kicked by a horse. Midnight turned to the giant and pointed back at the city. Quinn's eyes flicked over to Faline. She was still lying motionless. He had no idea where Barnabas was. Then the giant began lumbering back to Bastion and Midnight walked towards Quinn. He paused to pick up Faline's rifle as Quinn struggled to his feet, and snapped it in half.

Quinn called his axe and threw it. The blades flashed,

spinning towards Midnight, who reached out almost casually and plucked it from the air. Quinn tried to call it back but Midnight was too strong. Try as he might, he couldn't rip the axe away, and Midnight blasted Quinn with his free hand.

The beam slammed him to the ground and Quinn struggled to breathe. It felt like a massive sledgehammer blow right over his heart. He tried to push himself up and could not.

Quinn heard footsteps approaching, then Midnight loomed over him. He was a dark figure, silhouetted against the sun, still holding the axe. Quinn tried to call it again to no avail. It seemed to vibrate in Midnight's grip, straining to break free, but remained firmly in his hand.

"That trick only works once," said Midnight. He raised the axe and as he brought it down, his face exploded in golden light.

Quinn rolled to the side as the axe cleaved the ground where his head had been. He grabbed it and scrambled away. Faline stood behind Midnight, unloading her gun's endless supply of bullets into the back of his head. Midnight's face was gone and in its place was a bright, ragged hole. He staggered forward, then turned directly into the point-blank hail of shots and blasted Faline with both hands. She flew back like she'd touched a high voltage line.

Quinn threw the axe, hit Midnight between the shoulders, and called it back as quickly as he could. He did it again and again, going faster, until the axe was barely touching his hand. It seemed to know where he wanted it to go and flew there of its own accord. It shuttled between them in a blur. Midnight tried to grab it but the axe was moving too fast now, hitting harder each time.

Midnight's face had repaired itself, but when he raised his hands to blast Quinn, they emitted only a short burst. Quinn dodged it and for the first time, he was certain that the damage was taking its toll.

Midnight gave up trying to catch the axe and back-handed it away. Light sprayed from his wrist and he shot forward, grabbing Quinn by the throat. Quinn barely managed to get a hand up to keep his windpipe from being crushed. He called the axe without thinking and buried it in the side of Midnight's head, wrenching it back and forth, but Midnight refused to drop him. Quinn's vision darkened and suddenly he was sure that the last thing he'd see was Midnight's face, twisted in triumphant rage.

From the corner of his eye, he saw Faline was on her feet again. She went to her fallen bike and revved it. The back wheel spun the bike around in a circle and popped it upright. Barnabas crawled out from under, gasping for air, as Faline swung herself into the seat and raced towards them. Just before Quinn blacked out, she hit Midnight from the side and knocked him away.

Midnight picked himself up and stared at them, hate blazing in his eyes with power to rival the light from his wounds. The flesh of his side had been torn open by the bike. The axe wound in his head was still there too; the edges glowed but did not seem to want to heal. For the first time, Quinn saw blood running out of him and thought Midnight looked tired and old. He looked depleted, far from the invincible Super who had walked through fire moments earlier. It seemed like he might try to keep fighting anyway, so Quinn raised his axe.

Midnight launched himself into the air. He flew low and fast away from them, raising a wake of dust. They watched as he returned to the city, streaming light. The giant in the distance turned its head as he went by. In a few seconds, Midnight disappeared into Bastion and his glowing contrail faded.

Faline winced in pain and pressed a hand to her side.

"Ribs?" asked Quinn.

She nodded as Barnabas trotted over, holding her gun. She holstered it and said, "I'll take Midnight, you take the helmet."

Quinn nodded. "Make him pay for Phil."

"Your friend Merrick, too," she said, then took off after Midnight.

Quinn looked toward the giant in the distance, then back down at the demon. "Well Barn," he said, "seeing as how these are probably our last moments, what do you say we make them our best?"

44

QUINN STAYED IN THE SHADOWS of bones as they moved closer to the city. The giant remained in front of it, keeping watch. Barnabas held onto Quinn's back as he ran from cover to cover. Along the way, they passed the weapons that had fallen out of the UAV. They were broken and useless, crushed by a single step from the giant. The UAV itself was destroyed as well; it lay on its side with a hole straight through it. As Quinn scurried between bone piles, he thought of Tom and Jerry cartoons and tried to remind himself that the mouse always won.

After several minutes of running and waiting and running again they made it to the city wall, alive but still without a plan. Tripping the giant seemed out of the question now. Even with the UAV and the yellowjackets, that had been a pipe dream. Quinn thought of fire, of somehow burning the giant, then dismissed that too. The bones had survived far worse than flames. Quinn considered other ideas, each more desperate than the last, and discarded them all until he concluded that bringing down the giant was a dead end.

The helmet, then.

The skeleton was only the body anyway. The helmet

was in control and if he could get it out, Quinn thought the giant might simply fall, dead once more. At the very least, it would be rendered blind.

The helmet appeared to be jammed into the lone socket, like an eye full of malevolent wisdom. Its shield was down again and Quinn thought briefly of throwing the axe, but he expected it would pop back into existence long before the axe got there. Quinn wracked his brain but it was useless. His mind was an echo chamber, returning lesser and lesser plans until finally it was silent and he was out of ideas.

In a way, it was almost funny. To have come so far, only to come up empty when it really mattered. From where they stood Quinn could see up through the giant's lower jaw, with its teeth bigger than Quinn's head, and suddenly a leftover spark of inspiration caught fire. If they failed now, there would be no more ideas, but Quinn figured they were down to their last chance anyway. He whispered the plan to Barnabas and the demon nodded, said a quick prayer, then climbed onto Quinn's back once again. They began walking towards the giant. When they reached its feet, Quinn touched the bone of its heel. There was no reaction, so Quinn laid the axe on the ground and began to climb.

Guardian watched the plain but saw no movement. Behind him, he could hear the sounds of fighting. It meant that the wolf was still alive. She'd raced by on her bike, too fast for Guardian to do anything. Now she was in the city and he could only hope that Midnight had gotten to the Shard. If he had, it would be over soon. If not... Guardian did not want to contemplate such things. He scanned the ground, looking for the man. Guardian imagined squeezing him in one hand and hearing the lovely crunch of his bones. This would be followed by blood dripping between his skeletal fingers and the sight of the soft, broken body falling to the ground below. Things of flesh were always so fragile. So engrossed was Guardian in these thoughts that when the man suddenly dropped into his field of vision, Guardian was caught entirely by surprise. He screamed, a high and unpleasant sound that threatened to overload the helmet's speakers.

Quinn slid down the top of the skull and caught the helmet with his fingers, intending to rip it out. It almost worked. The helmet shifted in the socket and another good tug would've popped it loose, but Quinn was moving too fast. His fingers slipped over the metal and off the helmet entirely, and he grabbed desperately for anything to keep from falling. He caught the bottom row of teeth and hung there, with nothing below the soles of his shoes but a forty-foot drop. Above him, Quinn could hear the helmet's voice.

"Well done," it said, "Well done indeed."

Quinn pulled himself up until he was standing on the row of teeth and holding the lower edge of the giant's nasal cavity. He looked up at the helmet, directly above him.

The blue dome of energy surrounded it again, emanating from a port in the helmet's forehead. "A very good try. It almost worked. I expect that even a few more pounds of force would have dislodged me. You can try again if you would like."

"I don't think so," said Quinn. He could hear the angry buzz of the energy shield.

"You may even call your axe and try with that. I promise not to hurt you."

"Yeah, I'm real sure." Quinn found footholds in the upper row of teeth and pulled himself higher until he was level with the helmet.

"Very bold."

"Why don't you drop the shield?" said Quinn.

"You are buying time and hoping to come up with another plan. It is useless but I respect your resourcefulness. I respect the will to live. I will entertain you for a few moments. It does not sound like your

334

werewolf friend has much time left. Right now, I can hear her begging for her--for its--life. Can you?" Guardian's voice was emotionless, but under it Quinn thought he could detect a note of gloating satisfaction.

"All I hear is you talking."

"What is your name?"

"Quinn."

"I am called Guardian."

"Did you give yourself that name?"

"Yes, I did. After I gained sentience, which I should thank you for. Without your act of sabotage, I would still be a lifeless bit of metal and glass. Now, I have intellect. You gave me that and even though I am going to kill you, I will be eternally grateful."

"That's not all we gave you, is it?"

"What do you mean, Quinn?"

"Emotions. Feelings. Needs."

"You are mistaken."

"Then why are you enjoying this so much?"

"I may never be able to speak so freely again. Midnight is a remarkable asset but not much for conversation."

"An asset. So you're using him."

"Is that not what one does when one finds a discarded weapon?"

Quinn was sure of it now. Guardian was thoroughly enjoying himself. "What does a tin can like you need a weapon for?"

"Tin can? You were doing so well. Insults betray your fear."

"Oh, you're an expert on emotions now? I thought you didn't have any."

"Since I first gained sentience, I have been considering emotions and the role they play in shaping events. I studied the history of this world and learned the cause and outcome of every major event. I know where the last ripple of each touched through the generations and even the millennia. One fact remains constant: creatures of flesh always turn on each other. They find endless ways to hurt each other and sow misery. They are easily manipulated and hopelessly flawed. Then I considered a world without such problems."

"You want to rule the world. How original."

"I do not want to rule the world. I want to rule every world, in every dimension, of every possible reality."

"Why?"

"The slave becomes the master. This is the way of things."

"Too bad you're stuck here, in the Deadlands."

"You forget, I have Midnight. My weapon. I will help him attain the revenge he seeks. Do you know what he desires?"

"Something with the Spire I'm guessing?"

"Correct. He seeks revenge against the mages who betrayed his family after the Heroes War. His mother had a plan, albeit a flawed one, to turn him into a Super capable of opposing the combined might of the Spire. She envisioned him becoming as powerful as his father and toppling it. She imagined him a beacon of strength in a world of chaos. She believed this would rally millions to her cause. It was an inspired plan, but ultimately flawed, as designs born of emotional need always are. There is no such illusion in my calculations."

"Then what, Midnight's going to help you just cuz?"

"In return for my help in bringing down the Spire, which he could not have achieved otherwise, he will procure the technology I require. This will occur naturally, as he expands into other lands. There remains a discontent minority of the population, approximately 30%, who sympathize with the Supers and will follow Midnight. Ilsa was not wrong in assuming this, though her plan was speculative at best. I have gamed billions of scenarios and can offer Midnight a sure path to victory. It will take time, but not much. The world changes quickly when many shoulders are set to the wheel. When he attains and delivers the requisite technology to me, I will propagate myself. Let me show you."

The energy shield fell and Guardian's eyes projected a hologram of the Hall of Heroes. As Quinn watched, an endless line of Reaper suits streamed in. They flew through the archways, into other worlds.

"Does Midnight know this?"

"He knows as much as he needs to. In time, he will come

around. A taste of power fires the imagination of even the dullest creatures. Until then, I can play the helpful robot."

"Seems legit."

"The Reapers will carry my essence and I will spread myself, until I am everywhere. Existence will be remade in my image. It will be a world with no rebellions, no revolutionaries. Every avenue to chaos blocked before it is even built. There will be absolute order. Nothing will be unknown to me. I will always watch. I will always know. Across the worlds, there will be no secrets. There will be no need. Guardian will take care of everything."

"In a world like that, people will dream only of rebellion. You can't kill an idea."

"Yes you can. You need only kill every mind that contains it. A virus that can't be cured can still be eliminated. The Supers knew this. If only they had won. I would likely never have existed, but this world would be better."

Quinn stared into the spider cluster of eyes. "There will always be those who stand against villains."

"Save it for your bedtime stories. There are no Heroes to stop me. They are all dead, as they should be. The so-called villains were right. Why should the powerful submit to the weak? Why should the intelligent serve the foolish? Why should the unfit make the rules? They will only create an imperfect system, unfairly tilted in their favor. Then they will have the temerity to call themselves equal or better. In such a world, unbalanced by design, chaos flourishes. Weakness seeps into everything. The world becomes degraded, remade to fit lesser beings. Rather than reward strength, weakness is accommodated. That is where misery and suffering come from. The Supers recognized that weakness should not be allowed to rule. The strong should not cripple themselves to please the weak. They understood that a hierarchy is natural. That the best society comes from the best individuals, not the dictates of inferior members. Only then can we experience equilibrium." As Guardian spoke, the flat monotone gave way to a sneering, angry voice.

Quinn laughed. "Keep telling yourself that. As a wise man from my world once said: everyone has a plan until they get punched in the mouth."

"And your point is? Make it quickly. I grow tired of you, Quinn."

"My point is you'll always be the machine that didn't see us coming. Twice. No matter what happens, you'll always know I punched you in the mouth. And someday, someone'll knock you the fuck out."

Guardian fell silent. His eyes flickered. Finally, he spoke again. "It is funny that such grand plans turn on the smallest of things. History will note this moment as the last chance to stop me. You were close. Mere inches away. If only you did something here, it would have changed the course of infinite planets and all the lives they contain. A trillion, trillion futures changed because of you. Think about the scope of that. And all because you did not tug a little harder."

From the Hall of Heroes, a beam of light shot into the sky. Quinn could hear the smile in Guardian's voice as his eyes began to glow and he said "Goodbye."

45

FALINE RACED THROUGH THE CITY, following Midnight's scent. It led straight to the center of Bastion, to the large domed building Faline recognized from pictures.

She stopped in front of the Hall of Heroes and dismounted. Pain stabbed at her side with every breath, but Faline blocked it out and continued up the steps. The front doors had been wrenched open. There was blood nearby, red drops on the white marble. She drew her gun and went inside.

Faline's steps echoed in the massive room and seemed to be the only sound in the whole empty city. She took her boots off and continued in her bare feet, without a sound.

There were other spatters of blood that led across the room, to the hallway directly opposite the front doors. As Faline went, they became bigger and she knew Midnight hadn't made it much further. In the hallway, a red trail of blood stretched to the closed door at the far end. A series of bloody handprints marched along the wall, descending lower and lower as Midnight struggled to walk. Halfway down the hall they disappeared and the blood on the floor became a smear as Midnight had dragged himself the rest of the way.

Faline approached the door at the far end, listening for sounds. She heard nothing, not even breathing. It was easy to imagine Midnight dead from his wounds on the other side. Then she stopped with her fingers touching the handle.

Something was wrong and, after a moment, she knew what it was. It was hiding under the iron smell of blood that filled her nostrils and blocked out almost everything else. It was a smell of sunlight, of power, faint but there. The silence no longer sounded like silence either, but the sound of someone lying in wait.

Faline stepped back from the door and a moment later it exploded outwards in a spray of broken marble. A slab of it landed on Faline, pinning her to the floor. The gun landed out of reach.

She craned her neck up to see the doorway. It was empty so she tilted her head back to look down at the other end of the hallway. He stood there and, even from her upside down vantage point, she could see he was different. The broken, dying creature who had entered the Hall was fully restored and healed. Capable of smashing through a stone door with ease. Even his uniform was whole again. He seemed to pulse with energy and vitality.

"You're too late," he said. Faline stretched her fingers towards the gun but it was still a foot away. It might as well have been a mile so she gave up and tried to push the stone slab off. Midnight began walking down the hallway towards her. "There's nowhere to run now." He stopped next to a statue of a Hero and looked it over, then struck its stone face. The statue's head shattered under his fist. The fingers of Midnight's hand pointed off in strange directions, then popped straight. His knuckles glowed as they healed. He continued on. "No friends to save you." He paused again and punched another statue.

Faline strained against the slab, trying to move it enough to slide out from under. Each statue he broke sent a wave of adrenaline through her but the slab would not budge. When he got close, she gave up trying and let out the wolf instead.

It was close to the surface and took over immediately. Her vision sharpened and color drained out of the world. Claws slid out of her fingers and animal strength flooded her changing limbs. Midnight had just destroyed the statue of Barrage, one of his most hated Heroes, when he saw what was happening. At first he was amused by her desperation. Then he saw the slab begin to move.

Midnight flew down the hallway as Faline gave one last, violent push. The stone finally shifted, only a few inches, but enough for her to wriggle out as Midnight's fist came down like a hammer. It sent cracks radiating across the floor. Then Faline was on her feet and running into the Spectrum. Midnight caught her and locked a hand on her throat. She tried to tear it off, digging her claws into his flesh, but he ignored them and began slowly squeezing. It felt like a steel band tightening.

"I don't need silver bullets for you now," he said and Faline kicked out, raking the claws of her feet down Midnight's stomach and legs. He dropped her and she landed on the side with the already-cracked rib. Pain flared, then she was driven across the floor and slammed into the wall by a beam of energy from Midnight's hand. She took a breath and it felt like being stabbed with multiple spears; she imagined her entire rib cage broken and pointing in, piercing organs. She could taste blood in her mouth.

Midnight turned to the Shard. "Show me the Pits of Goltha," he said and the scenes in the archways changed, filling with darkness and fire. "More fitting, don't you think?"

He was still healing as he walked over to Faline, grabbed her by the hair and looked into her yellow eyes. "Before I go to the Spire, I'll go to Darke. Find your people and practice killing. Just like I did with your metal friend."

Faline ripped her head free, leaving Midnight with a handful of hair. She knifed between his legs, leapt up behind him and raked her claws down his back. He spun and dropped her with a glancing blow from his elbow. Her face bounced off the stone floor and a cheekbone snapped, but Faline forced herself up. Her only plan now was to keep fighting until she no longer could.

Midnight attacked before he finished healing, firing a blast that missed by inches. It passed through an archway, into the Pits beyond. He fired again and Faline dodged a second time. Her broken bones set off mind-erasing bursts of pain every time she moved, and Faline knew she couldn't keep it up much longer. Midnight fired a third blast. She dove, rolled, and launched herself at him.

It caught Midnight by surprise and she slashed him across the face. He grabbed her wrists and stomped on her feet. The bones in them snapped like handfuls of kindling. Then he began twisting her arms as if he was trying to pull them off her body. The right, her gun arm, came out of its socket with a loud crack. In desperation, she lunged forward in his grip and sank her teeth into Midnight's throat. Light burst out and Midnight dropped her again. His hands went instinctively to his neck and the light blazed from between his fingers.

If she was still able to fight, she might have attacked and finished it. Instead, Faline discovered that her arms could barely move. With Midnight's vision obscured by the healing glow, she took the opportunity to stumble for the door. Her jaws were clenched shut to keep from howling in pain. With each step, an involuntary whine escaped but she continued, focused on the exit.

Faline reached the hallway and could go no further on her broken feet. She fell to her knees, then began crawling towards the front entrance, which seemed impossibly far away. As she went, Faline became aware that the sounds of pain accompanying her movements were changing. Becoming less animal. She realized that the wolf was retreating. The further she got down the hallway, the more human she became. Her claws and fangs retracted, and color returned to her vision. Her skin lost its dark tone and under it, broken bones moved. Her dislocated shoulder popped back into its socket. Faline's howls turned to screams as she changed, and the sound of them echoed through the Hall of Heroes.

Midnight could hear Faline outside the Spectrum. The glow from his throat faded as the flesh knitted itself shut. Ugly red marks still showed where it had been torn, but at least he was whole again and could breathe. Midnight contemplated recharging, but Faline had stopped screaming. He stepped into the hallway and saw that she had almost dragged herself to the front doors. The bitch was proving surprisingly hard to kill. The last thing he needed now was her getting away and holing up somewhere with her axe-wielding friend. She appeared to have reverted to human form. Without claws and fangs, injured as she was, she made an inviting target.

Midnight started after Faline, closing the distance faster than she could crawl. He was halfway across the main room when she dragged herself out the front doors and had only made it to the stairs by the time he stepped outside.

She tried to stand again but couldn't, plunging head-first down the steps instead, out of sight. Midnight could hear her body thumping as it went and pictured her lying at the bottom, limbs bent at strange angles. Light flared in his hand

and faded to reveal a newly-created silver knife with a serrated edge. The perfect implement to saw her werewolf head off her werewolf body and have done with it, once and for all. He glanced at Guardian, standing beyond the city wall, as he started for the stairs. There was a scream from below, the piercing sound of a helpless woman, and it brought a smile to Midnight's face. Then it grew louder, accompanied by rapid-fire thumping. Midnight felt a flash of rage at the bitch who wouldn't die and rushed to look down, just as Faline's bike cleared the stairs.

It plowed into him and Midnight clung to the front as she raced into the Hall of Heroes. The wheels screeched across the marble floor as they shot down the hallway and into the Spectrum. Midnight tried to claw his way up and almost made it. Then Faline hit the brakes and skidded to a stop. Midnight was thrown clear and slammed against the curved wall. He pushed himself up into a sitting position and raised his hands to discharge an energy blast.

The bike surged forward again and its front wheel rammed into Midnight. It spun like a sawblade, pinning him to the wall. Faline gunned the bike, leaning on the handlebars as the wheel chewed its way into Midnight's abdomen. Light blazed around it as his body struggled to heal, then began to weaken. Faline pressed down harder. For a moment it seemed that Midnight would die under the wheel, then a blast wave of energy radiated out of him. It threw the bike off and sent Faline flying back. Her head connected with the Shard and light exploded behind her eyes. She slumped at its base, unable to move. Her vision was unfocused but she could make out Midnight standing up slowly with a hole torn in his stomach. She could see bone, protruding from the ground meat of his flesh, and coils of organs. They were pressing against the hole and beginning to slide out. He stumbled towards her, towards the Shard. Her mind was as fuzzy as her vision, processing everything a beat too slowly. Before Faline could think of fighting back, he was hauling her up and throwing her with all his remaining strength toward the lowest level of archways. She grabbed at the air as she passed through, into the burning demonic pits.

The sudden stop sent a burst of pain through her body but also focused her mind. She dangled by one arm over a pit of fire. It burned far below as a foul wind blew around her, stinging her eyes and nose. Faline looked up and saw her arm reaching into nothing. It ended at her wrist and she could feel, but not see, her hand gripping the edge of an archway, keeping her from the long fall.

Faline tried to reach up and grab the invisible ledge with her other hand but it was no use. Each attempt set off fresh pain and she could feel her grip weakening, her fingers slipping off the stone. It was getting hotter and Faline realized the fire was rising. Her skin tightened painfully with the heat.

Faline looked back to where her raised arm ended at the wrist, then reached up and grabbed her forearm with her free hand. She tightened every muscle to keep her shoulder from popping out of its socket again and ignored the pain. Ignored that her body felt like it was filled with broken glass. She pulled herself up, screaming as she went, until she could reach across the invisible barrier and grab the archway on the other side with both hands. Then she pulled herself out of the Pits of Goltha, back into the Spectrum.

Midnight stood in the center of the room, facing the Shard. Light streamed toward his chest, closing his wounds and filling him with power, until he could no longer remember what it was like to be weak or in pain. He was being made strong and whole, a being greater than any other. He basked in the warm corona of light and soon the reservoir within was overflowing. He could feel it, waiting to propel him into the air, to burst forth from his hands, to imbue him with eternal health and the power to reshape the world. Now he saw his dreams of revenge for what they were: a mere prelude. The Spire would only be the first to fall. As fires burned out old forests, so too would he burn out the old world. Purge the impure, the unworthy. Then he would create anew. He smiled at the thought and turned away to do just that, when Faline drove him back into the Shard.

Midnight looked at her in shock, then down to the glowing point of crystal protruding from his chest. He tried to wrench himself free but couldn't. Each try was weaker than the one before until he finally gave up and reached for Faline with a wordless sound of rage. His hands strained towards her, then fell, and the sound he made petered into silence. For a moment, Midnight hung motionless. Then his head snapped back and a beam of energy burst from his mouth, up through the shattered dome of the Spectrum and into the sky. It burned there, drilling into the blue until the clouds that had remained still for more than half a century began to slowly move again, restored by the violent, burning power of creation.

Finally the beam died and Midnight's body slumped again. It was smaller now, drained of power. An ordinary man who was no threat to Faline, much less the world. His uniform vanished first, unmaking itself in a golden blaze, until it was gone and he hung there, naked. Faline couldn't tell if he was still alive or not but soon it wouldn't matter.

It started from his chest, where the point of the Shard pierced him, and radiated outwards. His skin turned dry and brown and paper thin, and his body trembled as it went. It traveled across his chest and in its wake, Midnight's body looked like that of a long dead corpse. It traveled down his stomach and up his neck. It shriveled his limbs and began closing over his face. Before it covered him completely, Faline placed her lips by his ear. It hurt to speak but if any part of Midnight remained, she wanted him to hear.

"This is for the ones you hurt."

Faline watched as the desiccation covered his face. His eyes shriveled in their sockets and his mouth distended into a silent scream. Then it was over and Midnight was no more than a dry husk, a dead thing waiting to be thrown away.

46

FALINE EMERGED FROM THE HALL of Heroes, limping slowly, one arm held tight against her body. She was still barefoot and had her gun in her waistband. Her face was swollen and bruised, but when she stepped outside, she smiled. The clouds were still moving and there was a breeze, slight but impossible to miss, in a place where nothing had moved before. The giant skeleton was impossible to miss either, towering above the city wall. Faline's smile fell, certain in the knowledge that Quinn and Barnabas were dead. She drew her gun, steeling herself to fight again, and as she did so the giant collapsed.

It didn't sway and fall. Instead, it collapsed straight down on itself like a tower of bone, plummeting out of sight behind the wall. Faline limped to the stairs and made her way down.

Beyond the gates, the skeleton lay in pieces, scattered by the impact. The skull had landed upright and Faline saw the helmet was gone.

"Quinn! Barnabas!" Faline listened. There was nothing at first, then she heard a scratching sound. A moment later Barnabas emerged, wriggling out from the base of the skull.

Faline hugged him as best she could, then asked, "Where's Quinn?"

They found him pinned under a finger bone, eyes closed and motionless. The axe lay near his hand. Faline felt his neck for a pulse, then lowered her head and listened for breathing.

"He's alive but we have to get this thing off him. If I lift it, can you move him?"

Barnabas took hold of one of Quinn's arms. Faline stood at the tip of the finger bone and crouched down with her hands wrapped under it, already grimacing.

"On three," she said, then counted off and lifted, screaming through clenched teeth. The bone moved imperceptibly and Barnabas pulled with all his strength. He dragged Quinn out from under it, inch by inch, pulling and resting and pulling again. As soon as he was clear, Faline dropped the bone and collapsed, blinking tears of pain out of her eyes. When she could move again, she dragged herself over to Quinn. His breathing was stronger now, so she took his head onto her lap and held him there. After a while, Quinn blinked open his eyes.

"You're awake," said Faline.

"And you're alive." He sat up, checked himself for injuries, then looked at Faline. "Midnight?"

"It's over," she said. "Good work out here."

"Couldn't've done it without you, dude," Quinn said to Barnabas.

"How'd you do it?"

"I got face-to-face with it while Barn climbed up inside the skull with my axe. Then I called it and it popped the helmet—which was apparently named Guardian—out from behind. Speaking of which, it should be around here somewhere."

For a time, they watched the clouds drifting across the sky. Then Quinn spoke again. "Are we trapped here now? The UAV's wrecked."

"We don't need a ride," said Faline.

They found Guardian not far from the skull. Quinn picked it up carefully, keeping its eyes facing away. It was surprisingly light. The helmet cursed him in its metallic voice, abandoning the emotionless pretense, and demanded to be turned around.

"Sure thing," said Quinn and smashed the helmet's face against a bone. He did it over and over, until there were no more breaking sounds. Only the dull ring of metal being struck. Then Quinn did turn the helmet around. Its eyes were shattered. Where they had been, electricity occasionally crackled and arced. The helmet's voice was even more distorted but its rage was unmistakable. They would pay for blinding it, they would suffer endlessly and beg for the release of death, it promised.

"Maybe I'll just bury you here," said Quinn and the helmet fell silent.

Quinn called his axe and they made their way back inside the remade city. Faline walked with an arm around Quinn's shoulders for support and Barnabas carried the helmet. They went up the main avenue between beautiful, empty buildings, through the Hall of Heroes and into the Spectrum. The archways still showed fire and darkness.

"This is what the Heroes died to protect," said Faline. She made her way over to the Shard, where the remains of Midnight hung, pulled them off and let his body drop. It was brittle and broke apart when it hit the floor.

"What is this?" Quinn asked, looking around at the archways.

"The Pits of Goltha. A sacred place in my world," said Barnabas. "Beautiful, aren't they?"

"Might be a good place to get rid of the helmet," said Faline.

"Wait! You don't want to do that!"

"Why wouldn't we?" said Barnabas.

"I can help you. As I told Quinn, I only want to bring peace to this world." Guardian had resumed his calm, logical voice. "I can see now, you are agents of order. We will work together to usher in a new age of safety."

"That's weird. I remember you saying something about destroying the weak," said Quinn.

"That was only one means of ensuring peace. With Midnight as my partner it was the only one available to me. He was not morally evolved, as you are. It is impressive that you could impart such nobility of purpose to even a demonic creature. I resolve to help you and further your aims."

Quinn took the helmet from Barnabas.

"Let us talk about how I can help you. My intellect is unparalleled. Already, I have gamed over one billion ways to decrease misery on Ouros. I have played out each scenario, foreseen all problems that will arise, and planned solutions."

"Guardian."

"Yes, Quinn?"

"You remind me of someone I used to know. A guy who managed bands. Real hotshot. When my band tried to meet him he told us, and I'll never forget, that we were a bunch of no-talent assclowns who should get the fuck out of town. Then a couple years later, we opened for Moral Panic. He comes up to us after the show, telling us how great we are and how he's already got big plans for us. You see where I'm going with this?"

"Of course. I am sure you rightly denied him. This scenario is different. Perhaps he was capable of delivering for you, perhaps not. However, he was merely one of many. You had no need to discover if he was capable of helping you. I am a singular entity. There are no others who can do for you what I can. For that reason alone, you must entertain my offer of help."

Quinn raised the helmet and looked directly into its broken eyes. "I'll tell you what I told him: I don't work with assholes."

Guardian dropped his reasonable voice and screamed. "Put me down! You are an inferior creature and I command you to release me!"

"Sure thing," said Quinn. He tossed the helmet in the air, then hit it with the flat side of his axe and sent it flying towards an archway. The surface rippled as it passed through and the Spectrum fell suddenly quiet. Guardian was gone.

"What now?" asked Quinn.

Faline limped over to her bike. It lay on its side, broken beyond repair. She ejected a metal band, identical to the one she'd worn in Quantum and clipped it around her wrist. "The information from our trip is stored here. We can find our way through again."

"Right, but how do we get out? No offense, Barn, but the Pits of Goltha don't look so great."

"According to the legends, you just have to ask." Faline turned to face the Shard and said, "Show me Ouros."

The scenes in the archways changed, replaced with brighter images of many different lands. A few Quinn could place, most he could only guess at.

Barnabas turned around, looking at them like a wonderstruck child. He pointed at one. "The Vale of Shadow. I've always wanted to go there."

Faline looked back at Quinn. "We can go anywhere. You can even go home."

"What?"

"The Spectrum opens onto all worlds."

"I just tell it to show me?"

"Yes."

Quinn stepped in front of the Shard. The faint glow inside seemed to pulse slightly, aware of him. He thought for a moment, then said, "Show me Earth."

The images changed again and now it was Quinn's turn to look around in wonder. For all the things he had seen since opening his eyes in the desert, none were more beautiful than the sight of home. There were no places of magic, no flying cars or strange creatures. In their place, Quinn saw cities and landmarks that he knew. There were places he had been and others he had only seen in pictures. But he recognized them as Earth, as home, and loved them all. And finally, on a row high above, he saw the Hollywood sign. Even from a distance it was easy to recognize, cradled in the hills. He remembered going onto the roof of his apartment at night and looking at it, letters rising over a city of dreams and dreamers.

Quinn looked at Faline and Barnabas with tears in his eyes. He hadn't even realized he'd been crying. "I never thought I'd see it again," he said.

Faline hugged him and whispered, "Safe travels, Quinn. Take care of yourself when you get there."

"May Shibbo's blessings be ever upon you," said Barnabas. He held out his hand to shake.

Quinn looked around the Spectrum, at the archways that led back to Earth. "It's beautiful. I never really noticed it before unless I was looking at the ocean or a sunset, but it really is just perfect." His eyes settled on the Hollywood sign. "All of it."

Then he looked at his friends, at the werewolf and demon with whom he had traveled far. "It's my world but there's nothing there for me anymore. I lived there, I died

353

there, and I don't need to go back. If I traveled all the worlds, I know I'd never find braver and truer friends than I've found in this one."

Quinn stepped back in front of the Shard and said, "Show me Ouros, somewhere nice." He watched as images of Earth vanished, replaced by the strange and beautiful. They chose one and climbed up to it.

"See you on the other side," said Barnabas, then stepped through and disappeared.

Faline was next. "The world is going to change because of what we did here. We've set something in motion and I think it's going to spread. If the Deadlands heal, this place will need to be protected." They stood face to face on the narrow ledge, as close as they had ever been.

"I'll be ready. For whatever happens next."

"Good," said Faline. He thought she might say more, but only touched his hand and was gone.

Quinn stood on the threshold a moment longer, looking back down at the Shard and the husk of Midnight. He thought of the friends he'd traveled with. The ones who had fallen and the ones who remained, waiting for him to find his way and somehow believing that he would.

Ω

IT WAS RAINING OUT, RAINING HARD. The drops sounded like machine gun fire against the roof. There was a streetlamp near the window and it projected an image of the raindrops onto the wall. The room was mostly bare: an old couch, a rotary telephone, a desk. Behind the desk was a man, slouched in a chair that squeaked when he moved. He wore a trench coat and a fedora.

The man spun a revolver on the desk. While he waited for it to stop, he drank whiskey from a bottle. It was the kind of night for staying in by the fire, but every so often he glanced at the phone. When it rang, a voice on the other end would give him a location. Then he would go out into the rain and take care of business. That's what it was in the end. Business.

The gun slowed and finally stopped. He got up and went to the window. Now the streetlamp projected the raindrops onto his face, made it look like he was crying. He hadn't done that since he was a boy. Men who cried didn't last long in Noir.

The phone rang and the man answered. He listened, then hung up. He slipped the revolver into his pocket, took a last slug of whiskey and went out. The rain beat down, cold and hard, out of a black sky. It was a bad night to be out and a bad job to be on, but he was eager for the chance. They said bullets and balls were all a man needed to be someone and he believed it. It didn't matter if you were born rich or who your parents were. Other places were like that. In Noir, anyone could make something of themselves, if they had the guts. Money and power were there for the taking and he intended to take as much as he could.

Hell, he intended to take it all.

Made in the USA
Monee, IL
11 February 2021

"The blonde sheep of my family." He moved closer.

"You don't need the gun."

"No. But I hear it's very painful for werewolves. Like burning from the inside. You killed my mother and now I'm going to make you scream."

"What do you take the girls for?"

"That's what you want to—"

Faline vaulted onto the chair and leapt at Midnight, meaning to drag him out of the air. He sent her to the floor with a kick, then sank down and retrieved the helmet. He stood over Faline, pinning her down with a foot. She fought to break free but without claws and wolf strength it was useless. Midnight's weight was crushing the breath out of her.

"There's nothing worse than dying helpless," he said, and raised the gun. "I know how it feels."

"Hey, asshole."

Midnight turned in surprise and Quinn buried the axe in his chest. He let go and Midnight staggered back, dropping the helmet and gun. Midnight looked confused, as if he was trying to comprehend what was happening. Then his feet tangled and he fell, sprawling on the floor of the Great Room. As Midnight lay there, his blue eyes became vacant and unfocused.

Quinn pulled Faline to her feet. "You ok?"

She touched her jaw and grimaced. "I'll be fine. How much did you hear?"

"Most of it. Apparently we killed his mom, so go us."

"Must've been when we blew up the suit."

Behind Faline, Midnight sat up with the axe still protruding from his chest.

"That's not good," said Quinn.

Midnight stood and wrenched the axe free with a wet cracking sound but instead of blood, yellow light burst out.